Beyond The FENCES

Beyond The FENCES

Muriel W. Sheubrooks

Archway Publishing books may be ordered through booksellers or by contacting:

Archway Publishing
1663 Liberty Drive
Bloomington, IN 47403
www.archwaypublishing.com
1 (888) 242-5904

ISBN: 978-1-4808-7623-1 (sc)
ISBN: 978-1-4808-7624-8 (hc)
ISBN: 978-1-4808-7622-4 (e)

Library of Congress Control Number: 2019906576

Print information available on the last page.

Archway Publishing rev. date: 06/05/2019

DEDICATION

For my husband Rich, who offers me the world,
Our combined children and their children, who color my world,
And in loving memory of my Kentucky parents,
Martha Belle and R. C. Wright, who left this world a better place.

The wide world is all about you; you can fence yourself in, but you cannot forever fence the world out.

—J. R. R. Tolkien, *The Lord of the Rings*

Part 1

CHAPTER 1

A few days before Christmas, I drove through the cemetery gates to place wreaths on my parents' and younger sister Maria's graves.

It was a bone-chilling day as snow flurries fell around me. Before I got the wreaths out of the trunk, I threw an heirloom quilt around my shoulders like a shawl for additional warmth and comfort. This sentimental visit, like this cherished quilt, always triggered memories of how my life was so different from my family's in rural Kentucky.

When I bent over Maria's grave to place the wreath on her headstone, I remembered my first meeting with her when I was four years old.

That morning was etched in my mind as Daddy scooted me out the kitchen door without an explanation of why Mama's bedcovers were bloody when I went to the bedroom to kiss her goodbye. He drove me to our neighbors' house, the Johnsons'.

He promised to be back soon when he and Dr. Johnson left. Mrs. Johnson sat me on a tiny, red chair in front of a wood-burning fireplace to warm up. Watching the flames dance, I had so many questions dancing in my head. *Why is Mama in pain? Is she going to die? Why didn't Daddy bring my big sister Beth with me to the Johnsons'?*

I patiently sat waiting in a room without children's toys or books, wishing I had brought Angela, my favorite doll, with me.

To my four-year-old mind, it seemed like an eternity until Mrs. Johnson called me for lunch. But just as I sat down at the table to eat a homemade biscuit with blackberry jam, I heard car tires crunch on the driveway.

It was Daddy. I knew he'd come back for me! When he came into the kitchen, stomping the snow off his boots, he pulled Mrs. Johnson aside and said in a low voice that Mama had had a hard labor. Mrs. Johnson nodded like she understood, but I didn't have a clue.

Because Daddy was in such a hurry to leave, I didn't get to eat lunch. Mrs. Johnson put some biscuits in a bag for me. As we were leaving, Daddy said, "Dr. Johnson will be home soon."

On the short drive to our house, Daddy didn't say anything, and because I didn't know what to say or ask, I counted the fences dividing each neighbor's property. Mama had taught me to count to ten.

When we got home, Daddy took me directly to Mama's bedroom. She was smiling and said, "Come look at your new baby sister, Maria."

I looked at the bundle in her arms, and I wanted to scream, *"I hate that ugly baby!"* But instead, I stood quietly and obediently, saying nothing.

I secretly wondered, *Where did that baby come from? Why was there blood on Mama's covers when I left her, but not now? Why is Daddy so worried about Mama? Why did I have to go to the Johnsons' alone? It must all be that baby's fault. She's to blame.*

CHAPTER 2

By the time Maria turned two, I decided she would be okay as a sister if she'd just leave my things alone. After all, I was six years old and ready to go to school that autumn, and I took special care of my toys and books. Beth, our older sister, was now eleven and didn't have anything to do with me unless it was to scold me for doing stupid things. Of course, I knew she teased me because she was jealous that I was so much better at climbing trees and riding horses.

But most of the time, she ignored me. She didn't have time for a little sister, although she thought Maria was special and paid attention to her, combing her hair, rubbing her back, and talking to her.

So life went on as usual at our house until one Sunday morning, when Mama said, "I'll stay home with Maria this morning. She has a fever." Mama never missed church, and it scared me. Mama sat on the bed next to Maria, touching her face with a cool washcloth. Daddy asked if he should call Dr. Johnson, but Mama said, "No, I hate to bother him now. You know he and his wife always go to the early morning Methodist church service."

Daddy ushered Beth and me out the door and into the car. I

made a mental note to pretend to be sick next Sunday so Mama would give me special treatment.

Mama was standing on the porch holding Maria when we drove up the driveway after church. She didn't wait for us to get out of the car; she just ran toward us.

"Girls, stay in the house while Daddy and I take Maria to the emergency room."

I had never seen Mama so frightened. She handed Maria to Daddy while she climbed into the back seat and then held out her arms for Maria. They sped away, leaving Beth and me standing in the driveway looking after them.

Daddy didn't come home until after dark. He sat us down and in a low voice explained, "Maria is very sick. Dr. Johnson is with her and your mother at the hospital." Daddy hesitated before he continued, "They're running tests, but they don't know what's wrong with her."

Days went by, and Maria didn't get any better. Beth and I tried to keep the house clean and prepared meals as if everything would soon be back to normal. Daddy worked as much as he could on the farm and went to the hospital every night to check on Maria and Mama. Everything changed after Dr. Johnson said they should take Maria to Mid-Atlantic Children's Hospital. It was three hours away.

Daddy arranged for neighbors to help out with the house and the farm. Neighbor women came to the house on a regular basis to help with household chores and to make sure we were never left alone for too long. The neighbor men took care of our livestock and crops while Daddy was away. It was a blur of adult faces coming and going in our house and on our land.

After two weeks at the children's hospital, Daddy and Mama came home with Maria. Daddy was carrying Maria, and he and Mama looked tired. Mama took the homemade quilt off their bed and folded it carefully to make a soft pallet that she put on the living room floor. Daddy laid the baby down so she would be closer to all of us.

Then Mama motioned for Beth and me to take a seat on the couch. She explained that Maria had been sick with a rare virus that attacked her brain and caused a high fever. The doctors weren't sure how to treat her.

"The virus has left Maria paralyzed. She can't move her limbs and will probably not advance mentally beyond the age of five or six," Mama said with her voice beginning to break. Beth began to cry. I sat frozen with fear, glued to the chair. Guilt swept over me, and my mind raced. *Wasn't I the one who didn't like Maria when she was born? Is her illness my fault?*

Finally, I jumped up and ran outside to find Rex, my dog. I threw my arms around his neck and began to sob. His cold nose nuzzled my neck, and he turned his head slightly and began licking the tears streaming down my face. He never budged until I got up much later and went slowly back into the house that now felt so strange.

In the days following, I found a special place to escape the reality of Maria's illness. My refuge was a tall, old oak tree that was as far from the house as possible but still on our property.

There was a fork in the tree's massive limbs that made a perfect saddle for me. I could settle into place and feel the rough texture of the tree bark making imprints on my skinny, tan legs as I looked out across the farms adjoining ours. I could count different shades of green as I watched the corn and tobacco crops swaying in the wind. I wondered what was beyond the fences that dotted those vast fields.

CHAPTER 3

In October 1949, I was eight years old and could help with milking the cows and feeding the livestock. Harvest time was a happy time for the farmers—and my favorite season. I loved the smell of the dry corn shucks and the feel of the kernels deeply embedded in the cob. Sometimes, I'd break the hard kernels off and chew them. They tasted sweet as they softened in my mouth.

But that autumn was different after a severe drought. I heard Daddy and Mama talking about money worries. They spoke in low voices, almost as if they had a secret code.

I overheard Daddy talking to other farmers at church or in town too. They were all worried about the drought. But we had an additional financial burden with Maria's health issues. In our farm community, doctors were called only in the case of emergencies. We saw Dr. Johnson a lot.

However, we never discussed Maria's medical issues or our fears of what might become of her. Instead, each of us learned to cope with her condition by throwing ourselves into our work.

By the time I was a teenager, I'd added another layer to cope with Maria's illness—my friendship with Grace Pender, my best friend. All the telephones in our area were on a party line, so instead of using the phone to confide secrets, I went to Grace's house.

Grace was a year ahead of me in school, and everyone thought we looked like sisters. We were both tall and slim. We could easily swap clothes. And we were both blue-eyed blondes with freckles. We did everything together. One afternoon, we bought a bottle of peroxide and used cotton balls to produce blonder highlights in our bangs.

When Mama saw what we had done, she said it made us look cheap. Her opinion didn't count. We knew it was the style and complimented each other on how cute we looked and how everyone would notice us at the county fair on Saturday night.

That outing was a big deal because we planned to show off our fashion savvy. Our mothers had made us matching outfits. The hot pink cotton fabric with large white polka dots was perfect for the split-necked, sleeveless blouses. We added layers and layers of stiff, starched crinoline petticoats under the skirts.

We had never considered that our ensemble might be more of a showpiece than we could handle. On our first ride, the Ferris wheel, it was nearly impossible to hold down our skirts—and that ride was tame compared to others we rode. We didn't even have to be on a ride to have trouble. If we walked too close on the midway, our skirts flipped up in the front or flew up in the back. And we couldn't eat or drink anything. For modesty's sake, we had to hold down our errant skirts with both hands.

Although they had more money than my family, the Penders were always welcoming to me. Grace's daddy owned the town's grocery store. People called him Mutt because with his tall, thin frame he resembled the character in the comic strip *Mutt and Jeff.*

Grace's mother, Sue, was short and round, a little like Jeff, and had a warm, inviting smile. She was also a wonderful cook. It was years later before I realized I'd traded my childhood oak tree refuge for Grace's family. The time I spent with them was my way of avoiding my home situation and the embarrassment I felt inviting friends to my house because my sister was not normal. None of my friends had a family member like Maria.

Another reason I preferred Grace's house to my own was her older brother, Andrew. I'd had a serious crush on him since fourth grade. Like his father, Andrew was tall, lean, and very handsome. I especially liked the freckles that peppered the bridge of his nose. He was four years older than me and could always sweet-talk Grace and me into waiting on him, although Grace was not as eager to please him as I was. I always avoided eye contact with Grace, who just rolled her eyes while I willingly complied with Andrew's requests so I could talk to him and get a little more time with him. I didn't care if it meant I had to iron a shirt or polish his shoes. But I hated it if it meant he was getting dressed for a date with the local beauty queen, Elizabeth. Of course, I knew someday he'd be crazy about me and leave Elizabeth in the dust.

If we weren't at Grace's house, we were together at her dad's grocery store, which was also the local gas station. Grace worked in the store on Saturdays, and when I finished my farm chores, I'd join her. At first, we got paid with our favorite candy—mine was a Clark Bar—or soft drinks from the big ice cooler near the gas pumps. My favorite soda was a Nehi Orange Soda.

Candy and sodas were fine, but as we grew older, Grace and I came up with a plan to make real money during our store workdays. When someone drove up to the gas pump, Grace would rush out to pump the gas. I sprang into action too, grabbing a can of car polish. While she pumped, I'd clean and polish a round spot the size of a skillet on the car's hood. When the driver came back from paying inside the store, we'd offer to clean and polish the complete car for *only* five dollars.

We got away with our semi-honest ruse and made a lot of

money that summer. Then we met our Waterloo. Old Man Ashby pulled in, and his ten-year-old Cadillac looked like it had never been polished. Old Man Ashby was shaped like a ball, as wide as he was tall, so we knew he couldn't shine his own car. We expected to score big, but when he saw the clean, polished circle on his hood, he ran to Mutt, demanding payment for the damage we'd done to his car. Mutt gave him the five dollars, and our punishment was polishing his car without collecting one dime.

After Mr. Ashby drove off in his polished car, Mutt shut down our uninvited service. Then, with a twinkle in his eye, he told us his favorite Ashby story.

"I wish you girls had seen Old Man Ashby when he came by the store one winter day and joined the rest of the fellows around the wood-burning stove to listen to the local gossip. In the middle of a good story, his chair collapsed, and he rolled around on the floor like a billiard ball. The men laughed so hard they could barely help him up. I was concerned when he told me he planned to sue for damage, but your daddy defended me, Marilyn."

"He said, 'Tell you what, Ashby. I have an old jackass that can't work anymore. I'll just give you that ass for your ass damages, and you can call it even.'" Mutt laughed as he finished by telling us how Old Man Ashby stomped out in a huff with a red face, a sore bottom, and a whole heap of indignation. "To this day, all those men remember the famous Ashby jackass story with uncontrollable snickers," he said. "If you want to get a chuckle out of your daddy, Marilyn, just ask him about Old Man Ashby's chair collapsing."

Then Grace's dad told us he was ready to ante up real money for our valuable services in the store. So, we legitimately became employed for money—not soft drinks and candy.

I have so many wonderful memories of my time at Grace's house, and some bittersweet ones—one in particular. I'd gone to Grace's house for lunch one Easter Sunday after church with my family. I wore a white piqué dress dotted with small navy flowers that Mama had tailored perfectly for my thin figure. With the money I'd saved from working at Mutt's store, I'd splurged on a pair of navy-blue heels, a perfect match for my outfit.

Sue had prepared an incredible Easter Sunday lunch, and as soon as we finished, Andrew announced he was going to take his two beautiful dining companions for a ride in his Nash Rambler convertible, which he had just cleaned and polished. Grace was suspicious and demanded to know what he expected in return. However, I was certain he wanted to be with me to show off his new girlfriend to his buddies.

Andrew put the top down, carefully making sure the folds were perfect. I crawled in next to him, close enough so he could easily put his arm around me. Grace sat next to me, and with the wind blowing in our hair, we rode along, singing, "Why Do Fools Fall in Love?" with Frankie Lymon and the Teenagers blaring on the radio. I felt like a queen—invincible—with the world at my fingertips.

And then it all slipped away. Suddenly, at the next curve, we collided head-on with another car. Andrew and I were ejected on impact. Grace clutched the passenger door with all her strength as Andrew's car careened into an embankment. When I regained consciousness in the ambulance, Andrew was on a stretcher beside me and Grace was sitting on the ambulance's bench seat crying.

We were all covered in mud and blood. My beautiful new white dress, now green with grass stains, was ripped beyond repair, and I was shoeless, which at that moment was more painful than my injuries. I mourned the loss of my new heels until the attendant, so reassuring in his white hospital uniform, produced them—unscratched. He'd found them in some bushes a few yards from my point of impact.

Maybe our family's guardian angel knew my mama and daddy

could not deal with any more troubles, because my injuries were minor. Or maybe I was just supposed to learn how fragile life is. I'm sure each of us gleaned something different from the accident, but I know we all felt very lucky when we walked out of the hospital several hours later. But I didn't feel lucky when I saw Elizabeth and Andrew exiting the hospital together—holding hands.

Riding home with Daddy, I apologized. "I'm so sorry I caused you and Mama such worry."

He quickly responded, "Quit feeling like you're responsible for bad things happening in our family." Then, more gently, he continued, "I know you blame yourself for Maria because you didn't like her when she was born. But her condition, like today's accident, is not your fault. Sometimes we are victims, and things that we can't control just happen."

I looked at Daddy and blinked back a tear, wondering how a farmer without a high school education could be so smart.

My father's words after the accident were my emotional epiphany. I began to see Maria in a different light. My internal anger toward her—because she was not like others—diminished. Her imperfection was a lesson to me about how fortunate I was in my life. I was healthy, popular, and a reasonably good high school student—and I was loved.

Although Maria was different, her life still counted. I recognized that she was entitled to be loved and to be happy, even if she was limited by her disabilities.

CHAPTER 4

I guess graduation, whether from high school or college, is always a time for reflection. I remember sitting in my senior English class and looking at my classmates, thinking how most of us had been together since first grade. Soon, we'd graduate and go our separate ways. Across the aisle from me was Barbara Coleman. Not only had we gone to school together for twelve years, but we also attended the same church. And she had played a role in a "Come to Jesus" episode involving our church.

My family was serious about going to church—we warmed the pews on Sunday morning, Sunday night, and Wednesday evening. Daddy and Mama were also active in church activities, like the Christmas pageant. Mama usually directed it.

When Barbara and I were eleven years old, we competed for the lead role of Mother Mary in the pageant. When I was chosen to play Mary, I assumed I'd won the role not because Mama was the director, but because I'd been so winsome at the tryouts. Everyone who saw my audition said it was flawless. Then I overheard two of the women in charge of the pageant's costumes talking in the vestibule. They said they would have had to almost remake Mary's robe if Barbara Coleman played Mary. I couldn't believe it. I was tapped as Mary by default, not because of my incredible acting ability. It was just easier because Mary's robe fit my small frame perfectly—no alterations required.

On the day of the pageant, I began to think about my role and the reason I was chosen—my size, not my acting ability—and I came down with a severe case of stage fright jitters. I went to Mama and firmly announced, "I'm not going to be in the pageant tonight. I have a stomachache."

She turned and announced just as firmly, "Marilyn, you made a commitment, and you will keep it." She often used the word *commitment.* In fact, her motto still resonates with me: "If you commit to doing something, then do it and do it right."

Usually, I was a dutiful daughter, but this time, I responded defiantly, "I said I *won't* be in the play tonight."

My father heard us. He said, "Marilyn, get your coat and boots. We're going for a walk."

The cold air did not change my resolve about the pageant. We walked in silence. At the edge of the woods, just past the pond, he stopped and stooped to my level, his face in front of mine. He spoke calmly. "So, you're not going to play the role in the pageant tonight, even though you rehearsed it so carefully. Is that correct?"

I nodded, feeling somewhat ashamed.

"Why did you change your mind?" he asked.

"I'm afraid, and my stomach hurts."

He straightened up to his full five-foot, ten-inch height and leaned back so the new falling snow began to dust his face. I could see a slight smile on his snow-moist lips when he said, "I think I understand why you don't want to play Mary. It's because someone else, like Barbara Coleman, probably knows this role better than you do. Right?"

Until then, I had assumed Daddy agreed with my decision not

to perform. His question surprised me, and I indignantly thought, *How could he say such a mean thing to me?*

I stomped my right foot so hard that snow came into my boot. I pictured Barbara as Mother Mary, and I threw back my shoulders and emphatically declared, "No one knows Mother Mary's role better than I do!"

That ended the discussion. There was no question about who was going to play Mary that night. I fit into Mary's robe and her role perfectly—no alterations required! I had made a commitment, and I was going to keep it.

To this day, if I have doubts about doing something that makes me feel unsure, I bolster my self-confidence by repeating a simple mental mantra: "No one knows this role better than I. No alterations needed!"

CHAPTER 5

It was the first day of my classes at Wesley University, and I had carefully dressed for the occasion. The sterling silver circle pin Grace had given me for my high school graduation fit perfectly on the Peter Pan collar of my newly purchased pale-yellow blouse. I'd picked the blouse because it was just right for the knee-length, yellow-and-green plaid skirt Mama had made. My new Bass Weejuns loafers looked so stylish with my forest-green knee socks. I caught my image in the long hallway mirror in the suite I shared with three other girls. At least I looked the part of a college coed—right out of the college issue of *Mademoiselle* magazine—even if I was apprehensive about this new venture.

The September air, cool against my face, calmed my nerves slightly as I walked the two blocks from the dormitory to the assembly hall for the first meeting in the week-long freshman orientation. If only Grace could have been here, I'd have felt more confident. She had traveled this same route alone as a freshman the year before so wouldn't be on campus until next week. Over the summer, Grace had tried to prepare me for this first week of college, and I'd thought I'd be fine. But now that I was here, I felt both apprehension and excitement.

The campus seemed so big. I knew every building was necessary to accommodate the total student enrollment at Wesley University, which was almost the size of Rockport, my hometown, in population. Still, I had a fear of getting lost.

Tree-lined brick walkways led to buildings of different architectural styles, some with ivy-covered walls. The tree-studded green grass, lush from summer, had that newly cut, fresh scent.

Rockport, a typical southwestern Kentucky small town, had similar brick sidewalks and trees at the little park in the town center. There were two drinking water fountains in the middle of the park with a sign over each: "White only" and "Colored only." At that time, this didn't seem strange to me. It was just the way it was. The message certainly incenses me today.

Rockport's main drag had two department stores, a hardware store, Mutt's grocery, two drugstores, and a few small restaurants, all neatly lined up and down Main Street. Two banks, like bookends, flanked the retail row. I knew every square inch of this small town and had so many memories of driving into Rockport with Daddy.

He would park on Main Street and tell me what time to meet him at the car. Then he'd give me a quarter to spend at Klein's Five and Dime Store, knowing it would take most of an afternoon for me to decide how to wisely spend twenty-five cents. The store's basement had child-height shelves lined with toys, kites, crayons, coloring books—everything to make a kid happy. So many choices—and complicated further by the large glass jars tempting customers with an assortment of candies and gum. My Daddy's brother, James, owned the dry goods store next door, but there were no child-friendly temptations there.

Every time I think of my uncle's store, I regress back to thirteen years old, when my mother said, "Marilyn, when you and your father are in town today, go by your Uncle James' store and buy your first bra. I wish I could help you, but I need to stay home with Maria. She's running a little fever."

Mortified that my uncle might see what I was buying, I went to the store next door. The saleslady asked me my bra size. I had no idea. I pointed at the counter display and said, "That one."

She looked at me skeptically. "Won't that be too big for you, honey?"

I responded, "Oh, it's not for me. It's for my mama."

When I got home, Mama asked to see the bra to check the fit. When I took it out of the other store's shopping bag, she looked at the tag and read it out loud—38-D!

Beth was listening and collapsed on the floor laughing. I was more than embarrassed—I was humiliated. Mama said on the next trip to Rockport, I was to take the bra back to the store for a full refund. Then I was to go to my uncle's store and ask my aunt to help me select the correct size.

The next week, with a red, flushed face, I returned the bra. Then I went next door and asked my aunt to help me. I came home with my first bra—a 28-AA cup. I felt a strange sense of dismay at having to trade my undershirt for a bra. That one act signaled the end of my tomboy self and the beginning of my development as a teenager. As an eighteen-year-old freshman in college, I remembered this embarrassing rite of passage as if it were yesterday.

When I entered the huge assembly hall, I was overwhelmed with the freshman class size. I found a seat on the aisle and sat down next to a guy. He turned to check me out, smiled, and introduced himself. "I'm Joe Bateson from New York. What's your name and where are you from?"

He was good-looking, with dark hair and soft brown eyes. Neatly pressed khaki-colored slacks were paired with a freshly starched oxford cloth blue shirt that complemented his tanned face, and of course, loafers.

For the first time in my life, I wanted to lie about my hometown, but I couldn't. "My name's Marilyn White, and I just graduated from Cannon High School in Rockport, Kentucky."

He smiled, then flippantly remarked, "Oh sure, I've heard of that place. That's where people don't wear shoes, right?"

I knew he was trying to be funny, but I was insulted. "Where I come from, folks with or without shoes know how to respect each other."

He looked sheepish and asked if he could treat me to a Coke at the end of the orientation. I accepted the peace offering and agreed to meet him at the Colony Café, near campus.

When we met for the apology Coca-Cola, I asked him why he had come to Kentucky to attend Wesley. It was so far from New York.

"There are two reasons. My mother and father didn't want to make a large donation to a college in the Northeast to get me admitted." He laughed.

I didn't understand what he meant, but I didn't interrupt.

He continued on a serious note,. "And I wanted to get as far away from New York City and my parents as possible."

My intuition told me not to ask why. If he wanted me to know, he'd tell me in time.

CHAPTER 6

Over the next few weeks, Joe and I spent many hours getting to know one another. I found him fascinating; his life was so different from mine. Joe was Jewish. He had one brother, Manny, a law student at Columbia University. His mother was a fashion designer and lived abroad most of the time, and his father was a doctor at a large New York City hospital. The family often spent vacations together in Europe.

The Batesons had an apartment in Manhattan, and they owned a country home on Long Island Sound that they used on weekends and holidays. The way Joe explained the country residence and its surrounding acreage, I knew it was very different from the country where I had grown up.

It was inconceivable to me that a family would have two homes.

"How does your mother manager to clean both houses when she spends most of her time in Europe?"

He laughed, but I'd gotten used to that. "We have a staff that helps at the country place and a full-time maid at the New York apartment."

Joe was as curious about how I grew up as I was about his upbringing. Neither of us could imagine the other's family or lifestyle. In comparison to his life, mine could only be described as drab and boring. In fact, I seriously considered making things up and downplaying how simply we lived on our farm until he asked, "Could I visit your home some weekend?"

I told him, "Of course you can." But I knew I would delay the visit for as long as I could.

The first weekend I went home from college, I looked around our farm with a critical eye. *Why does our life on this farm have to be so ordinary and humdrum?* I knew my parents would be crushed if they could read my thoughts. Then I wondered, *Has college turned me into a snob?*

My parents were happy to have me home. Mama cooked my favorite foods, and Daddy asked me all kinds of questions about school. Mama wanted to know all about my classes and professors. It was easy to give them the answers I knew they wanted to hear. Their questions weren't relevant to the college experience I was relishing—meeting interesting people who lived so differently than we did. I knew neither would understand. I was afraid it would hurt their feelings.

I remembered that when Beth had first gone to the University of Kentucky to get her degree in nursing, she was grumpy and short-tempered on her first freshmen weekend home. I didn't understand her negative attitude then, but we had never discussed it.

She was a nurse now and married. I drove to her house to confide my feelings. We sat at her kitchen table. I told her about Joe and his family, confessing that I was embarrassed about how unsophisticated our family appeared in comparison to his. Then I told her Joe wanted to come home with me and meet the family.

I groaned, "How can I ever bring him to our tiny farmhouse?"

"Marilyn, the way I learned to be happy was to associate with people on campus that I had things in common with, rather than to connect with snobs like Joe. Don't get so wrapped up in wanting what other people have that you fail to appreciate what you have. After all, our family's Christian faith is just as important to us as it is for Joe to be Jewish."

That's when I became defensive. "Beth, I can't help it if I want to expand my horizon. I am curious about the cultures and beliefs of others."

Beth shook her head. "Life is going to be tough for you. It's easier if you find some nice guy to marry, someone who shares your values, background, and religion. What I'm saying is, don't complicate your life—it's complicated enough."

When I got back to Wesley from my weekend on Sunday, Joe called and asked me to share a pizza. I was very quiet, and he kept asking me, "What's wrong with you?"

My feeble reply was, "Nothing—I guess I'm just tired."

"Did you tell your folks about me, and did they say I could come for a visit?" Joe asked, almost like a little kid. I nodded my head in agreement without saying a word.

"I talked to my father while you were gone," he said. "I asked him if I could bring you home at Thanksgiving. He not only agreed, but said he'd send me an airline ticket for you, too. We'll have a full house. Some family friends from Paris will also be with us. It would be terrific if you could join us for that long weekend—you'd get to see both the city and our country house in the Hamptons."

My head was spinning. Thanksgiving was always a big day for my family—a gathering like something Norman Rockwell might paint for a *Saturday Evening Post* cover. Aunts, uncles, cousins, and my family always gathered around my grandmother's table for the traditional turkey dinner. It was a sacred family event. Only Christmas was bigger.

One side of my brain thought, *There is no way you can miss this important family event!* The other side of my brain countered, *Are you nuts not to take advantage of this exciting invitation?*

I couldn't concentrate on eating when the pizza came. *What would I wear if I went to New York? How would I talk? Would his family find me too plain for Joe? Do Jews do anything different from Christians on Thanksgiving?*

I was emotionally strung out. "I guess I'm not very hungry. My stomach is upset, and I need to get back to the dormitory," I lied.

What I needed was to talk to Grace. Grace and I didn't always agree, but we had an unwritten pact to always talk through anything that disturbed us or needed to be discussed immediately. I knew she would be there for me.

I had to stand in line to use the telephone. I took my place behind Judy Richards, one of my favorite suitemates. She asked me if I was feeling okay and said I looked stressed. I let my body slide down the wall to a seated position on the floor and assured her I was fine—just a little tired.

While we waited, she told me about a new guy she'd just met. They'd gone out the night before, and she liked him. She said, "Imagine this. We went to school in the same county but never met until we came to Wesley! We had so much in common that we never stopped talking. We know so many of the same people back home."

She lowered her voice. "I've met some strange people since I've been to Wesley. You know, kids from different places and religions. It's hard to relate to them." Judy sounded like my sister Beth. I thought it was prudent not to respond.

Twenty minutes later, I got a phone. Thankfully, Grace was in her room, but talking on the phone with others waiting and able to hear my conversation was too much like the party line at home. Instead, we met at the Colony Café. In ten minutes, we had ordered Cokes, and she was ready to hear my crisis.

I told her about Joe's invitation. She listened intently and then began to lecture me on how I always created my own problems. "Why would you want to leave your family on such an important holiday to meet people you don't know, especially because they sound so different from you?"

The next day after class, I went to the library to do some research for geology. After I found what I needed, I wandered into the library's international section and selected a book about France. Leafing through it, I came across a section on Paris. The pictures were magnificent—wide, tree-lined boulevards and beautiful architecture, described in the photo captions as a hybrid of the decorative Rococo style and the more traditional neoclassical style.

Traveling to Paris was out of my reach, but couldn't I sample a piece of it by going to Joe's house for Thanksgiving and meeting people who lived in the City of Light, as we Americans called it, perhaps wrongly? The French translation in the book was *Ville Lumière,* meaning "city of enlightenment." That did it! I made up my mind and ran to call Joe. He was delighted but had one stipulation. He insisted he meet my family the next weekend. He wanted to be the one to tell them his family had invited me and his father was giving me an airline ticket as a gift.

I knew Daddy would consider the ticket a handout and oppose. But I also knew Daddy couldn't afford to purchase a ticket. Maybe I could come up with a plan so my family could reimburse Joe's father. When I tried to explain my dilemma to Joe, he laughed and said his parents would be glad to purchase the ticket for me. "My parents will be grateful to you for spending the long weekend with me."

I thought that was a strange thing for him to say about his parents. Even before I could question him, he elaborated, "My parents will have their friends to entertain and will prefer their company to mine. Your airline ticket is a small price to pay to lessen their guilt."

CHAPTER 7

By November first, a month had passed since I'd gone home. My parents were eager to see me and kept asking how long my Thanksgiving break would be.

To add to my stress, Joe kept badgering me about visiting the farm and meeting my parents. I'd run out of excuses; I couldn't delay his visit any longer. Maybe he wouldn't like my folks. That would be a perfect sign that I shouldn't go to New York with him for Thanksgiving.

We were at the Colony Café when I casually said, "I plan to go home this weekend; would you like to join me?" He jumped at the invitation and said he'd drive us to Rockport. Our game plan was to leave after his last class on Friday. I had no excuse now; I had to tell my parents I was bringing home a college buddy from the East.

When I called home, my heart was in my mouth. "Mama, would you put Daddy on the other line, so I can talk to you both at the same time?" I'd rehearsed this conversation carefully. I diplomatically wanted to let them know that Joe was very different from our family without sounding like I was ashamed to have him meet them.

"I hope it's okay if I bring a new friend of mine home this

weekend. He is interested in seeing a working farm. I met him the first day at Wesley. His name's Joe, and his family is from New York. Don't get any ideas—he isn't a special boyfriend," I explained cautiously.

"What's his last name?" Daddy asked

"Bateson."

"I don't believe I know any Batesons. Do you, Mary Beth?"

"No."

"What does his father do for a living?"

"He's a doctor."

"Well, that's nice," my mother approvingly said. "Where in New York does he live?"

"New York City."

There was a long pause before she said, "Is Bateson a Jewish name? I know there are a lot of Jews in New York City."

That question surprised me. I didn't reply. I hadn't thought they were prejudiced toward anyone. "I've got to go—someone is waiting for the phone." When we hung up, I felt a deep sense of relief. They knew I was bringing home a boy from college—who lived in New York City and had a car and a different religious faith.

As planned, Joe was in front of my dorm Friday at four. I was apprehensive about Joe meeting my parents. I calmed myself by saying over and over in my mind, *It's out of my control—it is what it is.*

Driving toward Rockport, Joe remarked on how quiet and peaceful the countryside seemed to him. "It's sure not Manhattan. The city is so fast-paced, with loud noises from honking cars and pungent smells from the ethnic restaurants. People stand in the street whistling through their fingers or madly waving their hands to hail taxicabs. And let's not forget those noisy, dirty subways where humanity is packed together underground like sardines in a can. Above ground, there are panhandlers and pickpockets competing for your money with the street performers who entertain under gaudy neon flashing lights against a background of concrete buildings as far as the eye can see."

I was enthralled by his colorful description of the city. New York sounded wonderful. And just think—in a few weeks, Joe would show me the city before we went to the Hamptons! The thought made me giddy.

As we approached the farm, I realized I had neglected to tell Joe about Maria. It wasn't fair to shock him when he met Maria, sitting in her wheelchair making grunting noises, trying to communicate. I told him quickly that I had a sister who was not normal. He joked, "That's nothing. My entire family isn't normal."

Making up for lost time, I went into detail about Maria's condition. Joe blushed and apologized. "I didn't know what you meant by 'not normal.'"

Putting a positive spin on my awkward relationship with Maria, I began to pontificate. "You know, there are certain advantages when you grow up with a disabled person. Maria reminds me of how fortunate I am to be healthy mentally and physically. She's also given me the gift of compassion toward those who are different from me."

"Is that why you accepted me as your friend?" Joe asked.

I hesitated before answering. "Maybe my experience with Maria influenced me to be open to everyone and everything and not let differences get in the way. When we were kids and I took Maria out in public in her wheelchair, people stared at us. I learned to cope with this unwanted attention by pretending I didn't see them. I concentrated on her needs. Today, I don't pity or shun people who are obviously handicapped. Maria taught me to look beyond the disability and see the person."

As we pulled into the drive, I saw my house as run down, with gutters hanging by only a few nails from the metal roof, no longer preventing rusty water from running down the sides. The white paint was cracked, exposing the wood. And I'd never noticed how dilapidated the barn and sheds looked. What must Joe be thinking? What a contrast to the beautiful New York apartment and country house he had described to me. I wanted him to turn the car around and head back to Wesley. But it was too late.

My parents were excitedly running down the driveway to greet us. I forced myself to push down my apprehension and gulped in quiet resignation, *This is who I am—it is what it is.*

CHAPTER 8

When Joe and I left on Sunday, he marveled at his driving a tractor, milking a cow—or at least trying to—and collecting eggs from live chickens. He'd also asked every question imaginable about crop and animal life cycles—to my father's delight. However, Daddy was reluctant to fully embrace this inquisitive stranger. He had never encountered anyone so enthusiastic or so interested in the things we took for granted on our farm. I know Daddy was thinking, "Is this guy for real?"

On the drive back, Joe gave the weekend a triple A rating. He raved about how gracious, warm, and friendly my family was to him. I didn't see it. I knew they had treated Joe just the way they would have treated any guest in our home. He didn't get any special treatment or attention. They were just being themselves—kind and thoughtful.

Eventually, our conversation shifted to Daddy's reaction to my upcoming New York City trip. I had told Joe that Daddy was a man of great pride and wouldn't allow Joe's father to send me an airline ticket. When Daddy objected, Joe tried to allay Daddy's objections by explaining that his family was providing transportation for all their out-of-town guests that weekend. My ticket was no exception.

Daddy finally agreed to the trip with one stipulation—he fully intended to pay Dr. Bateson for the ticket as soon as he could. Daddy seemed to consider the ticket a loan, similar to the annual bank loans he took out in planting and growing season and paid back after the harvest. Joe immediately countered, "That's not necessary. Providing tickets for his guests gives my father great pleasure."

We finally exhausted ourselves and fell silent. Both of us were tired, and I was mentally spent. I'd fretted all weekend about connecting Joe to the White family. And I had another bridge to cross: preparing myself for New York City—with only three weeks to get ready. I felt like I needed a lifetime. The prospect of meeting the Batesons was daunting.

However, I was a little concerned that even garrulous Joe was quiet. I wondered if he might be having some serious reservations about introducing his farm girlfriend to his family. But if that was the case, I didn't want to know. I had my heart set on seeing New York. Silently, I committed myself to doing everything in my power to fit into his lifestyle as enthusiastically as he had done this weekend with my folks.

Back at the dorm, I called Grace immediately. It would take clothes from both her closet and mine for this special trip. When the departure day arrived, Grace drove us to the airport in Joe's car. Her final words to me, whispered so Joe didn't hear, were to come back and share every detail from the trip. Since half my suitcase was filled with her clothes, I promised. After all, it was the least I could do for my best friend.

When we arrived in New York, I assumed that someone from Joe's family would greet us at the airport. But when we collected our luggage, nobody stepped forward to help. Joe seemed unconcerned and walked outside with our luggage. I followed him to the vehicle queue for arrivals. The first thing I noticed was a big, black limousine—like something out of the movies—in the middle of the row of taxis. A man in a uniform was standing next to it, and Joe shouted to him, "Hey Sidney, over here! Give us a hand with these bags."

Sidney rushed to us. "Great to see you, Master Bateson. I'll take those bags."

Realizing my confusion, Joe introduced me to Sidney, the family's chauffeur. *First time on a plane, first time in New York City, and now, first-tim e riding in a limo driven by a professional! Grace is going to love these details.*

Driving into Manhattan, Sidney told Joe his mother was arriving on a late-night flight from Milan, Italy, and we were to meet Dr. Bateson after his evening hospital rounds. He said, "Your dad has reservations at Eleven Madison Park Restaurant at 8:30 sharp, and you're to wear a dark suit and tie."

Joe nudged my arm. "That means it's a bit dressy."

Then he turned back to Sidney. "Is my brother Manny coming home for the holiday?"

Sidney shook his head. "You know Manny—nobody knows when he'll show up." Joe looked crestfallen. I wondered if he was disappointed that nobody—parents or brother—had made the effort to meet him at the airport, since he'd been away for more than three months. And why would it be so difficult for Manny to make it home for Thanksgiving—didn't he go to law school at Columbia, right here in the city?

However, my concern for Joe was fleeting. Selfishly, I turned away from brooding Joe to focus on the New York skyline, sparkling in the autumn sunlight. The scene exhilarated me. It was just like Joe had described it—car horns blaring from all directions, yellow taxis darting in and out of traffic to avoid one another like bumper cars at the county fair, smartly dressed people scurrying along the crowded sidewalks, high-rise buildings flanking the streets, and neon lights flashing gaudy colors. It was everything I had expected. No, it was much, much more. *Is it possible to have an instant affinity for a place? It must be—because this is mine!* We turned down Fifth Avenue. I had read somewhere that it was unrivaled as a shopping thoroughfare. I pictured myself walking confidently down this avenue, stylishly clad in a black wool suit with black leather knee-high boots. I turned to Joe and whispered, so Sidney couldn't hear, how overwhelmed I was. "It's all so beautiful."

Joe looked at me with a frown. "What do you mean?"

"This city has so much energy," I continued, dramatically, throwing my arms in the air to make my point—forgetting about Sidney. "I absolutely love it!" My revelry didn't change Joe's distracted mood. If anything, my enthusiasm seemed to irritate him. But I could not contain myself. This farmer's daughter was literally "over the moon." I felt as if I'd been dropped onto another planet.

Sidney pulled up in front of an apartment building with marble columns and a heavy, highly polished brass door. There was an awning over the front entry, and a uniformed doorman stood under it waiting for Sidney to help us out of the limo. When Sidney opened the car door, the sentinel tipped his hat and said, "Welcome home, Master Bateson. It's been a long time." Joe was polite, but not overly friendly to Sidney or this doorman, although they deferred to him. We took the elevator from the building's spacious lobby to Joe's parents' apartment.

As we entered the formal apartment foyer, another man in uniform, Samuel, and a woman named Sarah greeted us. Sarah wore a simple black starched dress covered by a soft, ruffled, organdy apron. Both were genuinely thrilled to see Joe. Joe's spirits lifted at once. He was obviously delighted to see them and hugged and kissed them both before he proudly introduced them to me.

There was only one word to describe my initial impression of the Batesons' magnificent apartment—awesome! Its sophisticated interior design and elegant furnishings reminded me of the exquisite rooms I'd seen when I leafed through the pages of *Town and Country* magazine at the Wesley library. A mammoth silk Oriental rug dominated the living room with long, finger-like fringe on each end. Its vibrant color accented the room's earth-toned furnishings perfectly. The down-filled cushions on the sofa were covered with a taupe-colored raw silk fabric. Did anyone ever sit on them?

The kitchen was so pristine it looked more like a showplace kitchen instead of an actual food preparation center. It had dark cherry wood cabinetry, stainless steel, commercial grade appliances, and shiny, mirror-like black marble counter tops. The other rooms, like the living room and kitchen, appeared uninhabited, almost as if the Batesons' interior designer had just finished the project and was ready for the initial unveiling to her client.

I gulped when I thought of the cost. I kept thinking that the furnishings in any one room cost far more than all the furniture in our farmhouse. The artwork alone must have been priceless. But everything was so sterile. In some ways, the formal living room reminded me of a museum with artwork adorning the walls and marble busts of famous people and other sculptured pieces positioned strategically around the enormous room. Of course, the *pièce de résistance* was the sweeping view of Central Park through the tastefully draped wall of windows.

Joe led me to my room—an inviting, feminine bedroom with chintz fabric window treatments that matched the dust ruffle on the double bed. He suggested I unpack before putting on comfortable walking shoes for the guided tour of his urban neighborhood. As soon as he closed the bedroom door, I threw my arms in the air and pirouetted around the room in total exhilaration. How could

I explain all this to Grace? My first journal entry simply described New York as "something out of the movies. It can't be real."

After a long walk through the streets near the apartment, we went to Central Park and sat down on a park bench. Joe was tired and ready to go back home. I, of course, was operating under a full adrenaline rush and wanted a little more time to scout out the neighborhood. I asked if I could stay out a little longer on my own. After he carefully explained that the street's grid pattern made it easy to explore, he wrote out precise instructions and drew a map of notable landmarks nearby. Then he meticulously instructed me on how to get back to the apartment. As he started to leave, he added one cautionary note. "Be home and ready to leave for the restaurant at 8:00 p.m."

CHAPTER 9

When I got back to the apartment to freshen up for the evening's adventure, I learned that Sidney was off-duty and we'd take a taxi to meet Joe's dad. As we stepped off the elevator, the doorman hailed a taxi and helped me into the cab. On the drive to the restaurant, the building lights and overhead streetlights fascinated me. The city sparkled brilliantly. The night was clear and crisp, but when I looked up to the sky, only a few stars were visible.

I asked Joe about the nearly starless sky, and he explained that the man-made city lights blocked out the natural starlight. "It's light pollution. The stars are there, but we don't see them. See what I miss by living in New York? One of the first things I noticed at your parents' farm was the mass of stars that filled the sky."

I wondered what was so great about the stars in Rockport. I'd looked at star-filled skies all my life and didn't find them particularly remarkable. Stars were just there—something everyone in the country took for granted on a cloudless night. Even when Beth and I looked up at the stars to say in unison, "Star light, star bright, first star I see tonight. I wish I may, I wish I might, have the wish I wish tonight," we certainly didn't have a sense of awe.

But thoughts of city lights and stars would soon disappear as

Joe paid the driver and we dodged groups of people to make our way to the restaurant's front door. When we walked in, I caught my breath as I gazed at the richly elegant, yet understated, setting. I was so glad I was wearing Grace's "Sunday best" dark brown wool sheath with its fashionable stand-away Italian neckline, paired with my dressy, camel-colored gabardine coat, which Joe checked.

Joe's dad was waiting for us in a dimly lit, long and narrow bar room. A mirrored wall behind the bartender reflected an imposing array of different-sized bottles of liquor and dinner liqueurs, with a special rack section for wines. Dr. Bateson was seated on one of the leather chairs, resting his elbow on the highly polished brass rail. He was holding court, the center of a small group of men at the bar. I recognized him immediately. He was an older version of Joe—dark, curly hair and brown eyes, olive complexion, and an open, round face. Joe shared his father's upright carriage and air of confidence. He walked toward us with a wide, warm smile that made his eyes dance and extended his hand to me. It was obvious he was a man of assertiveness and in control of most situations.

Dr. Bateson embraced Joe in a bear hug that let his son know he was genuinely happy to see him after the three-month absence. When they broke apart, Joe immediately introduced me. Dr. Bateson responded warmly. "Please call me Joseph—Dr. Bateson is way too formal for your soft southern accent. Nothing should be *that* formal in your lilting voice."

I knew Dr. Bateson was being cordial, but I was suddenly conscious of my accent and made a mental note to be very careful when I spoke. I didn't want to come off like a country bumpkin from Ohio County, Kentucky, and embarrass Joe. I had no idea how difficult this speaking metamorphosis would be during my long weekend with these sophisticated New York City northerners.

As soon as we sat down at the round leather booth in the dining room, Joe asked about Manny. Dr. Bateson responded, "I haven't spoken to Manny in several days. He wasn't sure of his plans but hoped he could be with us on Thanksgiving Day at the Sound."

Joe nodded, and then he and his dad shifted their conversational gear, skipping quickly from one topic to the next—Joe's college experience (I tuned in), Dr. Bateson's latest medical research (I tuned out), shared foreign travel experiences, and the long hours Joe's mother spent in her fashion world in Milan (my ears perked up). Every now and then, Joe or his dad would try to bring me into the conversation. I knew they were being polite and didn't want to exclude me, but I assured them I was enjoying just listening. I felt safer in my silence, although it was pleasant to listen to them banter with each other so easily. There was another advantage in not having to worry about contributing to the conversation. I was free to scope out the restaurant so I could report every detail to Grace. It was only fair, since I was wearing her dress.

There was only one way to describe the restaurant's ambiance. Pure elegance! The evening was the epitome of a lavish dining experience—menu selections sounded wonderful, and thankfully, the descriptions contained no unfamiliar ingredients or foreign phrases. However, I was amazed that there were no prices listed. Miraculously, our waiter anticipated our every need as if we were the only people in the restaurant who required his service, although I knew he was serving several other tables. In fact, the room was filled with stylishly dressed people chatting in low tones and clinking crystal glasses. The heavy silverware made scraping noises as the diners ate the beautifully presented food from the delicate china.

The humming sounds of conversations and background restaurant noises presented an imaginary symphony performance. I imagined the waiters in their black tuxedos and stiffly starched white shirts as musicians, moving effortlessly from one table to the next, performing their individual parts to an orchestra score.

Once we ordered our appetizers and main course from the

leather-bound menus, Dr. Bateson ordered a bottle of wine with a French-sounding name from the miniature leather-bound wine list. The waiter brought the bottle wrapped in a linen napkin and showed Dr. Bateson the label before placing three globe-shaped stemmed wine glasses on the table. After expertly uncorking the bottle, he handed the cork to Dr. Bateson and then poured a small amount for him. Dr. Bateson swirled the wine in the glass, sniffed the bouquet (I learned that term later that evening), and held it to the table's candlelight before tasting it. He nodded approvingly to the waiter, who filled my glass half full. He poured the same amount in Joe's glass and then served Dr. Bateson before placing the bottle in a silver wine holder next to our table.

I'd never had a glass of wine or an alcoholic beverage with my parents, so the wine presentation was quite impressive. When Dr. Bateson had held the glass to the candle in the centerpiece of fresh flowers at our table, I marveled at its deep garnet color. Now with my filled wine glass in front of me, I worried about not spilling any wine on the pristine table linens—but only briefly—because the wine in our glasses teased to be tasted. And I felt so grown-up!

Dr. Bateson raised his wine glass in a toast: "'Yesterday is history; tomorrow is a mystery; today is a gift. That is why we call it the present.' Let's enjoy the present together and welcome Marilyn to New York." We raised our glasses and touched rims. I had a feeling there would be many new experiences in the next five days—and many tales for Grace.

As I took my first sip of wine, I vowed to enjoy the present—after all, it was a gift. "Hear, hear."

CHAPTER 10

We returned to the apartment in high spirits. As we walked down the apartment's corridor to our bedrooms, Joe noticed the note on his bedroom door in his mother's handwriting. He read the message from her:

> Joe, darling—
>
> I arrived from Milan exhausted this evening while you were out to dinner. Apologize to Marilyn, your houseguest, for me. I'm eager to meet her. Will see you both in the morning when I'm more rested.
>
> Love, Mother

Joe went down to the bedroom door at the end of the hallway. It was closed tight, and no light filtered under the door. Joe stood in front of the door for a few minutes; then he turned and came back to me standing in the middle of the hallway. "Sweet dreams, Marilyn. I'll see you in the morning," Joe said flatly. He could not hide the disappointment of his mother not waiting up for him. It was the same dejected look he had had when Sidney picked us up at the airport.

I opened the door to the bedroom assigned to me. Too wound up to go to sleep, I sat down in the soft, cushioned armchair, putting my feet up on the matching ottoman. I looked around the room, studying the interior detail in the soft lighting. My bed was quite high and had a solid off-white "Matelassé" (that's what its label said) coverlet spread with a quilted design of flora and fauna. This coverlet met a chintz pastel patterned dust ruffle matching the drapery window treatments. The walls were painted a very pale aquamarine color that was the same color in the chintz pattern along with yellows, white, and lavender. The room was welcoming and soothing. Obviously, it was a guest room, since there was nothing in the bureau drawers or closet. I noticed this when I unpacked and hung some of my dresses and coat on the empty hangers. You couldn't miss the scented paper liner in all the bureau and vanity drawers when you opened them.

What luxury! I even had my own bathroom with fluffy white bath-sized towels with a turquoise-colored monogram *B* on each towel neatly lined up on the chrome towel racks. The large bar of soap had a scent of crushed roses embedded with the words, "French milled soap." Other toiletries—bath salts and shampoo—were included on the bathtub ledge.

I wondered who had stayed in this room before me—perhaps someone who was visiting from across the Atlantic. When I got into bed, the sheets were ironed and smelled so clean. I'm not sure how long it was before I went to sleep, but the next thing I knew, I heard sounds of people moving around in the apartment.

Having no idea what time it was, I jumped out of bed and went into the bathroom to wash my face, brush my teeth, and to make myself presentable to meet Joe's mother. When I looked into the closet, I realized I had not really packed anything that was "nicely" casual—an outfit to wear before I dressed to go out. All I had that would be somewhat comparable was a pair of clean, pressed jeans and my Wesley sweatshirt. Then I brushed my hair and pulled it back off my face into a ponytail. I was as ready as I would ever be to meet Joe's mother. After taking a deep breath, I opened my bedroom door and peered into the hallway.

Joe's bedroom door was open, and I could see him standing at the end of the hallway in the bedroom doorframe that I assumed was his parents' bedroom. It was where he had stood the night before after reading his mother's note.

Suddenly, the door opened across from Joe's bedroom, and his dad entered into the hallway. I realized that Dr. Bateson and his wife didn't share the same bedroom. How strange—I never knew a husband and wife would have their own separate bedrooms. Dr. Bateson headed toward the living and kitchen area of the apartment.

My thoughts halted in considering the bedroom situation when a tall, willowy woman, impeccably dressed, entered the hallway too, approached Joe, and hugged him. She was wearing a gray silk pantsuit with a purple scarf at the neck. Her flat leather shoes were the exact same color as her suit. Her haircut was short and chic, set off by pearl earrings. She looked like a French model or a fashion clone of Audrey Hepburn. I wanted to rush back into my bedroom and put on the best-looking outfit I had packed, but Grace and I owned nothing that had this timeless style—she was pure class from her head to her toes. I felt like a waif.

Joe turned and saw me standing in the hallway looking at them. He motioned for me to join them at his mother's bedroom entrance. His mom extended her hand to me as I entered her room to stand next to Joe. She had the most beautiful emerald-and-diamond ring on her left hand that almost knocked my eyes out.

After Joe made the formal introduction, she interjected, "Dear, please call me Chloe." The tone of her voice was low, modulated, and businesslike. She then turned to a lady standing near the closet who was dressed as elegantly as Chloe. "Marilyn, I would like for you to meet my business partner, Janice. We were very tired when we arrived home last night. I'm sorry for not seeing you and Joe until this morning," she apologized. Joe looked worried, and he herded me toward the door. He obviously wanted to usher me out of the room as quickly as possible. I wondered if he was ashamed of the way I was dressed next to these perfectly groomed and stylish women.

As we were going down the stairs to the kitchen, Joe stopped abruptly and turned to face me, saying, "I'm embarrassed about my mother."

Shocked, I responded, "Why in the world would you be embarrassed about your mother? She was just tired when she got in last night, and right now, she's probably feeling guilty for not having the stamina to wait up for us and greet us when we came from the restaurant last night—that's all."

He shook his head and said, "You have no idea what it is like for me." Joe was right. I couldn't understand how he could be ashamed of his mother—she looked flawless to me. Then I had a flashback of Joe and me driving up the gravel driveway to the farm. I remembered the knots in my stomach and the embarrassment I had felt in Joe seeing my family and where I grew up for the first time. Was it déjà vu for him?

CHAPTER 11

On the day before Thanksgiving Day, I wasn't ready to leave for the country house on Long Island Sound—I just wanted to settle down right here in the city. My stay had been way too short. When I stepped off that plane, I'd never felt so alive.

As we drove away, leaving the high-rise buildings of New York behind in the rearview mirror, I knew I'd go back to work and live there one day. I tried to explain my feelings to Joe, but he just laughed. "Marilyn, you're just seeing the obvious differences between farm life and city life. If you lived in New York, you'd soon see the city's flaws and warts. Ironically, I felt the same way about your farm when I visited your family in Rockport." And that ended our conversation. We rode in silence for the rest of the trip—together, yet apart, in the back seat of the Mercedes. Sidney was silent, too. He drove, his eyes fixed on the road ahead—straight ahead.

We left the main road and drove down a narrow, tree-lined road. Occasionally, we spied a house on a knoll or in an open field—always surrounded by towering trees and well-manicured lawns. Sometimes we glimpsed the Atlantic Ocean. This was not my familiar Kentucky countryside, and these were not farmhouses.

But I still wasn't prepared for the massive English Tudor-style house when we arrived at the end of the long, circular, paved driveway. Flawlessly landscaped grounds, rising to a bluff overlooking the bay, encircled the house.

The car halted in front of the house. Sidney turned to us and announced the obvious: "We're here." As I stepped out of the car, I caught a glimpse of a smaller Tudor-style house behind the main house that I learned later was a three-bedroom guesthouse. Beyond these two houses with their expansive lawns was a barn, except it was the stable for the estate's horses. In utter astonishment, I turned to Joe and said, "Wow! This is what you call a second country home?"

Joe blushed and responded, a little sheepishly. "I know, I know. It's decadent to have a place of this size that we only visit occasionally. What can I say?"

When we entered the house, Samuel and Sarah came out of the kitchen area to greet us. Sidney came behind us with our suitcases. I started to ask him if he needed a hand, but caught myself. Joe made no move to help.

I heard voices in the kitchen area as Sarah took Joe's arm, directing him toward the voices. I followed dutifully. She smiled at me and said, "Come say hello to the rest of the staff." As she ushered us into the kitchen, she said, "Joe, everyone had been asking questions about your arrival." I took that to mean everyone was asking questions about the farm girl he had invited for Thanksgiving.

The kitchen buzzed. Two men and two women, dressed in uniforms like those Sarah and Samuel wore, were scurrying around preparing food. "Well, here he is!" Sarah announced. Everyone stopped working, wiped their hands, and rushed to welcome Joe with a handshake or kiss on the cheek, crooning "Hello, and how are you doing?" Joe was encircled like a celebrity at an opening night. Obviously, the house staff was genuinely happy to see him.

Joe's warm smile turned into a broad grin as he greeted each one. He was so naturally animated and enthusiastic with them—quite the opposite of the way he had greeted his mother and father. His behavior seemed so peculiar to me.

When Samuel joined us in the kitchen, he announced, "Now it's my turn to take your pretty guest out to meet the outside staff. I assume you'll be joining us, Joe."

We walked out the back door onto an expansive terrace that overlooked a swimming pool and formal gardens. I saw a waterfall at the end of the pool, and the sound of its falling water reminded me of the Tennessee mountain waterfalls I had seen when my family traveled on rare weekend getaways. Ice had formed along the edges of the pool's waterfall. It created a natural ice sculpture like the ice formations on the rocks of mountain waterfalls and streams.

Strangely, this ice formation reminded me of Joe. He had been raised in perfectly sculptured surroundings. However, the flow of Joe's relationship with his parents had formed icy edges, and there was no apparent warmth to change him. It was evident that the staff had softened Joe's reserve, dissolving his rigidity and the distance he displayed around his parents. I made yet another mental note to talk about this observation—and so many others—when I got back to Grace at Wesley. How I wished my best friend was here to share these experiences with me.

After I met the stable staff, Joe gave me the grand tour, including the three-bedroom guesthouse. As I expected, it was royally furnished. I conjured up visions of executives of industry, celebrities, and intellectuals sinking into the luxurious beds after an evening of scintillating conversation and exquisite meals. It was easy to let my imagination roam in this fabulous setting.

I asked Joe if he knew how many people would be arriving

for Thanksgiving. There were enough staff and rooms to handle a multitude of guests. "Mom and Dad use holidays as a perfect time to entertain clients," he said.

My next question seemed so natural to me. "Will your other relatives join your parents' guests—grandparents, aunts, uncles, and cousins?"

He smiled sadly, "You don't understand, do you? We have never had a holiday with family like the ones you have in your family."

He continued, "My parents will arrive at the house later tonight after finishing work. Their guests will begin arriving tonight or tomorrow morning. They'll be coming from New York City, Washington, DC, Milan, and Paris. Since Thanksgiving is only celebrated in America, my mother invites special European clients to come across the pond for a long weekend."

I was thrilled at the prospect of meeting people from Italy and France, but I worried about a language barrier. When I asked Joe about difficulties in communicating with the European guests, he assured me they spoke English. "Some of them may speak broken English, but Mother speaks perfect French and Italian. She'll interpret. She always does for Dad's sake because he speaks English—period."

I remembered that Joe was taking French at Wesley. "Are you fluent in French?"

He dropped his head and said, "A little." Then he hurried to reassure me, "Please don't worry, Marilyn. You'll have no problem communicating with them." I still had doubts.

CHAPTER 12

After the tour of the grounds, Joe showed me the bedroom where I would be staying and explained that my bathroom, just off the bedroom, connected to the adjoining bedroom. He laughingly apologized. "When you use the bathroom, remember to lock the door and then unlock it for the other guests in the adjoining room sharing the bathroom with you."

I grinned at him and asked, "Do you have any idea how many girls in our dorm at Wesley must share a bathroom? And don't you remember that we have only one bathroom in my family's house?"

When Joe left me to get settled, I hung my clothes in the huge closet. My minimal wardrobe looked both scant and plain in the closet's roominess. I assessed what would be appropriate for me to wear to dinner and settled on a tan corduroy skirt and brown sweater set. With the decision made, I had a flashback of my mother sitting at the sewing machine making the skirt for me just before I had left to go to Wesley.

It reminded me of my first week of school, when all freshmen were invited to a garden tea on campus on Sunday afternoon. I had called my parents in a panic, telling them that I needed something very dressy for the occasion. With her good common sense, Mama suggested I shop for a basic black dress on sale and use the pearl necklace and earrings given to me when I graduated from Cannon High School to accessorize the dress. Today, I was grateful for that garden tea invitation and Mama's suggestion—especially since I had found a fitted straight-lined black knit dress on sale and had packed it for this trip. Of course, my little black dress would be perfect for this Thanksgiving dinner rather than my initial choice of a skirt and sweater. I smiled ironically when I realized the contrast of what I would have worn to my grandparents' house for Thanksgiving Day had I been at home—my favorite faded blue jeans and a comfortable, soft sweatshirt.

Joe said everyone would begin to arrive around 7:00 in the evening and I should meet him downstairs around that time dressed for dinner. I took a long, hot bubble bath in the fancy tub banked in a white marble ledge with brass fixtures in the shape of swans with the water flowing from their mouths. I relaxed in the warm water with bubbles surrounding my chin and hiding my nakedness. I could see myself luxuriating like this for the rest of my life—how wonderful it would be. I also wondered how Joe could be so unhappy with the life he led in his family.

Sitting in this luxury bathtub, I sat straight upright and vowed that if I did get married and have children, I would not live out my life on a farm. I now knew there was a big, wide world out there of many choices and luxuries, and I would work to get my fair share of this lifestyle.

When I heard voices downstairs, I jumped out of the tub and began to get dressed. I remembered to unlock the bathroom door for the other bedroom. I examined my image in the bedroom mirror and added a little blush, mascara, and lipstick to give me color and enhance the slight flush on my face from my hot bath.

My hair was long, thick, and blond, with a bit of a natural curl that gave me a more feminine appearance when I wore it loose to frame my face. I knew my hair was one of my best assets. Daddy used to say my hair was like the coat of a good animal that had been cared for with the right diet and grooming. Many times at night, he would ask me to sit in front of him on the floor while he brushed my hair. His theory was that brushing hair with one hundred strokes a day made it shiny.

When he'd look at me with a fatherly smile and tell me I was pretty, Mama would always chide him, "Clark, don't tell her she's good-looking—it'll only make her conceited."

He'd laugh and say, "She can't help it if she has my good looks. You know how everyone tells her she looks like me."

Mama would shake her head and walk away, muttering, "You're absolutely impossible." This form of banter between the two of them made me feel secure about my appearance. However, my family's reinforcement did not make me feel confident in these present surroundings.

Precisely at 7:00, I left my room to go downstairs. I heard many different voices below, some speaking in foreign languages. Before descending the stairs, I peered over the stair railing to see if I could spot Joe. Chloe saw me and called up for me to come down and meet everyone.

She took my arm and guided me through the sea of faces, stopping abruptly to introduce me to Jacque Morin. Chloe confidentially whispered to me, "He's a brilliant fashion designer from Paris, now working with the house of Yves Saint Laurent." Introductions were made, and Chloe explained to me that Jacque had recently designed his own clothing line, called Mouldin, and that it would be debuted the next spring in Paris.

Jacque smiled at us and spoke with such a thick French accent that it was difficult for me to understand him at first. However, I was struck by his impeccable appearance. Unlike the conservative Brooks Brothers conformity of most American men's dress in the room, he wore a plaid navy-and-red wool blazer with a white silk T-shirt and a folded silk handkerchief in his breast pocket. His navy soft wool slacks fitted his tall, thin frame perfectly. His shoes were supple navy woven leather. His curly salt-and-pepper hair came to the nape of his neck and looked wind-blown.

Jacque turned to another man standing across the room who was about his same size and height and said something to him in French, motioning him to join us. The man gracefully glided toward us, moving as if he wore ice skates. He was dressed in an elegant black cashmere wool suit beautifully tailored for his frame. His dark brown hair was brushed back off his face and emphasized his strong cheekbones.

Jacque introduced me to his "partner," named Phillipe. I assumed that he was Jacque's business partner, but I noticed both men oddly enough wore the same filigree designed gold ring on their right hands. When introduced to me, both these Frenchmen leaned in slightly and lightly kissed my right cheek then my left cheek. This gesture naturally caused me to slightly brush each of their cheeks. I thought this was the warmest greeting I had ever had and instinctively liked both men. They both seemed genuinely interested in me, questioning me about my school and where I lived, commenting on my unusual accent. I reminded myself to speak distinctly to cover up my country drawl with all these "worldly" people.

As more people joined us in the room, they all seemed to do the little kiss, a peck on one cheek and then the other, as a greeting. Joe saw me with the Frenchmen and came over to us and spoke to me. "I want you to meet Alberto Benenitto, if Jacque and Phillipe will excuse you for a moment." He took my arm and guided me across the room to meet Alberto, a rotund, short man with jet-black hair slicked back as if it were just oiled into place.

Alberto had his own confident fashion style, quite different from the two Frenchmen. He wore a black leather sport coat with a pair of dove-gray wool slacks. A gray-fringed scarf set off his black-and-gray striped shirt. His shoes were a type of leather that reminded me of the newly broken-in leather saddles hanging in my family's tack room in the barn. They had just weathered enough to look comfortable, yet new enough to look as if they were recently taken out of a store box. Joe explained, "Alberto has worked for the House of Gucci for many years."

As the introductions went on, the room kept filling with people. I turned to Joe finally and said, "I sure am underdressed compared to your parents' guests."

Joe put his arm around my shoulder and whispered in my ear, "Nonsense, you look fabulous. Every woman in the room would kill to look as good as you do. They wear makeup, clothes, and jewelry to try to achieve what you do so naturally."

Even with Joe's compliment, I still felt plain among the glamorous women in the room. They either wore silk flowing pants with colorful blouses or short, soft wool dresses with splashes of accent colors from their jewelry, belts, or scarf accessories. Their shoes were unmistakably fashionable, too. My Capezio black flats looked so out of place and made me feel frumpy. Then I looked up at Joe for the first time that evening, surveying him from head to toe. He looked so handsome in his tan cashmere sport coat and black wool slacks. I had never seen him dress like this before and remarked at how terrific he looked.

Suddenly, a loud commotion came from the foyer, causing all the guests to stop in their conversations to check out what had caused the noise. A tall, handsome young man with long, brown unkempt hair, dressed in well-worn jeans and a flannel shirt, had burst through the front door. He was loaded down with bongos, a backpack, and what appeared to be his wardrobe thrown over his arm. When he dropped everything in the middle of the marble floor of the entryway, there was an ungodly clatter. He entered the guest-filled room, extended both hands in the air, and dramatically shouted, "So, where's my family to greet this weary traveler who made it out to the Sound in a bus and taxi? Come here and show me some love."

Joe's parents simultaneously moved toward the boisterous young man. Joe looked at me and said sarcastically, "Well, my brother Manny has arrived."

Manny hugged Chloe and looked around asking, "So where's Janice, my other mother?" Chloe did not respond and quickly stepped back from him. Joseph moved in and gave Manny a bear hug. Joseph summoned Samuel in the foyer to take Manny's things up to his assigned room. After greeting his parents and Janice, Manny turned his attention toward Joe and yelled, "Come here, little brother, and give me a big hug."

When Joe introduced me to Manny, instead of a kiss on the cheek, as I had received from others that evening, Manny jumped back as if he were in a cartoon and gave me the once-over. Then he gave a wolf whistle and turned to Joe, asking facetiously, "Did you meet this good-looking farm girl at college? Who knew they grew beautiful blonds with such long legs in bluegrass country? Thought they were only known for their race horses."

Embarrassed, Joe started to apologize when Manny leaned forward, kissed me quickly on the right cheek, and whispered, "I'd like to see you later. Perhaps our rooms are adjoining so we can meet in the bathroom." He then winked, and I blushed, wondering if the adjoining room was in fact Manny's.

I saw Joseph say something to Manny in a low voice. Then Manny responded defiantly in a loud voice, "What's wrong with the way I look, Dad? The food will taste the same to me in these clothes as any others that I've brought with me." I wondered what kind of clothes Manny would have changed into if he had gone upstairs as his father had requested. Anytime Manny spoke, his voice boomed over all others. He was a total contrast to his younger brother, who was so soft-spoken, gentle, and proper. It was hard to believe that these two brothers came out of the same womb.

"Let's all go to dinner," announced Joseph. We left the living room and entered the formal dining room with its mahogany-paneled walls and a crystal chandelier hanging above the table, giving off the perfect amount of light to mix with candlelight. The long dining room table was dressed in a pristine white linen tablecloth with beautifully folded damask linen napkins at each place. A fresh autumn floral arrangement of yellow mums, white roses, and orange tiger lilies in greenery added color in the middle of the table, banked by sets of silver candelabras that ran up and down the table. White bone china plates were placed in silver charger plates, set off by a hefty collection of monogrammed sterling silver flatware choices. Four stemmed crystal glasses of different shapes and sizes were at each place setting, with ice water in the largest one. I blinked at the sight. The table was sumptuous. I had never seen a table so splendidly set.

On special occasions, Mama would use the china she had inherited from her favorite aunt, who had died and willed the set to her. We did not own sterling silverware, but we did have nice stainless-steel flatware that had come with the pots and pans Mama bought when one of our neighbors had a cookware party. I remembered Mama and Daddy discussing how much money had been spent on this cookware. Mama rationalized the expense by trying to convince Daddy how healthy it was to cook in good, heavy aluminum pans. She reasoned that the stainless-steel place settings were just a bonus to healthy cooking.

As everyone assembled around the table, Joseph, acting as the perfect host, directed each of us to our place before any food was served. What a contrast this was to the mental image I had of our family's Thanksgiving table, laden with food, when we all charged into my grandmother's dining room, maneuvering to sit closest to where most of the main dishes were located.

After everyone was seated, a man dressed in a tuxedo came into the room with a silver tray holding two bottles of champagne with labels that read "Champagne Lanson." Jacque eyed the label and remarked, "Fabulous choice—that's a fine French champagne." Chloe agreed, saying she had ordered a whole case of it from Reims, France, and would not think of drinking anything else. As the server poured the bubbly wine into each person's champagne flute, Manny raised his voice above the buzz of conversation and told the waiter to bring him a beer in a frosted mug. Joseph looked down at his plate, and Chloe acted as if she did not hear her son's rude request.

After everyone was served, Joseph raised his glass and offered a toast. We all saluted one another, and I began to take a sip. The champagne's tiny little bubbles went simultaneously into my nose and throat, making me feel totally euphoric.

I had only had champagne once before, as a senior in high school. It was "Great Western Brut" from New York State. A twenty-one-year-old sister in our group had purchased this bottle of sparkling wine for us to celebrate like adults to bring in the new year. This French champagne was far superior in taste to my New York State initiation to the bubbly wine experience.

With each course of the meal, a new wine was served. There was a dry white Bordeaux served with the soup and salad course, a red Bordeaux with the pasta, and dark Burgundy with the main course of a selection of different meats. When the dessert was brought to the table, I passed on the rich dark chocolate torte and port wine. I had eaten and drunk so much that I thought my stomach might pop, or more realistically, I might not be able to rise from the table.

My dinner companions seated on my left and right were a man who was a New York corporate attorney and appeared to be the age of my father and a woman who was a Washington, DC, fashion editor. Manny was positioned directly across the table from me. Throughout the meal, Manny kept looking at me with a smile (or was it a smirk?) on his face. He casually admonished me as the main course was served, "You'll explode if you eat everything that is presented to you."

The fashion editor from the *Washington Post* laughed too much as the wine courses continued, and she constantly addressed me by asking what a young person like me would do in a similar situation. I heard very little of what she said, since I was diverted by a foot without a shoe that kept going up and down my leg under the table. The attorney on my other side would turn to talk to me in my ear, and then the foot would devilishly move up and down my leg. Shifting in my seat, I tried to tuck my legs under my chair. Manny continued to grin at me knowingly, as if he knew my discomfort—not from the meal, but from what was going on under the table. When Joseph announced we would all move to the living room for cognac to help digestion, I was relieved to leave the table.

Joe recommended the two of us go for a walk to help our dinners settle. It was lightly snowing and very cold, but it felt good to be outside and moving around. The food and wine had left me feeling heavy and uncomfortably stuffed. Joe was very quiet and unresponsive. I wanted to ask him a million questions about the people and the evening, but the timing seemed off.

I said to him, "Tell me more about Manny."

Joe responded, "Manny and I are very different people. He's always been a troublemaker and always defiant. In prep school, our mother and dad made several visits to Wakefield Academy in Connecticut to try to keep him in line when the headmaster complained about Manny's behavior and threatened his expulsion.

When cajoling didn't work with remedying Manny's behavior, our parents ended up giving enough money to the school to name a building after our family to keep Manny enrolled until he could graduate with his class."

Joe continued, "Typical Manny—he was accepted to several small coed colleges of his choice, but Mother and Father insisted that he attend Columbia University. Again, a large donation was made to the school for him to get an undergraduate degree and then be accepted into their law school. Manny is a hit-and-miss student and academically just got by, although he has a high IQ. He always banked on the fact that our parents would bail him out when expulsion seemed imminent."

With a catch in his voice, Joe continued, "The irony of the two of us is that I am the dutiful son that my parents want Manny to be, but they never notice me. He is the son that demands and gets their attention. This irony was not lost on our house staff, who literally took on the role of loving and supportive parents when I was a small and lonely child. Manny was cruel and imperious toward the staff when we were young, and they avoided him like the plague."

It was like a light went on in my head in seeing Joe in this personal revelation. Yet, I did not know what to say to comfort him. There had been times in my family when my parents seemed to provide more love to Maria and it felt like they neglected Beth and me. Of course, we were a little exasperated and jealous of their constant attention to Maria because of the demands of her health issues. However, our sibling rivalry was nothing like what Joe had experienced with his incorrigible brother and the indifference his parents demonstrated toward Joe. No wonder he appeared formal and distant with them.

CHAPTER 13

"Joe, I'm cold and tired. Do you mind if we head back to the house now?" Our walk ended, but my mind was reeling from Joe's confession about his parental alienation and everything that had unfolded for me today. As we walked through the front door, many of the guests who lived within driving distance had left to go back to their homes and the houseguests were retiring to their assigned rooms.

Chloe cleverly had printed names on hand-painted ceramic signs that hung on each of the bedroom doors. When I entered my room, the bed covers had been turned down, and a crystal carafe of ice water with a glass was placed on a tray beside the bedside table. Lying on my pillow was a small wrapped gift. At first, I did not know if I was supposed to open it or not. When I saw the gift tag with my name printed on it, my curiosity got the better of me, and I opened the wrapper. To my surprise, it was a crystal etched perfume bottle from France with a note that read, "Enjoy your stay in our home. May you always carry with you the memory of this holiday with us." Little did the gift giver know how true this statement was for me already.

In my shared bathroom, there was a lock on the door leading

into each bedroom. As I locked the side of the door going into the other room so I could have privacy in the bathroom, I reminded myself I must remember to unlock it so the person staying in the room next to me could have access to the bathroom when it was not in use. I had peeked at the door next to mine to see who that party guest might be. Like my bedroom door, there was no ceramic sign on it. I deduced that it must be Joe staying in that room. However, another odd happening was that I saw Chloe and Janice go into the same bedroom down the hall, and Joseph went into another one. I was too exhausted to try to figure out this mystery. After brushing my teeth and washing my face, I unlocked the adjoining room door.

As I turned to go back to my bedroom, a sweet smell of smoke rose from under the door. Much too heavy a scent; I assumed it was not cigarette smoke. Since Joe wasn't a smoker, I also knew that it was not his room. I knocked on the door to inform the other guest that I was finished in the bathroom and that it was now available. As soon as I heard the voice behind the door respond, I knew it was Manny's voice.

He came to the door, opening it quickly. He had a smile on his face that lit up the room and made my heart race. This time, his smile seemed genuine, not diabolical as I thought it might have been at the dinner table. He leaned against the door holding a cigarette in his hand that was hand-rolled, like the ones I had seen Daddy roll with loose tobacco. He extended his other hand and slid it around my waist, pulling me into his room. I struggled slightly but hesitated to make a commotion in case the noise roused others.

Manny put his mouth close to my neck and told me how he had watched me during dinner knowing that John Humphries, his mom's attorney, seated next to me was probably trying to do something suggestive to me under the table. "I could tell something was up by the look on John's face, that he was aroused by you and was acting flirtatious. Joe is so naïve he had no idea what was going on, and even if he had, he would not want to make a scene."

Manny continued by saying that he wanted to jump up and tell John, "John, go ahead and get her really hot and bothered because I want her next." I had never had anyone talk to me like this. I was shocked, but also intrigued. I felt my face flush, and at the same time, I felt something tingle deep inside me. I wanted to explore this feeling further with Manny. It was like throwing caution to the winds. Manny was as thrilling to my psyche as he was dangerous to my body.

There had been many instances with Joe that I had wanted to have this tingle, this sense of pure sexual excitement, when Joe made advances toward me physically. But each time, I felt nothing, and I'd retreat from him physically. My usual excuse from pulling away with Joe was that I wasn't ready for an intimate relationship. I knew he felt rejected, but the truth of the matter was that I felt no passion for Joe and could not even fake it with him. But Joe was my best male friend, and I did not want to give up my relationship with him.

Manny turned to me and pulled me up against him. I felt the bulging hardness behind the zipper in his jeans. He pulled me over to the bed and put the cigarette in an ashtray beside the bed. He asked me if I had ever smoked marijuana, better known as "pot." I shook my head, and he said, "Well, baby, tonight is the night for some new experiences for you to take back to college."

The wine buzz from dinner and the intoxication of Manny's personality made me behave in a kind of out-of-body experience. I took a drag from his cigarette, inhaling the smoke into my lungs. I gave him back the cigarette. It had a peculiar taste as well as the odd smell, but on my third shared drag, I felt like I was floating. There was also a tingle between my legs. I had an insatiable urge to rip the clothes off Manny.

His seduction of me was direct and welcomed. His hands unzipped the back of my little black dress, and in one quick swoop, he unhooked my bra. He began to kiss my mouth and neck and then moved his lips to my breasts. I groped for his belt to begin removing his shirt and jeans. All I wanted to do was feel his bare skin on mine. He told me gently, "Slow down, baby—let's make it last."

He then laid me back on the bed. "Let's take off your dress so we don't wrinkle it," he offered. I slithered out of my dress like a snake slipping off its skin. My bra just fell away. *My, my,* I thought to myself, *I can't believe I'm lying in bed with my college boyfriend's older brother, who I assume will take my virginity at any moment.* I wasn't afraid about this prospect, only exhilarated, with undisguised anticipation of what was to come.

Manny kissed me so deeply I thought I would lose consciousness—my head felt like it was spinning off my neck as our tongues were intertwined. He moved down my body, kissing every part of it, exploring every nook and cranny.

He stood up from the bed to remove his shirt and jeans. He leaned over the bed in his total nakedness removing my slip and panties until I, too, was naked. Then, he slowly lay on top of me and continued to fondle me, kissing me all over and moving our hips back and forth together in a sensual dance. With the friction between our two bodies locked together, I began to softly moan. He fumbled on the bedside table and found the condom package. He opened the package adroitly and rolled the condom over his penis. He had obviously done this before.

My legs separated, allowing him to enter me. I could feel the pressure of him being inside me, and fireworks went off in my head as well as between my legs. I did not have to tell him it was my first time. He knew and proved to be an exciting teacher. He showed me how to move my hips simultaneously with the rhythm of his hips. After a while, everything exploded in my head and my body. At the same time, Manny became very still on top of me.

Then he rolled off me and lay beside me. He propped up on his elbow with his face near mine. He took his other hand and smoothed my hair away from my face. He said I could go back to my room and act like this never happened, or I could tell Joe everything. It would be up to me. He would never tell Joe anything.

At this moment, I did not want to think about what I would do in the morning. I just wanted to savor every sensual moment of what had just happened to me. Tomorrow, I would deal with the guilt—and what I should do about Joe.

CHAPTER 14

I consciously repressed the seduction scene when I awoke Thursday morning in my own bedroom. I vowed not to acknowledge this monumental occurrence and behaved as if nothing extraordinary had happened after my walk with Joe. I even dressed down—choosing the rejected skirt and sweater set for Thanksgiving dinner. It was the perfect choice.

Although the table was elegantly set, dinner was more like a traditional holiday feast than last evening's dinner party soiree with its assortment of courses and multiple wines. The centerpiece was now a medley of vibrantly colored autumn flowers, small pumpkins, and yellow gourds, intermingled with fall greenery. Again, candles ran the length of the table. Alberto was seated to my left, and an old family friend from DC was on my right. I relaxed.

Alberto was a charming, friendly, and inquisitive dinner companion. He insisted Joe and I come to Milan to visit him during spring break. The very thought of the trip thrilled me, but I knew it was only a dream. My family could never afford airfare to Europe—even if I could bring myself to ask them for the money. Allowing me to go to New York had been such a big deal for Mama and Daddy; it would be ludicrous to ask for airfare to Italy.

But at least I had Alberto for a dinner party companion, and he proved to be an engaging one. He painted a picture of Milan and all its amenities and freely shared a wealth of information about his homeland. His descriptions were so vivid I could picture myself in each setting. And he treated me as adult, discussing his work with me. By the time dinner and his captivating conversation ended, I was determined to go to Italy one day—if only to see if everything he said was true. I felt my connection to Italy was more than a coincidental dinner pairing. Meeting Alberto and listening to his verbal tour of Italy and Milan was fate.

Manny made no effort to approach me on Thanksgiving Day. And I purposefully avoided eye contact with him. On Friday, I looked out my bedroom window and saw Sidney open the town car door for Manny; then I watched it slowly disappear along the long driveway and sighed with relief. Manny was leaving my life to return to his in New York as fast as he had come into it, and I was filled with conflicting emotions—relief, sorrow, and guilt. But in that brief time, he had changed me irrevocably, introducing me to a sexual excitement and freedom that I'd never experienced before. However, Manny was his own person, obviously not influenced by convention, and I had to be honest with myself. We were different people. Still, I was inexplicably drawn to him as dangerously as a moth is drawn to a flame. His dynamic energy and bravado easily conquered those around him. I felt deep remorse that I had so quickly and so willingly chosen Manny over dear and unassuming Joe, my treasured friend. I eased my self-reproach by rationalizing that Joe would never have to know of my indiscretion with his older brother. It was just an accidental tryst because of an adjoining bathroom.

By Sunday morning, all the guests were gone, and Joe and I, comfortable in jeans and Wesley sweatshirts, were watching a movie on television in the den when Joseph came in. "I have to get back to the city early; I have a 7:00 a.m. surgery. But you can just relax. Sidney will drive you to the airport for your 5:00 flight," he said. "I've enjoyed meeting you, Marilyn, and hope you'll come back to see us. I can see why you and Joe are such good friends." I got up and gave him a hug.

I looked back at Joe, expecting him to hug his father. I shuddered when I saw the painful flash that swept over Joe's face—as if he'd just been sucker-punched.

Ten minutes later, Chloe came into the room to tell us she and Janice were headed back to the city with Joseph because they had so much work to do before an early morning meeting. Joe kept his eyes lowered and mumbled, "Sure, I understand."

After his parents had left for New York, I suggested we forget the movie and go for a long walk or a horseback ride. "Have you ever ridden bareback, Joe?" I was searching for something to change the tension in the room, and thankfully, that seemed to work.

Joe looked interested and said, "No."

Without giving him time to reconsider, I grabbed his arm and pulled him off the sofa, challenging him to a race to the barn. "You're on," he said, "as soon as we get our jackets and boots." We arrived at the barn, ready for our adventure, in a dead heat. The barn was deserted, so we took two of the horses from their stalls and put a harness on each, but no saddle. We led them to a gate to use as a mounting block to get a boost onto the horses' backs. Joe was a bit reluctant at first, but I promised we would go slowly until he felt comfortable riding bareback.

After we were mounted, I showed him how to press his knees into the horse's sides so he would feel more secure. The concentrated look on his face told me he was now in the moment, focusing on this new experience—exactly what he needed to get out of his depression.

We rode through the field and then down a wooded path that led to a stream. A stump near the stream was perfect for our dismount, and we tied the horses to a sturdy tree limb. There was ice on the stream, and a gentle snow had begun to fall, covering the ground. I was completely unprepared when Joe put his arms around me and kissed me more passionately than ever before.

"Marilyn, it meant the world to me for you to be with me this holiday. You charmed my parents and even my brother Manny. I have to confess—I'm falling head over heels in love with you," he said.

Those words, spoken so earnestly, shattered my complacent mood. Guilt swept over me, and my regret over what Manny and I had done so intimately and secretly was now painfully real. How could I have been so deceitful to Joe, my dear and sensitive good friend? Besides the guilt, I also felt profound shame. Joe had innocently poured out his heart to me, confessing his deep affection for me. And I had double-crossed him by losing my virginity to Manny, his big brother, his nemesis. And what was even more dishonest, I had anticipated and enjoyed this seduction and my deflowering with undisguised pleasure.

My head was spinning. *How should I react to Joe's ardent declaration of love for me? What should I say?* I quickly took refuge in my past reactions to Joe's affection. I pulled away, changing the subject and expressing my gratitude for the long weekend. "Joe, this Thanksgiving holiday with you and your family and their sophisticated friends is a memory I'll cherish forever. You can't imagine how thrilling it's been for this little country girl to experience New York City and be welcomed so warmly into your lovely apartment and magnificent home here on the Sound. You're one of my dearest friends and I've loved sharing this time with you."

Even as I spoke, I found myself at mental odds. I heard a little voice in my head urging me to confess my indiscretion to him, but another little voice counseled, wisely, that I should keep this secret to myself. Why should I add to the hurt he had already suffered because of his parents and brother's indifference toward him?

Almost without realizing I was still speaking, I heard my voice, strong and resolved, say, "Joe, you know you are a very special person in my life, but I'm just not in the same place as you. I'm not sure about my feelings toward you. Perhaps, when we get back to Wesley, we should spend more time with other people to define our feelings for each other. We should expand our circle. I need more time—and more experiences—to know what I really want." The despondent look on his face hurt me as much as I knew he was stung by my words. But I was right. I couldn't continue with Joe in good faith after Manny. I had a life barometer called a conscience, and lucky for me, it was still intact.

"Let's walk the horses along the edge of the stream and then head back to the barn. I need to finish my packing, and it's beginning to snow harder," I said, hoping to break the tension. He agreed quickly, obviously relieved to have a reason to leave the scene he had created.

At the house, Sarah fixed hot chocolate for us but urged us to drink quickly and leave for the airport early because of the snow. We hurried to change into traveling clothes and collect our luggage. Before we left, I hugged Sarah. "I know my parents would love you, and I hope they can meet you, Samuel, and Sidney someday." Joe hugged Sarah and Samuel before he said his goodbyes.

Our ride to the airport was quiet. I was thankful that Joe didn't want to talk because I was too busy sorting through all the memories of the people and events of the past few days to be coherent. How could I ever begin to relate everything that had occurred to Grace? Of course, there was one thing I could never tell her—that secret I would take to my grave.

For the first time, I realized I couldn't confide everything to my best girlfriend. I couldn't sit on the bed and babble every detail about my visit with Joe and his family. Some things were too intimate, and she would never understand the relationships or the emotions behind them. There were also some things I would never share with my family, especially the Batesons' luxurious lifestyle—a lifestyle they could never achieve.

When we returned to campus, Joe called Grace and talked about the weekend and my reaction toward him at the end of the trip. I learned about that meeting when Grace came to my room immediately after her conference with Joe. She chided me for not caring more about his feelings. My only defense was to say, "Grace, I really do care about Joe, but not in the same way he cares about me. I feel compelled to be completely honest with him because I love him—but only as a friend." She still didn't understand.

After my trip to New York, I reviewed my college plans. My Thanksgiving trip to Joe's home in New York had turned out to be much more than a weekend visit. It had provided a focus that literally changed my life. Before the fall semester ended, I talked with an advisor about a major in international studies with an emphasis in economics. The advisor's plan for me included a one-semester study abroad, a new program available only to students in the international major. I didn't see that happening, but I did see myself making changes in my life.

I now knew what I must do to make my dreams a reality, and that didn't leave me much time for Joe or Grace. But in one of those twists of fate, Joe and Grace didn't seem to notice my lack of interest or time. They were spending—and enjoying—too much time together to miss me.

CHAPTER 15

I looked forward to my junior year with conflicting emotions. I applied to the University of Milan for a semester study abroad. When I was accepted, I still hadn't broached the subject with my parents, fearing I'd be putting an even greater financial strain on them.

I was now living off campus, sharing an apartment with Grace to save money, and when the letter of acceptance arrived, I sat in the middle of my bed and screamed out of pure joy. Grace, startled by the outburst, came in, and I waved the acceptance in her face. She read it quickly. "Marilyn, I just can't understand why you want to leave your family and friends and go so far away." She was baffled by my hunger for adventure. "Why can't you be content to stay at Wesley and then go home to Rockport? Kentucky is home." She thought of Europe as a world apart and had no desire to go there. She tried to understand my desire to leave Kentucky for a foreign experience, but it made no sense to her. I understood her difficulty in accepting my plans. She just wanted to stay close to friends and family.

Grace and Joe were now seriously dating, and I knew they cared deeply for each other. I was content with this development.

I still counted Joe as my dear male friend and confidant, and it just seemed natural to me that he and Grace, my other dear friend, were together.

Earlier in the year, I had casually mentioned to my parents the possibility of my studying abroad, but I purposefully avoided the topic until I was certain it could be a reality. Now I had to convince them that this opportunity for me to continue my studies in international business in the country of my choice was an honor—recognition of my hard work at Wesley. I knew Mama would understand and accept my decision; Daddy would be reluctant. He'd always said he hoped I'd come back to our hometown, perhaps teach at the high school, marry, raise a family, and live close to them and my two sisters.

Those plans didn't include Italy. However, I did have one bargaining chip that I hoped would win him over. Although I hadn't seen Joe's parents since my New York visit in my freshman year, I'd occasionally received a note from Chloe, always on engraved, monogrammed Crane stationery. I always responded, but on far less elegant notepaper—often with an embossed Wesley crest on it. I was never sure if Chloe wrote the notes or if Janice handled the correspondence. It didn't matter because I was sure Chloe approved the content. I treasured these notes because I envied their lifestyle and, perhaps selfishly, wanted to continue their friendship. My personal goal—my dream—was to have a brilliant career, to travel and see the world as they did, to meet and deal with people from different cultures and backgrounds.

More personally, I'd heard nothing from Manny since that fateful November night two years ago. I knew we could never be together, but still, I had a crush on him and had hoped he felt something for me. Whenever Joe mentioned Manny, my ears would perk up and I'd question Joe, trying to tie my question into his comments. I tried to be subtle and nonchalant about my interest in Manny; I didn't want Joe to suspect my attraction to his brother.

So, truthfully, I had to admit that one of my reasons for keeping in touch with Chloe and Janice was to keep that connection alive on the slight chance that I might see Manny again. Since that physical encounter, I'd dated several guys at Wesley, but had no special feelings for any of them—at least, not like I did for Manny. To keep from obsessing about Manny, I concentrated on my studies. I dreamed that one day I would study in Europe for a semester and then return after college to begin my career there.

When those dreams became a closer reality with the acceptance to study in Milan, I shared that information in a long letter to Chloe and Janice. Within a few days, I received a letter from Chloe congratulating me on my acceptance to the University of Milan and inviting me to live with her and Janice for the semester. She sounded genuinely pleased with my news, and her invitation was my chance to make this study program a reality.

On the following weekend, I scheduled a trip home to talk to my parents about these new developments. Time was of essence to convince them, since I had to give my advisor my answer no later than the following week. I'd already begun my strategic planning—like crafting a battle plan. If I could convince Mama and Daddy that Milan was a critical career move in my international economics studies, I'd be on my way to Italy—and my life of adventure!

CHAPTER 16

My exhilaration battled my anxiety! How could I concentrate on classes when all I could think about was how to broach the subject of Milan to my parents? Between the excitement about the possibility of going to school at the University of Milan and the trepidation about how my parents would react to the proposal, it became difficult to focus on classes. I only wanted to think about how to secure my parents' buy-in for a semester abroad, but a little voice in my head kept repeating, *Focus on your schoolwork. If your grades slip, the Milan study program will slip through your fingers*. Somehow, I did force myself to read assignments and participate in class. But it was difficult.

I spent countless hours trying to determine the best way to win my parents' support. To demonstrate my financial acumen, I'd put together a bare-bones budget for the study program, including living in Chloe's apartment to eliminate housing expenses. And I outlined ways that I could raise money to reduce family contributions. I listed every way possible to come up with my own money between now and September. I'd save every penny earned in my summer job at Elaine's Dress Shop in downtown Rockport, and I'd use the few hundred dollars earmarked for my education sitting in the Southern Deposit Bank. I could also sell my ten-year-old Plymouth sedan before leaving. My financial plan would work. All I needed now was approval from my parents.

Driving home, I rehearsed my speech, vacillating between requesting permission and declaring that I knew how to pay for the semester abroad. All I knew was that I was resolved to go.

What if they said no? What would be my next step? The closer I got to our farm, the more apprehensive I became. I was so into my script that I barely noticed a strange car in the driveway, only fleetingly wondering who could be visiting on a late Friday afternoon.

As I pulled up to the car, Dr. Johnson, his black bag in hand, walked through the front door. A sense of foreboding swept over me. Who was ill—Daddy, Mama, or Maria?

For as long as I could remember, Dr. Johnson, a general practitioner, had cared for our family. His kind face had always appeared tired and old to me as a little girl. Today, he wore his customary black suit, and I realized it was too large for him, making him appear smaller in stature than I remembered from my childhood. His piercing blue eyes were now watery and framed by eyelids encircled in paper-thin reddish skin. Bags under his eyes gave him a raccoon look. His chosen profession had certainly weathered him, and I wondered how many patients in his career of healing he had outlived.

I opened my car door as Dr. Johnson hurried over. Eschewing his usual warm greeting, he said, "Marilyn, your dad has suffered a heart attack, and I'm not sure how much damage has been done. He refuses to go to the hospital, so I've sedated him because I want him to rest. I'll check back this evening after my hospital rounds. If he still refuses to go to the hospital, your mother must insist that he go."

Dumbstruck, I just looked at Dr. Johnson, nodding my head like a bobble-head doll. My initial fear had been well founded.

As I turned to go into the house, I fought back panic. My chest felt tight, as if there was a balloon inside me—one with too much forced air that might pop. I began to hyperventilate, breathing rapidly, as my hand grasped the knob. Then I hesitated, waiting until my breathing finally slowed to its normal rate before I opened the front door.

Mama was in Maria's bedroom trying to calm her. Maria's tear-streaked face clearly showed her fear and anxiety. She couldn't understand what was going on, but she sensed that something was terribly wrong. When my mother looked up, her face was ashen and mirrored Maria's stricken look. She jumped up and threw her arms around my neck, holding me tightly as if trying to extract strength from my presence. She finally broke away and held my face in both hands. "Marilyn, I'm so relieved you're here. I tried to call you at school, but you had already left. I didn't want you to be blindsided by your father's condition. I've called your sister Beth at work, and she'll be here as soon as she makes arrangements for little Dana and Sammy."

I was surprised at how steady my voice was when I asked, "How did this happen to Daddy?"

Her response was measured as she struggled to keep her voice from breaking. "Your father wasn't feeling well this morning, but he insisted on going to work in the fields. About an hour after lunchtime, one of the farmhands came running to the house shouting that Mr. White had collapsed and was unconscious.

"I rushed to the phone and called Dr. Johnson, and he said he'd be here in twenty minutes and that we should try to get Daddy to the house. The farmhands carried him back before Dr. Johnson arrived."

There was a tinge of regret in Mama's voice as she continued. "I wanted to call an ambulance at once, but I knew when he gained consciousness he would be upset that I had acted so impulsively, not waiting for Dr. Johnson to examine him. I also thought the doctor and the ambulance might arrive at the same time, so it was probably best to wait for Dr. Johnson's diagnosis. I guess I was hoping the ambulance wouldn't be necessary. You know how your father is about hospitals and added expenses."

"May I look in on him?" I asked.

She nodded yes, but warned me, "Be prepared. He's heavily sedated and may not recognize you—he drifts in and out of consciousness."

The door to the bedroom was closed, and I cracked it a little to see if he was awake. The draperies were pulled, so it took a few minutes for my eyes to adjust to the unnatural dimness in the room. Daddy loved seeing the sun streaming through the windows each morning, and Mama never drew the draperies at night. He insisted his morning energy came from the sunlight shining on him. Mama claimed it came from the two cups of coffee he drank on his way to the barn.

Lying so still under the covers, Daddy looked smaller than normal, and his complexion was sallow. Timidly, I approached his bedside and quietly pulled a chair up beside him. I looked at his motionless body, and suddenly, the reason I was here came flooding back to me. *What if I had been in Milan when this happened? How would I have felt being so far from my family during this crisis?* I quickly dismissed the thought. Right now, all I wanted was for Daddy to recover and get back to his feisty self. Nothing else mattered.

I sat quietly next to my father as total darkness enveloped the room and so many thoughts raced through my head. *Why was I so lucky to have been born to my parents and to have had such a magical childhood on the farm?* My parents had always made me feel loved and secure. Was I selfish—or maybe just plain nuts—to want to leave them for a foreign adventure? Why did I want to be independent—to leave everything I knew was safe and good? As I anxiously watched over my father, I questioned, for the first time, my eagerness to separate from my family—and even my ability to do so.

Mama looked in several times to see if everything was okay and asked if I wanted to get some rest. I told her I would stay with Daddy until Dr. Johnson finished the exam.

Removing his stethoscope, Dr. Johnson instructed us, "Call an ambulance. I want him in the hospital at once. Don't worry. I'll take full responsibility for the ambulance and hospital decision. If he's furious about the expense, I'll deal with it."

He continued, "He's stable enough for us to move him now. In the hospital, we can run tests to determine the extent of damage to his heart muscle. We need this information to know his medical treatment protocol."

Daddy had never been a hospital patient. The only time he'd been in the hospital's green corridors was when he visited Maria or seriously ill friends. He was adamant that, if possible, illnesses should be treated at home. Even as Mama was calling for the ambulance, his voice was playing in my head: "Hospitals are serious business and come with a hefty price tag."

When the ambulance arrived, Mama asked me to stay with Maria so she could ride with Daddy to the hospital. Dr. Johnson would meet them there.

The siren's wail and the flashing red lights from the ambulance reinforced how serious Daddy's condition was. I peered out the window to follow the vehicle's descent down the drive, and I shivered from fear. Although the temperature in the house was warm, my body felt cold and clammy. There were so many things I wanted to say to Daddy. I'd never put my feelings of love and appreciation for him into words. I just assumed he and Mama knew; I vowed to change that pattern *now*.

Shortly after the ambulance left, Beth arrived. As soon as she heard all the details, she jumped in her car and sped off to the hospital to be with Daddy and Mama. I was angry and resentful. Why did I have to stay with Maria? I wanted to be the one with Daddy. Maria, always attuned to everyone's emotions, sensed my hostility and looked at me with a sad, confused expression.

Instantly, I regretted my selfish thoughts and ran across the room to hug her, telling her, in my most soothing voice, that I loved her and would take care of her as long as necessary. Mama often said that Daddy was the only one who could make Maria smile instantly just by walking into the room. I couldn't imagine how traumatic it must have been for her to see Daddy on a stretcher being taken out of the house by strangers. I looked deep into her expressionless eyes and wondered just how much she could comprehend about the world around her. Then I had a startling thought: perhaps Maria was luckier than the rest of us precisely because of her limited ability to feel and experience fear, pain, and anger.

Mama came home the next morning and gave me all the details and the report of Daddy's progress. She said the cardiologist had determined there was some permanent damage to the left ventricle of the heart, but with proper care, he should recover. However, he'd be in the hospital for another week before coming home, and he'd have to limit strenuous work around the farm to avoid placing an added strain on his weakened heart muscle.

This report confirmed my worst fears. Instantly, I shifted my summer work plans. Instead of the job at Elaine's Dress Shop, I'd be working on the farm. Daddy would need extra hands as he recovered. Sadly, I called Elaine Poplin, the shop's owner, and told her I needed to help my father this summer as he recovered from his heart attack.

Then I retreated to my bedroom. How quickly my circumstances had changed. I was no longer the optimistic college girl who had driven down the driveway yesterday afternoon rehearsing the best scenario to gain her parents' approval for study abroad. Instead, I was the dutiful daughter, committed and resolved to do what was best for her family on the family farm.

I sat on my bed and studied the undisturbed memorabilia from my childhood and high school days: dried corsages with drooping satin ribbons, photos of friends with laughing faces, yellowing prom invitations, special notes from friends. I still had a piece of the plaster cast from my sophomore year when I had broken my leg sliding into home base for the winning run in a crucial softball game. Even my rag doll, Angela, still kept watch, seated in a prominent place between the bed pillows. Before I left for Wesley, I had asked Mama to leave all my things intact, and she had moved nothing. All these personal collectibles had meant so much to me at one time that I insisted on saving them. Now I felt compelled to sort through each tangible keepsake in much the same way as I was sorting through my emotional baggage.

CHAPTER 17

Depression set in when I got back to Wesley. There were mornings when I couldn't get out of bed to attend classes. My disappointment was overwhelming, and Daddy's heart attack was only part of it. I was distressed over his health, but I was also bitter that the heart attack had dashed my study abroad plans. Guilt and anger were an equal measure of my emotional decline.

A dark cloud hung over my head and affected my relationships. When Grace brought up my summer plans, I snapped at her, "Don't remind me!"

I resented the farm, my family, and most of all, my station in life. Why couldn't my family be like Joe's? Why did our livelihood depend on the weather and the success of each year's crops? Why would anyone choose the farming life? And it was easy to shift my resentment from the farm to the family. Why did Maria contract such a debilitating virus as a baby that would affect her physically and mentally the rest of her life? Why did Mama have to give up college and her dream of a teaching career? Why did Daddy's health fail at the most important juncture of my life?

Eventually, I tried to change my attitude—rise above my selfish "doom and gloom" thinking. Daddy was recuperating at home, following the doctor's orders and limiting his activities. I certainly was grateful for his recovery. But I knew he was worrying about the farm, and I needed to alleviate that worry. It was my responsibility to pitch in this summer and help with the farm until he was "back up to snuff." To reinforce this resolve, I decided to go home for the weekend and tell him he could count on me to take up any slack in the farm chores.

I was gathering my dirty laundry to take home when the phone rang. It was Joe. It seemed odd to hear his voice; I hadn't talked to him for some time. "Joe, Grace is not here. She headed home for the weekend yesterday," I said curtly. "I'm in a rush to get packed to go home this weekend myself."

"I know Grace is not there, but I didn't phone for Grace; I wanted to talk to you directly," Joe insisted. "I'll only take a few minutes. I'll be right over." I hung up the phone and felt the anger returning. Everyone and everything was controlling my life—everyone and everything but me!

Joe appeared at the door in a few minutes and asked me to sit on the porch steps. "I know you're in a hurry to get on the road, but I wanted you to know that I'm in your corner. I care about you deeply. Grace told me about your dad's heart attack."

Unsympathetically, I retorted, "Save your platitudes for Grace—I don't need them or you!"

He grabbed my shoulders and turned me to face him, "Listen! I care about you as one of my best friends. Grace told me your dad is to limit his work and that you've cancelled your summer job at the dress shop to help on the farm."

Suddenly, I was listening very closely to Joe. I'd been very guarded with Grace about Milan, not sharing the full details because I was afraid she'd discuss my study abroad opportunity with

Joe before I talked to my parents. I did not want anyone to know my plans until I had Mama and Daddy's blessing.

Since Daddy's heart attack had killed that opportunity, I didn't want anyone to know about Milan. Only Chloe and Janice knew the specific details about my initial plans, and I had dashed off a letter to Chloe explaining that I had postponed my study abroad semester because of my father's illness. I also asked them to not mention our communication to Joe, explaining that I didn't want anyone else to know about the Milan opportunity under these circumstances—especially my parents.

"Marilyn, Grace and I have seen how your father's illness has changed you. We're concerned and wish to help you get over this rough patch in your life. So I really want you to seriously consider what I'm going to propose. First, as background, my parents have offered to send me anywhere in the world this summer. I can't tell you how much that offer offended me. It was just their way of not having to deal with me for three months."

He lowered his head and looked at the broken bricks on the step below. Once again, Joe had made himself totally vulnerable—a rare occurrence—and my heart melted. But I also saw the irony in his confession. He could go anywhere in the world for the summer, and he was offended by the offer. I wanted to go anywhere in the world and couldn't and was deeply disappointed. How could we coexist in such different worlds?

His voice was barely audible when he said, "What I want to do is to help you on your family's farm this summer. I want to live with your family and work. I don't know how to do anything, but I want to learn. Please consider it."

He got up and hurried down the walkway, not waiting for my response. I knew he would have been embarrassed for me to see the tears he was brushing from his eyes. I wanted to call to him and tell him how moved I was by his offer. But I didn't. I initially thought he'd lost his mind to even consider a summer on the farm. In my confusion of processing his idea, I did nothing but watch him retreat. Then I got up, went into the house, finished packing, got in the car, and drove to Rockport. I felt numb.

CHAPTER 18

On the drive home, my mind was in turmoil. How could my good fortune—a chance to study in Milan—have gone so sour? The more I thought about it, the angrier I became. I banged my hand on the steering wheel as hard as I could and screamed an obscenity at the top of my lungs. I couldn't help myself. I had to let off the steam from the emotions boiling inside me—anger, disappointment, and frustration.

How would I be able to mask these pent-up feelings for an entire weekend? Dr. Johnson didn't want Daddy to have any added stress while he was recovering, and I sure didn't want to violate those instructions. Mama was already stressed from caring for both Daddy and Maria; I didn't want to add to her burdens. Plus, I believed that Mama would not empathize with me. I just had to be strong.

Grace was also in Rockport that weekend, catching up with her family. Since she had no Friday classes, she had arrived a day earlier, and when I got home, Mama said Grace had called and wanted me to call her back when I arrived. I didn't want to talk to anyone, particularly Grace, but I knew she'd just keep calling until I phoned her.

When we connected, Grace insisted I come by after dinner. She made it clear that she needed to talk to me, in private, as soon as possible.

I spent the afternoon talking with Daddy about how he was feeling and how the farm was doing. After the family dinner, I helped Mama with the dishes before I told her I was going to Grace's house because she needed to talk to me about something important to her. "My goodness, Marilyn, you two live together. What could be so urgent that it can't wait till Sunday when you're back at school? After all, you're both here to spend time with your families."

Once more, I felt pulled by intense emotional pressure from family and friends, exacerbated by my personal secrets. My emotional state was like a torn piece of fabric held together by only one fragile thread. Quickly, I manufactured an excuse. "Grace needs my help with a school project that's due before one of her final exams next week," I blurted out. Since Grace was getting her degree in elementary education, I knew this fib would resonate with Mama, who seemed to live vicariously through Grace's studies. Mama would have loved to follow Grace's career path. She was not into farm work. Other than taking care of her garden, Mama avoided all outdoor chores. Daddy often remarked proudly that Mama had the hands of a lady—soft with beautifully manicured fingernails—unlike the rough, calloused hands of a farmer. With that thought, I buried my hands in my pockets. Not calloused, but no stranger to farm work.

When I arrived at Grace's house, her parents—Mutt and Sue—hugged me and asked about Daddy's progress and my schoolwork. Then Sue invited us to sit down and visit. "I just baked a chocolate cake and want to make sure I haven't lost my touch with fudge frosting. I'll get some cold milk, too, and you can let me know if I still have a chance for the blue ribbon at the state fair." We all obediently sat down around the kitchen table and promptly dubbed the cake a shoo-in for a ribbon.

Sue continued, "I don't know how your mother manages these days, Marilyn, caring for both Maria and your father—she is amazing and never complains."

We finished our cake and milk, and Grace piped up, "If you all don't mind, Marilyn and I are going to Central City to see what movie is playing in the theater there. We won't be late coming home."

Once in the car, Grace let me know that whatever she wanted to discuss didn't entail driving to Central City. "Marilyn, I hope you'll listen with an open mind. If you can't hash things out with your best friend, who can you talk to? I know something is eating away at you. Ever since your daddy's heart attack, you've been so distant, sad—even rude. Joe and I are worried about how your dad's heart attack has changed you. And we're also wondering if something else is bothering you. Are you worried about your grades? Are you uncomfortable that Joe and I are discussing marriage?"

Then, more harshly, she continued. "You're acting like a real jackass, shutting out your two best friends. And I can't believe how insensitively you dismissed Joe after his offer to live with your family this summer and help with the farm. He called me at home this afternoon because he was so concerned about your reaction. Congratulations, you did an excellent job of hurting his feelings."

Suddenly, that final, fragile thread snapped. My emotional floodwaters broke, and I began to cry uncontrollably. Grace pulled into the grocery store parking lot and reached across the seat to comfort me. I continued sobbing, not able to catch my breath. I knew Grace thought I was crying because of the stress of Daddy's heart attack, but my tears were more from embarrassment. Shamefully, I realized my behavior was from the loss of studying abroad rather than from my family's problems.

As soon as I gained some composure, I unloaded on Grace. My secrets spilled out one at time, beginning with that fateful Thanksgiving night with Manny two years earlier when I was Joe's houseguest. "Grace, I was consumed with Manny. My instant emotional and physical attraction to him was overwhelming. It was so easy and natural for me to lose my virginity to him. You can't imagine my shame when Manny never acknowledged me the next day. And he's never tried to get in touch with me, although he knew he could write to me at Wesley. I've carried this guilt around for so long because that New York trip, made possible by Joe, was a pivotal time for me. The things I experienced in those four days changed my life and the direction I should take to achieve it.

"For the past two years, I've carried on a clandestine correspondence with Joe's mother in Milan. I shared the wonderful news about my chance to study at the University of Milan only with her. And that brought the unexpected offer to live with her for fall semester. The weekend I came to break this news to my parents and tell them how I had figured out my finances to make this happen, I arrived home to Daddy's heart attack. I never mentioned my opportunity to them. How could I? How totally inappropriate, given the circumstances! I came back to campus and told Mrs. Steadman to give the study opportunity to someone who could take advantage of it. I couldn't go because of my father's health.

"Grace, I hate the farm and my family's difficult circumstances. I can't believe you're content to marry Joe when there are so many exciting men out there. Joe is so mundane. God, I feel sorry for you."

Grace sat quietly as I ranted and raved. Once I stopped, she said, "Marilyn, look at me. You have to forgive yourself. You can have the life you want and desire. But don't condemn people who make different choices and are content with their decisions."

My fears and anxieties seemed to subside after my confession to Grace. I had a real epiphany at that moment, gaining an understanding of my motivations and looking at them now with clarity and calmness. I knew instinctively I didn't need to tell Grace to keep my diatribe in confidence. She was my best friend, and I knew from our long history that she would guard my secrets.

CHAPTER 19

When I got back to the house, Mama was in the kitchen. I went in and helped myself to the leftover rice pudding. Daddy was already asleep, and Mama said she'd put Maria to bed and come back to hear about my evening with Grace. I knew she'd want to know about the school project, and I was too exhausted to try to expand on my lie, so I said, "It's been a long day. I just want to go to bed and read a little before going to sleep. We'll catch up tomorrow."

As I walked up the worn steps to my bedroom, I felt a sense of comfort in being with family and friends. Everything was familiar, yet strangely unfamiliar. I had an uneasy feeling that I didn't belong here anymore. Or was it just because I felt so emotionally depleted after confessing to Grace? Once in my room, I put on my comfortable sweat pants and a faded T-shirt that doubled as a pajama top, crawled into bed, and reached for my pen and notebook. I was going to draft an action plan, mapping out my next five years on a grid. It seemed imperative that I answer two big questions that loomed before me: "Who are you now?" and "Whom do you want to be after graduation?"

But before I wrote the first step on how to move my grid plan to reality, I wrote in bold letters at the top of the page, "ACCEPT YOUR CHALLENGES AS YOUR OWN. DO NOT BLAME OTHERS FOR YOUR SHORTCOMINGS IN DEALING WITH THESE CHALLENGES!" This would be a constant reminder of my responsibility for my decisions. That was easy.

Writing my action plan was not. It was much more difficult to define than I had initially thought. So I lay back in my bed, propped up by pillows, and closed my eyes to envision what it would be like to study in Milan. I pictured myself walking down the narrow streets of the city and standing in the square in awe of the famous cathedral, Duomo di Milano, comparing it to the pictures and descriptions in the books I'd read. Milan would be peppered with fashionably dressed people clad in designer clothing from Gucci or Louis Vuitton, purchased at the Galleria, the glass-covered arcade with its upscale shops and restaurants. After wandering through the city's cobblestone streets or visiting its many museums, I'd relax in a small café and choose either an espresso or a cappuccino—depending on the time of day—while I listened to the lilting Italian language from the adjoining tables.

Then my thoughts turned to Chloe. I tried to picture her apartment, hoping that the invitation to live with her would still be open. Would it be small and cozy, with exquisite antiques, or light and airy, with contemporary furnishings? These Italian images filled my mind—a kaleidoscope of form and color whirling around in my head. I had to go to Milan. I had to see everything for myself. I had to seize this opportunity. I had to make it happen. Now all I needed to do was write my action plan so I could spring into action tomorrow—*Carpe Diem*—"Seize the day!"

My brain was moving faster than my pen, so I invented my own shorthand as I raced to keep up. The first thing I wrote down was, "You are a student in Milan with little or no money. First hurdle identified. Solution: Work out a budget and put it in writing."

While I was juggling figures, I realized a top priority had to be bringing my best friends—Grace and Joe—on board. I'd meet them on campus on Sunday and brief them. On Monday morning, I'd talk with Mrs. Steadman, my advisor, to confirm studying abroad next September. I wouldn't permit any negative thoughts. No one had been given my spot in the week since I'd turned it down because of Daddy's heart attack. My closing thought was positive: *I'm on my way.*

I didn't need an alarm on Saturday. I was electrified, bursting with energy to launch my attack plan. First, I phoned Joe. He answered the phone on the fifth ring, sounding groggy. He seemed surprised to hear my voice. I didn't want to tell him my plans over the phone, so I just said I'd like to meet him when I got back to Wesley on Sunday to talk about something urgent that concerned him. "Please call Grace. I'm going to be busy all day, and I want her to join us. Just pick a time and place that works for you. I'll adjust."

I pulled on my jeans, threw a sweatshirt over my T-shirt, and dashed into the kitchen. Mama looked at me skeptically as I slathered the toast with jam. No time to sit down and eat; I just ran for the door while I took a bite and, with my mouth full, called back, "I'll see you later. I've got something to do first thing today."

More than a little miffed, she called after me, "How many times have I told you not to slam the door? You act like you're going to a fire. And don't forget—you came home to be with your family!'"

My first stop was at Jimmy and Jane Ashley's farm, our closest neighbors. When I walked up to the back porch, I saw them through the glass storm door, relaxing over breakfast. My knock must have startled them because Jimmy jumped up and rushed to the door, anxiously asking, "Is anything wrong?"

I realized that I must look like a crazy fool, so I tried to catch my breath and calm down before answering. "Everything's fine.

I'm sorry I startled you with such an early morning visit, but my time is so limited, and I have a lot to do this morning. The first thing is to ask you for a special favor."

Jane steered me to the kitchen table and got a plate for me. I didn't want to be rude, but I didn't have time for ham and eggs. "I ate at home, but I'd love a cup of coffee," I said. I did want coffee to wash down the toast that felt like it was stuck in my throat. She put a cup of steaming coffee in front of me and then began drilling me. She started with questions about Daddy, quickly moved to the rest of the family, and finally reached me. I answered each one as quickly as possible and then looked directly at Jimmy.

"Jimmy, you know the doctors have told Daddy not to do any strenuous farm work?"

Jimmy nodded and said, "Marilyn, I've told him countless times that I'm ready to help at the farm. I'm there for him—whenever he needs help. That's a given."

"I know that, Jimmy, but I'm going to ask you to do even more—and this will sound really off-the-wall. My dear friend Joe—I've known him since my freshman year at Wesley—is from New York City and has probably never gotten his hands dirty. But he wants to live with my family this summer, learn how to farm, and help out while Daddy recuperates. Joe genuinely wants to get firsthand farming experience; I know he'll work hard. And I can't think of a better instructor than you. Of course, I have to tell you Joe may have a personal reason for his offer, too. He and Grace are dating, and I know they'd like to see each other this summer, but I also know he really is interested in learning about farming."

Jimmy tilted back in his chair and gave a deep belly laugh. "So, this is your favor? You want me to take this 'city slicker' under my wing so he can help on your daddy's farm. I can't wait to see your friend's face when we shovel the horse and cow manure out of the barns and spread it in the fields like peanut butter on bread.

Just wait until the end of a twelve-hour day—then we'll see how much he loves spending his summer vacation working on a farm. Bet he'll be hightailing it back to New York before a week's out."

Jane smiled and gently scolded Jimmy for being so sassy. "Jimmy, did you ever consider that this might be the city boy's only opportunity to prove himself as a solid worker? His family's probably never given him a chance to work with his hands. This could be a valuable lesson in responsibility for him."

Jane could not have imagined how little responsibility Joe had ever been given or how different his wealthy, spoiled life was from a farmer's. But I knew, based on their reaction, that I could check this off my to-do list. We chatted for a few more minutes, and then I thanked Jimmy and Jane for their constant kindness to my family and me. "Jimmy, if you're willing to help Joe, I'll bring him home next weekend so he can meet his agricultural mentor." I said goodbye and left for my next stop, the Allisons' farm, and a second unusual request for a member of the farming community.

When I knocked at the Allisons', Myrtle came to the front door and invited me in. "Thanks, Myrtle, but I really need to speak to Samuel. Is he here?" She said he was at the barn with the horses. We talked briefly, mainly about how Daddy was doing, and then I trotted down the hill toward the barn.

Samuel was older than Daddy and Jimmy, and he leased out his land instead of farming it himself. But he still cared for his livestock. When I got to the barn door, he was saddling one of his horses. "Howdy, Marilyn. Want to saddle up one of my horses and join me for a ride down to the river? We haven't had much rain, and I need to get down there to check out the water level."

My time was limited, and I hadn't planned to go riding, but something told me to saddle up and join him if I wanted him to agree to the favor. "I'd love to take a ride. Should I saddle your gray mare?" I responded. We left the barn and rode through narrow passages flanked by poplar trees. The smell of mulch was pungent, yet it had a calming effect on me. It was nice to be outdoors and riding a horse in a light mist of fog that permeated the air and created interesting shadows in the sunlight.

We rode to the edge of the river and dismounted so the horses could drink while Samuel surveyed the water levels. We'd spoken very little on the ride. It almost seemed as if Samuel thought I'd come by his farm to be his riding companion and nothing more. Finally, he turned to me and asked, "Marilyn, what in tarnation does a pretty little girl like you want from an old buzzard like me? I know you didn't come by this morning to take a joyride. What's on your mind?"

I sat on a nearby rock, cleared my throat, crossed my fingers, and said, "Samuel, you know the doctor told Daddy he couldn't handle the strenuous farm work as he recuperates from the heart attack? Daddy's got to limit his physical activity." Samuel nodded.

I didn't give him a chance to interrupt. "I have a young, healthy friend at school who doesn't know much about farming. Actually, he doesn't know anything about farming, but he's offered to help us this summer. I've just talked to Jimmy Ashley, and he's agreed to work with Joe, my friend, and teach him how to farm the land. I'm hoping that you'll work with Joe, so he can learn how to care for livestock."

"So, you have a friend who wants to become a farmer? Is he studying farming at your school? Where is this kid from, anyway?"

Reluctantly, I launched into my description of Joe. "He's from New York City—definitely a city boy. But he's offered to help my family this summer, and he is interested in farming. Of course, he's going to need good direction from real farmers to be of any help to us. That's why I thought of you and Jimmy—you're the best. Joe's a hard worker and very reliable," I added for encouragement.

When Samuel finally responded, I was shocked. "Well, he ain't no Jew, is he? You know there's a lot of Jews in New York City."

"Joe is from a Jewish family. I was lucky enough to be invited to his home for Thanksgiving my freshman year, so I've met his family and visited New York City. They were very gracious to me." I'd played all my cards; now I just waited for Samuel's response. If he turned me down, I'd have to come up with a plan B for this weekend.

Samuel sat down beside me on the rock, moved closer than I liked, and put his arm around my shoulders. He was invading my personal space, and suddenly, I just wanted to ride back to the barn and safety immediately. Then Samuel asked me in a low, intimate voice, "Has this Jew boy ever done anything to you?"

I responded indignantly. "What are you implying? Joe has always been a real gentleman."

He laughed when he said, "Well, you know how these young men are that do things to young, pretty girls like you." The hair on my arms rose. I found his comments and behavior bordering on lewd. His breath was so close to my face that I could smell breakfast coffee and his morning cigarette. When I jumped up to get away from him, my left foot slipped on the damp rock, and Samuel caught me around the waist to break the fall. He pulled me toward him, and I made a soft landing on my fanny, back on the rock next to him.

He cautioned, "Don't be in such a hurry, little lady. We need to talk about your friend." This time, I stood up more carefully and moved toward our horses. I wanted him to know this conversation was over.

As I mounted the gray mare, I turned to Samuel and, trying very hard to control my voice, said, "I'm sorry you're not interested in helping my friend learn about livestock. I came to you because you know so much about animal husbandry I thought you would be a great teacher for him. And I thought you would understand that Joe was kind and generous and just wanted to help my family while Daddy recovers. I've got to get back home now. Mama is expecting me, and the ride has taken more time than I thought."

"Wait just a minute, young lady. Did I tell you I wasn't interested in teaching this boy how to take care of livestock? I got more time on my hands than I know what to do with. Plus, Myrtle don't want me around the house all the time. I guess I got some knowledge that this boy needs. I'm sure willing to help him," he said as he walked toward his horse.

We rode back without saying a word. As I was taking the saddle and harness off my horse, Samuel walked over to me and said, "You know, Marilyn, I've always cared about your family. I'm glad to help your daddy out any way I can. That's what neighbors are all about. But I think you should know that I don't think your mama thinks too good of me."

His comment about Mama surprised me. I wondered why she would have a negative opinion of Samuel. What had he tried to do to her in the past? There must be some reason why he'd say this about her. Would she even want him around the farm this summer?

I didn't know how to respond, so I just said, "Thanks, Samuel. I'll bring Joe by next weekend so you can meet him." I finished currying my horse, waved goodbye, and headed for my car and home.

The first part of my Milan plan was in place. I'd accomplished everything I had set out to do this morning. But I wondered what kind of problems I might have created. Too late, I realized that I'd only considered what I wanted. I should have consulted Mama and Daddy to see what they might want.

Driving home, I was overwhelmed with questions. I was apprehensive, and tiny fingers of guilt were creeping into my head. *Mission accomplished—but what are my folks going to say? Joe was fine for a weekend, but how will they feel about a summer? How will Daddy react when I tell him I've arranged for someone else to do his work? How could I have been so presumptuous? And why doesn't Mama like Samuel? I've never known her to say anything negative about another person.*

CHAPTER 20

When I returned to school on Sunday, I barely had time to drop off my things and rush to the coffee shop to meet Joe and Grace. I couldn't wait to tell them all I'd accomplished to pave the way so Joe could spend the summer on the farm. After I related every little detail, Joe dashed my enthusiasm by bursting into the popular country song "Mockingbird Hill." He even had the audacity to sing it as a parody, with a country twang and cartoonish hand gyrations.

Was he mocking me through the song's title, my plan for him to help on our farm, or my country background? Grace, however, read nothing malicious in his reaction—only levity. "I sure hope you're better at farming than you are at country singing," she told him with a laugh, poking him on the shoulder.

My facial expression went from annoyed surprise to indifference as I collected myself. They seemed genuinely excited about the plan and the prospect of being close to one another for the whole summer. Once I'd outlined my complete plan and answered their many questions, I felt like a third wheel. These two lovebird friends of mine didn't completely ignore me, but it was clear their summer plans didn't include me. Heads close together, with intimate smiles on their faces, they discussed their summer in low, hushed tones. I excused myself and left them to their reverie.

I walked out of the café feeling so deflated and alone. There were many reasons for my dejection, but I wasn't ready to explore them. I decided to delay the trip back to my apartment by walking through, instead of around, the small city park across from the café. I needed to sort out my thoughts. My hasty plans from the weekend had buoyed me up; now they depressed me. I dissected my many hurried decisions, and now I wondered if they were the right decisions. Why hadn't I discussed my ulterior motive with anyone—especially Grace? If only I had shared my dreams and fears with her, I was sure I'd feel better than I did right now as I tried to sort out my personal conflicts by myself.

The park was quiet. I stopped at a World War II memorial and read the plaque honoring the fallen soldiers. I sat on a bench close to the memorial and looked at the monument for a long time. I read the names and wondered how each of these young people must have felt as they left familiar surroundings, family, and friends to join the military and face the threat of combat and death.

I sat in silence and thought about these young people. What had their lives been like before they were ended so abruptly and prematurely? The magnitude of their sacrifice helped me get a better perspective on my life. I just wanted to study in Milan—it was an opportunity, not a military deployment with a life-altering threat of death behind it. Those young people had had no choice. They were called to serve, and they did. I wondered how many of them thought they might not come back to family and friends—ever. I shivered.

My decision now seemed so simple and easy in comparison to their separation from the familiar. Once more energized, I walked to the plaque and bent to kiss it, whispering a thankful prayer for these soldiers who had sacrificed their lives so other young people, like me, would have the freedom to make personal choices. I ran back to the apartment, filled with a sense of possibility and already beginning to craft the next step in my plan. First thing tomorrow morning, I would see my advisor and tell her I wanted to study in Milan.

CHAPTER 21

Monday morning, I hurried to my advisor's office. Mrs. Steadman wasn't there, but a handwritten note on her door read, "I'll be back in my office today at 4:30 p.m. Please sign up for an appointment on this schedule." I wrote my name for her first appointment.

Mrs. Steadman's office was on the second floor of the decrepit administration building, the first building constructed on Wesley's campus. It was showing its age. The building smelled old, with odors of smoke and steam heat mingling with stale air. How different from the new life I envisioned for myself in Milan! As I started down the stairs, I was suddenly overcome by a spontaneous giddiness.

Clutching my books and pocketbook in my right hand, I hopped on the staircase railing as if I were mounting a horse. I steadied myself with my left hand and let gravity pull me to the first floor, yelping slightly when the newel post stopped my breakneck ride abruptly, digging into my backside.

As I swung my leg over the handrail in a less-than-ladylike dismount, the dean of students, Dr. Jefferson, came around the corner, catching me in the middle of this embarrassing maneuver. "Well,

Miss White, you certainly come downstairs in a more unusual manner than most of us. In case you didn't notice, the design of a staircase goes down just as predictably as it goes up."

I lowered my head sheepishly and said, "Dr. Jefferson, I'm sorry. I just couldn't resist, and I thought nobody was around to see me." I thought I noticed a slight upturn of his mouth, but I couldn't be sure. I was flabbergasted when he asked me to come by his office. He said he needed a word with me. I responded meekly, "I can come by now. I have an hour before my first class."

My heart was pounding with dread. What did he want with me? Was he upset about my banister plunge? Would I get a lecture on safety and the benefits of using good common sense? With my Milan plan in the balance, I couldn't afford any black marks at school.

We walked briskly to Dr. Jefferson's office; I had to jog slightly to keep up with his long strides. With each step, I felt more like a high school student called to the principal's office for some infraction. When we passed professors and other students on the way to his cross-campus office, I intentionally kept my head slightly bowed and made no eye contact. I was hoping nobody would recognize me shadowing the dean of students.

When we entered his office, he immediately apologized for the clutter. "I know my office looks like an explosion in a paper factory." After he removed magazines and papers from a chair across from the desk, I sat down. Half-full coffee cups with heavy rings of cream encircling the inside of each cup dotted the desk. Overflowing ashtrays mingled with the documents and files that covered the desk. Open file cabinet drawers bulged with papers. Piles of books were everywhere; some even had dust-covered jackets. However, as I viewed this disarray, I relaxed a little. Dr. Jefferson had a very noticeable human flaw—he was a slob.

"Mrs. Steadman advised me that you would not be able to take advantage of the foreign exchange program in Milan next fall," he began, taking his seat behind the desk. "The university was so proud when you were selected for this prestigious program. And when I looked over the criteria, it was clear that no one else was a more perfect candidate. We were looking forward to having you represent us."

He continued, "I'm curious about why you turned down this study opportunity. I believe you initially applied for the program. If the reason is finances, I assure you the university would help with a summer work program. Your first job could be to organize and clean my office," he laughed.

Total relief swept over me when I realized he wasn't angry with me and I wasn't in any trouble at school. The dean appeared genuinely interested in my reasons for reneging on my study abroad opportunity, so I elaborated on my father's recent heart attack and how it had altered my plans for Milan. "However, Dr. Jefferson, I now think I was too hasty in telling Mrs. Steadman I had to turn down the program. When you met me, I was coming from Mrs. Steadman's office. I'd already scheduled an appointment to tell her I had second thoughts about my decision and hoped the opportunity was still available."

Dean Jefferson said he was confident there would be a place for me in the exchange program, but it might not be in Milan. He urged me to tell Mrs. Steadman about my change of heart as soon as possible. I told him I had her first conference appointment that afternoon.

He nodded approval and then looked at his watch. "We better get moving, or you'll be late for your class and I'll be late for my staff meeting." I ran to my economics class and made it with seconds to spare. However, the lecture was totally lost on me. All I could think about was getting back into the Milan study program.

The rest of the day dragged. It was an eternity until 4:30—my designated time to meet with Mrs. Steadman.

Mrs. Steadman and I arrived at her office simultaneously, and even before she unlocked the door, she assured me I had a place in the exchange program and Milan was still available. "Marilyn, after we talked, I checked with the administration about including you in the summer work program. I wondered if earning money this summer might change your mind. I had planned to talk to you again to see if you might reconsider."

I thanked her profusely for intervening on my behalf but said I had a summer job at a dress shop in my hometown. I didn't think it was necessary to include one small detail in our conversation—the fact that I still hadn't told my parents about the study program abroad. I just knew that I would continue to methodically work my plan, one small step at a time, to make Milan a reality. I stood up to leave our conference and felt a painful twinge on my tailbone—a reminder of how not to descend the stairs to the first floor when I left her office.

CHAPTER 22

The following weekend, I went home to check on Daddy's progress and continue with my plan. Since Daddy felt better, I talked to Mama about working at Elaine's. I wanted her support when I tackled Daddy about the job. Mama quickly assured me that she didn't want me working on the farm with the men and had vehemently told Daddy so. After I told her that I'd arranged for Samuel Allison to help Joe with the livestock, she readily agreed to my summer job plans. And when I approached Daddy about permission to see Elaine and arrange to work at the dress shop that summer, I learned that Mama had already paved the way. Daddy said resignedly, "You can work in town. Your mama won that battle with me before you even asked."

Elaine's Dress Shop always smelled wonderful and welcoming. Its hallmark was the spicy aroma of the Russian tea Elaine served to her customers. They drank tea and ate little sugar cookies while she presented clothes to them. She knew every customer's preference and could always select clothes they'd want to try on and, hopefully, purchase. When we met in her tiny, makeshift office in the back of the shop, she offered me tea before we discussed when I could start, my hours, and my salary. After we agreed on my employment conditions, she asked if I could begin working on weekends before school was out for the summer. I walked out of the store with a new bounce in my step. One more hurdle cleared!

I was confident that my Milan plan was unfolding exactly as I'd hoped and decided it was the perfect time to broach the subject to Mama and Daddy. Back home, I took my notebook out and worked my budget figures for the semester one more time to insure the numbers added up. By leaving in August and returning to Wesley in December, I would receive full credit from Wesley for my semester abroad. Lodging was not a problem. Chloe had offered her apartment, so there would be no housing expense. My savings and summer earnings would cover transportation, meals, and incidentals. I'd talk to Mama and Daddy at our family suppertime, which always included Maria.

My luck held as Mama, unknowingly, had prepared Daddy's favorite dinner—meat loaf, mashed potatoes, green beans, and homemade biscuits. The stage was set for me to unveil my fantastic study abroad opportunity. I'd even scripted my opening line. I'd introduce the subject by thanking them for sending me to Wesley University and stressing the extraordinary learning opportunity it was affording me. I knew this would please Mama. She had always wanted to go to college and valued the higher education she and Daddy had provided for both daughters.

After my carefully crafted appreciation statement at dinner, I took a deep breath and continued, "Wesley has offered me an experience that I never dreamed could ever be part of my life. Please don't say anything until you have a chance to talk over what I'm about to share with you."

At this point, they eyed one another quizzically, not sure where I was going with this scenario. Within fifteen minutes, I'd presented my complete plan for my fall semester in Milan. Daddy looked shocked. He immediately opened his mouth to respond, but Mama interjected, "Clark, she asked us not to respond until we talked it over together." My heart jumped. I just knew I had Mama's approval.

That night, I could hear my parents discussing the subject in low, muffled voices. I thought about putting a glass to their bedroom wall so I could make out how the discussion was going, but good judgment prevailed, and I abandoned this idea. I just had to be patient and wait until they were ready to discuss it with me.

The next morning, I tried to act as if last night's dinner had been just another family dinner. However, it didn't take Daddy long to speak for both about my proposal. Between bites of homemade biscuits, sausage, and eggs, he said, "Marilyn, your mama and I are very proud of you and your accomplishments. You're our little girl, and we still want to protect you as much as possible; we also feel it's time to let you spread your wings as a young adult. We'll miss you every day during the semester. We'll also worry about you every day. You'll be so far away from us. But we both give you our blessing to go across the ocean to study."

The honey pot dropped from my hand, breaking my breakfast plate. When I jumped up to give each of them a big hug, I knocked over my empty milk glass. I didn't care. I just ran out the kitchen door, letting it bang shut, and stood on the back porch screaming to the world at the top of my lungs, "I'm really going to Milan!"

CHAPTER 23

The rest of the spring semester flew by. With studies, final exams, applying for my passport, checking plane connections, reserving my ticket, making—and remaking—lists for my Milan departure, and working weekends at Elaine's, I barely had time to breathe. Once I finished exams, I began working full time at the dress shop. Elaine was such an understanding boss. She never objected when I had to take an hour or more off to run errands to get ready for my trip.

A reporter from the *Rockport News* interviewed me about my upcoming studies abroad in late June. The article, a human-interest story with photos, ran in the July 4 edition, and I became an instant local celebrity. People stopped me on the street to congratulate me and ask about my preparations for Italy. Daddy and Mama were so proud of me and admitted they were enjoying the attention from church friends and neighbors. The publicity and attention added to the excitement surrounding my departure, but they also made the actual event seem less real—until my passport arrived. When the mail carrier delivered that blue passport with its official gold USA seal, all the hoopla became incidental. I was set—passport, photo ID, and credentials. *Look out, Milan—I'm coming!*

I'd written to Chloe in the spring telling her I was going to study at the University of Milan after all. She wrote back assuring me that the invitation to live in her apartment, which was near the school, was still open. She also sent a helpful list of items I should bring with me.

Earlier, I'd written to her about Joe's plans to work on our family farm instead of taking advantage of the summer opportunities she and his dad had offered him. I was apprehensive about her reaction, but her response was extremely positive. I immediately stopped worrying. Apparently, Joe had been so enthusiastic about his pending farming internship that she was delighted he'd found something to be passionate about. She even accepted his decision, made before he started his summer program, to change his major to agriculture.

A week before my departure, my family and a few close friends held a "bon voyage" dinner for me. Daddy, Mama, Maria, Beth, her husband Frank, their children, Elaine, Joe, and Grace were there, and Mama had prepared all my favorite dishes for the celebration.

After dinner, but before dessert, I was ushered to the seat of honor in the living room, and everyone presented me with going-away gifts. I felt like a birthday girl, unwrapping all these presents. I almost expected to see birthday candles on Mama's homemade coconut cake.

I was so touched when Daddy and Mama gave me a four-piece set of durable Samsonite luggage—"Strong enough to stand on." I wondered how many small pleasures they had sacrificed to purchase the set. The suitcases were cherry red with a pink interior lining—so beautiful that I almost cried. Grace and Joe gave me a Kodak Brownie camera, a set of flashbulbs, and two rolls of film. Beth and Frank gave me a beautiful leather-bound journal. Beth had written on the first page, "All my best wishes and hopes that your dreams out there—somewhere—will all come true." When she handed me the journal, she said she had one request: “Keep a full description of your experiences in Italy in this journal and share the adventures with us when you come home.” Elaine’s gift, a scrapbook for my Italian travel memorabilia and photographs, was the perfect companion gift to the journal.

I was now well prepared to pack for Italy and then chronicle my next five months. Little did I know that so much I would write in that journal could never be shared with these dear people.

CHAPTER 24

I was so focused on getting ready for my trip that I let days go by without seeing Joe and Grace—not that they noticed. They were content just being together.

There was so much to do that packing kept getting pushed back, and when I finally started to organize my clothes, I realized how humble my wardrobe was. Mama had washed and ironed everything I owned. My clothes hung neatly in my closet or folded in drawers, but what worked at Wesley seemed so inadequate for Milan, a recognized fashion capital. But even if I had had the money, I wouldn't have had the time to augment my scanty wardrobe.

The day before I left, I made my rounds to say goodbye to family and friends. Beth cried as I hugged her. She whispered, "I love you and wish I could go with you, but I know that my place is here on the farm with my family. They need me." I wondered if she would ever leave the farm and Rockport.

The next day, Mama helped Maria and Daddy, who still didn't drive much, into the car. I stacked my suitcases in the middle of the back seat, forming a divider between Maria and me. But so much more than suitcases divided us. We were worlds apart. She would never walk, talk, or plan a trip anywhere. I intuitively knew the space between us would become wider and wider as I seized the opportunities ahead of me. Two emotions—sadness and gratefulness—overwhelmed me. I reached across the suitcases and ran my hands through her hair. She reached up, took my hand, and squeezed it tightly. I thought I saw tears in her eyes. I wanted to promise her that someday I would do something to make her life better, but I didn't. Instead, I thought to myself, *If doctors can't help her, what could I possibly do?*

At the Nashville International Airport, Mama pulled up to the curb and told Daddy to stay in the car with Maria while she helped me with my luggage. Inside the terminal, she apologized for not walking me to the gate. "You know Daddy couldn't walk that far." Then she sighed, "And of course, there's Maria."

The child in me wanted her to be with me as I boarded the plane; the young adult in me realized I needed to board the plane on my own. I kissed her and promised to write often and call once a month. We'd already agreed on dates and times. As she turned to leave, she slipped a hundred-dollar bill into my hand. "Put that in your pocketbook. It's 'just-in-case money' for an emergency," she whispered.

I knew she and Daddy didn't have a hundred dollars to spare. "I promise you'll get the money back as soon as I graduate and start working."

The waiting area at my gate was almost deserted. It was still an hour before my flight to New York, where I'd change planes for Milan. I sat down and opened my book, *Exodus* by Leon Uris. I couldn't concentrate on this bestseller—too many butterflies in my stomach. Instead of reading, I reviewed the mixed emotions I felt about leaving my familiar community to embrace a bewildering world.

I took several deep breaths and calmed my anxiety by reassuring myself that someone would meet me at the Milan airport. My hostess Chloe had arranged for a driver and had sent me detailed instructions on where to meet him. Just in case anything went awry, I also had an address to hand to a cab driver. She said since I'd be arriving early, she'd be at the apartment and could get me settled before she left for work.

One worry was out of the way, but another surfaced immediately. And it was a big one: Chloe was a stranger. I'd never considered that. We'd written to one another, but the letters were more like a formal correspondence. Our one face-to-face meeting had been a few years ago—that Thanksgiving trip my freshman year. My real connection was through her son Joe, and she didn't seem to have a close relationship with him. Without Joe as my buffer, would she be embarrassed by the way I spoke, dressed, and behaved?

I was still wrestling with these fearful thoughts when the announcement came over the loudspeaker: "Boarding American Airlines 43 for New York." Mechanically, I moved to the plane, lining up behind the other passengers and then searching for my seat.

Once in New York, I concentrated on finding the international gate for my Pan American flight to Milan. Idlewild Airport was intimidating. It was huge, and in my first moments, I was completely absorbed in reading graphics to locate my gate. I was terrified that I'd make a mistake, and even though I thought I was on the right track, I double-checked my information at the ticket counter. Once I received confirmation, I quickly found the correct airport gate for Milan. I breathed a sigh of relief. My flight would not depart for several hours, so I walked around the concourse, looking in the duty-free shops. I couldn't buy anything, but I still felt so grown-up checking out the merchandise. Closer to boarding time, I returned to the waiting area and eavesdropped on fellow passengers, although I guess it wasn't eavesdropping. They were speaking what I assumed was Italian.

And that triggered another anxiety—how was I going to communicate in Milan with Italian students and teachers? But I calmed down quickly. My classes would be taught in English, and Chloe and Janice would talk to me in English—and help me assimilate. My first lesson would have to be how to order in a restaurant and a few important phrases, such as "Please help me, I only speak English." As the plane roared down the runway headed east, I settled back in my seat and began to relax. I was ready for my long flight across the Atlantic.

CHAPTER 25

We began our descent to the Milan Airport, and my heart rate started to ascend. Chloe had told me her driver would be waiting to take me to the apartment. But what if he wasn't there? I had that slip of paper with the address on it, but would I even recognize the address when I got there? And how would I know what to pay the cab driver?

Still panicked, I collected my red luggage and walked through customs with the other passengers, moving toward the terminal's exit. My anxiety kept escalating. How would I recognize my designated driver? How would I communicate with him? I didn't speak Italian. Then I saw the sign, and I was so relieved. The gray-haired man, neatly dressed in black, was searching the crowd and holding the sign "Marilyn White" over his head.

I walked to him and extended my hand. "I'm Marilyn White."

He replied in broken English, "Hello, my name is Mateo. Come with me." A sleek, black sedan with dazzling chrome trim was parked just outside the terminal. I'd never seen a car like this before (I learned later it was a Bentley), but it was certainly more luxurious than any car my family had ever owned.

As I started to walk toward the front passenger side door, Mateo opened the car's back door for me. I thought, *That's odd,* but then I remembered my long-ago trip to New York with Joe. We always rode in the back seat when we had a professional driver. I slid across the soft leather seats, pretending I was used to being driven. The strong scent of the supple leather reminded me of the smell of the saddles and harnesses that hung from wooden pegs in our barn's tack room. Now, as I climbed into this fancy car, I thought of home.

But once the car pulled into the road, the only thing on my mind was how narrow the streets in Italy were—and how fast and recklessly Italians drove, not at all like drivers in the States. I clutched the door to keep from sliding across the seat. After careening from side to side to maneuver through these needlelike streets, Mateo stopped abruptly in front of a row of three-story apartments. He put the emergency blinkers on, got out of the car, and walked around to open my door before gathering my luggage from the trunk. He motioned for me to follow and declined my offer to help with the luggage. He simply shook his head and muttered something in Italian.

He pressed several numbers on the keypad near the apartment door, and immediately, I heard a woman's voice that sounded like Chloe say, *"Si."* Mateo said something in Italian, and she answered in Italian. The lock clicked, and Mateo pushed the door open. We walked into a white-marble-floored lobby with a curving staircase that resembled a reverse corkscrew ascending as far as I could see. Mateo led me to a glass elevator trimmed in brass and stood aside to let me enter first. He followed me and pressed the top button, marked *"Attico."*

Why in the world would he take me to the attic? When the elevator stopped and the doors opened, Chloe was waiting. It was only 9:00 a.m. and she wore a full-length, silk, coral-colored robe with matching ballet-like slippers. But she had on makeup, and her hair was perfectly groomed. She reached out her arms in greeting and kissed me on both cheeks—continental style. In a warm, welcoming voice she said, *"Buongiorno!* Welcome to Italy and your new home for five months" as she stepped aside to let me see the apartment, the building's penthouse. I made a mental note of my first Italian word, *attico.*

Chloe directed Mateo to take my luggage to the room that I assumed would be mine during my stay. Speaking in Italian to Mateo, she obviously dismissed him with the phrase *"Ti ringrazio tanto."* Then she turned to me, smiled most welcomingly, and said, "Before I show you your room, let me give you the grand tour."

We were standing on marble floors in the pristine living room, and I couldn't help wondering if anyone ever sat on the two facing white sofas that dominated the room. The white rug that divided them looked soft and almost as inviting as the sofas. Beautiful glass accessories dotted the room, giving it a smattering of just the right amount of color. "Marilyn, all the glass comes from the island of Murano," said Chloe. "Before you return to the States, I must take you to Venice for a long weekend with a side excursion to the island."

Trying to mask the fact that I was having trouble concentrating because I was so awed and overwhelmed by this room, I enthusiastically gasped, "That would be great!"

An exquisite hand-blown glass chandelier hung over the long, polished dining room table. Chloe said it was also from Murano. The only way I could relate to all this glass artwork was by remembering a high school class trip to the Smoky Mountains in Tennessee, where we had watched a man blow glass into small animals. I had bought Mama a small glass giraffe that day.

In the kitchen, Chloe introduced me to Estella, the cook. Chloe said, "Anything you wish to eat, Estella will prepare for you. Her specialty is homemade pasta." This image reminded me of my aunt Margaret's spaghetti and meatballs.

Janice walked into the kitchen just as I was about to ask Chloe if the kitchen belonged to Estella or if she also cooked. Chloe and Janice exchanged a few words in Italian before Janice extended both her hands toward me and kissed me on both cheeks. This greeting was a little friendlier than a Rockport greeting, and I found it a nice custom. Chloe said she and Janice were going to get ready to go to the office and she'd show me my room. She suggested I could explore Milan on my own.

My bedroom had an off-white carpet and soft, salmon-colored walls. The comforter was off-white with light coral squares and matching throw pillows. My room was comfortably warm and welcoming. Chloe opened the door to the adjoining bathroom, and I noticed that the towels and shower curtain had the same soft salmon color as the bedroom walls. The bathtub had a shower, and next to the commode, I saw what looked like a second small toilet. Chloe must have realized I was confused; I was staring at it with a questioning look. She told me it was a bidet and explained its hygienic function. "Most European homes have one," she said.

After Chloe left, I began unpacking. My wardrobe and belongings seemed so simple and sparse in this lovely, well-appointed room. As I hung my cotton and wool dresses, plaid wool pants, corduroy skirts, sweaters, and blouses in that spacious closet, each garment reminded me of how unattractive my life back on the farm now seemed.

I owned only one "little black dress," which I wore with black pumps and a single strand of pearls. My other dressy dress was red wool that Elaine had allowed me to purchase at a discount when I worked at her shop during the summer. When I wore the black or red dresses back home, I felt so elegantly dressed. Somehow, I didn't think I'd have that same feeling in Italy when I slipped into either of them.

CHAPTER 26

Janice had placed a walking tour map and Milan guidebook on my bedside table with suggestions for my first day of sightseeing in Milan. Her handwritten note explained that the Duomo di Milano Cathedral, dedicated to Sister Chiesa di Santa Maria delle Grazie, was close to the apartment. I glanced at the guidebook and learned that the Duomo di Milano was a fifteenth-century Gothic-style cathedral that had taken six centuries to complete and was known for its variety of architectural styles. The convent next door housed Leonardo da Vinci's magnificent "The Last Supper" mural.

As I tucked the map and guidebook into my pocketbook, I saw another paper—instructions about getting back into the apartment and a schedule of mealtimes. The instructions also included a form I could fill out to request special foods, details of where I should leave any clothes that needed to be dry cleaned or laundered, and a fat envelope with lira that looked like a fortune to me. The note just said, "Welcome to Milan."

This generosity and thoughtfulness overwhelmed me. Still, I squirmed, shifting from foot to foot, trying to decide how to reciprocate. Should I go find Chloe and Janice and hug their necks?

Should I give them United States currency to replace the Italian lira? How? I didn't even know the exchange rate.

I started toward the door, but suddenly I felt exhausted. I blamed jet lag, no sleep on the airplane, and the excitement of being in Milan. I took a quick bath and changed clothes, thinking that would revive me. Then I stretched out on my bed for what I told myself would be a short nap. Much later, I was startled by the sound of someone in the room. When I opened my eyes and sat up, Estella was standing by the bed with a tray of food.

"Signora Chloe said you should not sleep all day or you will not be able to sleep tonight," Estella said in broken English. As I jumped up from the bed, I almost knocked the tray out of her hands. She asked if I would prefer my tray in bed or on the terrace, which I now saw was just through the double glass doors off my bedroom. *This scene can't be real. People don't live like this, do they? What is wrong with Joe? Why is he on the farm and I'm here?*

I gestured toward the terrace. When Estella settled me in a chair with the luncheon tray on my lap, I breathed in the cool air and basked in the warmth of the sun. Sounds of the city below—blowing automobile horns and chattering Italian voices—floated up. The scent of food cooking in nearby restaurants reminded me of the sense of exhilaration I'd felt in New York—only in a different language.

Just as I was lapping up the last bit of the food on my luncheon tray, Estella appeared with a light, fluffy dessert and a small cup of espresso, which did wonders in waking me up. This must have been what Joe was talking about when he said the Italians pulled off highways when they got tired to get a jolt of espresso at the Autogrill. He swore they always returned to their cars and finished the drive to their destinations at a much higher rate of speed once they ingested this brew.

I finished the dessert, picked up my tray, and went downstairs to the kitchen. Estella quickly ran to me and removed the tray from my hands. In broken English, she chided me, *"Ma Mia, Signorina,* I do the job." I was confused. Figuring out my new home was going to be complicated. I hoped I hadn't offended Estella.

CHAPTER 27

Clutching my map and guidebook, I left the apartment to explore. As soon as I stepped out into the bustling streets, I was gripped by a feeling of exuberance and unbounded energy. My classes would begin on Monday, so I had the whole weekend for my Milan sightseeing adventure. Of course, even if I walked all afternoon today, plus all day Saturday and Sunday, I'd only make a small dent in my guidebook's list of recommended sights. *But who cares? I have five whole months to explore this wonderful city.* I set a leisurely pace and headed to my first destination, the Plaza Del Duomo, the cathedral square.

At the Plaza, I realized my Kodak Brownie camera could not begin to capture the cathedral's total magnificence. I had to settle for just some of its lacy architectural detail. My guidebook described this Gothic cathedral as built in the shape of a Latin cross with an impressive construction history—more than six centuries—and said that when Napoleon had conquered Milan in the early nineteenth century, he added his own decorating ideas to the façade.

I climbed to the roof of the church, moving up through pinnacles, turrets, and marble statuary. A gilded Madonna towered over the tallest spire. As I stood in this spectacular structure, I couldn't stop myself from comparing this magnificent edifice with the simple little, white, wood-framed church where my family worshiped every week. And I briefly wondered—which structure did God value more, or did it matter to Him?

I spent most of the afternoon at the church, but I was never completely lost in my surroundings. I checked my watch constantly, remembering that Chloe had said cocktails would be served at 5:00 p.m. in the solarium off the study near the garden. I wasn't sure if I was expected to join them for the cocktail hour, but I felt I should return. I didn't want Chloe to be concerned about my whereabouts, and I had to change for dinner.

When I got back to the apartment, Chloe called me into the solarium. I hesitated at the door, thinking how underdressed I was. Chloe and Janice had changed from their work clothes into what appeared to be flowing velvet lounging outfits. Chloe's ensemble of emerald green emphasized her eyes; Janice was wearing pants and a top of off-white with gold trim, accentuated by strappy gold high heels.

They looked up as I entered the room. "So how did you spend your first day in Milan?" asked Chloe. I immediately began an excited monologue, interrupted by a gentleman dressed in black pants, short jacket, white shirt, and black bowtie, who offered me a glass of white wine from a silver tray. I took the glass and sipped the wine before continuing to expound upon my incredible adventure at the *Il Duomo.*

At first, Chloe and Janice seemed entertained by my animated description of the exploits of my day, but I didn't command their attention for very long. Almost, but not quite, abruptly, their expressions changed, and they began to dissect their afternoon business meeting with the House of Gucci. "I was thrilled when Marco seemed so interested in the design of our holiday wear line for next season. How did you interpret his interest, Janice?" asked Chloe.

I'm not sure whether I wanted to capture their attention again or just to contribute to their conversation, but I interjected, "You should have seen the huge holiday season order Elaine's Dress Shop received before I left for Milan. It was so large we had to store the merchandise in boxes in the back until Elaine had her fall sale and we had room for the winter and holiday stock," I said authoritatively. They looked at each other in surprise and then smiled.

I blushed and stared at the second glass of wine I'd accepted from the same gentleman, who now appeared and announced that dinner was served. Chloe and Janice continued their conversation at dinner and made no effort to include me. They discussed clothing design and rattled off the names of people who should be on the invitation list for the party they were planning in November. Since I wasn't participating in their conversation, all my thoughts were now on how soon I could escape to my bedroom.

When Chloe and Janice rose to go to the study for their brandy nightcaps, I excused myself. Not only was I sleepy from the wine and the three-course dinner, but I was also totally exhausted from my first day of sightseeing in Milan, as well as from the time change and my new lifestyle.

I spent the rest of the weekend exploring Milan's art and science museum, *Museo D'Arte e Scienza,* and the cathedral's museum, *Museo della Fabbrica del Duomo.* I also discovered the *Quadrilatero della Moda,* the world-famous high-fashion clothing district near the cathedral, which promised to be one of the most fascinating sections in the city. This was Milan's hub for big designer names and luxurious stores that would soon be part of my education into Milan simply by living with Chloe and Janice.

As I strolled through the district, I began to see that Chloe and Janice's lifestyle fit perfectly into this sophisticated fashion world. They dressed like the displays in the windows. They talked about the colors, fabrics, and styles that dominated the storefronts along my window-shopping route. Although I couldn't afford one garment in the fashion district shops, I still wanted to know the perfect stylish trend. And I carried that thought to an even broader perspective: I wanted to know how fashion translated into business—my true intellectual interest.

That night at dinner, I told Chloe and Janice about my glorious venture into the fashion district that afternoon. I recounted peering into the windows and finding myself intrigued by the fashions and the fashion industry. I wanted to learn so much more about fashion as a business. Both seemed impressed by my observations and determination to delve more deeply into this important business. "You know, dear, you must be willing to be an individual first and know yourself before you can create design in fashion, art, or architecture," Chloe said. "When you design what you think is cutting edge or a perfect runway-ready creation, there always will be someone to judge your design and criticize your creativity. You must have both the intrinsic talent and the acquired confidence to continue to create despite your critics."

I listened carefully to Chloe and then unexpectedly confided, "Although I've never told you, I grew up with a sister who is both physically and mentally handicapped. I had to learn to ignore the looks and disregard the comments that people made about her." I didn't say it, but I also thought, *And learn to accept her myself.* Silently, I thanked Maria for providing me with the ability to not let other people's opinions influence me or sway my confidence.

My revelation and obvious interest in fashion were apparently the only impetus that Chloe and Janice needed to welcome me into their work world. They began by showing me business plans made and scrapped, failed designs, colors that faded, and fabrics that raveled. They shared with me the difficult times and the challenges they—and others—faced in the industry. Chloe brought the session to a close. "It's past midnight, and we all have a big day tomorrow," she said. "We'll share our successes with you tomorrow night."

I went to sleep that night with my mind swirling in anticipation of my next evening of instruction from these two accomplished women.

CHAPTER 28

On Monday morning, I awoke in a panic. My first day of classes at the university, and I'd overslept by thirty minutes. I grabbed the first outfit I saw in my closet and, still buttoning my blouse, rushed downstairs. The breakfast of bread, cheese, cold meats, and coffee with milk in no way resembled my farm fare, but it didn't matter. I was way too hyper to eat.

Luckily, the university was only four blocks from the apartment. My schedule had been arranged before I left Wesley, and came with full instructions, but I still had those familiar butterflies fluttering in my stomach. This whole experience was uncannily like my first day at Wesley.

When I got to the address on my instruction sheet, I was a little puzzled. The building looked like an apartment to me. It was several stories high and painted a dark yellow-gold—no campus, not even a landscaped yard. Definitely not Wesley!

The doors on the building dwarfed me. They seemed twenty feet tall and quite thick. I used my full body weight to push open the door and walked into a dark hallway. The white stucco walls did nothing to lighten the space. When my eyes adjusted to the dim light, I saw numbered doors on both sides of the hallway. My instructions were to go to the door numbered twelve *(dodici)* to meet my advisor. At the end of the hallway, I found the door and knocked timidly on it. The answer came in Italian. *Oh no, this might not be as easy as I had hoped.*

I entered a small room, furnished with a desk and two chairs. An elderly man was seated behind the dark wooden desk, and he motioned for me to sit in the other chair. He began speaking in rapid Italian. Totally confused, I simply handed him my instruction sheet. He glanced at the paper, smiled warmly, and immediately transitioned into beautiful English with a lilting Italian accent. I calmed down at once, releasing most of those butterflies in my stomach.

"I'm Sandro Gamba, and I'll be your contact person during your tenure at the university. Let's get started." He reviewed my instructions and then walked me to my first classroom. Before he left, he said, "Don't hesitate to come to see me any time you have questions."

Several students were already seated in the classroom, even though it was still twenty minutes before the class was to begin. I took a seat next to a girl whom I thought looked like she might be an American. She had dark brown hair and blue eyes and introduced herself as Teresa Bennini. She was Italian but spoke perfect English.

She must have seen my surprised look because she said, "I grew up in Rome, but my parents are bilingual, so we spoke both Italian and English at home. I came to Milan two years ago to study fashion design. As you probably know, Milan has an excellent international reputation for elegant fashion design. We compete with Paris."

And she was a good example of that competition. Her outfit, a fitted gray dress accented by a black velvet-trimmed collar and sleeves and coordinated with black stockings and black patent shoes, demonstrated her personal sense of high style and the ease of finding fashionable clothing in Milan. My outfit, a plaid wool skirt, teamed with a pullover cable wool sweater, knee socks, and penny loafers, was frumpy in comparison.

Since I couldn't correct the situation, I shook off my feelings of inadequacy and introduced myself, explaining I was beginning my fourth year at Wesley, a small liberal arts college in Kentucky, majoring in international business studies. We chatted effortlessly until the classroom filled and the professor entered.

Each of my classes had about thirty English-speaking students—Americans as well as others from countries around the world. I was naturally drawn to the Americans, but after meeting with Teresa I purposefully promised myself I would seek out students from other cultures. I truly believed this would be the best way to maximize the impact of my time in Milan.

Learning Italian would be another way. I had confided to Teresa that I wanted to learn to speak Italian fluently. She immediately wrote down the name and contact information for a dear friend of hers who gave private Italian lessons. She offered to call her friend and arrange a meeting. Between classes, with me standing by, Teresa called her friend from a black rotary pay phone in the hallway. Luckily, her friend answered. We three agreed to meet at 4:00 p.m. in the coffee house across from the university.

When I arrived at our meeting point, Teresa was sitting at a table near the rear of the café with her friend, a lady who looked to be in her mid-thirties. I walked toward the table, and Teresa stood and greeted me with a kiss on both cheeks—a custom I was beginning to like very much.

"Marilyn, I'd like you to meet Erica Gabbinno, the friend I told you about. She has graciously agreed to teach you Italian at no charge in exchange for helping her become more fluent in English," Teresa said.

I liked Erica at once. Even before she stood for our introduction, her warm smile told me we would do well together. When she stood, I saw she was of average height, with flawless olive skin and dancing dark brown eyes—and a no-nonsense attitude. In Italian, Erica asked about a lesson schedule with Teresa translating in English for me. Although I was eager to get started on my Italian lessons, I knew my university studies had to be my first priority.

"I'd love to meet every day of the week to learn Italian as quickly as possible," I said, looking directly to Teresa. "But please convey to Erica that I'll have to give preference to my university studies. A more realistic schedule would be to meet here on Tuesday and Thursday afternoons at 4:30 for one-hour sessions, if that meets with her schedule." Once we settled the schedule, we relaxed over a cup of espresso and, with Teresa serving as our translator, the three of us got to know one another.

CHAPTER 29

At dinner, Chloe asked, "Well Marilyn, how did your first day go?" I gave a quick rundown of my classes and described the people I'd met. I also told her about meeting Erica Gabbinno and that she'd agreed to teach me Italian in exchange for English lessons.

"I'm thrilled that you want to learn Italian to talk to the people here in their language. It will be endearing to them. When you break down the language barrier, your foreign experience will be much more enriching for you, too."

Before we left the table, Chloe casually said, "I believe you remember my son, Manny. He was with us the Thanksgiving when you visited with Joe in New York."

My heart skipped a beat, and I felt heat rushing to my face. Did she have any inkling of what had transpired between Manny and me? Had she somehow found out my transgression and wanted me to leave?

I hesitated and then shyly replied, "Yes, I do remember Manny. I believe he attends Columbia Law School—unless he's graduated." I hoped my voice was steady.

Chloe lowered her head and sadly admitted, "Manny's been

dismissed from Columbia because of poor grades. He's coming to live with me until he can sort through what he should do next. His dad is so disappointed that he won't allow Manny to live with him in New York until he gets his act together." She wistfully added, "I wish Manny were more like Joe and knew what he wanted to do with his life. Manny has always been a challenge to us—and to himself."

The news that Manny was coming to Milan to live threw me into an emotional tailspin. I'd have to face him again—live under the same roof with him. I was embarrassed, but I also couldn't help being excited about seeing him again. And right now, I knew I had to escape to my bedroom to digest this disturbing news. However, Chloe had other plans. She asked me to join her and Janice in the study for an after-dinner drink. I lamely said, "I need to head upstairs to study."

She responded rather emphatically, "We need to talk to you; it won't take too long."

As I left the dining room to go into the study, I had flashes of scenes in which Chloe and Janice confronted me about my liaison with Manny during that fateful Thanksgiving when I was Joe's houseguest. I blushed remembering how easily and foolishly I'd given up my virginity to this guy—the guy who had never contacted me after that weekend at the Long Island Sound house.

When I joined Chloe and Janice, we settled into the study's comfortable chairs, but I didn't feel very comfortable. As usual, Chloe and Janice were dressed beautifully and looked so poised. I was in my schoolgirl outfit and a nervous wreck, fidgeting—not knowing what would be discussed and wondering how I would respond if they questioned me about my past behavior with Manny.

Chloe cleared her throat and began by saying, "Marilyn, Janice and I have been talking about your interest in the fashion industry, and we want to support you. We believe you have the potential for success in the business. We also have a suggestion and hope you won't be insulted by it." She continued in a low voice, "I must be candid with you about your college girl wardrobe. It diminishes your talent and fine qualities. And it will hinder you as you begin to transition into the professional world. It's not a unique problem—many young women face that difficult transition.

"Janice and I believe there's a market for a line of clothing we've created for women in their early twenties. We wondered if you might become our walking advertisement and wear samples of these creations to classes. You could provide us with feedback and comments from the university students. It would be particularly helpful since you're studying in the fashion design college."

I exhaled in relief when I realized Manny was not going to be the topic of this conversation. I jumped up enthusiastically, kissed each of them on both cheeks, and danced around the room, babbling. Finally, I settled down and asked when we could start the fashion show with me as their living model.

"Soon," Chloe said. Then in a more serious tone, she continued, "But first we need to tell you an intimate detail before Manny arrives. You may already be aware of the relationship between Janice and me. We are partners."

"Of course you are. You work together," I naively responded.

"Marilyn, you don't understand. Janice and I are in a lesbian relationship. We are intimate partners in our personal lives as well as partners in our professional career. Manny and Joe have never accepted this. They were upset when I split with their father and still resent that we are no longer husband and wife. I know Manny will make a big issue of this when he's here. We wanted you to hear it from us and not from him."

I was flabbergasted and didn't know how to respond. I finally collected my thoughts and said, "But Chloe, you and Dr. Bateson are still married, aren't you?"

"Yes, we have been married for thirty years, but you might say our marriage is one of financial convenience, friendship, and acceptance of our choices. Dr. Bateson has had a live-in girlfriend in New York for years. She's a nurse at the hospital where he's worked for the past fifteen years. He knows that Janice and I have a committed relationship with one another that must be kept private because of social mores in America. Dr. Bateson has no intention of marrying his girlfriend, so he tells her I won't give him a divorce. This arrangement works for the two of us financially, and we are both happier with our current partners."

Now I understood why Joe had been so uncomfortable around his parents when I visited the Batesons that Thanksgiving. Chloe added, "Neither of the boys has accepted that I'm a lesbian and that their father has a live-in girlfriend."

This conversation gave new meaning to the term *boggles the mind*. I was so confused. Nothing in my conservative Baptist upbringing had prepared me for this. I couldn't equate this relationship with anything I'd encountered in my farmland home in Kentucky. Of course, I had heard about infidelity in Rockport and read about homosexuality and lesbianism in literature and history, but I'd never known anyone who exhibited or admitted to this behavior—until now.

What would my parents think if they knew I was living with two lesbians in Milan? What would they think of Joe's father having an extramarital relationship in New York? What would they think of Joe's parents accepting one another's intimate choices outside their marriage? I was having difficulty absorbing this situation and struggling to accept it.

I mumbled something about understanding, although I'm sure they could see I was trying very hard to grasp their disclosure. In just a few minutes, Chloe said she knew I had some studying to do, and I escaped to my bedroom. Once alone, I rationalized this latest development and sorted through my thoughts. Chloe and Janice had always been gracious and kind to me. *Why should I judge them because they are different from me?*

It didn't take me long to make up my mind that these revelations weren't my business and would not influence my feelings toward Chloe and Dr. Bateson. And I was sure I wasn't going to leave Milan until my semester ended. I also realized how lucky I was to be under the tutelage of these two chic hostesses—Chloe and Janice—and to enjoy their hospitality. They were going to dress me in their designer clothing line, and all I had to do in return was provide them with information on how others liked the style. *How lucky can one girl get? And I sure do need a wardrobe update!*

I opened my textbooks, but I had trouble concentrating on the words printed on the pages. Too many things were swirling around in my head. One thing I knew—life was never this complicated on our farm. You got up early, did your morning chores, ate breakfast, and then went to school. After school, you came home, did your chores, ate dinner, studied, and went to bed. The next day, you did it all over again. This familiar routine was so predictable.

I had no intention of going back to it. My unfolding adventure in Milan was too fascinating. I was like a moth drawn to a flame. I only hoped the consequences would not be the same for me as they were for the moth!

CHAPTER 30

When I woke the next morning, my homework was scattered over the bed. I'd fallen asleep while trying to study. *Great way to start school*, I thought. But as I gathered my papers and books, I realized I'd completed most of my assignments before I fell asleep. I showered, dressed quickly, and hurried downstairs for breakfast. Estella was alone in the kitchen, and I was greatly relieved that I didn't have to face Chloe or Janice before going to school.

School was my refuge, and I happily took a seat in the economics class next to Teresa. "Are you ready for your first Italian lesson today with Erica?" she whispered.

My lesson! With everything going on in my life, I had completely forgotten about it, but responded quickly, "Of course, I can't wait to get started!"

As soon as my classes ended, I met Erica at the café. She launched into my first Italian lesson immediately. We struggled at first without Teresa as our interpreter, but kept at it. At the end of the hour, my mind was filled with new words and phrases, but I realized that at our next session, I'd have to devote time to teaching Erica English. That was only fair.

By the time I got back to the apartment, it was dinnertime. When I entered the dining room, Manny was talking to Estella with his back to me. I tried to breathe. He must have heard the door because he turned and walked directly to me, kissing me softly on both cheeks. Since he had just showered from his journey, I could smell soap and shampoo. His hair was still wet and hung casually into his face. He smiled his crooked smile, showing his white, straight teeth. I melted.

"How do you like Milan?" he asked casually. Before I could answer, Estella broke in, ordering us to take our seats at the table, since dinner was ready to be served. Manny asked Estella if the two "dykes" would be joining us. His sarcastic tone and open disrespect for his mother shocked me.

Estella chided him. "Mind your manners, Manny!"

He hugged her and said, "I'll be a good boy if you'll bring me a beer." When I looked at Manny, I felt an unadulterated attraction to him—like electricity running through my body. He was everything I *should not* want in a man, yet he excited me beyond distraction. My feelings toward him were most confusing. He was such a contrast to "neat freak," button-down Joe.

Manny was always unkempt. He paired his well-worn jeans with denim shirts that looked like they would fall into shreds at the next washing, and his brown leather shoes were scruffy. His body language shouted, *I'm Manny, and I don't give a damn about you.* He seemed determined to go through life in a slouchy posture that screamed contempt. Was he deliberately trying to contrast himself with Joe, who always dressed as if he were going for a job interview and was extremely proper in his behavior and demeanor? The irony was that Joe—who was everything I *should* want in a man—did not fascinate me one iota, but Manny did monumentally. What was wrong with me?

Chloe and Janice entered the dining room together, looking

stunning as usual. We spoke briefly; Manny just kept looking at his beer. He did not stand or even acknowledge Chloe when she came up behind him and kissed him on top of his wet head.

The tension when we sat down at the table was palpable. I tried to break the ice by showing off some of the Italian I'd learned from Erica. I stumbled through a few words, struggling to make a sentence. Chloe and Janice were so supportive and encouraging. Chloe said, "The only way you will be able to really communicate in Italian is to practice the Italian you learn and not worry about making mistakes."

Manny winked at me and said, "I'd prefer to communicate with you in other ways." I avoided looking directly at him, fearing I'd stutter if I tried to say anything in retaliation. I'd never experienced anything like the magnetic charge I felt for him. *Maybe this is what's meant by an "approach-avoidance" conflict.*

CHAPTER 31

After dinner, I excused myself and went to my room. I resisted taking my dishes to the kitchen and offering to help clean up. Estella had made it clear that was her job.

I flipped back the bedcover, crawled onto the bed, and spread my books around me to start my homework. A few minutes later, I heard Manny entering his room down the hall. Just knowing we were now under the same roof made it difficult to concentrate on my work—but at least he wasn't in an adjoining room. Still, he was close enough that I heard him playing his guitar.

After a few minutes, there was a soft knock on my door. Since the music had stopped, I was sure it was Manny. I sat quietly. Should I pretend to be asleep and hope he'd go away? Then I glanced at the clock and knew he'd know it was too early for me to be asleep. So with my heart racing, I crawled out of bed and slowly cracked my bedroom door.

Manny was leaning against the doorframe but didn't move to enter the room. Instead, he whispered, "Take a walk with me to get coffee." My first reaction to his invitation was that I needed to study, but there was something in his voice and the sad look in his eyes that made me accept. I felt he needed someone to talk to, and I grabbed my jacket and scarf and left the apartment with him.

We walked for two or three blocks in silence. I spoke first. "How long do you plan to be in Milan?"

He didn't answer. He just steered me toward a cozy-looking café and said, "Let's go in here and talk." He ordered two espressos and then turned to me and apologized. "I'm sorry. I should have let you use your newly learned Italian to order. You'll never learn without practice, right?"

"Do you speak Italian?" I asked.

"I have no reason to try to do things to please my mother," he snarled. I jumped to Chloe and Janice's defense, but he cut me off, attacking me in a loud, confrontational voice. "Don't tell me I've fucked a dyke. Are you one of them? Is that why you are living with them?"

His aggressive reaction mortified me. My only consolation was that there were only a few people who could hear him in this quiet café, and probably none of them spoke English. At least, that was my fervent hope.

"Manny, please sit down and calm yourself. First, I'm not a lesbian. I was surprised by your mother's revelation, and I know it must be difficult for you and Joe to understand your parents' life choices. However, they love you and Joe."

He responded sarcastically, "Really? Ask either of them if they love me. I'm not easy to love, you know, but it would be easier for them to accept me if I had gotten that law degree from Columbia and become a successful corporate lawyer on Wall Street. That's the type of unconditional surrender that parents like mine need to really love their kids.

"I've tried alcohol, drugs, and anything else they find objectionable. That's my way of trying to fit into my dysfunctional family. I'm jealous of Joe, yet I admire the hell out of his ability to rise above it all."

I quickly corrected him. "Manny, Joe struggles with the same issues you do, just in a very different way. He excels in all he does to gain your parents' approval. He even dresses the way he thinks they want him to dress. He's always seeking their validation, but without much success." Manny's demeanor changed abruptly when I spoke about how Joe tried to cope with their parents. He seemed puzzled—as if he'd never considered Joe's behavior as a coping strategy. I wanted to take Manny in my arms and console him and reassure him that everything was going to be okay. Instead, I sat quietly. Was I afraid to make the gesture because of his erratic behavior? I wasn't sure, but I could tell he needed a friend to confide in and support him, and I was ready to fill that role.

Manny suddenly dropped his defenses. "It was my father's idea to get me into Columbia Law School. He was the one who jumped through hoops to make it happen. He never asked me if it was what I wanted to do. He just told me this was his dream. I didn't want to go, but I didn't have the balls to resist. I suppose that's my 'Achilles heel'—no guts, no glory."

"If you could do anything you wanted in your life, what would it be?" I asked him. I was serious; Manny wasn't.

He smiled diabolically, leaned across the table, almost touching my face, and said, "I would fuck you day and night."

Rude or crazy? I didn't care. I'd had enough of him. I got up to leave, but he grabbed my arm, pulled me back into the chair, and said in a wavering voice, "The scary thing is, I don't know what I want to do with my life. I love playing the guitar. I'd be perfectly happy just going into the streets of New York or Milan and playing for the coins people dropped in my guitar case in appreciation. If I did that, my parents would probably have me committed to

Bellevue Psychiatric Hospital. Yup, my parents *definitely* would have me committed!"

"If you like music so much, why didn't you study it and pursue a career in music?" I asked him. "You could teach and compose."

"Are you kidding? My parents would never have approved, and they sure wouldn't have paid for a musical education so I could squander my life. At least, that's how they'd view making music as your life's work."

I didn't have an answer, so I looked at my watch and panicked. "I absolutely have to get back to my assignments. They're due tomorrow. Let's continue this conversation later." I said in what I hoped was a soothing voice.

The walk back to the apartment was as quiet as our walk to the café. But it was a comfortable silence. I hoped the walk was the beginning of a better understanding of each other.

CHAPTER 32

I woke up, and my first thought was, *I need to talk to a friend about last night.* I'd been so confused by Manny's bizarre behavior at the café that I wanted to see how someone else would interpret his mood swings. I couldn't wait for economics class to see Teresa. She was already in the classroom when I got there, talking animatedly with two people I didn't know. I waved to her as I approached the group and began speaking before I was next to her. "Excuse me, Teresa, I hate to interrupt, but I need to talk to you after class. Do you have time?"

She responded at once, "Let's go for coffee right after class."

As soon as the lecture ended, we headed to a small coffee house. Once we were seated, Teresa asked, "What's up with you, Marilyn? You look exhausted—and stressed."

I broke down and confided about Manny. "I met him a few years ago when I was dating his younger brother and was a houseguest over Thanksgiving with the family. From that first meeting, I knew instinctively that Manny was dangerous, rebellious, and unreliable. But I couldn't help myself. He fascinated me. I had this overwhelming attraction to him," I confessed. "I can't get him out of my head. And now we've been thrown together again. We'd had no communication since that weekend of several years ago, which made me very uncomfortable, and then last night, he sought me out. I agreed to go for coffee because he looked as if he needed to talk to someone. But the evening ended so strangely I don't know what to think."

I briefed her on our excursion to a café after dinner and how he had switched from vulgar and rude to endearing during the evening. "He seems to delight in keeping me off balance when we're together," I said, trying to wrap up the whole relationship for Teresa.

She listened intently and then said, "He does sound like a complicated and very intriguing guy—I would certainly like to meet him." Her reaction prompted a slight tinge of jealousy.

But I quickly suppressed it, telling myself she probably wanted to meet him before she tried to advise me on the relationship. Her next sentence reinforced that thought. "A friend of mine is throwing a party Saturday night at her apartment. Why don't you and Manny come? I'll call and get you both on her invitation list. I'll meet Manny, and you'll meet some new, interesting people." She gave me her friend's name and address and the time the party would begin. I thanked Teresa and said I'd ask Manny and let her know if he would come. I'd already decided to go—with or without Manny.

After dinner, I told Manny about the party and asked him if he'd like to go with me. I should have expected a flippant response, but I was still unprepared when he said, "So if I go with you, can you guarantee I'll be able to meet some good-looking nymphomaniacs there?"

I wondered, *Is he just trying to shock me, or is he serious about what he expects at the party?* And it irked me that he still viewed me as a naïve and prudish little farm girl—especially since he had seduced me and taken my virginity at his family's country home. Then I realized that he might not be trying to shock me. He had no idea how many lovers I might have had since that night. He didn't know he was my one and only sexual encounter. And he certainly wouldn't learn that fact from me.

I ignored his "nympho" reference and replied nonchalantly. At least, I hoped that was how it seemed. "I have no idea who'll be there. But if Teresa is an example of the people who are invited, I think it should be a fun evening. I know I'm looking forward to it."

He agreed to go with one caveat. "Marilyn, we can make the scene at this party together only if you promise me we'll immediately find a dark corner so we can make out the whole evening." I blushed, which only reinforced his suspicion that he could get a reaction from me with personal sexual remarks. He recognized his power instantly, too. His eyes locked with mine, and he leaned closer, giving a deep, throaty laugh that seemed to drip with sexual implications. I blushed again, averting my eyes. I hated that he had the ability to control my responses, but I loved hearing his naughty laugh. I'd never had such feelings for any other guy. What was it about Manny?

The week passed quickly. Manny was still in bed when I left for school, and when I saw him at dinner, he usually was his obstinate, taciturn self. Chloe sensed his hostility and kept her distance, making only perfunctory dinner conversation with Janice and me. I found it easier to be quiet. I had no idea how to operate in this awkward family dynamic.

The only relief came when Estella was in a room with Manny. There was a genuine feeling of warmth between them. He complimented her on her cooking, and every single day, he told her how beautiful she was after she delivered his cold beer. And she doted on him and was not afraid to joke and scold him openly.

After dinner on Saturday, I reminded Manny of the party at Teresa's friend's apartment. He smiled and winked at me wickedly, adding, "And how should I dress for our dark corner this evening?" I blushed, and then he gave that laugh again, and I melted.

The party was within walking distance of our apartment. I met Manny in the hallway around 10:00 p.m. Teresa had said most of the guests would be arriving about then or a little later. When we left the apartment, Manny fished a pillbox out of his jacket pocket, took a pill, and gulped it down. He offered me one, but I shook my head. I didn't know what he had just swallowed, but I certainly wasn't going to find out by swallowing one.

"Marilyn, this party will be a lot more fun if you take one of these little blue pills. The sex we'll have in that dark corner will be a mind bender for you!" He threw his head back and laughed. Indignant, I walked faster to get away from him, but he grabbed me, pulled me close, and kissed me passionately. My body and mind went limp. He released me, and we continued to walk to the party—without exchanging any words. I wondered what he felt when he kissed me. *Or did he feel anything?*

At the apartment building, we pressed the appropriate numbers in the keypad beside the door. A voice answered (the accent sounded much like Teresa's), and I gave our names. We were buzzed into the lobby and walked up two flights of stairs toward an apartment with blaring music. Obviously, the party had started.

The apartment was dimly lit. Candles flickered throughout the compact one-bedroom unit, and there was a scent of sweet-smelling smoke. Some guests were weaving back and forth to the rhythm of the music—dancing together or alone.

Teresa greeted us and introduced us to several other guests. By now, I was completely comfortable with the customary greeting of a kiss on each cheek. Manny seemed to relax when Teresa guided us to the small kitchenette and its supply of beer and wine. "Please help yourselves," she said. I took a glass of wine, and Manny grabbed a beer before we followed Teresa back to the living room.

I was surprised when Teresa took Manny's arm and pulled him onto the sofa next to her. She put her mouth close to Manny's ear so he could hear her over the loud music. I sat in a chair opposite the sofa, watching them. I couldn't take my eyes off Manny. It was painful, but I wanted to see his reaction to Teresa. I was now totally aware of every movement, every gesture between the two of them.

I felt like a voyeur, but I couldn't help myself. Neither one of them noticed my presence. After they consumed several beers, they shared a marijuana joint, inhaling deeply. Then Teresa moved even closer to Manny, draping her right leg over his lap. He was obviously enjoying her attention despite the loud music. I could hear that deep-throat laughter as his hand caressed her bare leg. I was stunned and hurt, but I couldn't look away.

I was grateful when an Italian guy from my accounting class asked me to dance. He introduced himself as Paulo. He moved close and, like Teresa with Manny, put his mouth to my ear so I could hear him over the music. As we began to dance, he pressed his body against me and pulled me in very close. Since I had been drinking, I didn't pull away, but I wasn't thinking about my partner. Instead, I kept looking at Manny and Teresa. They had gotten up to slow dance next to us and were grinding their bodies against each other.

By 2:00 a.m., I was exhausted from drinking, dancing, and talking to strangers. And I was embarrassed by Manny and Teresa's overt behavior toward one another. I resented him for abandoning me for the entire evening, letting me fend for myself in a room full of strangers. I was ready to leave. Just to be courteous, I found Manny and told him I was going to take a taxi home. He excused himself from Teresa and said he'd walk me back to the apartment and then return to the party.

I was silent as we walked home, but Manny was animated. "You were right, Marilyn—your friends are amazing, and I'm glad to meet some people my own age in Milan." He continued to rave about the party, and when I didn't respond, he finally sensed my lack of enthusiasm. He grabbed my shoulders and turned me toward him. "What's wrong with you?"

I tried to stifle my rage when I answered, "I just don't understand you. You passionately kissed me on the way to the party and then immediately abandoned me when you met my friend Teresa. The two of you were all over one another!"

He threw his head back and laughed. "Marilyn, Marilyn, Marilyn. There is so much in life to experience; no one should be limited to just one person. I learned that lesson perfectly from my parents."

I found my rage turning to sadness for Manny and the warped way he viewed his family. He didn't understand loving relationships. My experience with my parents was just the opposite. In Rockport, I had never known anything but unconditional love, support, and devotion. And even after a night of too much to drink, betrayal, and humiliation, my understanding of this was crystal clear.

CHAPTER 33

It was like a combination of Christmas and my birthday when I went into the study to see the array of clothes and accessories Chloe had selected for me. A full-length mirror was propped in the center of the room so I could check out each outfit as I modeled it for Chloe.

The clothing line was over the top in style, beauty, and craftsmanship. As I caressed the fabrics—cashmeres, silks, soft, draping wools, and supple leathers—I kept thinking that I would never be able to afford these clothes on my budget. But someday …!

Chloe had chosen garments in colors ranging from bright reds to subdued grays and blacks. There were scarves, jewelry, stockings, boots, and multiple pairs of shoes. This private fashion show included a lesson in how to mix and match colors and accessories. Our congenial agreement was that I would wear something different to class each day and record comments made by others on the individual pieces and the complete outfits. To capture these comments, Chloe handed me a leather-bound journal—top of the line, just like the clothes. I couldn't believe how easy this would be—and I couldn't wait to begin.

I greeted Monday morning with undisguised anticipation. *Let the experiment begin!* My first-day strategy was to wear an outfit that was not too flashy. My classmates were used to seeing me in conservative wool skirts, sweaters, knee socks, and penny loafers—a typical American coed college girl.

I carefully went through the different outfits that now lined my closet, putting together different combinations of accessories and shoes. Once I'd settled on a black cashmere straight-line dress with a mock turtleneck and small buttons that ran down the sleeves from the elbow to the wrist, I selected black tights with a woven gray pattern to match short, gray boots with a slight heel that lifted them out of the sporty fashion category. By the end of school on Monday, my notebook was filled with copious notes—all positive comments from my classmates.

Still wearing the outfit, I triumphantly bounced into the dining room for dinner. I eagerly launched into an excited report to Chloe. Then I spotted Manny. He was standing between the kitchen and the dining room teasing Estella, but he stopped when I made my entrance. Putting his fingers in his mouth and pushing back on his tongue, he gave a loud whistle of ear-splitting appreciation. Then disrespectfully he addressed Chloe and Janice, who were standing at their places ready to take their seats. "I like this updated look on the farm girl. Thank God, it's not quite the artificial high style my queer mother emulates—yet."

I glared at him, but was silent. Keeping my thoughts to myself seemed best. Chloe dropped her head and, controlling her voice, sarcastically scolded him. "Manny, when did you become a fashion critic?"

He ignored her, turned to me, and warned, "Don't let her change you!"

After dinner, I was reading in the living room when Manny came in. I looked up and asked, "Why are you so cruel to your mother?"

He gave a wicked laugh and said, "Don't worry about Mother; she has Janice to kiss away the pain if her skin is too thin to take her eldest son's criticism."

I shot back, "Manny, you have a lot of deep-seated anger. You need help."

"Good God, Marilyn, you're starting to sound just like her! You're dressing to her specifications, mimicking her mannerisms, and now using her same tone of voice—what's next? Falling in love with a woman just like her? Can't you see she's carefully grooming you for this role?"

I'd had enough of his verbal abuse and jumped off the couch, grabbed my book, and ran out of the room. When I reached my bedroom, I quickly closed the door, leaning against it as if I was physically trying to block him from my mind. I just wanted to forget his cruel—and baseless—prediction. As a diversion, I went to my closet to select Tuesday's outfit. I stepped back, looked at all the beautiful clothes, and felt my angry feelings dissipating. Gradually, my feelings of elation returned. I had had a wonderful day at school, basking in the compliments from my classmates and dutifully recording them in my journal. I vowed to remember the exhilaration of the day and not Manny's vicious observations.

Why should I let this outrageous law school dropout get under my skin? Who in the hell does he think he is, anyway? This asshole is not going to rain on my parade.

After our unpleasant exchange, I consciously blocked Manny from my thoughts. Instead of thinking about him, I spent my days focused on my wardrobe, enthusiastically putting together each day's outfits and recording a multitude of positive journal entries. When I did think about Manny, it was easy to dismiss the thought. Since he was rarely at the house, I assumed that he spent most of his time with Teresa. My friendship with Teresa was almost non-existent, so there was no way to know if the two were an item or not. In fact, she avoided me like I had the plague and acknowledged me only by nodding hello to me in classes we shared or if our paths crossed in the building or on the street.

As the days went by, I became totally preoccupied with pleasing my hostesses and providing them with feedback from my daily fashion show at the university. The success of this experiment reinforced my resolve to continue seriously pursuing my studies in international business, concentrating on the fashion industry. Chloe and Janice were proving to be invaluable role models and mentors in this pursuit.

As the days turned into weeks, my studies and Italian lessons consumed more and more of my time and energy. I practiced my Italian as much as possible, particularly at dinner. Chloe and Janice were as helpful with my Italian as with my wardrobe. Although I made a lot of mistakes, they were so patient and forgiving that I never felt self-conscious. These table lessons served a dual purpose: they reinforced my tutor's efforts—and they effectively shut Manny out of our conversations. He could only speak to Estella. Impolite? Probably, but I felt so smug!

Once I had worn each of the outfits in my closet (almost a month), I developed a formal written report for Chloe and Janice. After I presented this business summary, they announced the next step in their strategy—and it was an exciting one. They wanted to brand the line of clothes.

"Based on your research, Marilyn, we want to produce a label called Bourne Innocence, targeted to young twenty- and thirty-year-old women who have a fashionable inclination and the money to support it," explained Chloe.

"Could you take your report and produce a more complete analysis—something that could become a business plan for this innovative line when we roll out the brand?" she asked.

Could I? My mind was already reeling with questions and plans, as well as additional analysis of my unsolicited research findings. Now that the brand name was set and the target audience identified, I knew exactly how to proceed. The first order of business—develop a price point for the garments and accessories.

Why would I waste any more time or energy on someone like Manny? I had too many exciting opportunities and prospects in my own life—Manny was now so easy to repress. In my mind, he was out of the picture!

CHAPTER 34

Every Tuesday and Thursday, Erica and I met in our favorite coffee shop for our Italian and English lessons. She had become not just my language instructor, but also a trusted friend.

During one of our Tuesday English tutoring lessons, she confided her concern about her friend Teresa. I had also noticed Teresa had been absent lately from classes, so I questioned Erica more thoroughly in English. Erica slipped into Italian to describe Teresa as *"letargo"* and then back to English to express her real concern: "She perhaps plans to harm herself."

"Are you saying she's deeply depressed?" I asked in English with alarm in my voice, before elaborating in broken Italian, using lots of hand gestures to convey what I meant. We continued to discuss Teresa in broken Italian and broken English, something we'd learned to do during our lessons. We'd almost created our own personal language.

I told Erica I, too, feared something was wrong, since Teresa was skipping too many classes and probably spending too much time with Manny—not the most stable influence. Erica shook her head sadly in agreement, "Unfortunately, Teresa is madly in love with *that* Manny. He's a no-good cheat, you know—her American

Don Juan. He even flirts openly with other girls when he is with her. He's a heartbreaker."

My first thought after hearing this news was, *Welcome to Manny's Broken Hearts Club—just one more victim! His personal entertainment network continues to grow.*

Since Erica didn't know my background with Manny, I spared her my cynicism or elaboration on what a hateful person he was. Instead, I told her I'd try to talk to Teresa the next time I saw her in class, just to make sure she was okay. I also realized how lucky I was that Teresa had no idea how deeply Manny had wounded me at that fateful party when he had tossed me aside and openly pursued her, even though I had invited him to be my escort for the evening. It was bad enough she knew my history with him.

The following Tuesday, Teresa wasn't in economics class, and my worries about her became so escalated and compelling that I rushed to my tutoring session. I told Erica that Teresa hadn't been to class in two weeks and I thought we should check on her. Erica said that since we'd talked last week, she had telephoned Teresa several times but never received an answer. She suggested we skip the tutoring session and go to Teresa's apartment immediately. I agreed. I believed Teresa needed a friend right now to help her confront her despondency.

It only took us a few minutes to get to Teresa's apartment, but when we buzzed for entry, there was no answer. We decided to go to the corner phone booth and call her. No answer.

We retraced our steps and stood on the front stoop, bewildered and wondering what to do next. Just then, a woman came out the building's front door, and Erica approached her and in rapid Italian asked if she knew Teresa. The woman nodded. Then the woman said thoughtfully, "It's odd, I used to see Teresa all the time going to or coming from her university classes, carrying many books in her arms. But recently, I haven't seen her at all."

The woman buzzed us into the building, and the three of us went to Teresa's door. We knocked loudly and took turns calling out to her. No response. Our concerns rocketed. Then the woman said she would contact the landlord. He lived on another floor and could unlock the apartment door for us to check on her. She brought him back to Teresa's apartment a few minutes later.

After we explained our concern and told him how many times we had tried to contact Teresa, he agreed to let us in so we could make sure she was not ill. Reluctantly, he opened her apartment door and said he would remain at the door until we checked all the rooms. "Please don't disturb anything," he cautioned. "I'll lock up as soon as you make sure everything is okay and leave."

The three of us entered the apartment. The window blinds were closed so tight that the apartment was pitch black. The woman opened the blinds, and Erica and I turned on some lights. We were shocked at the disarray, and I put my handkerchief over my nose because of a peculiar stench.

Plates of uneaten and rotting food were piled on the table in front of the television, and dirty dishes were stacked in the sink and on the kitchenette counter. Beer cans littered the room and kitchenette, strewn about as if they had been emptied and then thrown helter-skelter. My heart began to race. Something was very wrong.

Erica and I moved toward the bedroom and entered together. Erica fumbled for the overhead light switch, and suddenly, the room was bathed in a harsh light, revealing a ghastly sight. Teresa was lying face down on her bed with an empty medicine bottle beside her. I rushed to her and turned her head to see if she was still breathing. Her body was cold and stiff, and there was no breath. Erica screamed and ran from the room.

The landlord and the neighbor rushed in when they heard Erica scream. I yelled for someone to call an ambulance. The neighbor and I turned Teresa's body over to see if we could find any life. It was too late. I looked in horror at her face with its gaping mouth and open eyes and tried to remember the beautiful girl who had befriended me that first day.

When the medics arrived, they said it appeared she had overdosed on pills and been dead for more than twenty-four hours. I was numb. Guilt, mingled with deep regret, swept over me. *If only* I had checked on her last week as soon as Erica warned me of her mental state. *If only* I had been a better friend and not pulled back, jealous over her relationship with Manny. *If only* I had not taken Manny to that party. *If only* any of these circumstances had been different, would she still be alive now? How could I have let this happen? Suddenly, I realized I wasn't the only guilty party in this tragedy. How could Manny have let this happen? My anger at Manny blazed. He was just as responsible as I for Teresa's death. But even as I blamed him, I still wanted to shield him—to keep the real reason for her apparent suicide from him. I recognized him as a selfish, uncaring individual, but I still wanted to protect him. What was his hold over me?

Erica and I stayed at Teresa's apartment until her body was removed and the police had questioned us about our relationship to the "deceased." *What a cold, impersonal word!* After we answered their questions and gave them our contact information, one officer said, "We have no more questions of you now. Please leave and don't touch anything. We won't begin our investigation until we're sure of the cause of death. It looks as if it was self-inflicted, but we'll need to determine that for a certainty. We'll be in touch. Thank you for your help."

As Erica and I turned to leave, I had to resist a strong compulsion to straighten up the apartment—to put this sad, disheveled scene back into order—almost as if the act of restoring order would restore Teresa. Instead, we both obeyed the officers and left the apartment as we had found it, except for the open blinds and burning lights.

Erica and I walked together for blocks without speaking, almost as if in a trance. When we came to the café, we said goodbye and parted. She headed toward her apartment, and I slowly crossed the street to go toward mine. We left each other at twilight, but I continued to walk even after I reached my apartment—perhaps in a state of shock. It was almost the 8:00 dinner hour when I let myself into the apartment.

I found Estella in the kitchen and told her I wouldn't be joining them for dinner, lying that I had eaten an early dinner with friends and now planned to study for a test tomorrow. "Please let Chloe know that I need to excuse myself from dinner this evening to concentrate on preparing for this big test." Estella asked if I wanted a tray sent up later, but I declined. The lump in my throat would guarantee that I couldn't get food down. Of course, I also knew there was another reason for avoiding dinner. I absolutely could not look at Manny across the dinner table and pretend that everything was normal.

I entered my room and sat on my bed, looking around for something to divert my attention. I wanted to put thoughts of Teresa and the afternoon's shocking events out of my mind. My whole world had been upended in minutes. I needed to calm myself—and thoughts of home flooded my mind. I quickly retrieved a box of letters from the top shelf of my closet. My parents, sister, and friends from Rockport wrote on a weekly basis, and I had saved them all. I began with the first letter, reading each in date order as if I had never read them before.

Reading the letters from home proved to be therapeutic—almost like having Mama here to put her arms around me to comfort me and tell me everything was going to be okay.

Mama's letters reassured me that Daddy's health was improving and that he couldn't be more pleased with Joe, crediting Joe's leadership with the workers for getting the crops out. Joe seemed to be adjusting to the routine of farm life remarkably well. Joe's letters detailed his farm work, which had continued on weekends after the fall semester started. He was getting credit toward his degree in agriculture for the work. Although he was only at the farm on weekends, Mama wrote that with his help and Jimmy and Samuel, the farm was running smoothly. Mama described Joe as a hard worker who had adapted to life on the farm quite naturally. She said he and Grace were spending a lot of time together but assured me he wasn't letting that interfere with his work. Mama said Grace teased him, accusing him of loving the farm more than her.

Daddy's letters were brief—just a few lines to let me know I was never far from his thoughts—and that he was very proud of me.

The letters from Grace and Joe were as reassuring as those from Mama and Daddy. They were so obviously head over heels in love that every letter just confirmed how right they were together. Joe's excitement over his agriculture major was evident, and Grace supported him fully in his future career decision. There was so much sensibility, order, and purpose to life in their letters. They truly were devoted to each other.

Beth's letters always closed with the same thought: "I hope you find what you are looking for in life. We all miss and love you." Reading this closing statement, tears blurred my eyes and streamed down my cheeks. It seemed so long ago since I was that little girl sitting in the oak tree and wondering what was beyond the fences. And now I was following an internal force that was propelling me forward to find out.

CHAPTER 35

After reading the letters from home, I tried to collect myself enough to tell Chloe and Janice about my horrific day. Walking into their study, bathed in soft lighting, I saw the two women sipping brandy from tiny snifters and discussing their day in hushed tones. It looked so normal. What a contrast to my world that seemed so dark and ominous. Both looked up when I entered the room. "I'm so sorry I couldn't make dinner this evening, but this has been the worst day of my life. I can truly say these events have shaken me to my core," I began.

Chloe and Janice listened intently as I recounted my story. When I told them of finding Teresa, they were shocked and quickly expressed their concern that I had to deal with Teresa's suicide. I omitted Erica's conclusion that Manny had broken Teresa's heart with his philandering and betrayals. But I did tell them I would discuss Teresa's death with Manny because I knew they had spent time together. However, that conversation would have to wait until morning; I was simply too exhausted to go over the details again this evening. They agreed, and as I left the study, they called after me with words of support.

That night, I fell asleep thinking about how I should tell Manny that Teresa was dead. In the morning, I made sure I saw Manny at breakfast. As much as I dreaded the conversation, I knew I had to get it over with before my late morning class. "Go for a walk with me, Manny. I have to tell you something that involves you."

As usual, he had a smart comment and said, "Only if I get lucky."

My blood boiled, and it took all my self-restraint not to scream, "You asshole!" I forced myself to ignore his obnoxious remark and just said, "Let's go."

We left the apartment in silence. I clutched my coat against the cold wind. It was a dark, cloudy day, perfect for this moment. I was as cold inside as the outside weather. I tried to compose myself so I could talk to Manny quietly and rationally about Teresa and the terrible events of yesterday. We walked for some time before he finally said, "What in the hell is wrong with you? You look like you're about to break into tears every time I look at you."

That was all I needed to destroy the fragile emotional reserve I was struggling to preserve. My tears broke, flowing like water through a fissure in the Hoover Dam. My crying was punctuated by loud gulps and gasps for air. The more I tried to stop crying, the harder it became to gain control. Manny surprised me by taking me in his arms to comfort me, whispering in my ear, "It's okay, Marilyn. Let go of whatever it is that's upset you."

I finally gained my composure enough to pull away from him and fumble in my coat pocket for a tissue. I wiped away my tears and blew my nose. Then I heard myself screaming at him in a high, accusatory tone. "You want to know what's wrong with me? I found Teresa dead yesterday in her bed from a presumed drug overdose. She killed herself because of your betrayal."

Manny stumbled back from me. His face registered shock and disbelief. He looked as if I had smacked him across the mouth. Now it was his turn to compose himself. The color drained from his face, and his voice cracked as he said, "What are you saying? Teresa did what?" He tried to swallow the tears collecting in the back of his throat, but he couldn't get any more words out.

I pointed to a bench. "Let's sit down over there, and I'll tell you all the gory details from beginning to end."

I began my story with Erica's conversation with me about how Teresa was in deep depression because of the way Manny, her lover, was treating her. Their relationship was deteriorating, and she was despondent over his blatant infidelity and disrespect toward her. I ended with my discovery of Teresa's body and the subsequent arrival of the medics and the police at the scene. "There was an empty pill bottle by her side. When I rolled her over to check her breathing, her eyes and mouth were wide open. I can't get this ghastly sight out of my mind," I concluded in an amazingly matter-of-fact way.

Manny's face was still ashen, and he was speechless. Several minutes later, he took my hands, looked straight into my eyes, and said, "You probably won't believe anything I say right now, but I need to tell you my side of the story with Teresa."

He immediately launched into his explanation of their relationship. "It's true I found Teresa to be very sexy, lively, and alluring from the moment you introduced us. It was easy to spend time with her. But you of all people, Marilyn, know that I'm a flirt and can't get too serious about any woman for an extended amount of time. And that was particularly true when I learned more about Teresa's inner demons.

"Early in our relationship, we shared drugs and drinks together to heighten our feelings toward one another. We relished getting high together—laughing, talking, and making love. But the more I was with her, the more I realized the severity of her addictions and the extent of her destructive personality. Even I was shocked at how many amphetamines she dropped when we were together. She also was a user of opium, as well as my drug of choice, marijuana."

He continued as I sat stunned. "You have no idea the many nights I spent with her in that apartment trying to calm her down and building up her weak self-esteem. After we would make love, I would plead with her to get a handle on her drug usage. She would sort of agree—just to placate me—and then launch into a diatribe about how she was no good to anyone and often toyed with the idea of doing herself in. Her self-destructive comments frightened me and at the same time turned me off. I started to dread seeing her and spent less and less time with her.

"Ironically, through my connection with Teresa, I had made other friends and acquaintances with whom I enjoyed passing time. And they enjoyed being with a good party boy like me. I admit I was often cruel to her socially—trying to make her despise me. The real sorrow in this tragedy is that she called me two nights ago around 3:00 a.m. at one of our friends' apartments. She knew I crashed there frequently. She begged me to come over to her apartment. She needed me. My response was brutally uncaring. I told her I was tired of trying to help her and getting no results, and I was through trying. I hung up. That must have been what took her over the edge and caused her to take an overdose. Marilyn, if I am guilty of anything involving her suicide, it would be not going to help her get through that night."

To my surprise, I was seeing a side of Manny I'd never seen before—an authentic compassion and concern for another. He reached out to me, and I cradled him in my arms. His body was convulsing with tears. He tried to talk, but was totally incoherent.

He became quiet and said, "I feel like such a failure. Everything I touch seems to be the 'Midas touch' in reverse," he added feebly, trying to lighten the moment. "Marilyn, I see such innocence and goodness in you that I'm afraid I might destroy you by just by being around you. That's why I've used sarcasm and often rudeness to repel you."

Manny's words struck a chord with me. How similar our lives seemed at this point. How many times had I felt I was responsible for bad things happening? Flashbacks reminded me I had felt responsible for Maria's disability when I was a little girl. Then I felt responsible for my Daddy's heart attack, chastising myself for leaving to go to college instead of helping my family on the farm.

Lastly, I remembered Daddy's talk when he drove me home from the hospital after Grace, Andrew, and I were in the car accident. He had told me to quit feeling responsible for bad things happening. He had patiently explained that a strong sense of responsibility was good, but bad things, as well as good things, happen, and they are totally out of our control. And then he had added a few sentences that I remembered so clearly: "You are giving yourself far too much credit to think you are so powerful that you can influence all the things that happen in your world. Just learn to focus on the challenges that are really in your control to overcome these obstacles."

In comforting Manny, I used my father's same approach and soothing voice. Stroking his hair, I told him to look at me. "Teresa was an abuser of drugs and alcohol before you ever met her. There was nothing you could do to change her behavior unless she wanted to make the change herself."

He gave me a sorrowful grin and asked, "How can you be so wise at such a young age?" I shrugged, knowing he was teasing me, but it still made me feel good. We walked back home silently, holding hands.

Erica, Manny, and I attended Teresa's memorial service together. Erica was standoffish with Manny. She still blamed him for Teresa's death. Manny asked me to keep his conversation on the park bench confidential, especially to Erica. "Nobody needs to know the extent of Teresa's drug abuse. Marilyn, I'd rather take the blame than to expose Teresa's real demons now," he said.

This simple request told me volumes about Manny's real personality, the one he kept hidden underneath his false bravado.

CHAPTER 36

Teresa's death forged an uneasy peace between Manny and me. We began spending time together. At first, it was casual—going to the movies, getting a pizza or coffee, or simply taking long walks. Eventually, our relationship morphed into intimacy and exclusivity.

As my time in Milan grew shorter and our relationship grew closer, we tried to fill our weekends with activities away from Milan. On several long, four-day weekends, we took the train to Lake Como and stayed in an apartment owned by one of Chloe's friends. This lake area, surrounded by the majestic Alps and foothills, is dotted with fabulous villas and quaint resort villages, and we spent hours exploring them. Hiking paths, boating, and water activities abounded, and we indulged in many of them. Lake Como was famed as a popular scenic and romantic destination, but the real draw for us was that it is a perfect spot for a budding photographer—Manny.

Ever since Manny had purchased a complicated Leica camera in a pawnshop in Milan, he had become obsessed with mastering its intricacies—reading everything he could find on the mechanics of operating a thirty-five millimeter camera. He was equally obsessed with learning the creative techniques of compositions—studying the best ways to capture landscapes and architecture and staging interesting candid people shots. On one visit, we took the boat to Bellagio so he could photograph the majestic Alps descending to Lake Como and hopefully capture a spectacular sunset while we sipped wine at an outdoor café. No dramatic sunset photograph on that trip, but the wine was delicious.

During our weekend getaways to the Lake Como region, I noticed a remarkable transformation in Manny's outlook and behavior. He relaxed with me and seemed at peace with himself. We had become a very compatible twosome during these explorations of the countryside and the villages. We loved walking through the narrow streets of villages, shopping for the best meats, cheeses, vegetables, and fruit for our evening meal. After making our selections, which sometimes took an entire afternoon, we'd return to the apartment and together cook wonderful dishes using our fresh produce and herb purchases to complement the meats and cheeses. We also delighted in sampling the Italian wine from the Lombardy region and did our best to ensure that our selections were perfect to enhance our creations.

Manny enjoyed our culinary adventures at Lake Como so much that he enrolled in cooking classes in Milan. Estella even consented to let him help her prepare dinner, although she teased him unmercifully about how he constantly got in her way in her kitchen. Their friendship, already strong, was now totally cemented through his enjoyment of cooking and his interest in Estella's recipes. He delighted in calling himself her sous-chef-in-training. Surprisingly, his new interests seemed to be softening the way he treated his mother and Janice. Now and then, he demonstrated glimmers of respect toward them.

During the next three months, Manny and I were both friends and lovers, but we struggled to keep our emotions in check.

Instinctively, I knew Manny's transformation was happening because I provided the support, energy, and intimacy he needed after he had opened up, allowing me to see his vulnerable side. Teresa's death had forced him to seek stable companionship and reevaluate his lifestyle.

However, I was cautious. I knew Manny had many good qualities, yet I knew he could easily abandon me once I returned to the States. I refused to allow myself to become too reliant on his attention. He thought I was an innocent and was fearful he might corrupt me. I knew that wasn't true. Manny didn't know me or understand the strength of my convictions and ambitions. In our intimacy, we shared serious conversations about our fears, our desires—almost everything about our lives. But it was obvious that we would be catapulting in different directions once I left Milan. We tried to guard ourselves emotionally from this eventuality by focusing on the present moment and the sheer joy of spending quality time together.

One beautiful, sunny weekend, we drove to the Italian Alps for a day-trip escape. As we drove to the higher elevations, it began snowing. The reflection of the sun off the pure white snow was so blinding it was difficult to take in the breathtaking scenery without painful squinting. Manny finally found a perfectly shaded spot and pulled over to photograph the landscape. He insisted I pose with the magnificent mountains in the background.

"I know you, Manny—you just want to show how insignificant I am in the grand scheme of things!" I teased.

In one of his more tender and revealing moments, he replied quietly, "You are wrong on that account. You are more significant to me than the tallest mountain or most beautiful scene in the world."

As we continued driving to the higher elevations, we came to a tunnel. When we exited, the Matterhorn was before us, stretching high into the atmosphere. The brilliant sun bathed the mountain, warming its snow-capped peak and creating a halo of steam reaching toward the sun.

This extraordinary sight was an epiphany for me—I felt I had just glimpsed what was beyond the farm fences of Kentucky and glimpsed it with my eyes wide open. I knew I would have many more adventures, discover and explore many more beautiful places, and meet and know many more interesting and extraordinary people in my lifetime. But I also realized I would never be able to experience everything the world offered—and I accepted that because I knew it would be okay to just focus on the here and now. The Latin idiom *"Carpe diem"* became my internal compass at that moment. I understood at that moment that the here and now was more than special, and so was my relationship with Manny—but it was for this place and time only.

Manny pulled the car into a snowy parking lot and took multiple pictures of the mountain scenery. We left the car and walked up a steep driveway to a quaint little ski lodge and restaurant. It was warm and cozy inside, and the welcoming, wood-burning fireplace invited us to relax. The aroma of Italian food mixing with the smoke from the fireplace was intoxicating. We lingered in the restaurant after lunch, watching skiers come and go. Finally, we moved to chairs directly in front of the fireplace, sipped coffee, and watched the dancing flames. We were now so comfortable with one another that conversation wasn't necessary. And when we did speak, we could discuss anything. We had become that self-assured with each other.

When he was alone with me, Manny was different—not agitated, hostile, and sarcastic, like he was with his family or when we had first met. At this ski lodge, Manny finally began to talk about his childhood and how damaging his upbringing had been.

He blamed his family's wealth—and the lifestyle it provided—as a main source of his self-loathing.

"Joe and I were raised by hired staff—not our parents," he confessed. "I can't tell you how many hours of counseling I've been through, beginning at a very impressionable age, to rationalize my family's dynamics and to curb my antisocial behavior. The conclusion I came to through these numerous sessions to cure my 'bad boy' tendencies is that I just don't fit into my family. However, I've learned to charm the world at large when I choose to—I'm almost a social con artist. And I've totally given up trying to please my parents. My bitterness and lashing out stem from the lack of unconditional love from my self-centered parents. I find it strange that they even had children."

I listened carefully to Manny and his parental criticism, which echoed the feelings of inadequacy and loneliness that Joe had expressed when we dated during my freshman year at Wesley. The two brothers dealt with their family dynamics differently—yet both were damaged from the same emotional isolation.

"It's hard for me to identify with your upbringing," I said. "I grew up in a caring, supportive environment with salt-of-the-earth parents who unequivocally loved me and my two sisters. Farm life in Kentucky is simple and very predictable. Each season follows its set pattern—winter planning, spring planting, summer cultivating, and fall harvesting. And my family's love is just as predictable. My family means everything to me—in good times and bad. I can always count on them to support and cheer me on as I try to find my way in the world. I love being with them. How sad that you and Joe never experienced this close family bonding—it's so reassuring," I added.

"But your brother seems to be gaining some idea about this kind of love now, Manny. Joe's adapted seamlessly into my parents' farm life as a working guest this semester. He has a real fan club there. My folks can't stop singing his praises. And he's also getting unconditional support from his college love interest—my best childhood friend—who's from Rockport, too." I couldn't help smiling, thinking of Joe and Grace. "It wouldn't surprise me at all if there was a wedding in the future."

"Joe and I almost never talk to each other. Maybe I should visit him in Kentucky once we're all back in the States," Manny said wistfully. "But don't think for a moment you could recruit me to farm life," he said with a grin.

I smiled back at Manny, picturing him in bib overalls mucking out the horse stables. And for that moment, everything seemed so right. But Manny broke the spell, looking at his watch and announcing it was time to head back to Milan. We had a long drive ahead of us.

It was late when we got back to the apartment, and we were exhausted. We said good night with a quick kiss and went to our separate bedrooms.

CHAPTER 37

With only two weeks left in Milan, I began to panic, trying to cram as much as possible into that short time. I began meeting Erica four times a week for intensive language sessions. I was a little disappointed that Erica's English had greatly improved while my Italian was stuck at a more basic level. She picked up English much more quickly than I mastered Italian. Still, I was pleased that I could now converse in simple sentences. I was even dreaming in Italian!

As I increased my focus on improving my Italian, I didn't neglect my schoolwork. I had a final project to complete before the semester ended—a business plan for Chloe's fashion design business. Chloe and Janice worked with me every night for a week. It helped that I drew on their experience, but I also incorporated my own ideas into the plan. And the plan's organization was all mine, so I was doubly pleased when they liked the direction I was taking. I had some definite ideas about how to expand their business.

As part of my research, the three of us had spent several days in Biella, Italy. It was the fashion manufacturing capital of Italy and only an hour's drive from Milan. Because Chloe and Janice had so many fashion industry connections, I toured some factories and saw how the production lines were set up—a unique opportunity for a university student. On one of these visits, I studied the process and found some areas where I thought the manufacturing could be streamlined without sacrificing the quality of the fabrics or garments. I was particularly fascinated with the weaving; I loved seeing the beautiful wools and cashmeres develop. Chloe and Janice were the creative designers, but my business sense would be my contribution to make their endeavor profitable. Research and analysis were my strengths, and unlike Chloe and Janice, I found crunching numbers captivating.

Like a child, I couldn't wait to tell Chloe and Janice the high mark I received on my business plan at the end of the semester. Both women glowed at the success of their business fashion ingénue. We celebrated with champagne before dinner, and after dinner, they invited me for a nightcap. Chloe wasted no time, saying immediately, "Janice and I want to share with you the parts of your business plan we definitely plan to implement when we roll out our brand. You've addressed the line's finances brilliantly."

I raised my glass to my two mentors and thanked them for all their help with the business plan. "Your direction led me to make my career choice, and I can't wait to begin my professional career in fashion."

Finally, I floated up to my room, and that's when the reality hit me—my stay in Milan was almost over. The prospect of leaving these dear women and this fantastic city made me incredibly sad. But the thought of reuniting with my family and friends was very exciting. I realized I'd have to be careful when everyone badgered me for all the details of my Milan experience. I'd have to edit many of my adventures, discoveries, and relationships.

I could never tell anyone that my hosts were two lesbian women who were life partners. Folks would be horrified to know about the drugs and alcohol abuse I had witnessed and my discovering

Teresa's body in a drug-induced suicide. I also had to be careful about Manny; I could never admit he was more than just a dear friend.

Safe topics would include the beautiful places I'd seen and the mind-expanding education I'd received during the past five months—educational opportunities that reached well beyond the walls of the university and Kentucky's farm fences. I knew my family and friends would be delighted when I regaled them in my newly acquired conversational Italian—which might be one way to steer the conversation away from forbidden topics. And I looked forward to modeling my new outfits and telling them about my business plan and the research I had done for it. But I was eager to see their faces when I presented them with the souvenirs and little gifts I'd carefully selected for everyone in my family.

In my last language lesson with Erica, we agreed to meet again at some point in the future when we were both fluent in our newly learned second languages. I had chosen a silk scarf as a parting gift for Erica because she had so often admired the scarves from Chloe and Janice's line. She had selected a book of Italian poems that she said would remind me of our lessons whenever I read it. We shared a tearful farewell hug. I whispered *"Ciao"* in her ear, and she whispered "Goodbye" in mine.

Estella offered to cook my favorite dish on my last night. I asked for her homemade pasta with a simple pomodoro and basil sauce. She nodded and then, with a poker face, asked, "Would you like a chocolate milkshake with your pasta?" We both laughed, remembering my telling her how my aunt would make spaghetti and meatballs and give me a chocolate milkshake.

"You know, Estella, my tastes have matured here in Italy, and I now prefer a dry Chianti with my pasta."

Manny tried to appear lighthearted at my parting dinner. As we entered the dining room, he grinned impishly and asked me if there were place cards for the chosen twelve who had been invited to my "last supper." Daddy would have been scandalized at such a sacrilegious reference, but the four of us just burst into laughter.

Instinctively, I knew Manny, like me, was grappling with our approaching separation. We had spent so much time together during the short time since Teresa's death and had forged a deeply intimate friendship, but that would probably change with an ocean between us. During this brief period, I had seen Manny begin to work on positive directions in his life. He enjoyed cooking and photography, but his real passion remained music. He told me he might return to New York and open his own restaurant or music shop but pledged me to silence about his budding plans.

After dinner, Chloe and Janice asked us to come to the living room. They were seated on the sofa when we entered; Manny and I took the two Queen Anne chairs that faced the couch. Chloe took the stage, saying she had prepared a little going-away speech. She began with how much she and Janice had enjoyed having me with them for these five months, winking at Manny when she said, "And I know you've enjoyed her company, too, but I'll let you speak for yourself on that topic."

She continued, "Marilyn, you have great potential in the fashion design business. And, selfishly, Janice and I want to see you develop that potential. We'd like to offer you a position in our company after you've completed your university studies and have your business degree. Quite frankly, we need your business sense. And your progress with Italian is another reason we feel you would be such an asset to our company.

"Of course, my dear, all the clothes you've worn to show off our line, Bourne Innocence, are yours. But we don't want to lose the valuable input of your modeling experiment, so we want you to continue to gather information on the line and let us know how well it's received in your American circles. We plan to ship you an appropriate wardrobe each season until you come back to join our company to handle its business side." She ended her proposal by lifting her glass to me then taking a sip.

My jaw dropped. I was speechless. "Thank you" seemed so inadequate for everything they had done for me for the past five months—much less the job offer. I would walk off the stage with my degree in hand and walk into a dream job. And in my last semester in college, I'd be the best-dressed coed on campus! I jumped up and ran to Chloe and then to Janice to hug them both and enthusiastically repeat, "Thank you."

When I finally came down from my feeling of elation and disbelief, Manny and I excused ourselves to go for a walk. He had asked earlier if we could spend my last night revisiting some of our favorite spots. When we left the apartment, I could barely contain my excitement. I was grinning and talking nonstop about the job offer and how it meshed so perfectly with my career goals following graduation.

We were holding hands, and he was very quiet as I gushed and bounced around next to him. I finally settled down to a more sedate pace and looked at him. I knew we shared a special bond, but I also knew in my heart—and my mind—that our relationship would not be permanent. We would not be a couple.

"Marilyn, I hate to see the best friend I've ever had leave tomorrow, but I'll always remember these past few months as the happiest time I've ever experienced—with anyone. Your goodness hasn't worn off on me, and my corrupt ways haven't changed you at all," he said with a laugh.

Then sadly, he acknowledged what I already knew. "However, I think we both know I'm not who you would want as a permanent partner—you know, the 'till death do us part' bit." I became very still and nodded in agreement. "But, Marilyn, I'm serious about coming to Kentucky to reunite with Joe, to meet his girl and your family and to just be with you again."

We stopped at our favorite coffee shop and talked until midnight. We could have stayed longer, but I had an early morning flight and still had some packing to finish. I also needed to get a little sleep before the car came to take me to the airport.

When we got back home, we held each other for a long time in the hallway. There was a brief goodbye kiss, and then he turned and went to his room and I went to mine. It was a bittersweet farewell.

Chloe and Janice woke early to see me off. Estella was there, too, with a small sack full of her special breakfast rolls. Manny didn't come out of his bedroom, although I thought I heard him moving about. I wasn't surprised that he chose not to see me off. We had said our goodbyes the night before.

The driver piled my luggage (so much more for the return trip) in the trunk of the black limo, and we headed to the airport. I struggled with my mixed emotions. I was sad as I walked into the terminal, but I was equally glad to be going home. One thing I knew as I checked my bags at the counter—all the new things inside my suitcases could not begin to equal all the new things I was taking home inside my heart and head.

CHAPTER 38

During the long plane trip from Milan to New York, I took out Erica's going-away gift and reread the heartfelt, handwritten note inscribed in English on the book's title page. I reclined my seat slightly and began to read the poems. Immediately, I stumbled over Italian words I did not recognize. Unfortunately, my Italian-English dictionary was packed in my suitcase. Struggling to decipher the poems, I found my thoughts returning to Milan. I missed my life there already. And I had a very real fear that I might lose the little Italian I'd learned without hearing it or being able to speak to someone in this beautiful language. Then I dozed off.

I was surprised to awake as we prepared for landing at Idlewild Airport. I joined passengers in the long lines that snaked through the cavernous customs room. The scene reminded me of herding cattle at the farm. Blurry-eyed and feeling totally disoriented, I finally cleared customs and headed to the gate for Nashville—the last lap of my journey home. In a little over three hours, I'd be with my family.

As soon as I deplaned, I saw Daddy, Mama, and Beth smiling and excitedly waving their hands in unison. Beth held a "welcome home" sign and fresh flowers. Joe and Grace had volunteered to watch Maria and Beth's children so she could drive Daddy and Mama to the airport to pick me up. My excitement at seeing my family eclipsed my earlier reluctance about having to leave behind a lifestyle I now coveted.

But even my joy at seeing these beloved faces couldn't overcome my jet lag. My energy was depleted from the long trip back to Nashville, and I was so looking forward to some rest. Then I looked at Daddy—focused on him. He looked like an old man. Mama was standing beside him with her arm curled through his, clearly propping him up. My father had always been a strong, suntanned, vigorous man working industriously on his farm. In front of me stood a ghostly, hunched-over figure that slightly resembled the man I knew and loved deeply. This stranger had hollow cheeks, weary eyes, and a gray pallor. His hair had turned shockingly white during my Milan semester. Why had all the letters from home reiterated glowing reports about his health? I was completely unprepared for this transformation.

I covered my shock as best I could when we all exchanged hugs, kissed, and talked excitedly as we walked toward the baggage claim. It broke my heart when we had to stop numerous times so Daddy could catch his breath—his breathing was alarmingly labored.

Beth left us at the front door of the terminal outside baggage claim to get the car. Seated on a bench, Mama, Daddy, and I waited for my luggage to arrive. When Beth drove up, Mama helped Daddy into the front seat of the car and said, "As soon as we get all her suitcases, we'll come out through this door. See you shortly."

Once we reentered the terminal for my baggage, I accused Mama of keeping Daddy's failing health from me. "Why did you all tell me Daddy was fine when he's obviously not?"

She responded quickly, "He made us promise not to mention

his declining health for fear you'd hop on a plane and return home immediately." We collected my luggage in silence as I tried to adjust to this new, unsettling situation.

On the ride home, Mama and Beth bombarded me with questions. It was a friendly interrogation, but I had to be careful with my responses. I tried to answer their many questions in a circumspect way, elaborating on details I thought would not disturb them. Daddy was very quiet, only commenting or asking questions infrequently.

Exhausted, I sprawled out in the back seat of the car. To divert their nonstop questioning, I began rapidly firing questions at them. "What's been happening on the farm? How did Joe and the others manage? How's Maria? How are your kids doing, Beth? Any exciting news in Rockport?"

My questions focused on the family and home. I was eager to catch up, but it was also a cover-up as I tried to grapple with Daddy's health issues and how rapidly he had deteriorated during my absence. I tried to project an enthusiasm and eagerness in my voice, but it was difficult to mask my concerns. The oxygen tank on the passenger side where Daddy was sitting seemed to confirm my worst worries. *No wonder we had to stop while we were walking to the baggage claim. He couldn't breathe!*

It seemed like an eternity just getting out of the airport. When we entered the highway heading toward the Kentucky border, I acknowledged the oxygen tank. "Daddy, why didn't you bring your oxygen tank with you into the terminal?"

He responded in his usual straightforward way, "I didn't want that to be the first thing you saw when you spotted us." A tear crept down my cheek, and I turned my face to the window, looking out at the familiar, farm-dotted countryside.

I only allowed myself a moment to turn away from my family. I pulled myself together quickly—for Daddy's sake—and we spent the ninety-minute ride from Nashville to Rockport catching up on the most important highlights of life in Rockport during my time abroad. Instinctively, I knew I couldn't discuss the employment opportunity in Milan waiting for me after graduation in May. Everyone was just reveling in my return and wanted to hear about my incredible adventure. I told myself the right time would present itself to tell them about this exciting job prospect in Italy. I'd wait for that right time.

Daddy spoke glowingly about Joe. "He was so smart—going to the administration office at Wesley to get approval to combine his classes in agriculture with his work on the farm. He traveled back and forth for the entire semester—and that wasn't easy." Daddy's breathing was so labored I asked him to stop, but he insisted on continuing. "Joe even received academic credit for his work as an intern on the farm. I'm sure his professors were impressed at his practical experience. Joe, Jimmy, and Samuel were a terrific team, Marilyn. And you deserve credit for having the good sense to arrange this help. As you can see, I haven't gained back my strength from that heart attack."

We finished the last few miles in silence, and as we drove up the gravel driveway toward our farmhouse, I had mixed feelings. I was relieved to be home, yet I felt a sense of detachment from this familiar place. Grace and Joe were in the front yard, waving and grinning—so glad to see me. Maria was bundled up outside in her wheelchair, sitting in the winter sun and watching Beth's kids play. It looked like a Norman Rockwell painting of a family that belonged together. Sadly, I didn't see myself in that picture.

Joe and Grace ran to meet the car. I tumbled out of the back seat, and we hugged each other. Before I could say anything, Grace waved her left hand in my face. "Joe and I are getting married. Look at my ring!" With our arms now locked in a circle, we exuberantly jumped up and down to celebrate their match, one clearly made in heaven.

"I gave her the ring last night," Joe explained as he beamed at Grace. "I haven't even told my family. I wanted to give Grace her ring while we were both here in Rockport. I'll take her to New York to meet my father and tell him the good news before my classes begin in a few weeks."

When we finally moved into the house, nothing had changed. Everything was in its right place. Mama's welcome-home dinner included all my favorite foods, and the dining room table was set with the Sunday-best china. Daddy blessed our food and gave a prayer of thanksgiving that I was home where I belonged. When he stressed the word *belong,* it was a poignant moment for me because I was torn between my home and my ambitions. But those thoughts drifted into the background, and my mood shifted during the boisterous dinner. Everyone was talking at once, laughing and sharing stories.

Joe talked nonstop about his terrific experience on the farm. Daddy punctuated Joe's stories with quips about how Joe was a natural farmer and lucky to have landed Grace as his soon-to-be perfect farmer's wife.

Joe stopped the good-natured kidding when he asked Daddy and Mama if he and Grace could have their wedding reception at our farm. They planned to put up a tent in the backyard. There was no question what my parents' answer would be. Daddy and Mama just beamed. Joe continued, "Your place is really what brought Grace and me together this past year—and you two are like family to me. Grace and I will be married in the Baptist church here in the summer after my Wesley graduation."

I tried to visualize Joseph, Chloe, and Janice seated on the groom's side of the Baptist church and then attending the reception in our farmhouse backyard—under a tent. No doubt Joe had already thought about this ironic meshing of the two camps of parents, but he didn't seem to care. *Maybe he wants his folks to see his life as it is now—and their son happy and pursuing his chosen life's work with a wife named Grace.*

Then another thought crossed my mind: *Will Manny attend the nuptials? Will he be good Manny or evil Manny? Was he sincere when he told me in the Italian Alps that he wanted to come to Rockport and reunite with his brother and meet Grace and my folks? Did he mean it when he said he wanted to see me again?*

I shuddered with this thought and knew it was time to call it a night. "I feel like a walking zombie. I'll pick up with the stories tomorrow morning after a good night's sleep," I promised as I excused myself from the table. Somehow, I knew Joe suspected there was "a story behind the story" I relayed about my experiences—especially since many of the anecdotes were peppered with references to Manny. Each time I mentioned his brother, Joe looked at me with a raised eyebrow.

Grace innocently said she could not wait to meet Manny. "If he's anything like Joe, I know I'll love him!"

"No way, Grace, we're as different as night and day," Joe said.

I backed Joe up in this assessment by stating, "Manny has a tender heart like Joe, but he's *definitely* different!"

CHAPTER 39

On Sunday morning, we went to church as a family. As I walked through the front door, I realized this was the first time I'd been to a church service in over five months. In good conscience, I couldn't count the number of cathedrals I'd visited in Italy. They were just part of my "to see" list, and each time I checked one off my list, I felt rather smug about my progress.

I looked around the congregation and saw so many familiar faces—people I'd known since childhood. I tried to focus on the minister's sermon, but instead, I found myself daydreaming about my favorite topic—Italy. I smiled slightly as I looked down at my Rockport church outfit. I'd selected a simple woolen dress from my Wesley college wardrobe. I'd still not shown anyone the clothes Chloe and Janice had given me in Milan.

Time passed so quickly in Rockport. Two weeks seemed like two days, and suddenly I was packing again—getting ready to begin my last semester at Wesley. I carefully folded my Italian clothes and laid them in my luggage, each piece cradled in tissue. I was eager to wear them and get some reactions to share with my two mentors. Since I'd sold my car almost a year ago, I was thrilled when Beth offered to drive me to school. It would be the first time since my return that we'd have some one-on-one girl talk time with no interruptions from her husband, her children, or our parents.

As soon as we left the driveway, I began drilling Beth about Daddy's real condition. I had skirted this subject when the family was together, and I particularly didn't want to broach any questions to Mama. She always looked so worried and frazzled from taking care of Daddy and Maria.

"Marilyn, the doctor said Daddy is living on borrowed time, but I guess you could see how much he's declined for yourself," Beth said. Then she continued, and her voice and message were clearly intended to make me feel guilty. "I sure hope you've gotten that foreign travel bug out of your system—you're needed around home more than ever now."

Her words chilled me, and I drew back, even physically shrinking into the seat. I knew there was no way I could share my exciting job offer with her. Beth's words jolted me back to reality. I had to face my daddy's serious illness and my obligation to my family during this crisis.

As we drove through the lush countryside, I looked out the window and stared at the fences that had been built to contain the livestock and delineate the property lines of the farmers who owned the property. I had been home only a short time, but already I felt fenced in and my hope of pursuing greener pastures was far beyond the fences—and fading.

After a brief silence, Beth changed the subject. Our conversation focused on more mundane topics until we reached my apartment building. Beth helped me unload my suitcases and boxes, and I asked her to stay and have a cup of coffee with me. "It will only take a few minutes to brew, and I want to show you something special. It's very important to my future career."

She said callously, "No coffee. I've got to get back to the kids and Mama and Daddy. Make your show-and-tell brief."

I opened my suitcases and began to carefully unfold my beautiful Italian outfits. I laid each outfit on my bed so she could see and touch. Beth's expression morphed into one of anger, and she spewed out, "Miss Prissy, where do you think you'll wear these things? Are you too uppity for us now that you've lived in Italy? Please tell me you didn't spend Mama and Daddy's hard-earned money to buy these ridiculous clothes! What's gotten into you? I don't know you anymore."

"Beth, calm down!" My voice sounded shrill. Clearly, I wasn't in total control of myself. "These are some fashion samples from a line I'll be working on when I finish college and enter the business side of the fashion industry. I didn't buy these outfits. They're a gift from Joe's mother. She's a fashion designer and worked with me on a business plan assignment I had last semester." I was trying to control my voice and hold back tears of indignation, so I said in a more conciliatory tone, "I thought you'd be curious to see samples of Chloe's new clothing line for young women. Don't you want to touch the fabrics and examine the masterful detailing on each garment? This is where I hope my future career will take me—that's all it means."

Beth glared at me and the clothing display on my bed before turning and stomping out of my apartment without saying goodbye. I called after her, "Beth, thanks for driving me back to school. I love you." But it sounded so lame after her tirade. During that Sunday afternoon drive, I had gone from simple elation at being alone with my sister to abject despair. She had cut me to the core with her criticism.

Monday morning was the start of winter semester, and my first assignment was going to my advisor's office with the forms from the University of Milan. I wanted to make sure I received full credit for my semester abroad. Knowing she would be supportive, I didn't hesitate to tell her how I planned to use my business degree. "I'll be entering the world of fashion design. It's a fascinating industry, and I believe I'll be successful."

I was puzzled when she looked perplexed. "Marilyn, how do you plan to accomplish that? Wesley offers no coursework in fashion design."

I responded quickly. "I plan to go into the business management side of fashion design." Then I expanded, telling her about the business plan I'd developed for a newly branded fashion line of clothes. "It was part of my studies at the University in Milan, and I received a very high mark. I've also got a potential job offer."

She smiled and then replied, "Well, let's get you signed up for the classes you'll need to graduate with a business degree."

After I left her office, I studied the ambitious schedule of courses she'd outlined. I had to complete a course-load heavy semester before I could graduate with that business degree. It would be a tough semester, but my motivation was stronger than ever. I was completely focused on the captivating prize before me—working in fashion.

As I hurried down the corridor to go to my first class, I saw Joe heading into a classroom. He yelled out. "Hey, Marilyn, let's grab a 'catch-up' Coke together at the Colony around 4:00 this afternoon. Okay?"

"Sounds good to me—I have so much to tell you," I said.

Joe's response was glib, almost a Manny response. "I bet you do."

At the Colony, our conversations leapfrogged from one topic to the next. We talked about the different lifestyles of Joe's parents, Manny and his struggles to find himself, and Joe's recent trip to New York to introduce Grace to his father. I told Joe how much I had enjoyed living with his mom and Janice. Not only were they gracious hostesses, they were invaluable resources with my business courses. I even showed off some of the Italian phrases I'd learned and confided that his mom, Janice, and I had often spoken Italian at dinner to exclude Manny from the conversation. Joe laughed at this wicked little scenario. Finally, I launched into the proverbial "elephant in the room" question about his upcoming wedding.

"Joe, what's your take on your parents and Manny attending your wedding in dinky Rockport? Will you be embarrassed?" I asked.

He countered, "Strange that you should bring this up, Marilyn. I could care less what my parents think of my marrying Grace and where we'll have our wedding. I'm much more concerned that they will embarrass me in front of your family and friends!"

I blinked. Immediately, I realized our feelings of embarrassment would be coming from totally opposite directions. *Joe and I are as similar as we are different—both of us were born square pegs expected to fit into our own designated family circle's round holes.*

CHAPTER 40

I started the semester determined to focus on my studies and ace my classes, even though I'd be carrying a heavy course load. I wasn't going to be distracted. Good intentions, but translating them into concentration on my studies was proving a little more difficult. Too often, I found myself daydreaming about Milan and planning my return to that wonderful, exciting city.

Chloe regularly fueled this fire by sending letters filled with riveting tidbits about the fashion world. Not that I needed her letters to keep me zeroed in on fashion. The notebook of report forms Chloe had given me would ensure that priority. I was to complete a form recording the comments from students and others on campus and in town about each outfit I wore. These findings would give her relevant feedback and help her determine if there would be a market for her Bourne Innocence line on college campuses in the States.

I was a little timid when I wore my outfits on the first few days, and my initial findings were quite enlightening. The girls reacted much like Beth had. Some even made snide remarks, clearly audible to me, about showing off my semester abroad wardrobe. The guys were much more positive, and I collected many unsolicited compliments. Faculty members seemed intrigued. They asked a lot of questions about the clothing line and how I had become involved with the company. They were often the first to compliment me on the different outfits.

The positive reactions from the guys and faculty boosted my confidence, and I was soon wearing these high-fashion clothes with more assurance. I also became comfortable questioning different segments of the campus population, interviewing individuals to learn specifically what they liked or disliked about each outfit. And the last bit of negativity from the girls disappeared after a front-page story in the college newspaper featured me modeling an outfit and explaining my research study for a new foreign clothing line soon to be introduced in the States. Suddenly, everyone wanted to be a fashion critic and contribute to the reports for Milan. My circle of acquaintances greatly expanded after this publicity.

My weekly feedback to Chloe highlighted the differences between Wesley students and those at the University of Milan. Coeds, particularly sorority girls, at Wesley said they'd prefer clothes that were a little more tailored. They said something more conservative—with less flair—would work better for their college classes, games, and parties.

After reporting for two months, I received a large box from Chloe. I tore off the wrapping and found myself looking at a whole new wardrobe. There were skirts, cashmere sweaters, woolen jackets, and simple, straight-line dresses in soft cottons, linens, and wools—and all in more conservative designs and colors. The reaction to my new wardrobe was immediate. Everyone, including the guys, loved this look. I rushed back after my last class and wrote to Chloe in large block letters:

WE ARE IN BUSINESS IN THE USA WITH THE LINE OF CLOTHING YOU JUST SENT

ME–RECEIVING RAVE REVIEWS. CAN WE MAKE AFFORDABLE?

What a triumph!

But the euphoria wouldn't last. Life was about to intrude. I was in my accounting class the next day when the professor was interrupted by a knock on the door. He answered it, nodded briefly, turned back to the class, and motioned for me to join him. My heart began to race. What could it be? I didn't think I had done anything to create dismissal from school. Surely the fraternity party I had attended the previous Saturday night wouldn't have put me in jeopardy, although it had spun out of control with revelers drinking illegal Tennessee moonshine mixed with ginger ale and grape juice. The police had received a call about a wild party and raided the house. According to the campus rumor mill, this fraternity would be on probation for the rest of the year. Since my date and I had sampled the concoction enthusiastically that evening, we prudently slipped out of the back door when we heard the commotion as the police came through the front door. Had someone seen us sneak out, and were we being called to task for participating?

Mr. Humphrey, the dean of students, was standing just outside the classroom door, and he wasn't smiling when he asked me to come to his office. Once there, he pointed to the chair in front of his desk and said to sit down. My heart was pounding, and I could feel my anxiety level rising.

He began, "Marilyn, your sister Beth just called. She wants you to come home immediately. I hate to be the bearer of sad news, but your father died in his sleep last evening."

I was stunned. Had I heard right? *No, not my daddy! He's so tough. He can overcome anything.*

Mr. Humphrey continued, "Beth also asked me to contact Joe

Bateson about the death. I understand he's a close family friend. Beth said she was sure he'd drive you to Rockport at once. We've located Joe, and he'll be at your apartment at 2:00 p.m." We rose, and Mr. Humphrey extended his hand. "My deepest condolences, Marilyn, to you and your family. Let me know if there is anything you need from us."

I walked back to the apartment slowly. I was numb. I couldn't cry. I couldn't think. Everything was a blur. *People talk about having an out-of-body experience; now I know what they mean.*

Opening my apartment door and crossing the threshold seemed like entering a different dimension. I sprang into action, pulling my red Samsonite suitcase from under the bed and starting to toss things into it. I was going through the motions, but it was still difficult for me to get my thoughts together enough to even decide what clothes I should pack. I stood in the middle of the room, dazed and confused, when the reality of the news finally hit me, and I began to sob uncontrollably. Tears streamed down my face, sprinkling the clothes in the suitcase—the red suitcase, my special gift from Mama and Daddy. I remembered how happy I'd been when I packed it for Milan—and how excited I'd been packing it with the beautiful clothes Chloe had given me for my return to the States and my family.

I suddenly saw my suitcase as a symbol of change—both good and bad. There is never any guarantee that the simple act of packing and unpacking will always lead to happiness and adventure. Sometimes it will lead to sadness and tribulation. I shuddered, and that physical act seemed to focus my mind on the task before me. I began to organize my thoughts—and my clothes—to prepare for my daddy's funeral.

But before I could resume packing, a knock on my bedroom door startled me. It opened slowly, and to my comfort and relief, it was Grace. Grace was taking graduate courses in library science for the next two semesters at Wesley after receiving her undergraduate degree in education the previous May. I ran to her. She held me, and we both sobbed so heavily that we had trouble catching our breath. She pulled back, held me at arm's length, and commanded, "Marilyn, just sit on the bed while I finish packing for you."

She shook her head as she began to rearrange the contents of the suitcase. "Look at this mess. You've packed five skirts and three pair of flats that don't match. But you packed no blouses or sweaters, no black dress, no heels, and no underwear." She proceeded to carefully lay out the clothes she thought I'd need for the next week at home. She even remembered to put in the necessary toiletry items—from toothbrush to talcum powder. When Joe arrived, we hugged and cried, and Grace circled her arms around the two of us.

It's funny, but when someone dies, people can't stop talking about the deceased. That person becomes the topic of everyone's conversation. Our ride back to Rockport was no exception. Joe reminisced about how much Daddy had meant to him. "I'll miss his guidance, his honesty, and kindness."

Grace, who had lovingly packed my clothes and then hurriedly packed for herself, shared our many childhood experiences. We were best friends and usually got into mischief together. "Remember how your dad would want to discipline us for our deviant ways, but couldn't bring himself to punish us?" she said. One remembrance of Daddy spawned another, and it was so comforting for me. I needed to talk about him on this sad ride home.

There were at least ten cars and trucks in the farm driveway when we pulled up. "Get ready," Grace said. "There will be lots of people, food, and flowers." She was right.

When neighboring farmers heard of Daddy's death, they came to the house to offer Mama their condolences and to tell her not to worry—they would make sure her farm ran smoothly. Their wives were already in the kitchen preparing food and organizing the house, making sure there were enough chairs for people to sit when they came to support the family and pay their respects to Daddy. Beautifully arranged flowers had already arrived from the florist in Rockport and had been placed throughout the house.

I found Mama in her bedroom. She was supposed to be resting, but she was standing by the window, gazing out wistfully, not focused on anything. When she saw me, she rushed to me with her arms open to gather me to her. She held me close, saying tearfully, "Honey, our strength and the love of our life is gone."

At that moment, I began to realize the magnitude of her pain and loss. My parents had been married for forty-one years, and their personalities were so integrated emotionally and spiritually. How could I have been so self-centered? When I learned of Daddy's death, I had only thought about my loss, about how I would go on. I'd never considered that others were also grieving.

We were all grieving, but the business of life had to go on. And that meant planning Daddy's funeral service. Beth, Mama, and I sat on her bed and tried to decide what Daddy would tell us if he was alive and helping us plan this event. From that perspective, all we could come up with was that he would not want us to be sad; he would want us to remember him—and smile. He would tell us that he would be present in our memories, and then he would say, "Get on with living your lives." And we did.

Beth, Mama, and I drove to the Simmons Funeral Home early in the evening, chose a casket, and made the necessary service arrangements. We all agreed Daddy would want the services to be in the church and to be buried next to his mother and father in the family plot at the church cemetery.

We moved from one decision to another, completing Daddy's funeral arrangements. But it all seemed so unreal—almost as if we were moving in a trance. Daddy's death eclipsed everything.

All other thoughts and plans faded. Maria sat in a chair in a corner of the living room and mirrored our sad feelings. The tears streaming down her face were her only way to communicate the way she felt.

A friend of Mama's volunteered to watch Maria while we were at church for the funeral. Other neighbors and church members suddenly appeared to support our family in so many ways. Their compassion and kindness demonstrated the value of community life. A community's support provides a foundation to help get through profoundly sad times. Daddy had been a pillar of our church and community. His funeral validated his life and showed the respect many people had for him and for the way he lived his life among them in Rockport.

I believe Daddy's funeral was exactly what he would have wanted to celebrate his life—from the processional and recessional organ music selections to the hymns, Bible readings, and prayers. A simple spray of white roses, intermingled with daisies and greenery, blanketed his casket at the front of the church. Our minister's deeply heartfelt eulogy was a tribute to Daddy's life. The pews were filled, and more people stood in the back and along the sides of the church aisles. Although Joe was Jewish, he was moved by the ceremony. He told Mama, "The spirit that prevailed at that service was so touching. I've never felt such a sense of community before. It was a memorable and uplifting testament to one of the finest men I've ever met."

After the funeral and the burial, Mama sat Beth and me down in her kitchen and, speaking in a matter-of-fact voice, said, "In the past few months, as your father's illness was becoming worse, the two of us had very heart-wrenching conversations about the farm and what I should do with it when he passed on. He told me to sell it as quickly as I could and to move into town with Maria. He wanted me to have fewer worries and responsibilities. I told him I just couldn't sell our place immediately. I'd need time before making such a major decision. He knew that was right, but he said I'd know what to do when the time seemed right. I hope you girls will trust me to do what's right when that time comes."

CHAPTER 41

Two weeks after the funeral, Joe called and asked to meet with Mama, Beth, and me. When he arrived, we gathered around the kitchen table, always the site where my family made important decisions.

"I called this meeting to order," Joe facetiously began—and then his tone turned serious. "It's no secret that your family is very dear to me, really like a second family. Because of you, I'm in closer contact with my dad—rekindling our father-son relationship. Mr. White's death taught me how fragile life is and the importance of family support. As I've watched you go through these past few weeks, I've come to realize I need to mend fences with my parents."

He continued, "And Dad says he's willing to build a stronger relationship with me. And to begin that new relationship, I want to ask him to fly to Nashville and come here to meet you all. I want him to know the people who mean so much to me. But before I invite him, I want your blessing for this trip, Mrs. White."

Mama's response was immediate—and gracious. "Of course, Joe, we'd be delighted to host your father. He can stay in Marilyn's room. She can sleep with me or go over to Grace's during his visit."

My face flushed when I pictured Joseph coming to our

farmhouse and staying in my little bedroom. Apprehension gave way to panic, and before Joe could answer, I said with authority, "Your dad might be more comfortable staying at the new Howard Johnson's Motor Lodge in town rather than here."

Joe thanked Mama for her offer but added, "I agree with Marilyn that Howard Johnson's will be best. You've got enough on your plate, and I don't want to add any burdens to your life."

A few weeks later, Joe drove to the Nashville airport to pick up his dad. Beth and her husband Frank came over to meet him, and Mama prepared a welcoming meal—her special Sunday supper—even if it wasn't Sunday. Her fried chicken, gravy, and homemade biscuits were my favorite, and after his double helping of chicken and three biscuits, I think I can say it was a hit with our special guest. Mama topped off dinner with chocolate cream pie that nobody refused.

After dinner, we sat around the table talking and waiting for our stomachs to recover from our feast. Joseph seemed very comfortable. He shared memories about his favorite childhood summers when he visited his grandparents at their farm in Louisiana. His father had grown up there but ventured north to attend college and medical school in New York. Instead of going back to Louisiana, after graduation he had set up his practice in Scarsdale, New York, married a local socialite, and raised his family in that village suburb, north of New York City.

"I followed in my father's footsteps and became a doctor, but I preferred Manhattan to Dad's Westchester County suburb. But even though I'm a city dweller, I've always treasured those summers I spent on my grandparents' farm. Tonight's dinner has brought back so many fond memories for me. Thank you," he said, smiling and patting his belly.

Joe slapped his forehead in jest. "No wonder I love farm life so much—it's in my blood!"

Mama, Beth, and I cleared the table and washed the dinner dishes, letting them drain dry, while the men stayed at the table sipping coffee and chatting. When we returned, Mama offered another round of coffee.

Joseph shook his head. When Mama sat down, he leaned toward her and began to talk. His tone was almost confidential but still included the rest of the family. "Since Mr. White's death, Joe and I have talked seriously about the future of your farm. I hope this isn't too presumptuous—and we don't want to rush you—but we want you to consider our proposal when you and your family are ready. Joe loves this farm and has been so happy here with you that I'd like to lend him the money to buy it and care for it with the same love and respect that Mr. White bestowed on it when he was alive.

"Of course, I don't expect an answer until you've examined all your options. But Joe is so passionate about receiving his agricultural degree, and he would be honored to continue the traditions he's learned here during his time with Mr. White. We want you to know this is a genuine offer of love and respect. The transaction would take place only when—and if—you're ready to sell."

When I looked at Mama's face, I couldn't read her reaction to Joseph's proposal. Her bottom lip quivered, but her eyes were expressionless, staring straight ahead. I couldn't tell if she was relieved by this suggestion or saddened at the reality of having to deal with her husband's death and a future without him—and without the farm. She had to know—at least intellectually—that she couldn't run the farm and care for Maria—but what about emotionally?

Suddenly, Beth jumped up from the table and ran through the kitchen to the back door, covering her mouth. Her tears started before she reached the door. Frank excused himself, thanked Mama for dinner, and said he thought it would be best if he and Beth went home to relieve the babysitter. Frank shook hands with Joseph and walked to the back door. When he opened the door, we could hear Beth's sobs through the screen.

Mama waited until she heard Frank's car on the driveway gravel before she broke the awkward silence. She was composed and looked Joseph in the eye, but her response was guarded. She was clearly measuring every word. "Our family has come to love and trust your son. He's done an outstanding job on the farm during my husband's illness. If I had a son, I'd want him to have all the fine qualities that Joe possesses. However, at this point, I can't give you a definitive answer about your generous proposal. We do need time. But I promise you we'll get back to you with our answer after we've discussed it as a family."

Mama rose from the table, extending her hand to Joseph. "Please excuse me now. I need to bathe Maria to get her ready for her early bedtime. I'm so glad we've met, Joseph. We'll talk again soon." Silently, we watched her walk to Maria's bedroom.

I finally broke the spell and, on a lighter note, began to tell Joseph about my incredible study time in Milan, weaving in stories about how much Chloe had helped me with my studies and touching on the business plan for her newly conceived fashion design line. Joe added several comments, but when I mentioned that Manny and I had become dear friends, even exploring the Italian Alps during my stay, Joe interrupted. "I'm sure you must be tired, Dad. Would you like to return to the motel?"

I wanted a little more time with them, so I asked if I could ride into town with them. Immediately, both men agreed. In the car, Joseph apologized for discussing the farm's future so soon after my father's death. "I'm sad that I had to bring this up now, but I thought it was important for your family to know they had an option that would keep the farm in caring, responsible hands." He finished his apology and quickly steered the conversation to Mama's dinner. "The dinner was wonderful, and I'm so glad I was able to meet your mother, your sisters, and Frank." Joseph had moved from the farm topic, but I could tell he was still embarrassed that it might have been too soon to broach the topic of purchasing the farm. I wanted to ease his discomfort.

"Joseph, your proposal was heartwarming. We're still reeling from Daddy's death. Everything has changed, and we just need time to decide, as a family, what to do with the farm. I know Mama can't manage the farm by herself, not with the full-time responsibility for Maria. We all know we need to deal with this new situation realistically—just not right now."

As I watched Joseph walk to his motel room, I hoped my words had soothed his reservations about bringing up the farm purchase too early in our grieving process. Driving back to the farm, Joe asked me how I felt about his dad's proposal to loan him the money to buy the farm. I tried to sort through my conflicting emotions before I answered, but I had to be honest with him. "I'm afraid. My family's home has always been my safe haven. No matter where I went, I knew I could always come home. It's going to be an adjustment, but I'll have to make it."

Joe reached for my hand and very gently said, "Marilyn, as long as Grace and I live as husband and wife at your family farm, you will always be welcome there. You're like our favorite sister—as well as our best friend."

I was so touched that I could only whisper, "Thanks Joe, that means a lot to me." We finished the drive in silence. I spent the time trying to process the day's events and thinking about the decisions our family would soon have to make. I considered the irony of my life. It had been so easy for me to venture beyond the fences because I knew I could always return to the security of my childhood boundaries. How easy would it be now?

However, I understood that Beth and I needed to set aside our selfish emotions of our childhood and support Mama in the tough decisions she would have to make about the farm. When Joe stopped in front of the farmhouse, he reached over and gave me a warm hug and a brotherly kiss on the cheek.

Always the gentleman, he came around to open my car door and added, "I need to go back to the motel for a one-on-one chat with Dad before the two of us turn in for the evening. And you need to go in and support your mother right now."

Mama was busy at the sink washing the last of the dinner cups and saucers when I came through the kitchen door. I knew that staying busy helped her deal with the profound absence of Daddy. Each of us—Mama, Beth, and I—had our own way of coping with grief. Mama turned to me and asked, "Would you put away the dry dishes in the drainer and dry these cups and saucers for me?"

We finished our task without a word and headed toward our bedrooms, still silent. We knew that tomorrow we'd have to deal with routine tasks, but that the pressing priorities and decisions would be taking center stage. I went into my bedroom and wondered how it was possible for a quiet house to scream such a deafening silence.

CHAPTER 42

For the first few weeks after Daddy's death, I stayed at the farm, and Beth, Frank, and I helped Mama with most of the chores. Neighboring farmers pitched in, too, taking over the more difficult tasks in the field and barn. But I knew that couldn't continue, and as the weeks went by, our neighbor volunteers had to curtail their help to care for their own farms.

Now in just a few days, I'd have to return to school for mid-term exams, and I was concerned that Mama would try to do more chores so Frank and Beth wouldn't have to spend more time helping. I was also worried because we hadn't discussed, much less finalized, anything about Joseph's proposal to finance Joe's purchase of the farm. Selfishly, I wanted to have something settled before I left for Wesley because I needed to concentrate on my studies—not worry about Mama and Maria and the farm. So I decided to take action on my own.

First, I looked over the "homes for sale" ads in the paper and decided to spend a day checking out the available housing in Rockport, which was only about ten miles from our farm. I couldn't tell Mama, so I lied when I asked to use her car. I told her Grace and I needed to shop in town. Mama agreed at once. She

rarely drove anywhere because it was difficult to get Maria into the car or to find someone to watch her at home. Although I did feel a little guilty about my deception, I felt my actions were justified.

I rationalized my proactive plan and the little white lie by remembering Daddy's philosophy: "Do the things you do not want to do first." He always justified that philosophy with a story about how easy it is for farmers to go fishing or hunting on a nice day—a day perfect for bringing in the hay—and then regretting their procrastination when the rains came on the following days and washed away their crops. I didn't want to do this, but I didn't want to regret not acting.

To assuage my guilt slightly, I stopped to have a cup of coffee with Grace before driving to Rockport. I didn't tell her the ulterior motive for my visit, either. I didn't want Joe to know our family hadn't even talked about his father's proposal. Of course, I hadn't pushed the subject because I believed I needed to know possible real estate options for Mama and Maria before I broached the topic. When I started to leave, Grace asked if we'd reached any decision about selling the farm to Joe. I just shook my head and replied quickly, "Not yet."

Fortunately, Rockport was small enough that I could ride up and down every street looking for the homes from the paper and for any others with "For Sale" signs in the yards. Two-story houses were out, since Mama couldn't get Maria up and down stairs. I only saw three houses for sale; all had two stories.

Frustrated, I took a break and stopped at Perry's Drugstore on the corner of Main and Fourth Streets. I couldn't begin to count the hours Grace and I had spent at Perry's when we were in high school, always sharing a bag of potato chips and sipping our cherry Cokes while we talked about everything going on in our lives.

Ugh Page was behind the chrome counter at Perry's. He'd been the soda jerk there for decades and watched a slew of kids grow up.

He loved to tease us when he served our fountain drinks, and when I walked in, he was polishing a glass and holding it to the light to check for spots—just like he'd done forever. I plopped down on one of the cracked vinyl bar stools, propped my elbows on the counter, and cradled my face in my hands.

Ugh acknowledged me with a wide grin. "Bet you'll have your regular, Marilyn. Right?" Before I could confirm the order, Ugh placed a bag of chips and a cherry Coke in front of me. Then he said, "Why such a long face?"

"Ugh, I've driven all over town for the past four hours looking for one-story houses for sale—something suitable for my mother. You might not know Mama is the prime caregiver for my little sister, who's disabled, and since Daddy's death, Mama can't stay on the farm. She just couldn't take care of it properly and watch Maria twenty-four-seven. I came to Rockport to do some real estate snooping before I go back to school tomorrow. But there's nothing here."

"Oh God, Marilyn, I was so sorry to hear about your Daddy's passing," Ugh said, blushing. "I should have said something to you as soon as you sat down instead of that silly quip. Forgive my rudeness.

"But maybe I can make up for my insensitivity. I know a one-floor house coming on the market very soon. My uncle Harry's going to a nursing home, and our family will be cleaning out his house and helping him sell it. He's now way too frail to do it himself."

Ugh continued, "It's a nice white cottage with two bedrooms on the first floor and a finished attic that was used as a third bedroom years ago. But I think the best part of the house is the back porch. It was recently screened in, and in warm weather, it's like another sitting room."

I couldn't believe my luck. The cottage sounded perfect. "Is there any way I could see it this afternoon?" I asked.

"Sure, I'll call my cousin and tell him you'll be dropping in to see the place—right after you finish your Coke and chips," he laughed.

The address Ugh gave me was in a well-kept neighborhood within walking distance of Rockport's downtown stores. As soon as I turned in the drive, I realized Ugh was spot on in his description. The cottage was neat and tidy. Mature trees shaded the front yard, and flower gardens lined each side of the house. Mama would love tending them. Ugh's cousin met me at the front door, introduced himself, and took me into the living room to meet his father Harry, who was sitting quietly at the window looking out with a vacant stare. "Please feel free to wander through the house, and be sure to look at the attic room and back porch. Ugh said you were hoping it would be right for your mother." Ugh was right. The attic would be a perfect guest room—or maybe just a quiet place for Mama to retreat to when Maria was asleep.

Once I'd seen the house, I checked out the backyard—just the right size for a vegetable garden. Mama would love that. Although I thought the house was just right, my inspection had convinced me that it would take a lot of cleaning, painting, and decorating to make the cottage Mama's home. I thought that would be good. This move would be a welcome distraction for her, helping her transition into her new lifestyle with Maria.

I went back to the living room and crossed my fingers when I asked Ugh's cousin what he thought the price of the cottage would be. Surprisingly, it was modest, and I knew Mama could handle it with the money from Daddy's insurance policy and the sale of the farm.

"This cottage would be perfect for my mother and disabled younger sister," I said. "I'm going back to school tomorrow, but

I'll talk to my mother and older sister this evening and have them get in touch with you very soon. May I have your phone number?"

I wasn't sure how Mama and Beth would feel about my real estate discovery, but I was convinced this cottage was right for Mama and Maria. I shook hands with Ugh's cousin, thanked him for showing me his father's place, and assured him we'd be in touch. I had to force myself to contain my excitement as I drove back to the farm. I kept repeating, "Hands on the wheel, Marilyn. No clapping!" I was sure I'd found the answer to Mama and Maria's future. Moving into town would make their lives so much easier.

Mama was setting the table for dinner when I got back. I asked if Beth could join us for supper. "Ask her yourself. She's in the barn finishing your chores." I cringed at that little dig but then shook it off. I knew I'd had a very productive day, one that would benefit the family.

Beth said she'd planned to stay. Frank had taken the children to visit his mother and would have dinner there. As soon as Mama finished grace, I launched into my real estate adventure. First, I confessed that Grace hadn't been with me. "We had coffee, but I didn't want to include her in my house hunting. At first, I didn't find anything, but then I stopped at Perry's and unloaded on Ugh. That's how I found out about a cottage that will soon be for sale—and it's perfect."

No one spoke for a minute. Mama finally said, "I know I've got to decide about the farm. I can't rely on Beth and Frank to continue to take care of the heavy-duty farm chores—it's not fair to their family."

Beth interrupted, "But Mama, we can hire someone for the farm. We don't have to sell it."

To my surprise, Mama responded instantly. "I appreciate everything you girls and Frank have done to help me with the farm, but we can't keep this up much longer. I called Joseph this morning and told him I'm ready to sell to Joe, contingent on my finding a place in town, Of course, Joe has this semester to finish his degree and won't be able to take on the farm—or marry Grace—until then.

"I told Joseph I'd expect Joe to take over the farm lock, stock, and barrel as soon as the deal was finalized. I thought that might be within three months. Joseph said Joe would hire someone to take care of the farm until he finished school and could move into the farmhouse.

"When I talked to Joseph, I had no idea Marilyn would locate a house before she went back to school. I thought I'd have to do the house hunting on my own. Leave it to my little planner. Marilyn, call and make an appointment for us to see your cottage tomorrow."

Maria was sitting in her wheelchair playing with her doll. Mama turned to her and said, "Maria, you and I are leaving the farm and going to live in town very soon. But I'm sure Beth and Marilyn will come visit us there. What do you think?" There was no way Maria understood all that was going on, but she sensed that Mama had shared something important with her. She raised her doll and smiled.

The next morning, Mama asked a neighbor to stay with Maria while she, Beth, and I went to see the cottage in Rockport. Ugh's cousin left us alone, and Mama moved from room to room slowly. I could tell she was beginning to fill the spaces with her furniture, and she even talked about colors for the walls. You could tell Mama had mentally moved into this property.

Beth was less enthusiastic about the cottage. She was noncommittal and expressed no interest in Mama's proposed furniture arrangement or the possibilities for landscaping the yard. But I wasn't worried that she'd influence Mama's decision. We had both learned long ago that when Mama made up her mind about something, a team of wild horses couldn't change it.

That afternoon, Beth drove me to Wesley, and we talked about all the details involved in selling the farm and purchasing the house. Beth had softened her attitude about the move after she talked with Frank, and now we agreed Mama should hire an attorney to help with the transactions. "Marilyn, I'll talk to Mama about hiring an attorney, and if she agrees, I'll make calls to find one and keep you posted."

When Beth and I pulled up to my apartment, we were in sync—committed to doing what was best for Mama and Maria. We hugged goodbye to seal the deal. As I watched her drive off, I was so relieved. Time to concentrate on my studies at last!

As soon as I opened the apartment door, Grace grabbed me, and we danced around the room celebrating. She was so excited about Joe buying our farm and their upcoming wedding that she couldn't stop whirling me around. She finally calmed down and said, "Everything's falling into place for us. We'll marry at my family's church in the summer, and the reception will be at the farm. It couldn't be better." Later, when Joe came to pick up Grace to go to a movie, he picked me up and swung me around, just as jubilant as Grace.

After they left, I went to my room to unpack and begin to study. But I had trouble concentrating. I felt sad and alone, but I couldn't pinpoint the source. Was it losing my father or the sale of the farm? Or was it that my two best friends were so happy with each other—happiness that didn't include me?

CHAPTER 43

It took a few weeks to catch up with my coursework when I got back to school, and suddenly, it was Easter break and back to Rockport—but without Grace. She'd be spending the spring break in New York with Joe's family and was completely focused on her trip. Her questions about clothes choices were the same ones I'd asked her before my fateful visit with the Batesons. And every question triggered another memory of that life-changing trip.

Joe was as excited as Grace. He was eager to spend some quality time with his dad to further cement their relationship. Although Joe hadn't had much communication with his mother, he'd confided to Grace that he planned to remedy that situation—before the wedding. Grace and I had never talked about his mother's lesbian relationship and her emotional and logistical separation from her husband, but I assumed she knew about Chloe and Janice. Joe and she didn't keep secrets from one another. Mostly, though, I wondered how he had described Manny.

Just thinking of Manny was fascinating. His occasional letters always produced the same reaction—anticipation and eagerness. My hands shook as I tore open the envelopes. He was still in Milan, taking music classes at the University of Milan, where I'd studied, but he wasn't living with Chloe. He had his own flat in the artistic area known as *Navigli*.

Every letter said the same thing about his future. He still didn't know what he should do when he finally grew up. And the letters always ended on a teasing note, begging me to come and live with him. His last letter had included a very tempting closing offer: "Wendy, fly to me so we can once again have wonderful Disney adventures together with no strings attached—your favorite Peter Pan."

Each time I read his letters—and I read every one many times—I thought nothing would make me happier than to spend the rest of my life with him. I relived those last days in Milan and convinced myself that we were truly compatible. Contributing to this fantasy was my demanding coursework. My studies were so time consuming that I often pictured myself throwing in the towel and flying to Milan to be with Manny.

But reality always intruded, and I'd brush those romantic fantasies from my mind and buckle down to tackle lengthy assignments, finish final reports, and study for my rapidly approaching exams. Despite my heavy academic workload—and frequent flights of fancy—I made time to work on Chloe's business plan, my ticket to eventually joining her firm. My fantasies were a fun diversion, but I knew I was too much of a realist and way too ambitious to act on them. I always understood my real goal was to prepare myself for a career that would challenge me intellectually and inspire me spiritually.

While I stayed busy at college, Mama and Beth were busy in Rockport. They had hired a real estate attorney, and the two transactions—sale of the farm and purchase of the cottage—had proceeded at jackrabbit speed. Mama culled her farmhouse furniture and household goods, keeping the things she'd need in town and putting everything else in a yard sale. Joe and Grace made a special trip to Rockport for the sale and were two of her best customers, purchasing things to set up housekeeping after they married. The farm sale included farm equipment and livestock, but no personal belongings.

As promised, Joseph and Joe had found a reliable caretaker couple, neighbors from a nearby farm whose house had had major damage in a fire. They needed temporary housing while they rebuilt and remodeled, so they moved into Mama's farmhouse as soon as she moved to Rockport. They would tend the livestock and farmland until Joe finished school and could move into the house with his new bride.

I had mixed emotions as I headed home for our spring break in the cottage—the first without Daddy. I arrived at Mama's new house just before dark on Wednesday, and Mama couldn't wait to show me everything she'd done to make the cottage her own. There was still a little daylight, so she steered me to the backyard to see her vegetable garden preparations before ushering me through the back door to show off the interior.

I was amazed at her accomplishments. The rooms were transformed—light and airy instead of dark and dreary. Her paint color selections were perfect. If I had to choose one word for the cottage—*sparkle* would win, hands down. Mama had blended the farmhouse furniture with several new pieces and chosen window treatments that added a finishing touch to each room. She explained she still had many ideas for the house and yard and warned me to expect more surprises in the future.

Mama's enthusiasm was contagious, and Maria appeared to be adjusting happily to her new home, but I felt sadness. Now that the move was a reality, I realized I'd lost my childhood sense of place. Strangely, this radical change symbolized my personal rite of passage, completing my education and striking out to create my own place. A shiver of fear went through me—I wasn't sure I was ready to fly from the nest, but I knew I had no choice. I'd just been kicked out!

Our Easter feast was at my aunt and uncle's house. As we gathered around the same traditional dinner, I couldn't help remembering other holidays. There was a void at this table. We remembered Daddy in the blessing, and I felt his spirit fill the room at that moment.

I went back to my apartment at Wesley a day early. With mounds of class work, papers due, and mid-semester exams in just a few weeks, I had to hit the books.

I had a full day and half of quiet study before Grace and Joe returned, and I was ready for a diversion when they burst into the apartment Monday night. It didn't take much convincing to get me to take a pizza break. I was hungry and couldn't wait for a blow-by-blow account of their New York trip.

"I finally got to meet the notorious Manny," said Grace. "I think he's madly in love with you, Marilyn. All he did was talk about you."

I cut her off quickly. "I don't think so. If he's wild about me, he sure has a strange way of showing it. Plus, I don't think he knows what he wants yet for himself, much less for another person." I smiled as I jokingly added, "Hey, Grace, wouldn't it be a scream if we ended up marrying brothers? We could have a double-ring wedding at the farm."

Then I pointedly changed the subject. I'd shared too much about my feelings for Manny—as well as confidences about his dark side, lack of motivation, and complete absence of direction in his life—to go down this conversational path. I also felt we'd entered dangerous waters because Joe was with us. He didn't need to hear girl banter about Manny—his nemesis.

However, I'm not sure my subject choice was any better. I

thought it was a simple question. "Joe, how are Chloe and Janice doing?" I was angling for an update on their business, their health, maybe a few comments about their wardrobe. I was hoping to hear if any of the people I knew from Milan had come to New York with them or if they had brought new acquaintances. Joe had a different take on my question. He immediately launched into a description of his conversation with his mother, not on how she and Janice were faring.

With a chill in his voice, he began, "You know Mother and Janice are a package deal. They're both well, if that's what you are asking. But here's the real kicker from our visit—although the behavior is so typical of Mother I don't know why I was surprised. It took her two days to set aside enough time to talk to Grace and me. Why? Well, as usual, she was too preoccupied with more important things, like the proper wine to pair with each different menu and the perfect seating arrangements for the dinner parties. You know, her usual agenda of priorities," he ended sarcastically.

When he paused for breath, Grace jumped in. "When we finally had a few minutes for our chat, Janice joined us. Joe formally thanked his mother for taking time to meet with us—as if she were granting us an audience. I was shocked—really …"

Joe put his hand on Grace's arm, stopping her in midsentence. "Marilyn, I really tried. I began gently, looking her in the eye. Then I told her I didn't think she loved me and asked her why she didn't like to spend time with me. Chloe and Janice mirrored each other's reaction, recoiling at the same moment, shocked at my accusations."

Joe continued, "Mother recovered quickly and responded to my accusations by asking, 'What are you talking about, Joe? You know I love you. I give you all the money you need to do whatever you want. You've always been so obedient and accommodating. I never had to ride your case like I had to with your brother.' Once again, she refused to accept any blame for my feelings."

Joe stopped and bowed his head as if it was too painful to continue. Grace filled in, saying that Joe had released the floodgates and all his frustrations and hurt had spilled out when he went into detail about how no amount of money could make up for her absence during his childhood. "He even told her that Manny and he shared the same anger about her actions, saying they just acted out that anger in different ways to capture her attention."

Grace continued, "Janice kept patting Chloe's hand to comfort her during Joe's diatribe. It was unreal. Chloe is not my favorite person right now, but I guess you can tell that."

I turned to Joe to find out the result of this scene. "Do you think this confrontation has broken through the wall separating you and your mother?"

He shook his head negatively. "I really don't think Mother is capable of understanding what her parental role should be—and how her actions have scarred our family. She's just too narcissistic. Lucky for me, I have Grace, and we're going to build our future together. I'll still try to have a relationship with Mother going forward, but now I know it will always be on her terms."

I wondered how Joe and I could have such different perceptions of a person. Chloe had always been generous, kind, and thoughtful to me, even spending an inordinate amount of time with me. Was it because our relationship was built on a business level rather than a personal one? No matter the differences, I was glad Joe and Grace felt they could discuss this intimate conversation with me, especially since they knew how much I respected Chloe and Janice and considered them valued mentors.

"Joe, you are a dear friend of mine. And your mother and I have an amicable, professional respect for one another. However, I want you to know I'm proud of you for taking the lead to try to change the dynamics of your relationship with her. It was a valiant effort on your part, since she has such a forceful personality," I added. That seemed to settle it, but I knew when Grace and I got back to the apartment, I could ask her all the questions I wanted to about Chloe and Janice.

But right now, I couldn't wait any longer to open the box of clothes Chloe had sent from New York—her latest designs. I excused myself, saying, "Grace, I'll see you at the apartment. I'm glad you're both back safe and sound."

By the time Grace came home, I'd spread all the items out on my bed and was busy mixing and matching clothes from my closet with these new garments. I was so busy fussing with the new clothes and the different combinations that I didn't hear Grace come into my room. I jumped a mile when I realized she was standing behind me.

When I turned to face her, I was stunned by the unfamiliar and unforgiving look on her face. "I can't understand the relationship you share with Chloe and Janice," she said bluntly.

I moved the outfits so we could sit on the bed facing one another Indian style, legs crossed. We had sat this way as kids to share our true confessions with one another during sessions we called our powwows. But we weren't kids anymore, and Grace was clearly upset.

"Marilyn, you and I were brought up to know that being queer is a sin," she began hesitantly. I started to respond, but she stopped me. "Let me finish. I'm disgusted by Chloe and Janice's lifestyle and the way they put on airs to impress people. They're despicable. I don't understand how you could have let them suck you in. It's beyond my comprehension. We've been best friends forever, but sometimes, I don't understand you at all. And I'm shocked to see how self-centered and egotistical you've become under the influence of these lesbians. You're willing to sacrifice the principles of your own family for personal gain. You should be ashamed. I know your mother and Beth would be equally alarmed if they knew the extent you've been taken in by these women. And you're jeopardizing your friendship with Joe because of your strong alliance with them. You need to decide: Joe or Chloe."

Grace was so emotional that she began to cry, and I was so angry with her that I was shaking. What a pair! Finally, both of us took a deep breath. I knew I shouldn't respond to her ultimatum when I was so upset, but I couldn't contain myself.

"I spent five months with those two women in a strange country, thousands of miles from home. They could not have been more generous and thoughtful. They welcomed me into their home and taught me so much about the fashion industry. Although I've never told you, they've offered me a job with their company in Milan when I get my degree. These clothes are a project we're working on, research on their business plan—a plan I worked on as a class project in Milan. Yes, I'm ambitious and long for a more sophisticated lifestyle, but I expect to work hard for it."

With each sentence, I became more livid. My voice was shaking as I continued. "How dare you be so pious as to judge two beautiful people because they don't fit into your worldview? They've stepped out of the mainstream and endured criticism because of their love for each other. And yes, they do love each other. But who are you to judge?"

I finally realized Grace had stopped crying, but when I looked at her, I saw her arms were folded over her chest—an obvious posture to shut me out and shut me down. "Tell me, Grace, did you speak for Joe or yourself when you said I had to choose between Joe and Chloe?"

Grace softened her voice. "Joe has never questioned your relationship with his mother and Janice, and he's never said you couldn't be friends with him and them. It was my observation. It's something I've wanted to get off my chest for a long time. The New York trip just pushed me into telling you how I feel."

We sat silently for several minutes, collecting our thoughts and taming our emotions. "Grace, you are my dearest and oldest friend, so I hope you'll seriously consider what I'm going to say. Please respect my decision to join Chloe and Janice in the fashion business. It's a business deal—not a personal commitment. With you and Joe, it's personal. I love you like my brother and sister. Are you still my best friend?"

Grace unfolded her arms, and we hugged, losing our balance and falling back on the beautiful clothes, now a jumble on the bed. I closed my eyes, and then I realized the clothes had created a wedge between us physically, just as our words had created a wedge in our friendship. But the separation only strengthened my resolve to make my own decisions—even if they were not acceptable to my family and friends. I was not going to be defined by a small, culturally conservative Southern town.

CHAPTER 44

After our dramatic heart-to-heart talk, Grace and I maintained an uneasy peace during our final semester at Wesley. We were friendly but no longer shared our intimate thoughts as we had before her ultimatum that I choose between Joe and his mother. And since our classes, exams, and social obligations took us in different directions, we had little opportunity to mend the relationship.

As Grace, Joe, and I prepared for our May graduation from Wesley, I reflected on how different our futures would be. Grace and Joe would marry in two months, and Grace, having completed her graduate educational coursework, would begin her teaching career at Rockport Elementary School in the fall. Joe would be busy caring for the farm and helping Grace set up the farmhouse. They planned to completely redecorate the house, but over the summer they would remodel the kitchen and master bedroom so they could move in after their honeymoon.

Graduation was a big event for my family. An in-town neighbor offered to take care of Maria and Beth and Frank's young children so everyone could attend the commencement. Mama had even made herself a new dress for the occasion, although she brushed off my compliment and said the best outfit for the day was my cap and gown.

Grace's family was here, and Joseph had flown in from New York to see Joe walk across the stage. True to form, Chloe sent Joe a check—one thousand dollars and a note promising that both she and Janice would be there for his wedding.

Beth and Frank added to the day's excitement when she announced they were expecting their third child. She had come from an early appointment with her doctor that confirmed her morning sickness was a pregnancy, not a virus. Mama was thrilled that she'd have another grandchild to love. Beth's life script seemed to be perfect theater: daughter, nurse, wife, and mother. I wondered if she had chosen a nursing degree to enhance her role as caregiver for her family. Mama had never had to worry about Beth's future. However, she seemed quite anxious about mine and for the past three months had kept asking if I planned to look for work in Rockport. She even hinted that the attic room would be perfect for a bedroom and office. I dodged her job-hunting questions. I wasn't ready to disclose my career plans just yet.

I was waiting for the perfect moment to tell Mama I planned to begin my career in Italy. My graduation gift from Chloe was an open ticket to Italy—and an invitation to stay with her and Janice until I found my own flat. Wickedly, I thought of Manny's invitation to live with him in his apartment. He assured me there was room. It was so absurd that I laughed out loud. I wasn't quite ready to breach social mores by blatantly living with a man without marriage.

Graduation Day! After we received our degrees and tossed our caps in the air, we joined our families for dinner at a lovely country inn on the outskirts of town. Everyone was celebrating, and I noticed how affable Joe's dad was with my family and Grace's parents. Since my freshman visit, Dr. Bateson and I had developed a special friendship, so I purposely jockeyed to sit next to him at dinner. When the conversation turned to Joe, I lowered my voice and said, "You know, Dr. Bateson, it's meant the world to Joe that you've taken such an interest in his career and marriage plans."

"Oh, Marilyn, it's easy to get close to Joe. Manny is a different story. He sees me as the enemy and is always quite prickly with me and his mother," Joseph confided.

A perfect opening! I quickly told him that I'd befriended Manny in Italy. "It wasn't easy, but we became friends when I studied there last fall. He let me see a more vulnerable and sensitive side. But, I too, had my challenges peeling that prickly veneer off him." Almost on cue, Joseph and I laughed at a vision of Manny protected by rows of spiky thorns, as if he were a thistle.

"I've given up on him," Joseph confessed. "Lord knows I've tried to give him direction, but nothing I've ever suggested registered with him. He's fought me all the way. When he dropped out of law school, that was the last straw. He's rebellious, defensive, spoiled, and self-centered." Joseph's expression was sad, but then he looked at me and smiled, and I knew he was glad we'd shared these confidences.

After dinner, Mama, Beth, Frank, and I went back to the apartment to collect the last of my belongings. Grace came in as we were carrying things to the car, but she didn't offer to help. She seemed distant and avoided looking at me. I assumed she was so aloof because she disapproved of my plans to bail from Rockport and begin my career in Milan—far away from family and friends. I know she viewed me as a turncoat, but she had kept her word and hadn't mentioned my job offer to anyone. She'd promised to keep my secret until after I told Mama, who should have been the first to know.

When the last suitcase was loaded into the trunk, Mama and I climbed in the back seat, and Frank slipped behind the wheel, next to Beth. As we pulled away from the apartment, I felt sad. One chapter of my life was closing—symbolized by Grace standing in front of the building waiting for her parents to help her load her things. I waved goodbye. She didn't respond.

We weren't more than ten minutes from campus when Mama—true to form—said, "You know, your first job isn't going to come knocking on your door in Rockport. You're going to have to go after it."

Another perfect opening! This was the right time to tell her. "As a matter of fact, a job did come knocking on my door, but not in Rockport. It's in Italy." Before she could interrupt, I continued. "I plan to move to Italy permanently. Joe's mother and her business partner Janice have invited me to become a partner with them." Mama recoiled. She looked as if I had just thrown hot grease on her face. Frank and Beth said nothing.

Mama recovered quickly. She snorted and said, "You sound just like your daddy—always saying outrageous things to get a rise out of folks. So, you're going to Italy, are you? I guess the airlines will give you a free flight and someone nice will give you a place to live."

I pulled the airline ticket out of my purse, showed it to her, and told her Chloe had invited me to live with her until I was settled and found a place of my own. When Mama realized I was serious, she began to quietly sob and softly responded, "I knew our fences could never hold you."

Beth's voice was icy when she turned to me. "I hope you find happiness one day." I didn't respond, but silently, I hoped so too.

CHAPTER 45

The scent of coffee woke me the next morning—a new day—my first as a full adult, not a student. For just a few minutes, I snuggled under the covers, remembering the days when Mama and Daddy rose before any of us to share a quiet cup of coffee and a Biblical passage before beginning their chores. Mama still read the Bible with her coffee before getting Maria up and preparing breakfast.

These were comforting memories, but in an instant, I felt an urgency to spring out of bed for a trip to the kitchen to pour a cup of that aromatic coffee. When Mama heard me, she came out of Maria's bedroom to join me on the back porch. Yesterday's despondence after my announcement was gone. She was eager to talk, and her face was animated. "Isn't it wonderful about Joe and Grace's wedding in a few months? I hope the two of them will be as happy at our farm as our family was over the years," she added wistfully.

Instinctively, I knew she was alluding to my future. I wanted to reassure her, so I responded quickly, "I think it's wonderful, too, about Joe and Grace. But that's not the only direction. Some of us take a different path. I think marriage and children are great, just not at this juncture in my life—maybe that's because the right person hasn't come along. Right now, my passion is not for marriage. It's for using my business degree and pursuing a career in the fashion industry. And I'm very lucky to have everything in place for me in Milan. I know you understand, Mama. After all, you and Daddy raised me to be my own person and make my own decisions. The best thing you two did for Beth and me was to give us roots—not to anchor us here—but to let us grow and reach for the sky. My sky just happens to be in Italy."

Just then, Maria cried out. Mama jumped up with her "duty calls" look on her face and went to Maria's bedroom to wheel her into the kitchen for breakfast. I always marveled at Mama's patience with Maria. She was so calm and resigned to the constant care Maria required, but she never seemed to resent the caregiving, no matter how difficult.

I stayed on the back porch after Mama left. Although I had displayed a cavalier attitude with Mama about not having a special someone in my life, I spent a lot of time thinking about it—sometimes more time than I spent thinking about building a successful career. My single state was quite evident in Rockport when I attended engagement parties, weddings, teas, and bridal and baby showers. Everywhere I turned, I was besieged by people my age getting married or having babies. It was the next natural progression—you finished school, you got married, you had babies. This was Mama's world. No wonder she was concerned about my future. It just wasn't my world. I wanted something different. Still, I had some self-doubt now about my choice to look for that something different in a foreign country. I needed Chloe and Janice back in my life to reinforce my fashion career goals and intellectually and culturally stimulate my mind and spirit. But I was in Rockport, and they were in Milan, and I wouldn't be flying to Italy until after Grace and Joe's wedding.

Then I smelled bacon frying and decided self-doubt would

have to wait. Right now, I was hungrier for breakfast than I was worried about my future.

In the following weeks, Grace and I spent so much time together immersed in her wedding preparations that our conflict faded away. I was thrilled when she asked me to be her maid of honor and happily became her unofficial wedding planner. Together with her mother, we addressed invitations, selected dresses, and arranged the rehearsal dinner, the wedding ceremony, and the reception.

Joe kept busy getting the farm in shape for the reception and arranging for his family's accommodations. One of my major assignments was to calm Joe whenever he began to panic about his family coming to the wedding. I reassured him that everyone would have a wonderful time, that there would not be any embarrassing outbursts, and that no one would focus on the very different lifestyles in these soon-to-be blended families. I never let him see that I was just as concerned about everything going off without a hitch as he was. Knowing all the players who were coming, it was impossible not to worry.

When the wedding weekend finally arrived, Joe had made travel arrangements for his family, so he didn't have to drive to the Nashville airport. The Batesons and Janice were staying at the local Howard Johnson Motor Court. Joe was anxious about seeing his mother and Janice and asked me to go to the motel when he welcomed them. They had arrived a few hours earlier and were resting in their room to recover from jet lag.

Joe gripped the steering wheel so hard on the drive to the motel that his fingers and knuckles were white. "What's wrong, Joe? You look as if you're dreading this visit."

"Marilyn, under the best of circumstances, I'm apprehensive when I meet my mother and Janice."

"That's nonsense, Joe. Why would you think your mother and Janice would be anything but charming at your wedding? I've always thoroughly enjoyed their company. They've been wonderful friends to me."

He angrily turned on me, and his answer was so cruel I couldn't believe he said it. "How would you like to have a mother who's a dyke? Or wouldn't it matter to you? Do you make a nice threesome for them?"

I dismissed his caustic remark because I knew how upset he was. But I also thought how much it was like something Manny would say. I thought Joe should compose himself, so I suggested we have a Coke before we went to the room. He turned off the engine and faced me, brushing the tears from his cheeks with the back of his hand. I understood his anxiety, but I didn't know how to comfort him. We sat in the car for a few moments while he composed himself. "I'm so sorry, Marilyn. I had no right to snap at you," he said in an apologetic voice. "My comment was uncalled for and disrespectful. It's just that I'm so frightened about Grace's family meeting my mother and Janice. What if they despise one another? I love Grace and her parents so much. I don't want anything to upset her folks at the wedding."

"Joe, we're in this wedding together. I'll do everything I can to help you with Chloe and Janice. But you have nothing to worry about. Both are such gracious ladies that they will be perfect wedding guests," I reassured him with a smile.

"Well, let's go, then," he resignedly said.

When we knocked at their motel door, Chloe's pleasant voice rang out: "I'm coming." She flung open the door, and I was standing right there—the first person she saw. She pulled me into the room, and Janice jumped up from the bed and joined her at the door. They kissed me on both cheeks in that typical European greeting style.

It was a little awkward because Joe was still standing in the open door. No one had ushered him into the room. I turned and grabbed his arm, drawing him to my side. Chloe and Janice both gave him a stiff hug and the kiss on both cheeks. I was uncomfortable witnessing their meeting.

Chloe broke the ice. "Tell us the weekend plans. Janice will take notes so we get to all the events on time." I was so rattled I began babbling. I was talking the proverbial mile a minute to brief them on what they should expect this weekend.

"Our wedding customs are very simple," I said. "We're country here, and the wedding will be nothing like what you're accustomed to in New York or Italy. The ceremony will be at Grace's family's church—they're Baptists. The reception will be in the backyard at Joe and Grace's farm. Oh, a heads-up, no alcohol is served at Baptist weddings."

I blushed when I realized I was apologizing for my upbringing. Chloe sensed my embarrassment and put both hands on my cheeks to draw my face close to hers. "Marilyn, you have nothing to worry about. We're looking forward to a wonderful weekend to celebrate this marriage."

Obviously, she understood the situation much better than I thought. She turned to Joe and grasped both his hands. "Son, I'm really happy for you and Grace. I think it's wonderful you've found one another, and I'm sincerely wishing you a lifetime of happiness.

"Now go on and tie up all those loose ends that are always there as the wedding gets closer. Janice and I plan to rest this afternoon to recuperate from our long flight, but we'll be ready to meet everyone this evening at the rehearsal dinner. It's at the Colonial Inn, right?"

Joe said, "Yes, that's right. We'll be here to pick you up at 7:00. I'm going to let Dad know the game plan for this evening now. I'll meet you at the car in fifteen minutes, Marilyn. We're due at the church at 4:00 for the rehearsal."

After Joe left, I hugged Chloe and Janice again. "You'll never know how happy I am to see both of you," I said. "I'm so excited about coming back to Milan. I've got a million questions." They laughed and assured me they wouldn't leave town before they answered all my questions.

When I joined Joe at the car, he was much more relaxed. I couldn't tell if it was because he'd seen his father or because the initial meeting with his mother and Janice had gone better than he expected. I squeezed his arm and joked, "Well, I don't see any bite marks on your arm from the meeting with your mother."

He lightened up a little, but then confessed, "I wish my mother could be as easy with me as she is with you, Marilyn." I didn't respond, and we drove in silence until he dropped me at Mama's so I could dress for the rehearsal and dinner.

CHAPTER 46

When Mama and I pulled up to the Colonial Inn, the place was buzzing with Grace's family members and close Rockport friends.

I scanned the reception area, looking over the diverse outfits the women had selected for this special dinner. Mama, in the cotton flowered dress she'd made for the occasion, fit right in. She'd splurged on yellow pumps and a strand of yellow beads to complete the outfit and confessed that she was quite proud of herself for putting the outfit together. Before we left, she twirled around the living room and demanded, "Well, what do you think?" I thought she was beautiful and was so pleased to see her bright smile—a rarity since Daddy's death.

"Mama, you look sensational. If there are any eligible men there this evening, I'm sure they'll be making passes at you! You look that good," I told her with a laugh.

She smiled, but then turned serious. "No man could ever take your father's place." Her comment made me wonder if I would ever have a special "one and only" man in my life.

Mama had dressed quickly for the dinner, but I spent more than an hour just trying to decide on the most appropriate outfit. I didn't want to dress frumpy, but I didn't want to appear "highfalutin'," either. My Italian outfits were out of place, and I didn't have the courage to wear the beautiful silk dress Chloe and Janice had given me that afternoon. It was way too fancy for dinner at the Colonial Inn. I knew Chloe and Janice's entrance in their sophisticated clothing would start the room buzzing, and I wasn't about to add to that buzz by emulating their fashion savvy.

I finally chose a simple, light blue linen dress with a string of pearls and matching earrings. I accessorized with black patent heels and a clutch purse, attempting to placate the different dress codes in my two worlds.

Joe had given me a warning that afternoon that Manny would arrive on a later flight and would probably just make the 8:00 p.m. dinner by renting a car at the airport. But I'd been so distracted with worrying about Chloe, Janice, Joe, Mama, and Grace's family and trying to decide what to wear that I'd given little thought to reconnecting with Manny that evening. All I knew was that I would be seeing him very soon, and the few times I thought about that, I got butterflies in my stomach.

Since Joe and his family weren't at the inn when Mama and I arrived, I still wasn't thinking about Manny. I was too busy checking out the clothes and accessories the local ladies and gentlemen had chosen to meet the sophisticated "big city" contingent. Once I'd finished that, it hit me like a ton of bricks—I'd be seeing Manny in less than an hour. My palms began to sweat, my breathing became shallow, and I felt lightheaded just thinking about seeing him. I knew my emotional reaction was not the way you feel about seeing "a dear friend."

While I was struggling with my emotional state, Joseph came through the door with Joe, their arms intertwined in a bond of unity and looking strikingly happy. Grace stepped forward to embrace them both. Every face was turned toward the door, and all conversation had stopped, so Joe didn't have to raise his voice to say, "I'd like you all to welcome my father, Dr. Joseph Bateson, from New York City."

Joseph looked genuinely happy to be in Rockport as he spoke to the guests. "I couldn't be more delighted to be here—in the presence of such warm and friendly people. You've welcomed my son, and he's blossomed from your hospitality and kindness. I'm looking forward to meeting each of you during this special weekend."

As he was finishing his comments, the door opened, and two regal women stepped into the room. I moved instantly to greet them.

Chloe and Janice looked as if they had walked from a cover of *Vogue* magazine into our *Farmers' Almanac* setting. I stepped between them, taking an arm in each hand, to announce, "These two wonderful women made my semester in Milañ truly an experience beyond my wildest expectations."

Joe joined me at the doorway to make the formal introduction. "This is my mother, Chloe, and her business partner, Janice, who have just arrived from Italy for the wedding. I hope each of you will welcome them to Rockport."

That was the signal for applause for Joe's parents and Janice—and to sit down for dinner. Everyone began searching the place cards for their seat assignments when the door flew open and a longhaired, bearded man in jeans and T-shirt burst in. He was a dead ringer for a Greenwich Village beatnik. As if his appearance wasn't dramatic enough, Manny shocked the crowd by shouting, "Where's my little brother and that gorgeous girl he plans to marry tomorrow?"

My heart was racing wildly. Without considering the consequences, I left Chloe and Janice's side and raced to greet Manny. Big mistake! I should have considered my audience because Manny was still in his typical anything-for-attention behavior mode. He threw his arms around me, picked me up, swung me around and announced, "Hope you all don't mind if there's a double wedding this weekend."

I was mortified. I couldn't imagine what Mama was thinking. Everyone was frozen in place, looking on in sheer amazement. And all I could do was beat on his chest and plead, "Put me down!"

Thank God, Joe had the presence of mind to say, "This is my brother, Manny. He's just arrived from Italy and no doubt is delirious from jet lag."

Manny wasn't ready to relinquish the spotlight just yet. He grabbed Joe and pulled him close, kissing him on both cheeks. Then, spotting his parents and Janice, he started toward them. I cringed, and we all braced, wondering what Manny would say next. But he surprised everyone—at least, those of us who knew him—by giving his father a hearty handshake and man hug and gently kissing his mother on both cheeks.

In a final theatrical gesture, the backpack slung over Manny's left shoulder went sailing into a corner, landing with a loud *thud.* Turning to me, he demanded, "And where are we sitting?"

I led him to the table assigned to bridesmaids and groomsmen, and once we were seated, I whispered to him, "Don't you dare ask for a beer. This is a dry wedding weekend—no alcohol."

He looked at me, pinched both my cheeks, and promised, "I won't embarrass you this weekend if we get married with Joe and Grace. What do you say?"

Why couldn't he be serious? I answered him with a warning. "Behave yourself for Joe and Grace's sake."

Since I was seated next to "Manny the Time Bomb," I expected this to be the longest dinner of my life. Fortunately, he did quiet down and said very little after his attention-getting scene in front of the guests.

When I got back to Mama's house, a wave of relief washed over me. I was off Bateson duty and could relax at last. Mama put the teakettle on, and I could tell she was in high gear, ready to revisit the dinner and all the events surrounding the festivities.

She handed me a cup of tea and said, "Bring it into the living room. We can have a nice long talk." I braced myself. I was sure she was going to analyze Joe's family. And I wasn't ready for that, so I took control of the conversation.

Before she had a chance to ask any questions, I said, "Mama, didn't you find it interesting that these two very distinct cultures blended so well this evening? Think how different we must appear to Joe's family. Probably as different as they seem to us! But if you whittle down to the core, I think we'd find we're more similar than different. Don't you agree?"

She did, but she wasn't ready to concede yet. She looked at me in the same way she had looked at me when I was a little girl trying to divert her attention. She clearly recognized I was trying to protect Joe's family. "I agree we're similar, but I just don't understand how a husband and wife could choose to live on separate continents like Dr. and Mrs. Bateson do. And Manny is a piece of work, isn't he?"

I nodded my head in agreement. We briefly rehashed the rehearsal dinner, but as soon as I finished the last dregs of tea, I stood up and kissed Mama good night, firmly declaring, "I'm exhausted and need to get my beauty rest for tomorrow's wedding activities. It certainly was an interesting evening."

When I was alone, I kept replaying dinner in my head. Manny had taken full advantage of the seating arrangement. In his flirtatious way, he kept putting his hand on my leg and pressing against me every chance he got. I knew he was testing me to see my reaction, and I tried to ignore his antics, but down deep inside, I liked his touch, and if I were honest with myself—I had missed his touch.

Considering that so many of us were on operating on high anxiety, the weekend events went off without a hitch. No more outrageous outbursts from Manny, who even got a haircut and shaved off his beard on Saturday morning. He looked quite respectable as his brother's best man. In fact, he looked drop-dead gorgeous when I came down the aisle as the maid of honor and saw him standing there, grinning broadly. Manny was pleasant at the reception to the wedding guests and didn't complain about the no-alcohol rule.

Chloe and Janice tried mixing with the wedding guests, but it was much more difficult for them than for Joseph and Manny. They were gracious but uncomfortably stiff. They had so little in common with the other guests they couldn't converse easily, although they certainly got an A for effort from me.

Joe's family and Janice were flying out Monday, but before they left, Chloe and Janice made a point of meeting with me. They brought me up to date on the business, and we set the date for my first day at work. I'd written to accept their invitation to live at their apartment until I found my own place, but I confirmed that during the meeting. They assured me I was welcome to stay as long as I wished, adding that my room was ready and the house rules and meal schedule hadn't changed.

"Marilyn, this weekend was fascinating—a perfect opportunity for us to see firsthand what young women in America's small towns are wearing when they dress up. You tried to warn us, but we couldn't quite get the full picture. Now we understand why you were suggesting we modify the clothing line, and we agree we need to go back to Milan and make adjustments to Bourne Innocence."

Talking with Chloe and Janice rekindled my excitement about beginning my career in Milan. I knew it would. But I still had a little bit of trepidation. This wasn't studying for a semester and returning home; this was leaving home—establishing a home in a foreign country. This was permanent.

Manny was going back to Italy, too. Joe and Manny had talked about Manny staying to help Joe on the farm, but Grace had discouraged it. I think Joe believed farm work would be good for Manny, but I agreed with Grace that he needed to return to Milan.

Joe and Grace left for their honeymoon on Sunday morning, heading for a Great Smoky Mountain getaway in Gatlinburg, Tennessee. Joseph had offered airline tickets and hotel accommodations for a week in Hawaii, but Joe had refused. He explained that he and Grace planned to stay in Gatlinburg a few days and then get back to the farm. Joseph understood.

Chloe was not as understanding. Joe was an enigma, and she clearly couldn't fathom why he refused to accept her wedding gift—a check that would have made his life with Grace easier. I admired Joe's independence but had a twinge of guilt, knowing how much Chloe and Janice were giving me. I resolved to work hard and give back more than I got from them.

I confess my guilt was brief. I cheered myself up by thinking that I'd soon be seeing Manny again and we could continue building the relationship we had started almost a year ago.

CHAPTER 47

I had three weeks in Rockport after Joe and Grace's wedding. Since I wouldn't be returning to Rockport for a long time, I tried to spend as much time as I could with Mama and the rest of my family, which meant putting off packing for Italy until the last day.

When I started my frantic, last-minute packing, I was grateful for the large attic room. It was perfect for sorting—Rockport clothes, Chloe outfits, accessories, and incidentals. I kept trying to add sentimental things to remind me of home to the pile of necessities but forced myself to make some brutal choices.

However, I refused to leave one sentimental item behind—Angela, my well-worn ragdoll. My earliest childhood memories included Angela. Not only was she symbolic of my growing up, but she defined my relationship with my family members, especially Beth, who used to hide her from me to be mean. I had quickly learned to hide Angela under my pillow when I made my bed to keep her from Beth's prying eyes—*Much the same way I now hide my feelings of ambition from her. The two of us have always had a "push-pull" relationship as sisters. We are so different, but sometimes I think we may envy one another's choices.*

Beth was a natural caregiver, a nurse, and the sister who stayed behind to help her mother with Maria and created her own loving family circle with husband Frank, their two children, and another on the way. Beth was always so sure of her future and content with her choice of "hearth and home." But I couldn't help thinking she must have wondered what it would be like to see other parts of the world—to be a little more like her curious younger sister, who boldly ventured out and traveled an ocean away from family and hometown to begin her career.

My last day in Rockport finally arrived, and my sturdy red Samsonite luggage stood in the corner, open and waiting for my belongings. I packed carefully and then sat on each bulging suitcase, bobbing up and down so I could snap the locks tight. When the last lock clicked, I was overwhelmed by feelings of apprehension and self-doubt. Tears streamed down my face, and I brushed them away while I fumbled for a handkerchief. *Good grief,* I thought as I collected myself, *I haven't even left home, and I'm feeling profoundly homesick!*

Once again, Mama carefully prepared all my favorite dishes for yet another final family dinner the night before I left. This was her last generous concession, a gesture of love and support for my decision to go to a foreign country thousands of miles away from her. Beth, Frank, and the children hugged me when they left after my "farewell dinner." Beth murmured in my ear, "Take good care, and know we love you!"

The next day, I loaded my luggage into Grace and Joe's car and then went back in the house to say goodbye to Mama and Maria.

Maria was sitting in her wheelchair near an open window. The August sun illuminated her face, and a gentle breeze ruffled her light auburn hair. She looked up at me, reached for my hand, and tightly clasped it. My family never knew how much Maria understood, since she was unable to communicate, but she had her own special way of displaying her feelings. When I bent down to kiss her forehead, she grabbed my neck and held me tight to her face. I whispered, "Be a good girl while I'm away, and take care of Mama." Her face lit up when I said "Mama." She clearly understood that word. I hope she understood my last words: "Remember, I love you, Maria."

Mama walked me to the car; we hugged, and neither of us could hold back the tears. She didn't say anything, just walked to the front porch, turning to wave goodbye until we were out of sight. We didn't talk much on the way to the airport. Joe and Grace instinctively sensed how emotional the departure was for me. We all knew, too, that I wouldn't be the same person when I returned to Rockport. I was leaving my hometown behind for a new life, one that would change me profoundly.

I didn't have a direct flight to Italy. My flight went from Nashville to Newark, where I had a three-hour layover. Sitting in the busy airport waiting for my international flight to board, I admitted my excitement about beginning my career adventure was coupled with total anxiety about leaving my old life behind. I tried to squelch the fear by telling myself that if my decision to go to Milan was wrong, I could always go back to Rockport and work in Elaine's Dress Shop. I could do a lot for her business with my management skills. Just the thought of that scenario made me cringe, and I vowed to make my career abroad a success.

Thoughts ran through my head. Was it my career or the chance to be close to Manny that was motivating me to move to Milan?

Just as Chloe had promised, her driver was waiting at the airport when I arrived in Milan. As we drove to Chloe's apartment, I had a sense that I was "home." I was here and committed to make my choice work.

When we arrived at the apartment, Chloe and Janice were working in their office, but when they heard the door open, they sprinted into the foyer to engulf me in a group hug. "You know the ropes, Marilyn; just unpack and relax. We're delighted to have you here. And we're giving you a two-day holiday before we put you to work full time," Chloe announced with a laugh.

Janice chimed in, "We've planned a trip north for you. You're going to Biella for an orientation on leathers; all the arrangements are made." I remembered that Biella was an Italian wool and textile center at the foot of the Italian Alps with multiple manufacturing facilities for all the leading fashion houses in Milan.

When I went to my room, I found an envelope on the bed. I recognized Manny's handwriting and tore it open. The note simply said, "Call me as soon as you arrive. Can't wait to see you."

My first inclination was to grab the phone. But calmer thoughts prevailed. *Not so fast! Don't jump just because he tells you to, and don't respond with "How high?" Play it cool and control your emotions—call him later, once you settle in.* Instead of reaching for a phone, I reached for a suitcase, systematically unlatched each of them, and proceeded to unpack everything, using a warm bath and a fresh change of clothes as my incentive to complete the task.

I was luxuriating in a bubble bath when I heard a loud knock on my bedroom door. Thinking it might be Chloe or Janice, I scrambled out of the tub and wrapped a large terrycloth bath sheet around me before tiptoeing to the door. I cracked the door—and there stood Manny.

He pushed his way in, locked the door behind him, grabbed the towel out of my clutched hands, spun me around, and pulled my dripping, naked body against him. I feebly attempted to stop him by beating my fists on his chest. He just laughed, and I couldn't help myself; I laughed too. So much for my earlier resolve to control my emotions with Manny!

Since my first sexual encounter with him at the Long Island house, we had always been careful not to have sex in a family home, certainly not under Chloe's roof in Milan. I had priggishly insisted on this rule because I thought it was disrespectful as a houseguest, as well as embarrassingly dangerous. I was simply not willing to risk being caught in a compromising position by anyone. After all, we shouldn't be doing what we were doing without the benefit of marriage.

Manny threw me on the bed and quickly disrobed. I protested, "No, not here."

He shushed me, putting a finger to my lips and assuring me, "Relax. Chloe and Janice have gone to a luncheon appointment, and we have the place to ourselves.

It didn't take much convincing for me to throw all caution to the wind. My physical desire for him was overwhelming. I simply abandoned myself to his lovemaking.

I fell asleep in his arms, exhausted from our sexual encounter and my travel. Manny cradled me in his arms and drifted off to sleep, too. I woke with a start and turned to look at the bedside clock. It was late afternoon. I'd slept for more than three hours!

Manny was still asleep, and I took a moment to marvel at the sweet, boyish expression on his face. I hesitated, wanting to just stay there with him for a little while longer. But then I panicked. I was mortified that on my first day as a career woman, I'd let him break my houseguest rule. *What was I thinking?*

I jumped up and threw on some casual slacks and a sweater, worrying what Chloe and Janice would think if they caught us emerging from my room together. I shook Manny and whispered, "Hurry. Get dressed. I don't want to get caught with you in my room."

Manny complied quickly, for once with no argument or snide comment. He opened the door slowly and looked up and down the hallway before leaving. He mouthed, "I'm headed to the kitchen to see what Estella plans for dinner." He then moved stealthily down the hall, and I marveled that I couldn't hear him, even though I was straining my ears.

I waited a respectable time, draining the bathtub, tidying up the rumpled bed covers, and adjusting my clothing before I ventured out. When I walked into the kitchen, Estella and Manny were chopping vegetables and laughing.

At dinner, Chloe briefed me about my upcoming trip to Biella. Knowing her attention to detail, I carried a small notebook to the table to record the details and names from her conversation. My Biella host at the leather factory would be Antonio DeGevonio, a leather expert.

According to Chloe, Antonio, whom she called Toni, was expecting me and knew what I needed to tour in the factory and learn about the process. I'm not sure exactly what Manny knew about Toni, but whenever Chloe mentioned his name, Manny muttered some clearly insulting comments under his breath.

He broke into our conversation, asking Chloe, in an earnest voice, "Don't you think I should go with her?"

Chloe raised her eyebrow before responding, "Marilyn is perfectly capable of taking care of herself. Besides, if you plan to graduate from the university, you should be buckling down and working a lot harder than you are right now," she cautioned.

Manny's letters during the past year had been full of details about his studies at the university. He was enthusiastic about his progress in his music studies and wrote that his goal was to receive his music degree. He'd even been playing weekend gigs with a band. He'd also confided that Chloe disapproved of his musical efforts. After dinner, he pulled me aside and said, "Chloe doesn't support me at all. But it makes little, if any, difference to me what Mother thinks of my pursuing music seriously. There's no way in hell to please that woman when it comes to me, so I retaliate by pleasing myself." Then he grinned devilishly and smugly added, "I know my attitude just drives her crazy."

CHAPTER 48

Although Chloe had offered a two-day break before beginning work, I was eager to start after a ten-hour sleep. I went to the kitchen to get coffee as soon as I woke. Estella said Chloe and Janice were having coffee and a light breakfast in the dining room for what she said was a morning ritual.

When I joined them, they outlined their thoughts about our business arrangement and suggested that I join them for the daily breakfast meeting to discuss our collaborative work activities, at least for as long as I was living in the apartment. *Collaborative* might have been a little strong to describe the working arrangement. Before the first meeting ended, I figured out there was a definite division of business responsibilities.

Chloe was the point person in fabric sourcing, marketing, and merchandising. Janice worked with designers and made sure they met product deadlines. I'd work with both on the financial side, as well as to oversee operations and develop projections for future expansion. We didn't discuss it, but I knew they expected me to continue in my role as the lead model of the Bourne Innocence line.

"As soon as you're back from the Biella week, you'll have to prepare for a meeting with officials at the Bank of Milan. Obtaining the necessary financing is critical, and you'll be the main presenter of our business plan for the rollout of the Bourne Innocence line," Chloe explained.

She continued sipping her coffee and peering at me over her half-rimmed glasses for a minute before elaborating. "We need a substantial line of credit to successfully launch in both the European market and shortly after in America. And by the way, do you think we should change our accounting procedures from a cash basis to accrual?"

She then briefed me on my upcoming trip to Biella. "Our driver will pick you up tomorrow morning around 10:00 so you can make your noon appointment with Toni. He'll meet you in your hotel lobby. Now it's time to discuss what you'll wear for your first business trip." Chloe rose from the table, and we headed to my bedroom. "You'll be staying at the Hotel Bella Casa, and you're going to love it. It's in the center of the city and has a rich history and classic ambiance," Chloe said.

When we got to my room, I pulled the largest red Samsonite bag from my closet and prepared to fill it with her suggestions for my week's trip. "Oh, no, Marilyn, I have the perfect suitcase for your visit to these leather facilities." She smiled and disappeared into the hallway. When she returned, she was carrying a buttery-soft leather tan valise that she placed on the bed and opened.

It was fully packed—boots, shoes, dresses, and accessories, everything I needed for the week. I blinked in astonishment as she began showing me how to put together the outfits. I ran my hands across the leathers and touched each of the fabrics. Never in my wildest dreams had I ever imagined owning such a wardrobe or having enough money to afford these clothes. I rifled through the garments, taking longer than necessary because I was very uncomfortable, unsure of how to react. I certainly didn't want to appear ungrateful, but this gift was way too much. *This is how a "kept" woman must feel.*

Chloe picked up on my reluctance and immediately reassured me that this was business. "These outfits are tools and a necessary part of your work for our company. We always need to project the image we wish to present to others, particularly when they are able to buy. You are *the* perfect representative for Bourne Innocence, as a model. But even more important to us is that you have the brains to be our company's business director, too. In your dual role, you must dress the part for instant professional credibility."

I felt better after her explanation. And I even understood why I needed to wear our clothing line professionally—it was essential to my business role. But secretly, I thought of these outfits as an unexpected and delightful perk.

When I climbed into the back seat of the chauffeured car on the departure morning, I felt so grown-up. Everything for the trip to Biella was arranged; all I had to do was sit back and gaze at the beautiful landscape as we drove toward the snow-capped Alps.

Chloe had described Biella as an affluent, scenic town in the Piedmont region at the base of the Alps. Its population was less than fifty thousand people. Her description hadn't prepared me for this beautiful city. When we drove into Biella, the city's historical architecture and piazzas, beautiful gardens, and fountains immediately enchanted me. Everything was immaculate.

We stopped in front of the Hotel Bella Casa, and a bellman greeted us and took my bag to the reception area. As the driver turned to go, he reminded me he would pick me up here at the hotel at 10:00 on Saturday morning for the return to Milan.

The hotel lobby's rich, dark woods were a perfect background for the polished marble columns and elegantly upholstered furniture. The tall windows were draped with equally luxurious fabric. I checked in at the desk, and when the bellman led me to my room, I realized I only had an hour to freshen up before meeting Toni.

The bellman asked if there was anything else he could get for me, but I simply thanked him and gave him some change, following Chloe's advice about the appropriate amount for tipping at the hotel. I hurried to hang my clothes in the closet to let the wrinkles fall out. I didn't have time for a major makeover, but I wanted to appear fresh, so I applied lipstick and combed my hair before taking the glass lift to the lobby.

When I entered the lobby, I noticed one of the most handsome men I'd ever seen lounging in a chair. My heart skipped a beat when he got up and walked toward me, extending his hand and asking, "Are you Marilyn White? Chloe didn't tell me I would be working with such a lovely woman this week." His voice was deep and mellow, and his Italian-accented English was very sexy.

I blushed and thought to myself, *And she never told me I would be working with a drop-dead gorgeous man either. Guess we're even.*

Toni was tall, had runway model posture, and was immaculately dressed. He was somewhere in his thirties, with a charming smile and raven-black hair that had a glimmer of premature salt-and-pepper strands at his hairline, a perfect frame for his chiseled face. His eyes were deep Delft blue with a piercing quality that seemed to look into one's soul. I certainly hoped he couldn't read my mind!

Toni suggested we have a light lunch in the hotel dining room. "It will give us a chance to get to know one other," he said. I thought, *Thank heavens, I can sit down and compose myself. This man has totally taken my breath away.*

I was preparing to answer questions about me, but Toni was all business, reviewing the schedule he had planned for the week. He was taking his guide role very seriously, and our days would begin at 9:00 a.m. when he picked me up in front of the hotel. The itinerary included high-end leather and textile operations, and we would meet with representatives from each company we toured. During the tours, I would be shown a detailed composite of the various qualities, weights, and cuts of each company's leathers. "All the houses we'll visit use some of Chloe and Janice's designs, so they are willing to share some of their proprietary information with us," he added.

After lunch, we began my initiation into the leather industry. Workers were busy cutting leather patterns for handbags and luggage at the first leather operation we visited. The luggage display in their showroom featured several pieces similar to the one Chloe had given me for my visit to Biella. I ran my hand across the soft, tanned skins lined up, waiting for their turn to become luxurious shoes, boots, bags, and wallets and for a fleeting moment, I marveled at how soft, even velvet-like, the skins were.

But then the farm girl in me shuddered at the terrible thought that these pelts came from farm animals raised specifically for slaughter. However, I rationalized that everything has a purpose, even if only to supply fashion items. And wasn't this tour an educational experience so I could understand the leather fashion industry? It wasn't a journey to make moral judgments.

After three hours touring the plant, Toni suggested we go for coffee at a nearby café before he took me back to the hotel. The aroma of roasted coffee beans wafted into our nostrils as we entered, and I sniffed several times while we waited to be served. When the coffee arrived, I teased Toni by holding up my tiny espresso cup as if I were toasting him. "It always amazes me how Italians can make a small cup of espresso like this one last for an hour-long conversation."

Toni flashed his dazzling smile and chided me. "You Americans need to slow down and savor the flavor of the conversation that accompanies our espresso. It's not called 'expresso,' you know."

Once more, Toni steered the conversation back to work, but only briefly. He said, "We have a whole week to explore many different leather and textile operations, but tonight will be a purely social evening. I'll take you back to your hotel now so you can have a little rest before we go to dinner this evening. I'm going to introduce you to my favorite restaurant." I nodded enthusiastically.

After a short nap and a warm bath, I carefully selected my outfit for dinner—a gray cashmere dress that clung in all the right places, gray stockings, and soft black suede boots. I wore the silver jewelry Chloe had loaned me. My black lightweight cashmere coat, accented with a red scarf for a touch of color, was perfect for the cool night. I looked at myself in the full-length mirror just before going downstairs to meet Toni and smiled at my reflection. This was the outward new me. I still wasn't sure who the inward me would become.

Toni smiled as I entered the lobby. He gave me the warm Italian two-cheek kiss greeting and told me I looked "ravishing." He put his arm around my waist and ushered me to his sleek Alfa Romeo convertible, parked at the front of the hotel. He opened the door for me and then went around to the driver's side.

"I feel honored to have you beside me tonight," he said, smiling flirtatiously. I wasn't sure how to respond, so I chose a semi-professional one, telling him it was I who was honored to have such a knowledgeable guide for the week.

"If I have my way, it will be more than a week in fashion operations," he said and smiled—a little bit too suggestively. Again, I blushed, but I also tingled all over from excitement. It was a heady experience for this little girl from Rockport—being with a debonair man in his fabulous sports car, in a romantic Italian setting, wearing a sophisticated outfit as if I were born to this role.

At the restaurant, the maître d' welcomed Toni as a "regular" and said his usual table was ready. Obviously, Toni squired many women to this restaurant. I felt a jealous pang before I reminded myself this was a business dinner arrangement, not a social engagement.

Toni's table was in a quiet, dimly lit corner of the restaurant.

Soft music was playing, and a wine bucket was at tableside with a bottle of Prosecco on ice waiting to be uncorked. The waiter approached with a tray of antipasto and opened the bottle, pouring a small amount in Toni's glass for his approval before pouring the sparkling wine in my glass.

After the waiter left, Toni said, "I hope you do not mind, but I've ordered for the two of us because I want you to sample typical foods of this region."

I responded in Italian with a slightly subdued, *"Eccellentissimo!"* However, I secretly wondered how many times he had used this line on the other women he brought here to dine.

Toni raised his glass to mine and toasted: "To our new friendship and what I hope will be a long and successful working relationship." I saluted him before taking a sip.

The Prosecco had a crisp, light taste in my mouth. I leaned back in the booth and consciously decided I would enjoy the evening and not obsess about Toni's social life or how many women had traipsed through this restaurant with him. After all, I was here on a business trip.

A wonderful small dish of pasta in a bubbling white clam sauce, paired with dry white wine, followed the Prosecco and appetizers. Next came a fillet of freshwater trout topped with asparagus spears, accompanied by more white wine. A homemade tiramisu with grappa capped our dinner, followed by espresso.

Throughout dinner, Toni touched my arm repeatedly as if wanting to make a point. He also looked intently into my eyes during the conversation. I was a bit unnerved by this attention, but by the time dinner ended, I was stuffed and happily tipsy—no longer thinking about his actions. I was grateful I didn't have to drive back to the hotel. I just hoped when I got up from the table, I could walk a straight line to the car and not embarrass myself in front of Toni and the maître d'.

I felt lightheaded when Toni and I entered the lobby of the hotel. He respectfully kissed me goodnight on each cheek and said he'd pick me up the next morning for our second appointment.

I muttered, *"Grazie"* and made my way to the elevator, concentrating on not staggering and hoping he had already exited the lobby.

In my room, I jumped into bed, praying the room wouldn't spin. It didn't. However, I couldn't keep my mind from spinning as I reviewed everything that had taken place at dinner. I concluded there was no way I could interpret Toni's intentions and decided to view the evening as the most romantic business dinner of my life with a man who was as gracious as he was handsome. That settled, I drifted into a deep, wine-induced sleep.

Toni arrived promptly at 9:00 a.m. to take me to our next appointment. He was freshly shaved and looked wide awake. I had risen early to have breakfast, hoping it would vanquish any "hung over" look. When he smiled at me, I knew I must have passed the test and looked at least normally refreshed.

The scent of leather in the workroom at our first appointment reminded me of the tack room back on the farm. Patterns of leather coats and jackets of all sizes were laid out on the table ready to be cut. "Do you like the leather blazer I'm wearing this morning?" Toni asked me. "It's from this house."

I touched the sleeve of his black leather jacket, admiring its softness—and the man wearing it. He looked like a male model in his jacket, black slacks, and soft cotton shirt with a hint of lavender. I quickly admonished myself to forget Toni's outfit. After all, I was here to learn the leather trade inside and out, not admire Toni and his wardrobe. It was midafternoon when we finished my leather lesson.

Toni and I returned to the hotel to make plans for the evening over a cup of coffee. "Get ready for another superb Italian dinner tonight," he told me with a devilish grin.

I said that would be difficult. "You'll have to raise the standards pretty high to top last night's gastronomic introduction," I said. He simply laughed.

I thanked Chloe dozens of times as I dressed for dinner. Since she'd pre-selected my outfits, I didn't have to worry that I would be over- or underdressed. *What a life! I am living the proverbial good life. Surely it can't always be this way, or can it?*

Toni's restaurant choice was in the center of the city, and we had to park the car and walk a short distance. Dinner and wine were a repeat performance of the night before—extraordinary!

After dinner, we walked through town, talking and laughing comfortably with one another. Toni put his hand through my arm to guide me toward the car. His voice was soft and low in my ear, and I pressed closer to hear him. I didn't resist when he removed his hand from my arm and put it around my waist. But a little voice in my head kept saying, *Be careful.*

Although I had spent two very concentrated days with Toni, I knew little about him personally. "Toni, I don't know anything about you," I ventured.

My comment seemed to amuse him. "What do you want to know about me? I am a simple working man."

That wasn't good enough, and I pressed him, "Promise me when we have dinner tomorrow evening, you'll tell me about yourself. It's only fair. I've chattered on about myself for two evenings." Without answering, he helped me into his car, and we drove back to the hotel. In the lobby, he gave me the same goodbye kiss on both cheeks before pulling me toward him in a lasting hug. I felt a surge of emotion when he held me in this embrace. Back in my room, I could still smell his cologne on my hands. Once again, I had to sternly admonish myself for allowing Toni's demeanor to become a distraction. I was here to learn about leather.

We visited two fashion houses on our third day. Both dealt

in leather, but the last stop had a high-fashion display of finished leather items—belts, vests, skirts, pants, shoes, wallets, briefcases, and other leather goods—the final step in the process. On the third day, Toni switched gears and took me to a house specializing in cashmere sweaters. "Look here, Marilyn. This sweater would look beautiful on you," he said, tempting me by insisting that I touch it and hold it up to my face.

The color reminded me of Toni's eyes, which, of course, cinched the purchase for me. I knew I should be watching my funds very carefully, but I wanted something to remind me of this enchanting week. When I dressed for dinner, I chose a pair of wool slacks to wear with my new sweater. I pulled the sweater over my head and struck a runway pose to admire myself in the mirror; I felt like a million dollars in my first purchase of fine clothes. I hoped this would be the first of many.

Toni departed from his local food itinerary, choosing a French restaurant for our third dinner. As soon as our wine was poured, I reminded him that this was his night to talk about himself. He hesitated at first, so I began asking him pointed questions.

I learned he had dual Italian and Swiss citizenship and was an only child. "My father was Italian, and my mother is Swiss. I was born in Zürich, but my family moved to Milan when I was four. After many years in Milan, my father and mother moved back to Zürich to be closer to her sister. After my father's death, my mother remained in Zürich, but I still see her quite often.

"In fact, I'm going to Zürich this weekend and would love you to come with me and meet my mother." I was shocked and unsure of how to respond to his invitation. He paused briefly and then said, "You should try to see as much of Europe as possible. Switzerland is a lovely country."

The idea thrilled me, but that didn't mean I should accept the invitation. I hardly knew this man. *Is this a question for Chloe? Do*

I need her permission? Or should I make my own decisions about my personal life as long as I do the work she and Janice expect of me? I finally replied, "Toni, let me give your invitation some thought, but please continue about you and your family."

"I started in the fashion business as a cleanup boy in the shops," he explained. "I was fascinated by the designs, materials, and marketing in the field. However, my father was a schooled architect, and he wanted me to join him in his architectural practice when I finished school.

"I studied architectural design at the University of Milan for one year, trying to please him. But the only thing I learned was that architectural design was not for me, so I dropped out after my first year and went into the fashion trade, learning it from the bottom up. My father refused to help me financially after I rejected architecture, and we became estranged—something I regret deeply since his death."

He stopped for a moment to compose himself and then continued, "Since I learned the fashion industry in the College of Hard Knocks, I met many people in the industry, including very generous people who shared their knowledge with me. I learned about fashion design from its beginning as fiber, fur, or hide to the final garment or accessory. I wasn't interested in creative designing, and I never wanted to work in or own a 'cut-and-sew' operation, but I was a natural at marketing fashion. That's why I became an entrepreneur. I opened my consulting business several years ago, contracting my knowledge out to people like Chloe and Janice, as well as various fashion houses."

He stopped here and said he felt guilty for charging Chloe for this week. "I should be paying her for this fabulous time I've spent with you." I was flattered, yet couldn't silence that little voice that kept saying I should be wondering how many times he had used this same line on other clients.

We walked back to the car slowly, and instead of reaching for the door handle, he took me in his arms and shocked me with a passionate kiss. I stumbled backward, and he grabbed my arm to keep me from falling. He quickly apologized.

I came to my senses and, trying to defuse the awkward situation, put my index finger on his lips and said, "Please don't apologize. I was just taken by surprise."

As usual, back in my bedroom, I played the evening over and over in my head, always ending with his surprising kiss. And I always reached the same conclusion: I was sorry I had such a short time left with him. Biella had suddenly become more than just a business trip.

After this evening, Toni gave me the perfunctory dual goodnight kiss on the cheeks; there was no repeat of that passionate kiss or lingering embrace. I was disappointed that neither of us had the courage to talk about our feelings. And I regretted that I might not see him—or spend time with him again. The driver was coming for me on Saturday morning to return me to Milan.

Toni simply kissed both cheeks on Friday night and began to walk toward the door. Then he turned and said, "By the way, Marilyn, the invitation to Zürich this weekend is still open if you'd like to come with me."

I'd had time now to think about his invitation and practice my response. I simply said, "Perhaps another time. Chloe and Janice will be eager to hear a full report on my Biella experience. They're sending their driver for me tomorrow. You've been a wonderful host and guide. Thank you for everything."

The doorman held the front door for Toni, and I couldn't see his face as he walked to the street. I wondered if he looked disappointed or relieved.

CHAPTER 49

The driver arrived promptly on Saturday morning. Driving out of Biella, I daydreamed about Toni with thoughts colored by a glimmer of hope that I would see him again—professionally or personally. *Would he contact me? Would he ask me again to go to Zürich? Had I missed that opportunity?*

As the car snaked down the winding roads toward Milan, I reminded myself that I had to stay focused on my career if I was going to succeed. Chloe and Janice had chosen me as their protégée, and I was not going to disappoint them. Men—especially men like Toni and Manny—could certainly become major distractions, even derail my ambitious career plans! I'd have to be careful.

This past week had been my first as an employee, and I'd have my paycheck waiting at the apartment. My game plan was to save enough to move into my own apartment in three months. Chloe had agreed to give me a bonus above my base pay each quarter if I met her business goals for that quarter. I was so confident that I'd factored this perk into my timetable. My marching orders in the company were clear: keep my nose out of design and follow the business plan the three of us had developed my senior year at Wesley. The plan had earned me an A when I presented it for my senior seminar in business my last semester. As soon as I had that grade, I had sent the plan to Chloe. She had made only minor modifications to it, and I expected we'd tweak it as we went along, but for now, it was my road map.

This comprehensive written report on my experiences in Biella was going to be my first real assignment for the company, and I wanted it to be perfect. I had tried to work on the report each day, but was woefully distracted by Toni. I'd made very little progress, jotting down only sketchy notes—not a good start for my career. I knew I'd have to write it as soon as I got back to Milan to meet my Monday morning deadline—it was like a term paper hanging over my head.

When I arrived at the apartment, Chloe and Janice were working feverishly in their office, preparing to leave later in the afternoon for a week's business trip to Paris. I decided to be proactive and asked if they'd like me to give them highlights of my week and a summary of what I had learned about the leather industry. I concluded my concise account by telling them a comprehensive written report would be in their office when they got back from Paris. I was grateful for the reprieve, although I still planned to write the report as soon as possible. My summary had only touched on business—nothing about Toni. But as I turned to go to my room to unpack, Janice stopped me. "How did things go with Toni?"

I tried to be circumspect in my reply. "He was most helpful in introducing me to all the fashion houses and giving me tips on what to look for in quality leather pieces. He was also the perfect gentleman and host and took me to fabulous restaurants each night." Darn! Why had I mentioned our evening dinners? How I wished I could take back that last sentence.

Janice turned to Chloe. "Toni certainly went beyond consultant duty."

Chloe responded, "Doesn't surprise me one bit. You see,

Marilyn, as a consultant, Toni was only responsible for providing you names of restaurants. Sounds as if you had a good first week on the job."

I was embarrassed and turned bright red. Had I blundered by accepting the dinner invitations? Picking up on my discomfort by the stricken look on my face, Chloe soothingly remarked, "Marilyn, you've done nothing wrong. Just take this as a good lesson to be on guard when dealing with the romantic personalities of Italian men in business situations."

When I got to my room, I began mentally berating myself about my conduct with Toni. *Did I assume too much in Toni's kindness? What about the kiss? Did it mean nothing to him? It certainly meant something to me. I don't go around allowing men to kiss me with such passion without some attraction to go with it.*

In my personal journal, I made a single entry: "Romantic behavior of Italian men. Don't be fooled by it!" I promised myself to follow that rule from now on. *Obviously, there's a lot more to learn in Italy than just the fashion business. Class is now in session.*

CHAPTER 50

I buried myself in that report for the whole weekend. It was my way of coping with the emotional upheaval of the past week. Since Chloe and Janice were in Paris, there were no household distractions, and I expected to have a full written report on their desk when they returned.

I was wrapping up the report on Sunday when Manny called and invited me to share a pizza. I declined. My excuse was too much paperwork and too little time. "I'm on deadline, Manny. I'll take a rain check," I said.

His response surprised me. "So, Marilyn, does this mean you're reserving all your attention and time for the handsome, debonair Toni?" His tone was icy and his voice clipped.

His sarcasm angered me, and I hoped my voice tone matched his when I responded, "My time in Italy isn't about any man. You should know, better than anyone, that my priority is to successfully launch my career in the fashion industry." He hung up in mid-sentence, but I'm sure he understood the sentiment. Looking back, I thought I probably had sounded a bit self-righteous, but he deserved my tirade. I shook my head, thinking, *Men certainly complicate my life—and I don't know how to react to matters of the heart when I'm with them or without them.*

When Chloe and Janice returned, we met to review my Biella trip and discuss their Paris excursion. Chloe read my report's executive summary but put the complete report aside to read later. Right now, she wanted to prepare me for my next travel assignment—going to Paris to meet with managers of designer stores to research how they would fit in the Bourne Innocence marketing plan. "Marilyn, the information you glean from this trip will help us when we visit the bank to get financing for our line.

"We need you to interview the managers and evaluate their customer demographics. Our goal is to learn what designs and fabrics sell best and the age groups making the purchases," Chloe explained. I blinked in astonishment. I was so proud. This strategy came directly from my Wesley business plan—a plan that was obviously no longer a pipe dream but a reality.

"You'll be leaving in two days," Chloe said as she handed me an envelope with my airline ticket, reservations at the luxury five-star Ritz Hotel, and a map of Paris with the locations for each targeted store flagged. All the shops listed carried the upscale C&J line, along with other designers, such as Versace, Hermès, Yves Saint Laurent, and Louis Vuitton.

The highlighted streets were Avenue Montaigne, Boulevard Haussmann, Rue du Faubourg Saint-Honoré, and Avenue Georges V. The last street housed the Hermès Store, steps away from the famous Champs-Élysées, where Louis Vuitton is located. Chloe also suggested I visit the Galeries Lafayette on the Rue de Châteauduneven, but not to include them in my research. My focus would be on high-end specialty shops. *This must be a dream. It can't be work. Will I wake up and find myself on the farm? I sure hope not.*

Two days later, I was riding in the back seat of a car again, this time on my way to the Milan airport to fly to Paris—the City of

Light. And once again, everything had been carefully planned. Janice had arranged for a driver to pick me up at the Charles de Gaulle Airport and take me to the Ritz.

My first glimpse of Paris from the airplane was overwhelming, and I suspected this visit would be even more thrilling than my first visit to New York City. The trip to the hotel was memorable, but not for the scenery. I soon learned that traffic lights in Paris are merely suggestions, not mandatory, and it seemed as if all drivers used their car horns more than their steering wheels.

Paris is meticulously laid out with wide boulevards and massive, beautiful buildings—museums, churches, apartments, business and government offices—surrounding public squares. Lush gardens and parks with fountains splashing water added beauty and invited lovers, families, and workers to linger. Tall wrought-iron fences with gold-painted gates protected many of the buildings, and I wondered how important they must be to deserve such stunning entrances.

People strolled on the sidewalks or in the parks, quite different from the rushed gait of New Yorkers. Dog walkers and mothers or nannies pushing baby strollers shared the sidewalks, and there were conveniently located benches everywhere, inviting you to rest and enjoy the landscaped beauty. Sidewalk cafés with bright umbrella tables were perfect for people watching. Paris was uniquely French and lived up to its hype—a city designed for memorable beauty and leisurely enjoyment.

When we arrived at the Ritz, I was amazed at the number of jewelry stores encircling the cobblestone plaza in front of the hotel. These shops added emphasis to my impression that Paris was very wealthy. I wondered if Chloe and Janice had ever considered including elegantly crafted jewelry in their fashion line and made a mental note to ask them about adding this accessory, which I thought could provide a profitable markup for the company. *Always the businesswoman!*

When I checked in, I was surprised when the desk clerk handed me an envelope addressed to me. I waited until I got to my room to open it. It was from Jacque and Phillipe, the two French gentlemen I had met that Thanksgiving at the Batesons' country home—an invitation to meet them in the lobby bar at 7:00 for a drink and then dinner. Typical Janice! Knowing I was a neophyte to world travel, she was covering all the bases to make sure my trip was as close to perfection as possible.

My five working days in Paris passed quickly. With no distractions involving the opposite sex, I used my working time to gather as much information as I could. I wanted to have a comprehensive report for Chloe and Janice. Since my evenings were free, I used the time to outline my findings, including as much detail as possible to help me develop a marketing plan to accompany the report. At dinner the first night back, I told Chloe and Janice I saw some real opportunities for expanding the business and would have a marketing plan drawn up within the next day or two. My goal was to go beyond their expectations and provide a marketing plan that would be a reliable guide for business expansion. I said I thought we could use it as a supplement to the business plan when we made our bank presentation. They looked at one another and smiled broadly. I knew they were pleased with my initiative.

I spent the next day writing madly, trying to pull together the marketing plan, so I wasn't too happy when a call from Manny interrupted, but his tone was so conciliatory I decided to let him talk. He asked me to meet him for coffee later in the afternoon. "I really want us to catch up with each other," he pleaded. I wanted to work on my marketing plan, but I also thought I needed to reconnect with Manny. I justified my "yes" by telling myself that after writing all day, my brain would need a break. And what better break than coffee with Manny?

We arranged to meet at a popular coffee house near the university. The smell of coffee was as familiar as the people working there. This had been a favorite haunt when I studied at the university, and it was like "old home week." So many acquaintances from a year ago rushed to hug me. We kissed on the cheeks and exchanged pleasantries in Italian, which reminded me how important it was for me to practice my Italian. Chloe and Janice had spoken only English to me since I arrived.

I had only been at the café a few minutes when a disheveled Manny came rushing in, his guitar slung over his shoulder. He had just come from a class at the university, and his happy smile went straight to my heart. He gave me a warm, friendly hug and slight kiss on the lips. "Okay, stand up now. I want to see how elegantly you're dressed," he teased.

"Manny, I'm a working girl now, and have to dress the part," I chided playfully.

He answered earnestly, "Please don't let Chloe and Janice change you too much. I love you just the way you were when we first met."

Did he just say he loved me? I'm sure he didn't mean truly loved me. He just liked the person I was when we met.

I shifted gears and moved on, asking him about his music and classes. When Manny spoke of his music, it was with a genuine passion and enthusiasm that lit up his whole face. "Marilyn, please come and hear my group play at a club Saturday night. I'd like you to meet my band members; it would be a fun time for both of us. Our set is over at eleven, and we can have a quiet drink at the bar when I'm finished. We need to catch up. I've missed you."

My first thought was about work. I believed it was important to present the final version of my plan and report to Chloe and Janice on Monday morning. But I knew how Manny would react to that, and I didn't want to alienate him again. I'd decided I'd just have to handle the work stress myself and not use it as an excuse, so I told Manny I wanted to hear him play. "It will be such a treat—an incentive to finish my report and reward myself. Besides, I'll probably need a break from writing, and it will be good to relax on Saturday night with you and your music."

Manny reached across the table and stroked my cheek. "Marilyn, this really means a lot to me." As always, his touch excited me. However, I knew I could never write the report and assemble the plan in one day. I'd probably work after seeing Manny and spend all day Sunday writing, too. That would be the only way I could meet my promised Monday deadline. Suddenly, I felt like I was back in school with deadlines looming. I looked into Manny's eyes and realized how important this relationship was for the both of us. I would just have to pull an all-nighter.

"Manny, your mother told me she's really proud that you're pursuing a degree in music, although she admits it's not a major she would have selected for you. I think it's terrific, too—you look happier now than I've ever seen you." Hearing my words, he grinned and ducked his head, just like a little boy.

Manny walked me back to the apartment and, without prompting, came in to say hello to his mother and Janice. As soon as he left, I went to my room to work on my project before dinner.

A little over an hour later, Chloe knocked on my door. She said Toni was on the phone and wanted to speak to me. I tried to mask my excitement; I hoped I succeeded. When I picked up the receiver, Toni's voice sounded so sexy and smooth. I felt a familiar tingle, remembering our one embrace. We exchanged small talk, and he apologized for not calling sooner, explaining that a major client had had him working day and night for the past week. "I understand completely. I'm working on a report on a trip to Paris that's completely taken over my life," I said.

"Marilyn, I really want to talk to you and see you again, but this call also has a business attachment. I'm hoping you can get away this weekend. I need to see a client—a watch company—in Zürich on Monday. I plan to take the train to Zürich early Saturday morning and visit my mother for the weekend. I'll finish my business on Monday and return to Milan on Tuesday. I'd love it if you would come with me to meet my mother and see Zürich. When I told Chloe why I was calling, she thought it would be great and suggested that you could come with me on Monday to meet my client. He designs watches, and there might be a business opportunity for your company."

I told him I planned to spend the weekend preparing my Paris trip report and marketing plan for Chloe and Janice for a Monday presentation. But Toni didn't accept that. "I think you should discuss this with Chloe and Janice. They may be willing to give you an extension. You can call me back later this evening with a final decision," he said. He gave me his number, and we said goodbye.

When I hung up the phone, my head was reeling. I knew I couldn't finish the report by Monday if I went to Zürich. But it was a terrific opportunity for business and an equally terrific opportunity to add to my travel experience. I was so caught up debating the trip that I totally forgot my Saturday night date with Manny.

I went to Chloe's office to let her know my dilemma: if I accepted Toni's invitation, I would renege on my promise to get my report and plan to her on Monday. She responded immediately, "Don't worry about the report. Go to Zürich this weekend with Toni." Obviously, Toni had already discussed this with Chloe because she continued by saying the client Toni would be meeting was prominent in the watch industry. "If we decide to add watches as an accessory in our line, this contact could be very valuable. And you could include your findings in your marketing plan."

Then I remembered my commitment to Manny. When I told Chloe about my Saturday date to hear Manny's band, she laughed. "There's nothing you get yourself into that you can't get yourself out of. You can hear Manny's band anytime, but this watch company contact is an opportunity for our company."

I thought her reaction was cavalier—completely insensitive to her son and his music. It was all about *her* business. "Manny was thrilled when I promised to hear the band and meet the members on Saturday, and I feel guilty bailing on his invitation. I think it's important that I tell him in person that I need a 'rain check' on our Saturday evening plan. I don't want to say that over the phone, but I'll be back before dinner and call Toni later."

It took Manny a few minutes to buzz me into his apartment building. He was practicing his music and playing so loudly he didn't hear me. I walked up the three flights of stairs to his apartment, formulating how I should tell him the reason I was canceling our Saturday night plans. He was leaning against the doorframe when I rounded the last turn in the stairs, smiling. "What a nice surprise."

"I have something to tell you that's very difficult for me—something I felt I couldn't say over the phone," I said as we walked into the apartment. We sat side by side on his well-worn, striped sofa. He kept his hands between his knees as if he were bracing for terrible news.

"Oh, for goodness's sakes, Manny, it's not that big a deal. I just wanted to tell you in person that I can't make our Saturday date because something has come up in business."

He cut me off. "Don't tell me that damn report is more important than us spending time together on Saturday."

There was a pregnant pause before I elaborated on the business trip to Zürich. I tried to sound casual when I told him about the early Monday appointment with the owner of a prominent watch company that Toni had arranged. I added that Chloe was thrilled about the appointment and kind of implied that she wanted me to go on Saturday to see Zürich before meeting with the client.

In disbelief and rage, Manny turned to look at me directly. "I knew that son of a bitch would try to seduce you. Just remember, you're not his first; you won't be his last. Toni's 'modus operandi' is to get his way every time. He's a smooth-talking, deceitful womanizer."

It was my turn to be incensed. I jumped up, screaming, "I didn't come here to listen to you trash talk Toni or to imply that I sleep around." With that, I swept past Manny and flew down the three flights to the street. Walking back to the apartment, my cheeks burned. I was furious with him. So much for my calculated "letting him down easy" visit!

After seeing the sulking look on my face, Chloe and Janice didn't ask for any details. They wisely kept the dinner conversation light, which gave me adequate time to cool off from my frustrating confrontation with Manny before I called Toni. We decided Toni would pick me up at the apartment early Saturday morning and take me to the railway station for our trip to Zürich. Toni's voice was soft and inviting—quite a contrast to Manny's verbal fury earlier in the evening.

When I think about Manny, I feel extreme exultation or outrage. Yet, nobody has ever touched me as viscerally as he does—both in my head and in my heart. Perhaps it's because Manny never keeps his emotions in check and puts me on an emotional roller coaster. I can love him and hate him—simultaneously.

CHAPTER 51

Toni cautioned me to pack light, since we would be carrying our luggage up and down the stairs at the Milan and Zürich railway stations. I asked Chloe for help with my clothing selections, carefully depositing each outfit into my newly acquired leather valise. With my "Chloe seal of approval" weekend wardrobe, I was confident I was ready for any situation. Toni smiled approvingly at my single piece of luggage, effortlessly loading it into the tiny trunk of his sports car. As I slid into my seat, I could barely contain my excitement over our trip.

After parking the car, we walked, suitcases in hand, to the Milan Centrale train station. I'd checked out the station in my tour book, so I knew this cavernous train station, built in 1864, was considered one of Europe's most beautiful. I was certainly impressed when we entered the imposing main hall of the terminal, which still retained many of the early architectural details.

Toni had purchased our first-class tickets in advance and gave me a quick lesson on reading the ticket, including how to find our assigned car and seat, while he checked the large electronic board in the main terminal for our departure time. "We'll have to hurry, Marilyn. The Zürich train is on the platform and ready for boarding. We have fifteen minutes, and the platform is on the other side of the terminal."

We made it with six minutes to spare, and I settled into my window seat. Toni stowed the luggage in the overhead bin before sitting next to me. He said our seating arrangement was perfect; I could look at the scenery, and he could look at me. I blushed and reminded myself not to read too much into his flirtation. Not long after we left Milan, the snow-capped Alps appeared, and I pressed my nose against the window, absorbed in the passing scenery. Toni opened his briefcase and took out papers that looked like contracts. He was soon engrossed in the paperwork, and I sat quietly and enjoyed the scenery.

When we arrived in Zürich, Toni switched from English to fluent German to give the taxi driver directions to his mother's house. I was impressed at how smoothly he transitioned from Italian to English and now German. "How many languages do you speak?" I asked.

He laughed and said, "If you add French to the mix, you'll have my entire repertoire. It's easier for Europeans to be multilingual, since we hear the different languages as we crisscross borders."

I found his explanation a little dismissive. "Perhaps you're right, but I think it must take a little more effort than just crisscrossing borders. And I'm no longer so proud of myself for speaking two languages, especially since I'm still learning to be more proficient with my Italian."

When we left Zürich's Hauptbahnhof rail station, our taxi driver, following Toni's instructions, immediately began a serpentine ascent up a mountain. After a five-mile climb, we stopped at a contemporary white stucco house with an expansive glass façade. Once we were inside, it was clear why the architect, probably Toni's father, had selected the floor-to-ceiling glass. The view was spectacular, showcasing the city and Lake Zürich against the backdrop of the snow-capped Alps. As I was admiring the view, a female voice behind me asked in English, with a German accent, "Is it not beautiful?"

I turned to greet a woman who was obviously Toni's mother. Like her son, she was tall and erect, with the same intense blue eyes. Her perfectly styled salt-and-pepper hair framed a heart-shaped face. She wore a black cashmere sweater with a shawl collar and fitted slacks. Her only jewelry was a pair of stunning black onyx and silver earrings. She appeared comfortably chic, contented with herself and her home.

She turned to Toni and said, "You forgot to mention your American weekend guest was a fashion model." I laughed and explained that Chloe and Janice, my colleagues and Toni's fashion clients, insisted I wear their designs in my professional and social life.

Toni broke in to introduce me to his mother, Zara. "Please call me Zara, and let me show you the guest bedroom, Marilyn. When you've finished unpacking, join Toni and me in the front living room for some light refreshments."

I soon learned that every room had a magnificent view of the mountains or the lake, with Zürich in either the background or foreground. My guest room had a mountain view. Later, Toni confirmed my suspicion that his father was indeed the architect of this amazing house.

When I joined Zara and Toni in the living room, Zara poured sherry from a crystal decanter into delicate stemmed cordial-sized glasses, handing me a glass and a tiny linen napkin with an intricate embroidered design. Canapés, beautifully arranged on a silver tray, were conveniently located on the table. "Zara, these glasses are exquisite," I said, holding mine to the light.

Zara said, "Thank you. We Swiss are known for our watches, chocolates, and crystal. You may wish to take some crystal back with you. Toni or I can show you lovely crystal shops in the city later this afternoon. You must do your shopping today. Our shops are not open on Sunday."

I quickly accepted her offer. "I'd like that. Crystal would be a wonderful hostess gift for Chloe. I'm living in her apartment until I'm established enough to afford my own flat," I explained. Then I immediately regretted being so enthusiastic about crystal as a gift. Although it would be a wonderful gesture, I was worried about the cost. Not only was I naturally frugal, but I'd also been watching every penny to save enough for an apartment. And I'd brought very little cash with me.

In the late afternoon before dinner, Zara, Toni, and I went to Zürich. Toni kept steering me into jewelry shops to look at watch designs; Zara was equally insistent that I visit the crystal shops, even explaining the differences in the processes used in the manufacture of some of the pieces. Finally, I selected a mirror with a crystal handle that didn't fit into my budget but was the least costly piece I found. I had enough Swiss francs to buy it, and I felt obligated to purchase something. I hoped Zara hadn't picked up that I was secretly looking for affordability, not beauty.

Once I made the purchase, Zara suggested we take her home and then use her car to explore the city that evening. Toni and I returned to the city a little later, driving to a quiet, cozy Swiss restaurant on Lake Zürich.

Toni's dinner conversation focused on watches and their design. It was a crash course on what I should know about watch manufacturers, preparing me for the Monday meeting with his client. Once he'd finished my lesson, I felt confident that I'd be able to ask intelligent questions about timepieces and their design. Toni's conversation and demeanor were strictly business, quite a contrast to our dinners in Biella.

He ended the evening by presenting his game plan for the next day. "Rest well tonight. Tomorrow, I'll give you the complete walking tour of Zürich," he said. "Wear your most comfortable shoes."

Our Sunday excursion in the city began early, and all morning long, our walk was accompanied by the magnificent sound of church bells ringing in the background. We started our tour by window-shopping the expensive stores on the world-famous street, *Bahnhofstrasse.*

Once I'd admired all the high fashions, Toni went into tour guide mode. He was well-versed in the city's history and delighted in recounting historical—and often humorous—anecdotes about the many different landmarks we visited. If my feet could have talked after hours of walking, I'm sure they would have exaggerated their pain by claiming they had never traipsed through so many buildings in the entire time they had been attached to my legs! We did see Zürich—countless museums, guild houses, churches, including Fraumünster Church with its famous Chagall stained glass windows, and my personal favorite—St. Peter's Church, which boasts the biggest clock face in Europe.

By the time we wrapped up the tour in *Altstadt,* or "Old Town," in mid-afternoon, my feet were crying for my broken-in penny loafers or the old beat-up Keds that Mama had thrown away when I left for Italy. My thin-soled, stylish Capezio flats gave little support on the cobblestone streets of "Old Town."

Finally, I couldn't disguise the discomfort, and Toni caught me grimacing in undisguised pain. He suggested we stop for coffee and a pastry in a quaint coffee house in "Old Town." Relaxing over coffee, Toni began to talk on a more personal level, telling me how his family went to and from Milan and Zürich on a regular basis when he was growing up.

"One day, I hope to retire to Switzerland with someone who can share my love for this country." He reached across the table tentatively and took my hand. "I have very strong feelings for you,

Marilyn. If I didn't feel a deep connection with you, I would never have brought you here to meet my mother and see this country." He paused for a moment, looking into my eyes, before continuing, "I have a difficult time keeping my hands to myself when I'm with you. I often think of our kiss in Biella."

I wasn't sure how to respond but decided to be honest. I lowered my head to avoid eye contact as I shyly confessed that I found him a most attractive and intelligent man. "I'm so glad we came to Zürich. I've enjoyed getting to know you—*immensely.*"

"Do you think we could see one another socially when we return to Milan?" he asked.

I responded quickly, this time looking into his eyes, "Nothing would please me more."

He leaned across the little table and lightly kissed my lips. My body responded immediately, and I felt my heart flutter as if it had just received an electric shock. My mind began racing with excitement. It would be wonderful to spend more time with Toni. He seemed to be everything a woman would want in a man. I went one step further in my daydream—he would be a wonderful husband and father.

The next morning, Toni left early for his appointment with the watch company owner, explaining he'd need three to four hours to consult with his client and would pick me up to join them for lunch. Toni gave me a little "cheat sheet" with a number of questions about the watch industry I should ask the client at lunch.

Zara and I had a leisurely morning, chatting over coffee and croissants. By the time noon came, I was dressed and ready for lunch, watching for Toni at the front door. As soon as he pulled up, I went out, and Toni came around to open the car door for me. "You look lovely. I hope Mr. Zuddick is not too distracted by your beauty. After all, this is supposed to be a business lunch."

I laughed, nudging him in his ribs. "Stop it! You're such a joker!" I said.

The first thing I noticed about Toni's client, Johann Zuddick, was the large gold watch on his arm. The elegantly designed watch face was a conversation piece. Toni "primed the pump" for me by telling Johann I was interested in watches as a design component for our fashion line. Taking my cue, I complimented Johann on his watch, explaining it was the first thing I had noticed about him.

Then I launched into my questions, grateful for Toni's coaching. Johann answered each of my questions, going into elaborate detail about watchmaking, as well as watch design. Lunch turned into an all-afternoon business session. When Johann rose to leave, I apologized. "I'm embarrassed to have taken up so much of your time. I can't begin to tell you how helpful you've been. I feel I've learned so much this afternoon. It's been a distinct privilege to meet you."

He responded graciously that the pleasure was all his, adding, "I hope you'll come back to Zürich soon, so I can show you my business operations."

On the way back up the mountain to his mother's house, Toni said, "You totally enchanted Johann. I believe he'll be a great connection for watches in your fashion line. Chloe and Janice would have been so proud of the way you handled yourself in the business meeting. You're a natural at business and selling."

Zara drove us to the train station on Tuesday morning. As we were getting our bags from the trunk, she told me how much she had enjoyed meeting me and said she hoped I would return to Zürich again. I thanked her for her hospitality and said I'd love to return to her beautiful city very soon. Toni interrupted, "I hope it will be many times with me!"

Zara winked at me and said, "He's such a romantic." That wink reminded me of Chloe's warning about Italian men.

CHAPTER 52

At the apartment, Toni walked me to the door. Before I could put my key in the lock, he put both hands on my shoulders and turned me to face him.

"Marilyn, I had an enchanting time with you in Zürich. I know both of us have busy careers, but I hope we can make time for each other."

I agreed, but warned him my schedule for the next two weeks was incredibly busy. "We're debuting our new spring and summer collection, and almost every moment will be filled with meetings or overseeing fittings, makeup sessions, and photography. It's going to be a circus, and Chloe, Janice, and I are the ringmasters."

Toni planted a light kiss on my cheek, turned, and walked back to his car, calling over his shoulder that he'd be in touch soon. For a fleeting moment, I thought about calling after him to tell him I'd make time, but I stopped. This time, my head overruled my heart; I knew my focus had to be on work. Admittedly, Toni had bowled me over with his attention and handsome looks, but I was unsure of his intentions and wanted to protect myself in case he was the romantic seducer I'd been warned about by Manny, Chloe, and even Zara, his mother. Concentrating on work was the wisest tack.

I briefed Chloe and Janice on my meeting with Johann, referring to my extensive interview notes to be sure I was presenting our conversation accurately. Based on my report, we discussed the pros and cons of adding a watch line to our collection. "Perhaps I should craft a full-cost plan to see if the market will support high-end watches to augment our clothing line," I suggested.

To my surprise, Chloe asked, "Wouldn't it be smart to bring Toni in as a consultant to help develop our plan? His fee would be worth our time—or I should say, the time Marilyn would spend on the plan, especially since she has so many other assignments." I felt an immediate conflict of interest with her recommendation. I knew I could pull all the information together without Toni's help. On the other hand, what better way for me to spend time with him?

At our breakfast meeting, Chloe told me she had contacted Toni last evening, and he had agreed to work with me. "Expect a call from him in the next day or two. He's traveling, but said he'd be in touch very soon."

I got the call the next day, and we scheduled an appointment at his office to begin the project. When I hung up the phone, I lectured myself on the merits of keeping this arrangement strictly professional.

Our first business meeting lasted two hours and tested my professional resolve. We began by reviewing my draft outline, the road map of the necessary steps to take to complete the plan. As we went through each section, Toni would frequently reach over the conference table to touch my arm or hand. Was this his way of agreeing with my ideas or a subtle advance to remind me of our Biella encounter? I tried to ignore his gestures and stay on track, but it was disconcerting. Even with the distractions, we managed to accomplish a lot, including distribution of duties. By the time we wrapped up the meeting, we both knew how to move the project forward. I closed my notebook and started toward the door, but Toni stopped me. "I'd like you to join me for a drink. I'm off Chloe's consultant clock when I'm having liquid refreshments with you," he reassured me. "I promise, no more business talk, okay?"

I wanted to leap at his invitation, and I was really surprised when I heard words of refusal coming from my mouth. "I'd love to join you, Toni, but I've got to get back to work. My stress level keeps rising when I think about everything that needs to be done for our meeting with the Bank of Milan."

He responded immediately. "I understand completely; perhaps another time, when you're not under so much work pressure and financial deadlines. I just hope that will be very soon." As I walked back to the apartment, I couldn't stop wondering: *Is he just being kind? Does he really want to spend time with me? Is he the Toni who seems so sincere or the playboy that Manny described?*

Over the next two weeks, Toni and I met several times to polish the plan. At the end of each of these meetings, he said, "We're off the clock; care to join me for a drink?"

And after each invitation, I said, "I'm sorry, but I have to decline." I always had a work-related excuse.

Our last scheduled meeting was to review the executive summary. Instead of Toni's typical end-of-meeting invitation for a drink, he began the session by adding a personal note to his invitation. "When we finish today, I need you to have a drink with me. I have a personal matter I want to discuss with you. It's important." He was so earnest that I didn't hesitate. I agreed to join him when we finished our meeting.

Once we concluded the review, we went to a quiet wine bar across the street from his office. Toni ordered a bottle of a Dolcetto red wine from the Piedmont area for us to share. We sipped our first glass of wine, and the conversation was mostly small talk. I began wondering when Toni would bring up this important matter. He began pouring a second glass, and suddenly there was a serious tone in his voice. "I need to be up-front with you. You know I have a genuine respect for you as a businesswoman, and I would never wish to jeopardize our business relationship in any way. However, because I believe we also have a personal relationship, I need to make you aware of some things in my past—serious mistakes that I've made and harsh lessons I've learned.

"Remember when you asked me to tell you about myself? I was evasive. I told you I dropped out of architectural school my first year at the university because I wasn't interested in architecture." He lowered his head, and his voice wavered as he began to explain his confession. "That played only a small part in my decision. It was more about meeting a beautiful girl named Alisa during my first semester. We spent an inordinate amount of time together, often skipping classes just to be together. One thing led to another. We were young and passionately obsessed with one another—Alisa became pregnant.

"Alisa said her family wouldn't support her during her pregnancy or help with a baby out of wedlock. I understood her despair. I knew my parents would finance my education, but not my premature and unexpected marriage.

"As weeks slipped by, Alisa became more depressed and despondent. When I visited her, I often found her sitting in a dark apartment—crying. I told her we were in this together and I would never abandon her. It didn't matter. I told her I would drop out of school and get a job so we could marry immediately. I told her this would make our baby legitimate and our parents would come around eventually and accept the baby. It didn't matter.

"Then one day, Alisa came by my apartment and insisted she had another option—abortion. Both of us were Catholic, and I was shocked at her solution. I vetoed it immediately. I spent the next few days looking for work, and when I went back to Alisa's apartment, I saw a woman coming out. She brushed past me quickly with her head lowered so I couldn't see her face, but I was filled with a sense of dread that was reinforced when I knocked on Alisa's door.

"It took some time, but she finally came to the door and let me in. All I remember was the blood—all over Alisa's clothing and a trail from her bedroom to the door." He stopped and sipped his wine, trying to compose himself before he continued.

"I was in shock. I picked her up and took her to her bed, which was also covered in blood. I told her I was going to call an ambulance. She screamed at me, 'Don't you dare. Just leave me alone. Haven't you done enough to ruin my life? Get out of my sight. I never want to see you again—ever.'"

Toni was obviously struggling, but after a brief pause, he explained, "I was terrified by the blood and alarmed by her rage and fury. I didn't know what to do—and foolishly fled the scene, leaving her alone. As you might guess, it ended tragically. When I went to class the next day, I learned that Alisa Rizzo had died after hemorrhaging from a botched abortion. No one suspected I was the father because we had been so secretive in our relationship. I couldn't even grieve openly. I loved Alisa, and I killed the person I loved. I am an unintended murderer and will go to my grave with her blood on my hands."

By the time he finished, tears streaked down Toni's face, and his shoulders were heaving and his body shaking. He tried to hide his face in his hands. I was deeply moved by his gruesome confession, but I wasn't sure how to comfort him. I didn't know what to say. I wanted to take him in my arms, but instead I just sat there, my hands in my lap. I wondered how he could appear to move through his life so effortlessly—as if he didn't have a care in the world.

Finally, I found my voice. "Toni, did you ever tell your parents?"

He shook his head, "I've told nobody but you. When I attended Alisa's funeral mass, her parents never acknowledged me, even though I paid my respects to them personally after the service. They thought I was just another university classmate."

Toni composed himself before he continued his story. "I was too much of a coward to step forward and take responsibility for my failure to act. I've asked myself a thousand times how I could have left Alisa. Why didn't I have the courage to call for help?

"I dropped out of school and used hating architecture as an excuse because I couldn't reveal my role in Alisa's death. I cut all ties with my mother and father and spent the next year working in a bar. I drank too much and wallowed in self-pity. When I finally reached rock bottom, I realized I had to save myself. That's when I stopped medicating my grief in alcohol and acknowledged I wanted to turn my life around.

"I'd had conversations with a regular at the bar. He'd come in almost every evening, have one drink, and leave. But several times, he'd asked me what I planned to do with my life, and that gave me the courage to approach him when I decided to get serious about a career—and not one as a bartender. He told me he was in the fashion industry, and if I wasn't afraid of hard work, he'd mentor me. He took me into his fashion business and gave me my first career break. I'll always be grateful to him."

Toni continued, "So that's how I entered the fashion world, but believe me, there was nothing glamorous about it in the beginning. I did all the dirty work—lifting and hauling, running errands, sweeping floors—just making myself available for whatever needed to be done.

"By starting at the bottom, I was able to study all aspects of fashion. That's how I realized the need for a person to connect the creative design people to sources and operations, the actual cutting and sewing of fabrics and tanning of leathers. Once I had some experience under my belt, I began to think about opening my own business. Five years ago, I opened my consulting firm.

Thanks to clients like Chloe and Janice, my company has thrived, and supportive clients have sustained me. I continue to grow my business and find new avenues in the world of fashion to constantly benefit my clients."

His voice was low, and I strained to hear him as he continued, "My work has been my salvation. I've embraced it instead of embracing a person. Since Alisa, I've never had a meaningful relationship with another woman. But I think that's changed, and that's the reason I had to tell you these ugly and secretive facts about myself. I'm crazy about you and have feelings for you that are genuine—your intuitive business savvy, your youthful innocence, your enthusiasm for living and your inward and outward beauty—to me you are the whole package.

"I know I have a reputation as a womanizer, and people say I'm a player. It's all an act, my way of masking my reluctance to get close to anyone. I have a fear that I'll destroy that special someone—like I did Alisa. I'm terrified of intimacy because of this long-harbored guilt."

How ironic! I thought. *The man I'm attracted to, but have resisted because I was afraid might hurt me if I let myself get emotionally close to him, has just confessed his fear of a deep relationship.* Suddenly, I realized I'd have to revise my thinking about Toni. Going forward, my feelings would be tied to his vulnerability and shame. I felt so privileged that he had shared this tragedy with only me. As we left the bar and walked back to the apartment, he began several sentences but never finished them. Finally, he said tentatively, "I hope what I've told you won't destroy our budding relationship."

I didn't hesitate, saying reassuringly, "Toni, your honesty has deeply touched me. I respect you for your openness and look forward to spending time with you in the future—both on and off the clock." He smiled.

CHAPTER 53

The next few weeks were so crammed with work that there was no time to think about Toni or Manny, much less have a relationship with either of them. And I simply avoided thinking too much about my last conversation with Toni. I needed more time to process his confession.

However, it proved impossible to block Manny from my mind; he appeared at the apartment every Wednesday to dine with us. At the end of each visit, he invited me to hear his band. Finally, my guilt triumphed, and I promised to come to the club the next weekend to hear him play and meet his band members. "You won't blow me off again and go to Zürich with Toni, will you?" he asked.

Why does he always have to say something to ruin a moment? But I let the remark pass and simply assured him next Saturday night was all his. "I'm looking forward to our 'rain check' date."

When I arrived at the club, he guided me to a small table near the front of the stage. During the sets, Manny kept looking at me and smiling. With the club's intimate ambiance, the low lights, and a glass of wine, I was truly "in the moment." And as I listened to Manny playing the guitar and looked at his happy face in the spotlight, I realized he was truly in his element.

The band finished playing a current hit song: *"Nel Blu Dipinto Di Blu."* Then Manny stepped to the microphone and announced he would be playing a solo of his own composition and dedicating it to a special someone in the audience. The piece was a beautifully haunting and melodic love song. When his song ended, he came to me and handed me a long-stemmed red rose, kissed me softly on each cheek, and whispered in my ear, "This is for you, my love."

In that moment, I could have told him I loved him very deeply, too, but I couldn't bring myself to say a word. As I struggled to control my emotions, I realized just how romantically conflicted I was about my feelings toward Manny and Toni. I knew I would have to sort out those feelings before I gave any encouragement to either of them.

After the band finished playing, Manny and I sat in a dark corner at the bar, sipping Campari and soda and talking until almost sunrise. As we walked back to the apartment, he said earnestly, "Marilyn, this evening has been simply magical."

I responded, "I loved the evening, too. Your music and band are extraordinary. Manny, you know you have a very special place in my heart that no other person could claim." Later, recapping the evening in my head, I thought, *What a lame response—stilted and noncommittal. It certainly gave no indication of how I secretly feel about him.*

On Monday, reality was back. The Bank of Milan called and said they were receptive to our request for a line of credit based on Chloe and Janice's reputation in fashion design. However, they would still have to see our comprehensive marketing program and long-term strategy for the business. The bank officer said they would also expect separate plans for the upscale design known as C&J Fashion Choice and the less expensive line for younger women, Bourne Innocence, before giving final approval.

In the weeks that followed, the three of us worked incredibly long hours to get these documents in final form to submit with the application. When we finished, Chloe and Janice secured a luncheon appointment with the bank president to present the plan and answer any of the bank's questions.

When they returned from the meeting, they asked me to join them in their "at-home office." As I entered the room, my heart began beating even more rapidly. *What if the line of credit hasn't been approved? What if the prospectus I prepared for the bank president wasn't good enough?*

Chloe was on the phone, and Janice was busy at the drawing board working on a design. She motioned for me to take a seat until Chloe was finished. The suspense was killing me. My palms were sweating, and my breathing was shallow.

When Chloe hung up the phone, she left the room without even acknowledging my presence. My heart sank. *It must be worse than I imagined.*

My back was to the door, and I didn't hear her come back, but when I heard the clinking of glass, I turned around. Only when I saw the bottle of champagne and three crystal glasses in her hands was I able to breathe again. My very audible sigh of relief brought a smile to their faces.

Both cheered loudly and embraced me, shouting in unison, "Congratulations!" The bank president had given them verbal approval for everything we had requested, including funding for the start-up watch business we had proposed to expand our offerings.

We had six months to present our strategic plans for the two distinct clothing lines and the marketing plan for our watch initiative. Chloe said, "You'll be working with a company in Milan by the name of CRS International Marketing, and I've already contracted with Toni to continue working with you to develop the watch business." I was so excited about the bank's approval and the opportunities we now had to grow the business that her last statement about working with Toni hardly registered.

My first jubilant inclination was to call Manny with our good news. He hadn't complained too much about the time I spent on the plan, but I knew he resented it. Now, with the bank's approval, I hoped he'd understand how important it was to get everything right. I just knew he would be as happy for me in my career beginning as I was for him in his.

When Manny answered the phone, I didn't even say hello. I just launched excitedly into the whole scenario that had just occurred, including how I was afraid my face would turn blue from holding my breath. I didn't give him a chance to say one word until I had gone through the complete scope of work and what we would be doing to develop the watch line in the next six months.

When I finished, there was only silence. I couldn't even hear him breathing on the other end, so I asked, "Are you still there?"

He responded, "Yes, I'm here." Then, in a low voice, he warily added, "I'm pleased for your success in getting the bank financing, much less pleased with the development stage. I'm leery of your working with Toni on the watch portion of the marketing plan. He's bad news."

Typical Manny, always managing to ruin a glorious moment! I was so angry I couldn't get off the phone fast enough. *Why couldn't he have just been happy for me? Why do I always allow my emotions to swing up and down so dramatically in response to his reactions? Why? Why? Why?*

CHAPTER 54

The next morning, Chloe and Janice called CRS International Marketing and set up an appointment for that afternoon. The company was in the heart of the fashion district on the second floor of an office building over a cosmetic and perfumery shop and spa. The office was small but laid out efficiently, and the lovely smell that wafted up from the perfume factory and spa below made meeting there almost restful.

Charles Caldwell, an American who had worked in the company's New York office for several years before being transferred to Milan, would be my contact. We connected immediately, and I was impressed at his business approach. His questions were targeted—seeking information about our past marketing efforts and what we hoped to accomplish in the future. I gave him as much information as I could—any small detail I thought would be helpful—when he began putting together a marketing plan. I explained he would focus on our present products, C&J Fashion Choice and Bourne Innocence, since we were still developing the watch business. Once he felt confident that he understood the scope of our program, he said he would develop an initial marketing plan outline and get back to me in a week to ten days.

Back at the apartment, I gave Chloe and Janice a full report, including Charles Caldwell's time frame for completing the initial draft. Once I finished, Chloe said I wouldn't be working with him. "Janice and I will work with him on the marketing plan. You're going to Zürich to work with Toni, gathering the information we'll need to make the right decision on how to expand the business by adding a line of watches."

I wasn't sure how I felt about this new assignment. I'd talked to Toni a few times on the phone since our Alisa conversation, but I hadn't seen him professionally or socially. And I felt that after that confessional conversation, our relationship seemed a bit strained. What if he was embarrassed about his candidness? Was our relationship going to be different now?

As usual, Janice's folder for the business trip included my train tickets, hotel reservations at the Royal Palace, and my first appointment with Toni. We were to meet for lunch on the day I arrived to work out the itinerary for the rest of the week.

Once on the train, I found myself rehashing my recent trip with Toni to meet his mother, Zara. That trip had been a mix of enjoyable personal and successful professional events—without the complication of his confession. I had to admit I was attracted to Toni. I kept reminding myself, *Toni is our consultant. He's helping structure the watch business plan for our business and nothing else. I need to keep my emotions in check.*

By the time I unpacked my suitcase at the Royal Palace, it was time to meet Toni in the hotel restaurant. He was seated at a corner table with his back to me. I walked over to him and extended my hand. He smiled, stood, and kissed me on both cheeks. "Marilyn, you know handshakes are for Americans, never Italians."

My first inclination was to provide ground rules for the week, but I kept silent. *Why should I think this would be anything other than a business arrangement?* Prudently, I kept my mouth shut and waited for Toni to offer his game plan.

After a few minutes of small talk, he told me he was looking forward to our time together and that we'd be covering a lot of territory. Workdays would begin at 9:00 each morning and end at dinner each night. "Marilyn, I plan to be your host for dinner, beginning tomorrow. I'll be off the clock, and our dinnertime will not be billable hours for Chloe and Janice. You can rest this evening and get ready for a busy week. I hope the schedule meets your approval." It certainly did; I agreed immediately. Then I relaxed and patted myself on the back for letting him set the ground rules.

The next morning, we met Johann and toured his operation. Toni and Johann obviously had a collegial business relationship, since Johann had blocked out the entire day to take us through the watch design process—from production to retail. As we walked through the cycle, I was grateful for Toni's coaching before my first meeting with Johann. I had no difficulty following the presentation.

It was late afternoon when Toni dropped me at the hotel and said he'd pick me up around eight. I knew having dinner with him was risky, but I rationalized that it would be foolish for us to dine alone, and I was certainly committed to keeping all our time together strictly professional. To be honest with myself, I admitted I wanted to spend time with him.

At the restaurant, I tried to set the tone by taking a notebook and pen from my handbag. He looked at me, smiled, and said, "Put that away. We have all week to conduct business. This is a time for relaxing and enjoying each other's company."

Feeling a little silly, I stowed the pen and paper in my purse and relaxed. Our dinner was perfect; conversation flowed effortlessly on a host of subjects. But I still watched my wine consumption carefully and was pleasantly surprised when Toni returned to the hotel without an incident or flirtatious pass.

Each day, we faithfully followed Toni's schedule. I took copious notes at every meeting, recording my impressions and observations on the design and incredible precision that goes into the production of timepieces. I quickly realized why Switzerland is known for producing the world's finest watches and clocks.

Although I maintained my professional resolve for the entire week, there were times when Toni slipped into a more personal level. I brushed off his familiarity as natural, based on what we knew about one another personally and the heart-wrenching story of his relationship with Alisa that he'd shared with me.

My last night in Zürich, Toni told me that Zara wanted to join us for dinner. I was delighted and looked forward to seeing her again. When Toni picked me up, Zara was in the back seat, and when she didn't get out, I opened the door to give her a hug and the customary kiss on each cheek before slipping into the front passenger seat next to Toni.

Momentarily, I wondered why Zara was sitting in the back of her car, but we began chatting, and I dismissed it from my mind. However, the reason became apparent when we reached the restaurant and Toni got a walker out of the trunk and helped Zara out of the car. Why hadn't Toni told me about her illness?

After we were seated, Zara explained. "I had a stroke since we last we met. I'm no longer able to care for myself. Even with a live-in housekeeper who cooks and cleans, I can't manage the steps in my house. I'll be moving in with my sister soon; she has a one-floor plan," she said sadly. Her face contorted in despair, and Toni lowered his head and appeared to be ready to cry.

I took Zara's hands in mine and looked into her beautiful eyes to tell her how sorry I was to learn of her health problems. She smiled slightly before saying there was a silver lining to her illness. "Now that I'll be leaving my house, Toni is going to move in and, I hope, eventually marry a wonderful girl like you and raise a family in our family's home." She squeezed my hands tightly. *Was she trying to send me a message?*

Toni added, "I'll be moving my office to Zürich from Milan within the next six months. I've always had business in Switzerland and traveled back and forth from Italy to Switzerland regularly. I'll just be reversing the travel pattern now."

Toni didn't smile much during dinner, and I wondered if he felt pushed into moving to the house his father had built to make his mother happy. He had told me on our first visit that his mother could not bear to sell the house. It held too many precious family memories.

We drove Zara back to her house, and Toni helped her to the door. I followed them. The housekeeper, as if on cue, opened the door and guided Zara inside. In the foyer, Zara held me close and whispered that Toni was a good man who cared for me. "You're right, Zara. He's a good man, and you have every reason to be proud of him."

When Toni and I were driving back down the mountain, I asked how he felt about the permanent move to Zürich. He paused and seemed to be struggling to find the right words before responding. Finally, he said, "I have no problem with the move or living in my parents' house; my only problem with leaving Milan is that we'll be separated. I don't want to leave you."

He pulled to the side of the road and took my hand. "I have such strong feelings for you that it's difficult to be with you and not be able to express my feelings. I want us to be a couple." He pulled me close, and we kissed.

I laid my head on his shoulder and told him I cared deeply for him. "My dilemma is separating our business relationship from our personal one."

He said softly, "I love you."

I admitted that my feelings for him were intense. "I'm just not sure if it's love. However, I can't deny that I admire and respect you—and yes, I'm very attracted to you." When I hesitated to say I loved him, he raised my hand to his lips and kissed the palm.

"Take your time. We'll let our commitment to one another grow. I don't want to push you into saying anything that you might regret later. Let's just let our relationship unfold. Although I warn you, I intend to pursue you."

When we got back to the hotel, Toni asked to come up to my room. I knew I was breaking all my well-intentioned rules when I took his hand and nodded yes. So much for letting our relationship grow slowly!

When we entered my room, he was calm and very methodical in his seduction. He began by kissing me tenderly and holding me close while he ran his hands through my hair. As he moved to my neck and upper chest, chills ran up and down my spine. *Why doesn't he move faster?*

Slowly, he removed my jacket and carefully unbuttoned each blouse button until I stood in my lace bra, but fully dressed from my waist down.

He sat down and positioned me facing him, and all I could think was, *For goodness's sake, can't you move faster?*

"Marilyn, I've waited so long for this moment. Let me look at you." I stood in front of him for what seemed like an unbearable amount of time until he removed my skirt. Finally, remaining seated, he pulled me closer and began to remove my shoes and stockings, moving his hand slowly up and down my legs.

My pace in disrobing him was quick, even though I tried to mimic his seduction moves. When he finally stood completely naked in front of me, I thought he was the most beautiful specimen of a man I'd ever seen.

He was just as deliberate in the sexual act as he had been in the preliminary stages of foreplay. He took the time to use protection.

I had never experienced such longevity or intensity in the sexual act—not even the first time I lost my virginity with Manny.

When we finished our lovemaking, we lay together entwined in one another's arms. Toni pushed my wet hair away from my face and said, "Marilyn, you are so beautiful. I want to stay as we are now—forever."

We slept for a few hours and made love again before he got up, dressed, and lightly kissed me before leaving my room. As he quietly departed, I stretched luxuriously, and in my dreamy and sexually satisfied state, I thought, *I could spend the rest of my life with this man.*

CHAPTER 55

As arranged, Toni picked me up at the hotel the next morning to drive me to the train station. He helped me with my luggage and gave me a long, lingering goodbye kiss. "I'll be back in Milan in a few days, and we'll make dinner plans."

I responded as if I were scripted, "I'll look forward to it." Our departure seemed so far removed from the intimate experience we had shared last night. *But what was I expecting in a crowded train station?*

When I settled into my train seat, I looked out the window and watched the countryside fly by as the train rocked gently and picked up speed. I rested my forehead on the cool window, trying to analyze everything that had transpired since I began my career in Milan. Our business was flourishing, and Toni had told me he loved me. I was floating on top of my world.

Could Toni be that someone with whom I could spend the rest of my life? Mentally, I listed all his qualities in my mind: *Smart, handsome, kind, and sensitive. What else would any woman want in a man?*

Back at the apartment, Chloe and Janice were working at home, and I joined them in the office. Chloe looked up from her half-rimmed glasses and asked playfully, "Well, what did you learn about the 'tick-tock' industry in Zürich? Should we pursue a business arrangement with a watchmaker?"

I pulled my notebook from my hand luggage and fanned the pages to show them the extent of my findings. "I'll need to organize these notes, but you'll have my written report in a few days. I think you'll agree we have enough information to put together a prospectus for the Bank of Milan's evaluation of financing for our start-up line of Swiss-designed watches. Like our clothing lines, our watch collection will make a unique fashion statement—plus have an impressive markup."

Once I finished my brief report, I shifted gears. "I have some sad news. Toni's mother has had a stroke and cannot navigate all the stairs in her home. She'll be moving into her sister's one-level chalet soon. Toni will move into the family house." I explained that Toni's father had designed and built the house and Zara wanted to keep this architectural gem in the family. She was deeding the house to Toni.

"Toni plans to move his office from Milan to Zürich in the next six months. His client load in both cities is similar, and it's an easy train commute between the two cities. He's really just reversing the commute he already makes."

"How convenient for us," Chloe mused. Turning to Janice, she continued, "If we manufacture our watch line in Zürich, Toni will be there to help us. What do you think of Marilyn running the watch business in Switzerland, assuming we get financing?"

Janice spoke up quickly. "It would be perfect. No doubt Toni would like this arrangement, too."

I was exhausted physically and mentally and knew this was not the time to challenge this "pie in the sky" idea. We had to finalize the watch plan and obtain financing for the start-up project before we could even discuss my role—or location. Those were a lot of *ifs*.

Manny joined us for dinner that evening. When Janice and

Chloe retired to the sitting room for their customary "nightcap," Manny asked me to take a walk. I didn't want to go, but I was afraid if I said no, he'd feel rejected. He'd been upset and angry about my spending the week with Toni, and I felt I needed to spend some one-on-one time to assuage him, so I said, "Just a second; I'll get a sweater."

The moon was full and bright, lighting a path on the sidewalk. Milan was quiet except for the chirping cicadas. With his arm hooked in mine, we walked quite a distance in silence. We were comfortable with one another without conversation. When I was with Manny, I believed he saw and knew my true essence, and I saw his. We seemed to bring out both the best and worst in each other. Our relationship was like fire and water—all-consuming, yet also healing and tranquil.

When we returned home, Manny held me close, nibbling around my ear. He whispered, "I'm glad you're back so we can spend time together. When you go away, I miss you terribly."

I lamely responded, "It's good to be back in Milan. I've had quite an exhausting week, and right now, I've got to get some sleep before I pass out on this front stoop." I kissed him on the cheek and told him I'd see him soon when I was rested and better company.

I had a haunting thought when I left Manny and got ready for bed that night. *What would Manny think if he knew Toni confessed that he loved me and we had shared a meaningful sexual encounter just last night?*

CHAPTER 56

After I completed my detailed business plan for the watch business, I met with the bank's "powers that be" to present it and answer any questions about our loan request. They seemed receptive, but I kept my fingers crossed. It was a relief—and a thrill—when the bank president called Chloe and said the loan committee felt comfortable in financing the start-up based on my findings.

Yes, I was thrilled, but I was also very tired. In every facet of my life, I was burning the candle at both ends. My work—churning out reports following extensive research and surveys to crunching the numbers for our three business initiatives—was exhausting. And my back-and-forth visits to Zürich to work on the watch line were physically and mentally tiring—not relaxing. During one of my Zürich trips, Charles Caldwell completed the strategic marketing plan for the two clothing lines and presented it to Chloe and Janice, who briefed me on my return. Charles proposed introducing the two lines in the States immediately—scheduling the launch during the February Fashion Week in New York City. The high-end line was to be simply C&J, a rebranding that Chloe and Janice loved, and would be sold only in specialty stores. Bourne Innocence would debut in large department stores, such as Macy's, Saks, and Bloomingdale's. Charles Caldwell had used his New York connections to schedule preliminary meetings with buyers from specialty stores and department stores, so Chloe and Janice would be leaving for New York in just a few weeks.

My weekends didn't provide much relief, since I frequently finished projects instead of resting. And Toni kept my weekend social calendar filled with cultural events—theater and concerts—as well as dinners and cocktail parties with Milan's prominent society figures. My Italian was now a natural second language, and I was comfortable carrying on a conversation with the other guests. I never gave a second thought to my wardrobe—I knew it was always perfect for these outings. I was riding high and enjoying Toni's attention. He was an attentive and considerate escort. The months had just flown by, and Toni and I spent quality time with each other—working and socializing. My feelings for him were growing stronger and stronger. Still, I was careful to guard against sharing these feelings with him or others.

Even with my busy schedule, I kept in touch with my family and friends through letters, since international phone calls were financially out of the question. Since arriving in Milan, I'd tried to write one letter to Mama at least once a week. It was a round-robin letter that she shared with my family and closest friends—mostly Joe and Grace. It was the easiest way for me to keep everyone informed about my career growth, travels, and special Italian beau. However, I was careful not to include too much information about the men in my life. I didn't want to raise false expectations.

The shadow of Toni's pending move was always in the background. He'd almost finished shutting down his office and would soon move his company to Zürich. Time had passed quickly, but it was still almost eight months since that evening with Zara when he'd told me his plans. He explained the delay to me during intermission at the symphony. "I've had to cover all my bases with my clients in Milan. I had to be sure they were comfortable with the relocation of my consulting business. Chloe and Janice have been unusually supportive of this move, and that's been helpful with my other clients."

Then, he casually dropped a bombshell. "Chloe and Janice have talked with me about your relocating to Zürich, too, once the finances for the watch line are in place. I agree wholeheartedly with them. From a business standpoint, your presence in Zürich will make the watch business launch a successful reality more quickly. Selfishly, I think the move will be wonderful for our relationship, which will be able to grow outside of our business dealings. What do you think?"

What do I think? What does it matter? It seemed my future had already been determined. However, I didn't let Toni know I resented the three of them discussing my business future without my knowledge or input. So instead of looking annoyed or angry, I smiled and said, "It's a little early to make any moving plans. There are a lot of details to work out before I can leave Milan. But I would have more autonomy in Zürich, away from the watchful gaze of Chloe and Janice."

I hoped my answer let me save professional face, since I didn't want Toni to know how I felt about Chloe and Janice. Often, I felt like their puppet; they pulled my strings and made decisions that directly affected me without consulting with me as an equal in their business dealings. This career move was just the latest manipulation. And it wasn't just in business that I felt like a puppet. They also were thwarting my personal independence. Each time I looked at apartments and made plans to move, Chloe insisted I stay with them. "Marilyn, I believe the synergy from the three of us sharing the same living quarters and office space allows for an unprecedented flow of creativity and information sharing for the business both day and night. Don't you agree?"

Would it matter if I disagreed? I didn't challenge her. I knew Chloe was benevolently manipulating me, but I also knew it was financially beneficial for me to live there rent-free and save my lira, especially with the upcoming relocation to Zürich. Yes, I'd go because I believed I'd finally be independent. And truthfully, I was grateful to Chloe and Janice for being my mentors and protectors as I entered the career world. My successful ventures were all related to their support and introductions into the world of fashion.

My grueling work schedule and social engagements with Toni had forced me to put Manny's friendship on the back burner. Although he still came to dinner once a week and we took our "catch up" stroll afterwards, we were distant from each other—going in totally different directions.

But with these new revelations, I needed to talk to Manny. I phoned him and asked him to drop everything and meet me at our favorite coffee house near the university. I tried to lighten my request by adding, "My treat."

Manny was at the shop when I arrived and jumped up as soon as I walked in the door. "You look like you need a big hug. Is everything okay with your family?"

"Mama, my family, Joe, and Grace are all fine. We write almost every week to keep up with one another's lives. But I do have some concerns, and I need more than a hug from you. I need you, my dear friend, to listen to me vent. I'm exhausted and so overwhelmed with my work right now that I need to talk things through—and you're my sounding board. Okay?"

First, I briefed him on the new strategy to launch the clothing line in New York City during Fashion Week in February. "Chloe and Janice are flying there today for preliminary meetings with buyers and to get ready for the runway show. And the Bank of

Milan has fully funded the watch line ..." And that's as far as I got. To Manny's surprise—and mine—I burst into tears.

"Let it out. Cry and let it all out," he said. "I'll wait until you can continue."

I was finally able to compose myself to speak. "I just feel betrayed and manipulated by your mother and Janice. They've been conniving with Toni, making plans for me to move to Zürich to oversee the watch business line from there without ever asking for my input."

My last statement set Manny off. He stood up, threw his hands in the air, and kicked over his chair in a rage. "Now you see what I've tried to tell you all along. Chloe is controlling your life, just as she tries to control her husband, her sons, and even Janice. You're just her latest prey. When it comes to her business, she is ruthless. As a child, I thought of her as the petulant Queen of Hearts in *Alice's Adventures in Wonderland.* Welcome to the special Chloe Club of Broken Hearts."

Because Manny was creating a scene, I tried to silence him. "Please sit down, Manny, and hear me out, I'm not finished yet. Chloe has been generous to me—in my salary, clothing, and business opportunities. Don't forget, she and Janice are my mentors, and I've been living in their apartment for almost two years now rent-free. She's introduced me to her circle of connections, and that has been a big boost up my career ladder. My Kentucky upbringing tells me I shouldn't 'look a gift horse in the mouth.'"

Manny had finally calmed down and suggested we carry on our conversation at his apartment. I agreed quickly. I didn't want to risk another outburst, and my observations about his mother had obviously pushed his crazy buttons. As we walked to the apartment, I talked constantly. He couldn't get a word in. Grace, my childhood sounding board, was an ocean away, and I needed to unload on Manny before I exploded.

But the conversation ended as soon as we entered the apartment. Manny picked me up, took me to his bedroom, and gently placed me on the bed. He lay down beside me and began to stroke my hair, still not saying a word. I propped myself up on one elbow, leaned over, and kissed him. He unbuttoned my blouse and removed my bra. As his hands moved down my body, I felt sensations of warmth and excitement. He continued to undress me and then quickly shed his clothes. Our lovemaking was passionate, hungry—more intense than ever before.

All the stress and emotions I'd been struggling with faded, calmed by his presence and our lovemaking. Chloe and Janice were on a flight to New York. I was free and chose to spend the night with Manny. We made love two more times, then just lay together, exhausted in the best possible way. Finally, I admitted I was famished and joked, "Let's see if you can be the perfect host and whip up dinner for your house guest."

He jumped out of bed, pulled on his jeans, and headed to the kitchenette. I could hear him clinking dishes and pots and pans, so I decided to join him and watch the master chef at work. He uncorked a bottle of Chianti, and we sipped it as he made a tomato-and-basil sauce for pasta. It was perfect—making love, sipping wine, and watching Manny cook.

With Manny, I was always in the moment. Nothing or no one seemed to matter, including Toni. Later, as I drifted off to sleep next to Manny, I thought of Toni and felt a tinge of guilt before I rationalized my behavior. There were no strings attached to either one of these men. I was a free agent—free to have intimate relations with both if I wanted—and obviously, I did. As I drifted off to sleep, a popular Cole Porter show tune line from *Kiss Me Kate* kept running through my mind: "I'm always true to you in my fashion; always true to you, Darling, in my way."

I compartmentalized Toni and Manny, keeping them separate

and somehow unequal. Any guilt surfaced only because of Toni's assumption that we were headed toward a more permanent relationship culminating in marriage and children—particularly with my upcoming move to Zürich.

CHAPTER 57

When Chloe and Janice returned from New York, their excitement gave new meaning to the phrase "over the moon." They were ecstatic about the reception of the clothing line samples. The clothing line introductions, though small, had been enthusiastically received, and there was a file bulging with orders. Once they recovered from jet lag, we huddled in their office and talked about all the possibilities for growth once we launched both lines in New York. But it was just speculation for now, and I resumed my focus on the watch project launch.

A few days later, Chloe asked me to join her and Janice before dinner. "We have some important things to discuss, and I don't want any distractions," she explained. We went to the living room instead of the office, and once we took our seats, Chloe turned to me and smiled brightly. "Marilyn, you've done an exemplary job since you joined us, and we're so proud of you and your work. Of course, what we do from now on will determine our success, and I believe the future growth of our company depends upon all of us playing our different roles. I know we talked about your moving to Zürich for the watch design initiative, but we believe we need to change those plans."

My back stiffened, and I could almost physically feel the strings of the puppeteer manipulating my future career. I held my breath and waited for the pronouncement, which I believed was already cast in stone. Chloe looked to Janice and said, "Why don't you give her the good news?"

When Janice finished outlining the role she and Chloe had decided would be best for me and the company, I was flabbergasted. At first, I couldn't respond to the proposal because the words stuck in my throat, but my thoughts, though silent, questioned everything I'd heard. *How could these women make this decision without consulting me? Is this the time to make my break and gain control of my own destiny? Should I assert my independence? Do I have the courage? Could I be satisfied managing Elaine's Dress Shop after my exciting life and fascinating work in Italy? What would my family and friends think if I didn't accept this offer and returned to Rockport?*

It seemed like an eternity, but was probably only a few seconds, before I could look at both women. "I'm so grateful for everything you've done for me in your business and …" I never finished that sentence because Toni burst into the room. He must have been waiting at the door for Chloe and Janice to finish briefing me on their organizational changes and my new role in the company. When Toni entered, Chloe and Janice, as if on cue, left the room and went to their office. They were smiling at each other so smugly—so sure they had scored another victory.

"Congratulations, Toni, on your appointment as president of C&J Enterprises in Zürich. I know the watch business will flourish with you as its head," I stammered.

Like Chloe and Janice, he had a satisfied grin on his face, and I immediately thought of Alice's Cheshire cat. He reached for my hand and said, "And congratulations to you, Marilyn, on your New York promotion. The successful American launch of the two clothing lines is now assured with you overseeing the operation."

I recoiled from his touch. *Conniving*—a word I never associated with Toni before—came to mind. He had been a partner with Chloe and Janice in this new business plan. I felt as betrayed and manipulated by him as I did by Chloe and Janice. There was no joy for me in my new role, even if it was a brilliant career move, a chance to shine in the New York fashion world.

I saw the whole picture clearly now, and it wasn't pretty. The three of them were playing me as their company pawn. I could feel my cheeks burning from anger and outrage at my naiveté. I had had no clue they had formed a secret league that didn't include me. I suddenly realized that for Toni, being president of the watch business trumped establishing our "permanent relationship" in Zürich. Ambition, one, personal relationship, zero! I wanted to slap that arrogant grin off his face.

But my better judgment—or maybe my ambition—kicked in, warning me to say nothing and not risk showing my true feelings by crying. Toni moved toward me as if to put his arms around me to console me or celebrate with me—right now I wasn't sure which one.

I instinctively pulled back from him and moved toward the door. He didn't follow, but called out, "Wait, Marilyn. You're thrilled about our new roles in the company, aren't you? It's an extraordinary career opportunity for you."

I looked directly at him and, struggling to control my voice, asked, "How long have you known about this new arrangement?"

"Chloe and Janice confided in me before they went to New York. I knew that if the trip went well and initial sales of the two clothing lines to buyers were promising, they wanted you to oversee the American launch. But it wasn't a firm decision. It depended on so many things that I didn't tell you. I was afraid it would build false hopes and expectations," he explained. "Actually, it's a wonderful career move for us both. You'll see."

I turned quickly and walked out of the apartment in a state of fury. My only thought was to get to Manny's apartment as fast as possible. I leaned on the doorbell with insistence and force until Manny finally yelled into the intercom, "Who in the hell is there, and what do you want?"

"Manny, let me in. It's Marilyn." He pressed the button to open the door, and as I entered the stairwell, I heard him running down the stairs to meet me.

One look at me, and his face registered panic. "What's wrong, Marilyn? You look like someone just died. Come up here and tell me what's wrong." Typical Manny; he was so concerned for me that he just wanted to hear the reason for my impromptu visit.

Once I was seated on the familiar, well-worn sofa in Manny's sparsely furnished apartment, I took a deep breath before blurting out the entire story. As I talked, he held both my hands and kept telling me to breathe deeply. When I finished, I collapsed in his arms, exhausted.

We clung together on the sofa, and Manny rocked me gently back and forth. I finally confessed, "I don't just resent this because of the manipulation, Manny. One reason I'm resisting this promotion is because we'll be separated by an ocean."

"Trust me, we'll work this out together," he said. He didn't elaborate, but strangely, he didn't need to. His reaction soothed me, calmed the savage beast in me that was reacting to my new work arrangement. And oddly enough, I trusted him completely.

CHAPTER 58

I adjusted to my career change after a few weeks and began looking forward to heading up C&J Enterprises in New York City. Although I'd been shaken to the core by the alliance of Chloe, Janice, and Toni, my angry resentment at my exclusion gradually melted away. I gained a new perspective on what the move meant for me personally and professionally. I kept repeating Eleanor Roosevelt's quote in my head: "Yesterday is history. Tomorrow is a mystery. Today is a gift." And I planned to take full advantage of that gift!

When I wrote Mama to tell her I'd be moving back to the States permanently, I made sure I broke the news with an elated and optimistic spin. After all, how many women my age could wield this much power? I'd be heading up two clothing lines in the "Big Apple," and everything I did for C&J Enterprises in the States would reflect on my business and sales savvy. Events in my personal life were falling into place, too.

When Mama's response came, I couldn't wait to share her letter with Manny. Our relationship had grown to a new and wonderful place of intimacy. I hurried to his apartment and, over a glass of our favorite red wine, read the letter to him.

My dearest Marilyn,

I read your letter over and over before sharing it with Beth and Grace's families. We're all thrilled you'll be moving back to the States and heading up the New York operations for Chloe and Janice's company. It sounds like a wonderful promotion for you—and great news for us. You'll be close enough to come home for holidays and visit us lots of other times. We've missed you so much. You add such a spark to our lives.

It's been almost two years since you left Rockport, and you'll be amazed at the changes. Get ready for some real culture shock in our family. You won't recognize Beth's three children; they've grown like weeds since you left. Her youngest—your namesake—is into everything. We watch her like a hawk. If we don't, she scampers out of our sight looking for adventure. She's almost ready to walk on her own, and we expect to be even more vigilant. Beth describes her this way: "She's exactly like her aunt Marilyn. She's not yet two years old and displays strong-willed and independent tendencies. I just hope she doesn't find a penny and try to see if it fits in an electrical outlet, like her Aunt Marilyn did."

I don't know what I would do without Beth taking on many of my daytime responsibilities with Maria while I substitute teach English at Cannon High School. Beth has a very special and loving bond with Maria. How did I get so lucky to have three beautiful and uniquely different daughters?

Remember Mrs. Ada Thompson from church? Her husband died a year ago, and she has time now to devote three nights a week to caring for Maria while I attend night classes at Wesley. Maria loves her company, and it gives Mrs. Thompson a sense of purpose and fills some of her lonely evening hours.

I can't believe it only takes forty minutes to drive from my house to the campus parking lot near the educational classroom building. Remember how we dreaded the drive to Wesley when you were there? The new four-lane highway shortens the drive.

If all goes well, I should finish my teaching degree in less than two years. Your daddy would be so proud to know that two of his gals graduated from Wesley—I'm trying my best to make sure I graduate with honors, like you did. By the way, I expect you to attend my college graduation and cheer when I flip my mortar board's tassel—don't forget, I was there to watch you flip yours! Make a mental note to place this event on your May calendar two years from now. No excuses! It's only a two-hour flight from New York City to Nashville.

I have permission to share a secret with you—Joe and Grace are expecting their first child. Grace is in her third month, but she hasn't told many people. She's waiting until she's sure she'll be carrying the baby to full term. I don't think they've told Joe's mother yet, although Joseph was told the news as soon as they found out. I think Joe wants to tell his mother himself in his own time and in his own way.

Joe and Grace can't wait to show you what they've done to the farmhouse. They've spent countless hours remodeling and decorating. It's been such fun for me to go over there to watch their progress and share their excitement. Joe is doing wonderful things to the farm, too. Daddy would have been so pleased.

Joe and Grace are getting ready to furnish the nursery now, but haven't selected the paint color yet. Grace is leaning toward a soft, buttery yellow color and plans to pick up the baby's colors in the fabrics and artwork, since they have no idea if it will be a boy or girl.

We were all curious about Manny's plans you mentioned in your last letter to move to New York City too, once he finishes his music degree at the University of Milan. What gives? We want details! Does he plan to live with Joseph as he looks for space to open his music store? That makes the most sense to Joe and me, since he won't have any income until he's set up for business. Of course, he'll want to get his own apartment as soon as possible.

Joe said, "Thank God Manny has found himself in music and not law." Both Joseph and Joe are so proud of him and the direction he's pursuing. You, too, sound excited for Manny. We're all happy you two have forged and retained a strong bond from your first meeting many years ago in New York. Isn't it ironic that you two are ending up there together?

Hurry and write back with specifics on your arrival in New York City. Give Chloe, Janice, and

> Manny a big hello from all of us in Rockport. We can't wait to see you, and that goes for Manny, too!
> Love,
> Mama
>
> P.S. "Mum" is the word on telling Joe and Grace's news to Chloe. Joe wants to tell her himself.

Manny hugged me when I finished the letter and beamed. "Life is perfect with you in it. It's like Willie Shakespeare and the Kingston Trio's famous chorus line from their song 'The Unfortunate Miss Bailey': 'All's well that ends well, I suppose.'"

"I suppose that's true."

Part 2

CHAPTER 59

Weeks had passed since Chloe and Janice announced my new job assignment: moving to New York City to launch the C&J and Bourne Innocence brands in America. I recognized it was a career challenge, and I'd almost begun to believe the optimistic spin I'd penned in my letter to Mama. But I hadn't quite shaken the feelings of betrayal I felt toward Chloe, Janice, and Toni for scheming behind my back to award Toni the plum C&J watch business in Zürich while banishing me to the States.

I hadn't seen Toni since the announcement, and all the hurt and anger rushed back when I was summoned to Chloe's office and saw the three instigators waiting for me. I sat as far from Toni as I could and waited, apprehensively, to learn the reason for the meeting. It didn't take long for Chloe to make a request that completely unnerved me. She wanted me to write Toni's business plan for the watch business launch in Zürich. I could feel my blood pressure climbing. Internally I kept repeating, *Hell will freeze over before I do that for him!* Externally, I kept a poker face and even managed a slight smile.

I counted to three to try to soften my voice before I answered

Chloe. "Of course, I'll have a plan in your hands before I leave for New York."

Then Toni, speaking for the first time, said, "I'll be providing input to you, Marilyn. I'm looking forward to working with you on the plan."

I ignored him, continuing to face Chloe as I repeated, "You'll have my plan before I leave Milan. If that's all, I need to get back to sorting and culling files." As I turned my back and walked out of the room, I congratulated myself on my feigned composure; I'd managed to get through the meeting without exploding and hurling angry expletives that I would probably have regretted.

During the next two weeks, when Toni called to invite me to dinner, I was always too busy wrapping up my professional affairs in Milan. I cringed every time I heard his smooth voice. Each call renewed my anger at his blatant betrayal. *How could someone propose marriage, declare undying love, and then swiftly accept a lucrative business offer that did not include me in his life—much less as his wife?* Toni seemed oblivious to my rancor—which only cemented my resolve to banish him from my life. And I was beginning to embrace the move because I had come to realize that I would be independent and no longer under Chloe and Janice's day-to-day scrutiny.

My only regret now was that preparing for the move—file organizing, packing, and writing Toni's business plan—left me little time for Manny. I briefly considered developing a plan of failure for the Zürich endeavor, but quickly rejected it. My responsible side won; I presented Chloe with a realistic and—I believed—a successful business strategy with solid research and tactics. And I had avoided Toni in the process.

The night before my departure, Estella cooked my favorite pasta. She hugged me and had tears in her eyes as I left the dining room to go upstairs to finish my packing. The next morning, as Chloe and Janice were having their usual coffee and Danish before beginning their workday, I walked toward them to hug them and thank them. I was struck by how much they had influenced me and no longer had bitter feelings toward them because of my job change. Now I was genuinely grateful to both these women who had molded me professionally and shared their lives with me in this incredible city.

I walked back to my empty Milan bedroom for one last look and was suddenly overwhelmed with sadness. I recalled my exhilaration in discovering Milan, Paris, and Zürich and the wonder in experiencing the beautiful countries of Italy and Switzerland with my two lovers. My European sojourn felt like a graduate school into adulthood, but I was ready to close this important chapter of my life and open a new chapter in New York City.

I smiled, remembering my introduction as a college freshman to New York City with Joe—an introduction that included losing my virginity to his brother Manny. I'd often wondered if Joe ever knew of the guilty pleasure I'd shared with Manny. It didn't matter now, since Joe and Grace were happily married and Manny and I had forged an intimate relationship over the years.

Chloe's driver was waiting to take me to the airport. As he was stowing my bags in the trunk, I looked up and saw Manny rushing toward us. He grabbed me in a bear hug and whirled me around on the sidewalk. "I meant to be here sooner to say a proper goodbye, but my alarm clock never went off," he stammered. When he released me and I could look at his face, I saw tears in his eyes.

I held back the tears that were forming in my eyes and said soothingly, "Manny, we'll be together in New York soon. I love you." As I jumped into the back seat of the car, I turned my head away, refusing to let him see my tears.

I regained my composure on the long ride to the airport. I tried to hide how upset I was about leaving from the driver. It didn't work. He sensed my sadness, and after helping me into the airport with my luggage, he said in soft Italian, "Miss Marilyn, you have a safe journey. You will be missed in Milan."

I had an aisle seat on the plane, so I leaned forward to look out the window as we departed Milan. So much had transpired since I had left home for college: I'd launched my career in Europe; Daddy had had a heart attack and then died; Joe had purchased our family farm and married Grace. Then I had an odd flashback—my visit to see if unsavory Samuel Allison would help Daddy and Joe with the farm. That had been a pivotal move in my career because when Mama learned of my meeting with Samuel, she immediately suggested I apply at Elaine's Dress Shop in town. She was protecting me—and unwittingly steering me toward a career in fashion.

Suddenly, everything fell into place—I was homesick for my family and trusted Rockport friends, people who loved and protected me. I would only be a two-hour plane ride from home once I landed in New York. I could have the best of both worlds. Wonderful possibilities presented themselves—and occupied my mind on the flight home.

CHAPTER 60

Flying across the Atlantic toward Idlewild Airport, my mind continued to race with past memories, as well as future fears about relocating to New York. I'd slept so little by the time we touched down that my first thought was to find an affordable hotel, get some rest, and then start apartment hunting. I took the cab driver's advice and registered at the historic Pennsylvania Hotel near Penn Station. I had saved some money in Milan but knew most of it would go for the deposit and first month's rent on a studio apartment. Would I even have enough left to buy a bed if my apartment didn't have a Murphy bed? What other unknown costs could crop up as I set up housekeeping? All I had were my clothes and business papers.

As soon as I got over my jet lag, I began my apartment search. I thought it boded well for my New York adventure when I found an available walk-up apartment within two days. It was a cozy studio on Madison Avenue in the Upper East Side, not far from Central Park. It had long windows that flooded the small space with light and made a perfect frame for my work desk and chair. I even had enough money for my utilities and some secondhand furniture.

I furnished my first home with essential furniture pieces (yes, I did have to purchase a bed) but minimal creature comforts. Once settled, I began the next daunting task—locating office space in the Garment District near Fifth Avenue, Chloe's choice. Each time I wired her about a space, she responded, *Too expensive, keep looking.* Since Chloe had been emphatic about the office location, I was puzzled. Did she have any idea of rents in that area? Finally, I found a walk-up, one-room office a block off Fifth Avenue that was affordable, and she approved the lease.

Chloe had given me permission to hire an assistant, and after interviewing several young women candidates at the deli near the office that substituted for a conference room, I hired Lindsey. She was a recent business school graduate from Katharine Gibbs. A natural beauty, she had a winsome smile, crystal-blue eyes, long, wavy blonde hair, and a bounce to her step that mirrored her high energy level.

Lindsey was eager to begin setting up the empty office space. She didn't flinch at her modest budget, quickly saying she was ready to start with one stipulation—I was not to see the space until it was completed. After a few days, Lindsey called to say she was ready to show off her efforts.

She barely controlled her excitement when she met me in front of the office building and led me up the stairs. "No peeking until I open the office door," she said. "Now, look!"

My jaw dropped at the unveiling.

Lindsey had painted the drab beige walls a soft lime green with a white trim. All the used furniture was glossy black. She'd transformed an old upholstered chair into a comfortable chair for clients by making a slipcover using material with a white background and geometric shapes of purple and lime green. A soft, striped black-and-white rug now covered most of the worn, broad-planked floor. Brightly colored fresh-cut flowers adorned both desks.

I blinked at her decorating transformation. "Lindsey, how much did you go over budget to achieve this fantastic scheme?" I asked.

Instead of answering me, she reached under a desk and pulled out a silver metal bucket filled with ice, chilling a bottle of champagne. She opened the desk drawer and pulled out two flute glasses before she popped the cork.

With a devilish grin she said, "Sorry, I used the last of our budgeted money to buy this bottle of Taylor Champagne—New York's finest." We toasted and then sat in our new little cozy office desk chairs and talked and laughed until we finished the champagne. Then I said, "Lindsey, you and I deserve dinner on Chloe's dime this evening—we've done a great job for her here!" We clinked our empty glasses, locked the office, and headed to a nearby restaurant.

Each weekend during my first month in New York, Chloe had wired me for an update on my progress. When she finally telephoned at the end of the month, I couldn't wait to give her all the details. I told her I knew I had hired the right assistant and that we couldn't wait to show off our new office space to her. "I know you and Janice will be pleased with what we've accomplished in such a short time," I said. "And we've done it within your budget."

I was a little deflated when Chloe replied, "Let Janice and me be the judge of that hire and the office when we come to New York in September for Fashion Week." After she gave me all the details of their planned arrival, she added, "By the way, we've purchased two additional tickets, so you and Lindsey can attend Fashion Week with us."

Although I resented Chloe's condescension, I couldn't show my displeasure to her. I also knew it would be prudent for me professionally to remain positive at all times, especially to my new assistant.

When I hung up the phone, I turned to Lindsey and mustered some enthusiasm. "Chloe and Janice are coming to New York for

Fashion Week in September, and we'll be attending the events with them. I believe it's their way of rewarding us for our hard work."

I was a good actress because Lindsey could barely contain her excitement at the prospect of attending New York's revered Fashion Week and meeting our exotic business owners. I just thought to myself, *If this job fails, maybe I have another career on Broadway.*

CHAPTER 61

To say launching two clothing lines in New York was overwhelming was quite an understatement. I felt such pressure to succeed that my game plan to visit Rockport at least every four months after my initial visit never got off the ground. In fact, the grind of work kept delaying that trip. After several phone conversations with Mama, I agreed to chisel out a weekend visit.

Mama, Beth, and Maria greeted me at the Nashville airport. After our round of hugs, we clambered into Beth's car. Rockport was an hour's drive from Nashville, and as we crossed the Kentucky state line, I looked at the familiar countryside of my youth. The tidy, fenced farmlands that grew corn, tobacco, wheat, and soybeans swept by the car window, and I remembered how Daddy used to point out the different crops and the work involved in getting them to market.

When we drove through Rockport, I was happy to see how little the town had physically changed. Mama had made her new house comfortable for Maria and her. As I looked around at our family's familiar furnishings, I was struck by how much I missed Daddy's presence. I was eager to visit our old family farmhouse, modernized by Joe and Grace, and catch up with them and their growing family. Even before I saw them, I knew I would feel a sense of continuity and comfort seeing family life carrying on there.

I wasn't quite prepared for the deep void I felt because of Daddy's death. I wished he was here so I could ask him how he coped with the challenges life hurled at him in this farm setting—from raising a family to watching a crop destroyed by a hailstorm or drought. As a child and young adult, I had always felt secure and never worried about how our lives would turn out, even with Maria's disability, failed crops in our community, and Daddy's death.

What I wouldn't give to sit down with him now as an adult and discuss how to deal with daily change and stress.

Then it hit me. Mama was still very present in my life, a perfect oral historian and sounding board for me as I sought answers to dealing with personal accomplishments, fears, and disillusionment. Her life had not been easy—she had encountered many difficulties in her lifetime, yet she played her hand with discipline, dignity, and grace of acceptance.

I'd see if she was willing to let me interview her and capture our family history through her eyes. When I asked her, she seemed skeptical. "Marilyn, my life has been so mundane. Why me?"

When I said emphatically, "Because you are the most important member of our family tree," I saw a shadow of a smile cross her face.

CHAPTER 62

First thing on Saturday, I visited Joe and Grace at our former family farmhouse. When I returned to Mama's, I was prepared to begin interviewing her, but as I expected, when I broached the subject again, she rebuffed me. "Marilyn, your time is so limited this weekend. Don't waste it asking me boring, ancient history questions."

I countered, "It's really important for me to know about you and our family tree. It will help me connect dots on the pages that I've always wondered about." I wasn't going to reveal my ulterior motive, which was that I was searching for answers to both clarify and reconcile my relationship with Manny. I wanted to learn as much about my family as I already knew about his.

When she finally agreed, I made a pitcher of sweet tea, filled two glasses, and asked Mama to join me in the living room. I settled comfortably on the sofa, and she pulled up a straight-backed wooden chair, stiffly facing me from across the room. I told her I'd be making notes as she spoke. Then I launched into my first question, ignoring her stilted posture.

"Mama, I know so little about my grandparents—your mother and father. What were they like?"

She swirled the ice cubes in her glass before she began slowly in a soft voice. "My mama was beautiful and so very kind. I can't recall her ever raising her voice to me." There was a pause as she thought about her own mother. "She had a melodious voice and would often sing to me, my younger sister Clara, and my younger brother Walter, the baby in the family. After Mama died, there was no more singing in our house," she mused. "It was like a spigot had been turned off."

Suddenly, I realized I'd never heard my mother sing. Daddy had loved to sing. He sang childhood songs around the house to my sisters and me and enjoyed belting out hymns in church. But I couldn't recall Mama ever singing one note. She never even held the hymnal in church.

"How old were you when your mama died?" I asked.

She responded in a faraway voice, "I was seven years old, Clara was five, and Walter was three." Tears rolled down her cheeks as she quietly began to tell me about her mother.

"The singing stopped when I was about six. That's when Mama got sick and stayed in bed most of the time. She was frail and sickly for almost a year. Her skin was pale, and she was thin, with a raspy cough. I thought she might strangle herself when she coughed. As the oldest child, I knew instinctively that I had to take over her household chores. At six, I became chief cook and bottle washer. And since we had little food in the house, preparing meals was a major task.

"Daddy was rarely home, and when he did come home, his breath smelled foul. He would throw things and stumble around as if he couldn't keep his balance. If Walter cried, he'd slap him. If Clara or I cried out in alarm or protest, he would yell at us and raise his hand as if he might strike us.

"We were terrified of him and tried to avoid him. I knew it was my responsibility to create calmness in the house, so when Daddy came home, I did everything I could to please him so he wouldn't get upset with us. As hard as this was, it didn't compare with my frustration in trying to get Mama to eat. I pleaded with her, cajoled her, and sometimes threatened her to try to get her to at least take a bite. I'd tell her how much we missed her and that she needed to eat to get better. Nothing worked, and she finally could not even swallow the water I gave her from a paper sipping straw.

"One snowy night, a loud commotion in the house woke me. I tiptoed into the hall and saw two men carrying my mother out of her bedroom on a stretcher. Daddy was crying and swearing up a blue streak. I was too young to understand his combination of profanities. They were incoherent and unintelligible, but I understood the bone-chilling keening in his voice. When he saw me peeking around the hall corner, he yelled at me to get back to bed before I woke up Clara and Walter. Daddy's behavior had always scared me, but this fury was so frightening I immediately retreated to my bed for a sleepless night.

"The next morning, Daddy told Clara, Walter, and me that Mama had died during the night. Even at seven, I instinctively understood the enormity of her death and what it meant to our family structure. I shivered at his news.

"The 'viewing' practice at that time was to bring the deceased home so family and friends could view the body and pay their respects to the immediate family. Mama's body was brought back to our living room in a coffin for this visitation. It was taboo for children to view a corpse, so we were banned from the living room. When people came for calling hours, we were banished to our bedroom.

"As the dutiful eldest daughter, I helped Clara and Walter change into their pajamas and tucked them into bed during these nights. On the last night of the wake, I sat on my bed for a long time, listening to the visitors' voices in the living room. Later that night, when the voices stopped, I tiptoed downstairs to the living room. Daddy's brother was sitting next to Mama's coffin, almost as if he were standing guard over her. I ventured down the hall and found Daddy sitting at the kitchen table with his head in his hands, his back to me, and a half-empty bottle next to him. Every few minutes, he took a long swig from the bottle and wiped his mouth with the back of his hand. I knew better than to disturb him.

"I crept back to the living room to find my uncle fast asleep in his chair next to Mama's coffin. The room was chilly because we had no heat in the house, so I put a throw over him and quietly pulled up a stool to get a better look at my mother. She appeared to be sleeping, but it was a different sleep, not the sleep I remembered when she was alive. I wanted to touch her and to kiss her goodbye, but I was too small to reach her lying in the coffin.

"As I turned to go back to bed, Daddy caught me leaving the living room. He was furious with me, snatched me up like a rag doll, and took me upstairs to my bedroom, throwing me down on my bed.

"Marilyn, it was such a traumatic experience for me. I've tried to bury it," she said. There was a shadow of sadness on her face as she turned to look at me. I walked over, put my arms around her, and apologized for taking her down memory lane to such an unhappy place. She began to sob and then abruptly stopped.

"Marilyn, perhaps it's right for you to learn more about my upbringing. I know you and Beth often had a tough time understanding me. Unlike your daddy, who seemed like an open book, I'm far more reserved with my emotions." Then she surprised me by saying, "I really do want to tell you my story. Perhaps we should include Beth in the process. I've never really shared my story with anyone but your father."

I responded quickly. "I think you should call Beth to invite her. I know it would be best coming from you."

"I'll call her now and see if she can come alone for dinner tonight—just the three of us. I'll begin my storytelling with 'Once upon a time,'" she said, smiling at her reference to childhood stories.

CHAPTER 63

Beth eagerly accepted Mama's invitation for dinner after she learned it came with a serving of Mama's life story. She, too, had always wondered why Mama was so serious and reserved while Daddy was so fun-loving and open.

After dinner, Beth and I settled on the sofa, sharing the patchwork quilt Mama had made. Mama pulled up the straight-backed, wooden chair from the corner of the room and placed it across from us. I quickly recounted Mama's story of the death of her mother and the emotional trauma she had experienced as a seven-year-old.

Mama picked up her story from there. "We were not allowed to attend Mama's funeral. A lady from the church came to stay with us while Daddy was at the service."

Mama continued, "The church lady, whose name I don't remember, was kind to us and fixed supper from the wide of variety food our neighbors had brought. Our kitchen counter was covered; I'd never seen so much food. Suddenly, I was hungry.

"When Daddy returned, he thanked the lady and then told her sternly that he needed to be alone with his children and she didn't need to stay any longer. He summed up the situation by saying, 'I've got these kids covered now.'

"As soon as the church lady closed the back door, Daddy pulled a bottle from a top cabinet and began to guzzle down the brown liquid from the bottle. He wiped the back of his hand across his mouth before he ordered us to hurry up, eat our dinner, and then get to bed.

"We gobbled down the food. The nice church lady had cleared the counter, so I knew we'd have food for several days and that I didn't have to worry about it spoiling. As soon as we finished eating, the three of us jumped down from our chairs and ran upstairs to our rooms. As usual, I helped Clara and Walter get ready for bed, feeling a little guilty at leaving the dishes unwashed downstairs. I briefly wondered if I would go to school the next day or have to stay home to care for Clara and Walter, but the thought disappeared quickly, and I fell into a sound sleep.

"When I woke, I went down to the kitchen to make breakfast. Daddy was fast asleep at the kitchen table, his head next to our dirty dishes. I quietly cleared the table, started the coffee pot for Daddy, and scrambled eggs for everyone. I just wanted to please him. However, when he woke up, he snarled at me and demanded to know why I wasn't ready for school.

"He ordered me to get dressed immediately and get to school without being tardy. He said he'd take care of Walter and Clara. I got my brother and sister up, dressed them quickly, and got ready for school. I told them Daddy would take care of them while I was at school.

"Not many days after Mama died, Rachel Whitfield began coming around our house. I didn't know much about Rachel, except that she didn't have a husband. I had heard the church ladies tell Mama that Rachael attracted men to her house like bees to a honey hive. They had all laughed and a few made disapproving *'tsk, tsk, tsk'* sounds, shaking their heads in disgust.

"Rachel's house was located directly across a cornfield from ours. I could look out the kitchen window and see her walking through the field toward our back door. When she came into our kitchen, Daddy ordered us to go upstairs and not come down until he called. We obeyed, but even with the door shut, we could hear their laughter.

"Clara told me Miss Rachael was there most days when I was at school and that she and Walter had to stay outside until she left. The summer after Mama died, Daddy sat us down for supper and told us he and Rachel Whitfield were getting married and she would take care of us.

"When we said nothing, Daddy said we should be happy because we would have a woman to take care of us now. But since we didn't know Rachel, we were baffled about how to react to Daddy's news.

"A few days later, Daddy and Rachel went to the courthouse to marry. We were not invited. Rachel moved into our house after she and Daddy were legally hitched. She didn't bring much. She'd been renting a furnished house. She brought her clothes and hung them in the closet in my parents' bedroom.

"When I looked into their bedroom when the door was open, a knot always formed in my stomach, and I fought back my tears so Clara and Walter wouldn't see me cry. After Rachel joined our household, life became even more of a nightmare for the three of us. She told Walter he was a stupid little boy who would amount to nothing. She tagged Clara as so ugly that she would never get a man to marry her. Rachel's conversations with me were limited to barking orders; she treated me like a maid. She expected me to keep the house clean and cook meals after school. Daddy rarely noticed us, and we felt like pieces of cellophane as we moved through the house.

"I really took on the role of Mama to Clara and Walter, making sure they were bathed, had clean clothes, and behaved so they stayed out of trouble. Even at four, Walter knew there had to be a better life. He wanted to run away from home and talked about it all the time.

"That fall, Clara entered first grade, and Walter was home alone with Rachel. On school days, he would follow us down the road toward school until Clara and I turned him around and pointed him back to the house. We could hear him sobbing as he slowly trudged back to spend his day without the shield of his two sisters. I'm sure he was verbally demeaned and probably physically harmed while his protectors were at school. No wonder he talked about running away all the time."

To Beth's and my surprise, Mama stood up abruptly and said, "Girls, Walter was such a cute little boy. My heart breaks thinking of what he endured." Beth and I jumped up and put our arms around her to comfort her. She continued, "I'm emotionally drained right now. Perhaps I can continue tomorrow."

CHAPTER 64

Mama did not continue her story on Sunday. As I flew back to New York that night, I realized how relieved I was that we hadn't revisited that emotional session. I replayed our conversation over and over, and each time, I felt a deep sorrow. I regretted telling her how important it was that I learn about her upbringing and wished I could erase the memory of her sad childhood from my mind.

On Monday morning, I briefly recalled the weekend events while I gulped my coffee, but when I got to the office, I was completely immersed in my professional life. Meetings with department store buyers, dinners with specialty shop owners, sales calls on jewelry store owners about our watch line—there never were enough hours to accomplish everything on my "to-do" list—or to dwell on personal problems or revelations.

And my stress level climbed a notch every time Chloe and Janice prodded me to get Bourne Innocence into department stores in Chicago. I wasn't even confident about New York, and they were pushing me to expand into another major market.

When I finally returned to my small studio apartment at night, all I wanted to do was eat dinner, fall into bed, and try to get enough sleep to face the next day's rat race. And that was when I wasn't up well past midnight to complete that day's paperwork.

My first week back from Rockport, Chloe wired that she, Janice, and Manny would be arriving from Milan in a few days. Shortly after I received the wire, Joseph called and invited me to dinner the night before their arrival. I knew Joseph had an agenda, but I couldn't figure out whether he wanted my thoughts about how to prepare for Manny moving in with him or to discuss Chloe and Janice's stay in New York.

Joseph and Chloe's relationship was so complicated. Joseph was quite open about the nurse who lived with him. They worked at the same hospital, and the relationship was longstanding. Manny had confided that Joseph had ruled out marriage, telling the nurse Chloe refused to divorce him. When I asked if the nurse knew that Chloe and Janice were more than business partners, Manny said no.

Over the years, I had had time to process all the drama and intrigue within this family and examine, at least from my limited psychological knowledge, the ramifications that influenced Joe and Manny's attitudes and values. And I'd also developed a strategy for dealing with all the family members—to walk a thin line with each one of them when they were together. Like my family, each was different, even though they had shared the same upbringing. Of course, you couldn't compare my family with Manny's; we were no way that complicated. Or at least, I didn't think we were, even remembering Mama's childhood disclosure.

As I prepared for dinner with Joseph, I thought about my evolving relationships with this family. I admitted I was apprehensive about Chloe and Janice's visit, but I was eager to connect with Manny again. He had finished his music degree at the University of Milan in May and then landed a musical gig in Milan for the summer. We had corresponded on a regular basis since my New York move and had even had one international phone conversation.

Although we'd both been counting the days until we were once again in the same city, I had to confess his early September arrival was contributing to the rise in my anxiety level. I was afraid I couldn't continue my frantic professional obligations and see Manny on a regular basis. And I knew from Milan that Manny would not be sympathetic to the self-imposed pressure I felt to perform in my work.

Joseph's dinner invitation helped me deal with that stress because it reminded me that Manny would have his own challenges in New York. Joseph had agreed to help Manny open a music store in Greenwich Village, and my experience in launching Bourne Innocence made me realize he would be so preoccupied getting this new venture off the ground that he might not have much time for me. Maybe I'd be the one looking for more time together!

I knew from Manny's letters that he and Chloe had forged a much closer relationship. He'd explained that the change was gradual as she came to accept his life choices and more rapid after he'd completed his studies and then worked in the band for the summer.

Now Manny would have to build another parental relationship, and this one might be an even more difficult adjustment. I was apprehensive about Manny living with his father in New York because of his volatile and often cruel temperament, which he couldn't control.

So many questions were swirling around in my mind when I met Joseph at a quiet Italian restaurant in the Village. I was glad we spent time over a glass of wine catching up with events in Rockport before ordering dinner. Joseph beamed with pride as he told me he tried to see Joe, Grace, and the baby at least once a month. And his interest in my family was genuine and sincere.

By the time the waiter brought dinner, we'd finished our small talk, and Joseph launched into the real reason for his invitation. "Marilyn, I wonder if you might suggest that Chloe go to

Rockport during this trip? I know it would mean the world to Joe and Grace if she made the effort. She won't listen to me. Heaven knows, I've told her so often that Joe always asks about her and wants to know when she'll be coming to the States to see them. She's only visited once since the birth of her grandchild.

"And one other thing: could you suggest that it would be best to make the trip without Janice? Grace's family and church friends are already suspicious about her relationship with 'that woman'—the term they've used to describe Janice after her past visits. As you know, Rockport is a very conservative community," he said, raising his eyebrow.

I was startled by Joseph's request. He had to know I'd be uncomfortable approaching my two bosses about their personal choices. "Joseph, you're really putting me in a difficult position. I'm reluctant to get involved in your family situation, but I do understand your concerns. Give me some time to think about it; I want to be sure I don't jeopardize my relationship with my bosses if I decide to approach them with your request." He nodded, and I quickly changed the subject by asking him how he felt about Manny living with him until the music shop was established.

"I think a four-bedroom apartment is large enough to keep us from having any privacy issues," he said with a slight smile. I blushed—was he talking about his nurse or me? Joseph paid the check, and when we left the restaurant, he hailed a cab and gave the driver the address of my tiny apartment. I relaxed as soon as I shut the door. Somehow, life seemed far less complicated in my studio home—at least for now.

CHAPTER 65

The morning Chloe, Janice, and Manny were to arrive from Milan, I woke before dawn, probably from anticipation and apprehension. Although I had no idea where they would be staying in New York, I assumed it would be at Joseph's apartment. I wondered if Joseph's significant other would move out for the duration.

Manny had written that he planned to only bring his personal belongings and musical equipment on the plane, shipping everything else. Since I knew his wardrobe consisted of well-worn jeans, long-sleeved flannel or cotton T-shirts, and underwear, I expected he would be traveling with one bag—his canvas hiking backpack.

When it came to fashion, Manny was the antithesis of his mother—and his brother Joe, an irony that always made me smile. At first, I thought it was Manny's way of rebelling, but as we became close, I realized he simply lacked interest in personal possessions.

Sartorially, the brothers were opposites. Joe's clothes were always neatly starched and pressed and his hair closely trimmed—never as disheveled as Manny's. Beth and Grace regularly teased Joe about winning Rockport's "best-dressed farmer" award, particularly when he was handsomely groomed for church or social gatherings. Joe would only raise an eyebrow before grinning sheepishly and acknowledging his compulsion for neatness and order.

Clothes weren't the only difference between the brothers. Their personalities were also completely opposite. And I often marveled at feeling so attracted to loud, obnoxious Manny, who always kept me off balance with his behavior—while rejecting quiet, thoughtful, and predictable Joe so many years ago.

This arrival day dragged for me. I waited for Manny and my two bosses with a growing, gnawing apprehension. How would my relationship with Manny evolve now that he was settling in New York? Would Chloe and Janice approve of my assistant selection and our newly decorated office? Would they be pleased with our sales for the past six months?

To prepare for the office debut and Lindsey's presentation, I had done everything in my power to have things in order. Lindsey worked with me on the last-minute adjustments, and she kept ribbing me about the crooked grin that sporadically appeared on my face. I fibbed, "It's just that I'm anticipating how pleased Chloe and Janice will be with our office." No need to introduce Manny into the conversation.

Chloe checked in at 3:00 p.m. They were at Joseph's apartment and would be at the office within an hour. There was no smile on my face when I hung up the phone. I was disappointed because she hadn't mentioned Manny.

True to form, Chloe and Janice arrived on time, looking as if they had just stepped out of the pages of *Harper's Bazaar* magazine. Talkative Lindsey was silent—probably in awe. She stepped forward and extended her hand when I introduced her, which Chloe and Janice ignored. They both gave her the customary Italian kiss on both cheeks before turning to me to hug me and kiss me on both cheeks.

As soon as the greetings were over—and Lindsey had recovered from her surprise—I quickly launched into my plans for their stay in New York.

"Slow down," Chloe said, raising her hand. "I want to look around the office." She surveyed the small room slowly, studying each detail, before turning to Lindsey. "You've done a magnificent job on the office on a very small budget. Very impressive." Lindsey beamed as she gestured toward the chairs, which she had augmented with a straight-backed chair from her apartment. At least no one had to perch on the desk.

Once seated, I outlined our itinerary for the week and then got a brief update on things in Milan. Then Chloe suggested we meet for dinner at 7:00 p.m. at a small French bistro near Joseph's apartment.

After dinner plans were settled and Chloe and Janice had left, Lindsey flopped down in the chair that Chloe had vacated, lamenting her clothing choices. "You should have clued me in—no, I should have known—that they would be fashion plates. I wore the best dress in my closet and still felt like a bag lady."

I laughed at her. "You are a fashion plate compared to my introduction. When I first met these two women, I was wearing a wool skirt my mama had sewn, a simple blouse, loafers, and knee socks."

Now it was Lindsey's turn to laugh, envisioning me in my college outfit as I continued with details of my fashion transformation. "Chloe and Janice totally revamped my wardrobe when I stayed with them in Milan. I became their living model, which allowed them to get valuable feedback from young women about their clothing line.

"Looking back now, I realize I was more than their fashion guinea pig. I'm sure they wanted to avoid professional embarrassment had I continued to dress as I had when they met me in my freshman year."

Lindsey and I laughed until tears were streaming down our

faces. It was the comic relief we needed after the pressure of hosting our bosses—the infamous Chloe and Janice—in our small office space. It helped also to hide my disappointment that neither had mentioned Manny during their visit. I tried to suppress my frustration by preparing an agenda for tonight's dinner meeting.

Lindsey and I arrived at the restaurant early, determined to feel comfortable in our surroundings before Chloe and Janice arrived. Lindsey wore a white silk blouse with a simple strand of pearls, a black Pendleton worsted wool straight skirt, and black leather pumps. She was still nervous about her appearance and asked me, "Is this outfit okay?" I assured her she was dressed appropriately.

"However, if you had worn the rattiest skirt in your closet, Chloe might have sprung for a new wardrobe. It worked for me." We were still laughing when Chloe and Janice joined us at the restaurant bar. They sat on either side of us and ordered drinks. I hadn't seen them arrive, since my back was to the door, and now my attention was focused on them. I was not prepared when two strong arms lifted me out of my chair.

I struggled to gain my balance and then tried to turn to indignantly face my accoster. It was Manny, wearing that wide, impish grin that always melted my heart.

Dramatically, he turned my shoulders to face him, firmly planting my feet on the floor before releasing me. Then, in an even more dramatic display, he bowed and presented me with my favorite fresh-cut flowers—daisies—wrapped in tissue paper.

When I leaned toward him to take the flowers, I smelled the earthy fragrance of the flowers mingled with his clean, masculine scent of soap and shampoo. He bent down and kissed me on the lips—right in front of everyone!

"Did you think I was still in Milan?" he asked with mirth.

Chloe interrupted. "Janice and I had to solemnly promise not to mention Manny's name this afternoon. He didn't want anything to spoil his grand entrance this evening."

Typical Manny—always wanting to be in control, including waving to the maître d' to show us to our table and ordering a bottle of Dom Pérignon champagne. "This is a night to celebrate. I'm finally in the same city with the woman I love," he proclaimed loudly. Chloe shook her head at the announcement. Janice didn't blink an eye, and Lindsey had a look of bewilderment.

After we each had a glass of champagne, Chloe excused Manny, explaining it was a business meeting. As Manny got up to leave, he gave me a hug and said, "Marilyn, I'll see you later this evening."

Realizing I was embarrassed, Chloe apologized for Manny. "I don't know what gets into him. Perhaps one day he'll grow out of his 'bad boy' behavior, but I'm not counting on it."

Chloe and Janice ordered appetizers but declined dinner, pleading jet lag. "We'll talk tomorrow when we're not so tired," Chloe said. "I'll arrange for dinner and drinks on my credit card. You two stay and order a nice dinner."

As soon as they left, Lindsey demanded a full explanation. "My God, tell me about this guy Manny!" We talked about my favorite topic until after ten. I expected Manny to be waiting outside my apartment, but I was disappointed. No Manny and no note on the door. I couldn't help myself. I wondered if he wanted to spend the night with me or if that scene in the restaurant was staged for shock value.

I got to the office early the next morning so I would be ready to review all the orders for the C&J and Bourne Innocence lines placed with specialty shops and department stores. Our analysis for the past six months showed that our clothing lines had positive sales, but the watch business was clearly not meeting our projections. And even though we hadn't discussed watches at the restaurant, I knew Chloe would expect me to suggest some strategies for improving watch sales.

Lindsey arrived shortly after I entered the office, and we began to work on our presentation. Chloe and Janice arrived promptly at 9:30 a.m. They seemed pleased with past sales results and future orders. However, they offered no encouragement when I began to present our ideas for the watch business. And that lack of response made me uneasy.

Finally, Chloe stopped me in mid-sentence and said she and Janice had talked things over and decided Toni must come to New York to evaluate the watch business to see if he felt there was a market for it. If he decided yes, he'd design a marketing plan. "After his analysis," Chloe said, "we'll be in a better position to decide if watches will be a profitable addition to our fashion lines."

Perhaps I should have anticipated this scenario. It would have made my disappointment less intense. I felt my professional opinion and work had been discounted. I closed the folder on the plan Lindsey and I had so diligently compiled and simply said softly, "I understand."

Chloe quickly changed the subject. "Now it's time to show you girls the new lines we'll be introducing for spring during Fashion Week. We're very excited that we'll be sharing the stage with such prominent designers as Oleg Cassini and Coco Chanel." Janice opened a portfolio with the design drawings.

Lindsey was both impressed and thrilled with the designs and began enthusiastically peppering Chloe and Janice with questions.

Still smarting from the rejection of the watch line suggestions and dreading Toni's arrival in New York, I remained painfully silent. I knew Manny would be livid when he learned Toni was coming to New York and would probably be monopolizing my time once again.

I recovered my composure and contributed to the discussion

about designs and sales potential. We were so engrossed in the numbers that we almost forgot to break for lunch. When hunger overtook us, Lindsey ran to the corner deli for sandwiches and coffee, and we worked until 5:00 p.m., breaking only because we needed to rest before dinner at 8:00 p.m.

After dinner, Lindsey and I walked to our apartments together, since our flats were not far from each other. She was bowled over by Chloe and Janice, repeating over and over, "I can't believe how lucky I am to be working for such elegant and worldly businesswomen."

Although I couldn't share her enthusiasm at that exact moment, I did appreciate her excitement. Not too long ago, I too had that same impression of these two women. Of course, my current view was colored by Manny's observations about how charismatic and controlling his mother was. He repeatedly warned me that I should be careful because once she had me in her spell, I'd be putty in her hands.

After Lindsey and I parted, I reviewed the day. My common sense told me Chloe had the right to bring Toni to New York. But my professional pride was wounded because she hadn't consulted me before making that decision. Instinctively, I knew I could not share my feelings with Lindsey, but I wanted to tell Manny about this situation. I was sure he'd counsel me wisely on how to handle this turn of events.

As I turned onto the block with my apartment building, I suddenly remembered Joseph's request that I ask Chloe to visit Rockport alone before she and Janice had to return to Milan. But since my attitude toward her was so negative, I decided to wait until later in Fashion Week before I broached that sensitive subject. My attitude needed one big adjustment—and I was about to get it!

Arriving at my apartment shortly after 10:00 p.m., I looked up and saw a light in my window. Manny had found the key I'd hidden for him! I raced up the stairs and opened the door, flinging myself at him. We embraced passionately and began the disrobing ritual—awkwardly at first, and then seductively. He gently pushed me onto the bed and began to undress me, beginning with my shoes and stockings. I unfastened his belt and unbuttoned his jeans, and as I unzipped his pants, I realized how hard he was. He laid me back on the bed, and we made love. It felt both magical and familiar.

During the night, he whispered over and over in my ear how much he had missed me and how much he loved me. Our love-making trumped my anger, and the stress of the day melted with each kiss.

Manny was up first the next morning. I heard him rummaging in the cabinets looking for coffee. I stretched between the bedcovers and waited for his plaintive request. "Marilyn, where the hell is the coffee?"

Flippantly, I answered, "At the deli." He scolded me for not having any food in the apartment. I had my answer ready. "Who needs food? Much better to shower together, dress, and go out for a big breakfast."

I took him to a neighborhood café, promising him that he'd have the best croissants and jam in New York City. Over coffee, Manny chided me about my relationship with Chloe. "She still controls your life, even though she lives on a different continent. I've given you fair warning. She's a master puppeteer who pulls the strings to get those around her to do as she pleases."

When he paused for breath, I jumped in and asked him about the Rockport trip. "Your dad wants me to talk to Chloe about visiting Joe, Grace, and the baby without Janice. What do you think I should do?"

Manny responded quickly, "Nothing. It's not your responsibility.

I'll talk to her. However, I'm sure she'll say she's too busy to take the time to visit them this trip."

When we got up from the table, Manny kissed me goodbye first on the tip of my nose and then on my lips. "I'm off to buy groceries to fill your pantry so you will not die of starvation in your apartment," he quipped.

CHAPTER 66

The rest of the week went smoothly. We focused on the C&J and Bourne Innocence lines, and Chloe and Janice accompanied us to several successful meetings with buyers and shop owners.

Of course, the highlight of their visit was the fashion show. Chloe and Janice looked as if they should be on the runway, not seated beside it. They were showstoppers in their elegant outfits.

Lindsey had bought a new C&J outfit for the occasion. She told me she had never felt so good about the way she looked, but confessed it set her back two months in salary, even with her discount.

I wore one of last year's C&J dresses. It was perfect for the show and the cocktail party that followed. During the party, Chloe and Janice introduced Lindsey and me to other designers. It reminded me of some the functions I had attended with Toni in Milan and Zürich.

I knew Lindsey's reaction to all the glamor was the same as mine when I was first introduced to Chloe and Janice's world. It was exciting and new—like a dream come true. However, now I knew how superficial that world could be. I kept wishing this evening was over and I was back in my comfortable little apartment with Manny.

When Manny came to my apartment later that evening, he told me he'd asked Chloe to visit Joe and his family in Rockport before returning to Milan. As he'd predicted, her response was that she didn't have time. She said she planned to send Joe the money to bring his family to Milan to visit her.

"Marilyn, I almost exploded at her dismissive response. I reminded her of Joe's pressing responsibilities on the farm, thinking that might convince her to change her mind and her flight reservations, but her response was clipped and calloused. All she said was, 'Manny, it's not my fault Joe chose farming in a backwater town so far from New York. It's just not convenient for me to travel to Kentucky now.'"

Manny was clearly upset over this exchange. "Marilyn, I tried to convince Mother to visit Joe, but she was unwavering. But don't worry, you're off the hook with Dad. I told him everything about her reaction." I just shrugged. There was nothing else I could do or say. I was just glad to be home with Manny, lying next to him in my bed.

On Chloe and Janice's last day, they came to the office with two huge boxes—one for me and one for Lindsey. "You both earned these," Chloe said. "It's our way of saying thank you for working so hard on our behalf."

Lindsey opened her box first, throwing the tissue paper aside and then uttering an ear-piercing, Christmas-morning squeal of delight. "Oh, my God! Oh, my God, look at these clothes. All of them just my size. Oh, my God."

Chloe and Janice beamed at her reaction. "We want you girls to look your best when you're representing the company." I couldn't help smiling at Lindsey's unbridled enthusiasm, remembering how excited I had been when I received my first clothes from Chloe and Janice. Although my reaction to the new clothes was more restrained, I still was touched by the gift and conveyed that feeling to Chloe and Janice.

Once Chloe and Janice were safely on the plane, I began to concentrate on my next challenge—preparing for Toni's arrival—and fulfilling an obligation before his arrival. I had promised Mama I'd visit once a quarter, so I ducked into a travel agency on my way home and purchased a round-trip ticket for the next weekend.

I'd explain to Manny this evening why I had to leave so abruptly. I was sure he'd understand. I was just as sure he wouldn't like the news that Toni would soon be coming to New York.

CHAPTER 67

Flying home for the weekend, I was relieved Beth was alone when she picked me up at the Nashville Airport to drive me to Rockport. It gave us an opportunity to talk openly about Mama's startling childhood revelations. If Mama wanted to resume her story, we agreed that we would listen carefully and support her. But it was her call to bring up the subject.

Beth quickly turned the conversation to New York, demanding to know the details of my love life.

"Who has time for romance?" I said. "My work is so demanding that I don't have time for a social life, much less romance."

My summation didn't satisfy Beth. "Marilyn, at your age, you should be looking for a life partner. Is Manny still in the picture?"

"Manny is now living with his father in New York."

That revelation brought a quick retort from her. "I bet that's going to last about a month."

I bristled and immediately jumped to his defense. "Manny is planning to open a music store in the Village. He's a very talented musician and can't wait to open his own shop. Dr. Bateson gave Manny the same amount of money he gave Joe to buy our farm."

But secretly, I agreed with my sister's quick assessment—Manny's follow-through record was dismal.

I felt Beth wasn't going to drop the subject, but I wasn't prepared when she turned toward me, smiling wickedly. "You're in love with Manny, aren't you?"

I hesitated for a minute before answering her. "You know Manny and I have always had an intense relationship—it's definitely an approach-avoidance connection. But like you, I question his reliability. Is he marriage material? I don't know. This match would not be smooth—or as stable and reliable as the relationship you have with Frank. When I consider my future, I do ask myself if I'm in love with him and, even more importantly, if I could live with him for a lifetime."

That confession ended our conversation. We pulled into Mama's driveway, and Beth dropped me off. She told me Mama was teaching at Cannon High School and I'd be relieving Maria's caregiver until she came home.

As soon as I opened the door, Maria started laughing and reaching out to me. Words were not necessary. Her joyous laughter and radiant face clearly showed how happy she was to see me. However, when I saw her animated face, I felt guilty. Why hadn't I made time for a visit before now? My last visit had been at Easter in April. Too long!

I passed the time just sitting near Maria and holding her hands, but as soon as I heard Mama's car, I rushed outside. She gathered me in her arms, hugging me for a long time. "Oh, Marilyn, I hope you've set aside time for a long visit."

"I'm sorry, Mama, but I only have four days before I absolutely must get back to the fashion rat race," I said. "But I promise every moment here will be family focused."

I could tell Mama had hoped for more time, but she only said. "That's grand. I'm always afraid you're letting your work absorb you completely. It's so important that you don't neglect other relationships."

She and Beth had been conspiring to probe into my life options during this visit. I got the feeling their assessment of my career priority—often at the expense of family and friends—would be a conversation topic during the next few days.

Beth joined us that evening, and we only touched briefly on the importance of relationships during dinner. The three of us cleared the table and then shared the dishwashing chore—Mama washed, Beth dried, and I put away, just as we had done growing up. As Mama was wiping her hands on her apron, she said, "Let's get started. I think I left off where Daddy and Rachel had gotten married."

Beth and I nodded in agreement, and then we sat side-by-side on the couch covered with the quilt Mama had on the back of the sofa. Mama pulled up her straight-backed chair and faced us.

"After only two years, their marriage began to sour. Their daily quarrels always ended with Daddy grabbing his liquor bottle, slamming the back door, and heading to the barn to be alone and brood.

"Walter, Clara, and I tried to stay out of the way. We spent most of our time outside, as far from the house as possible, until dark. Then we headed in for a quick supper before retreating to the safety of our bedroom. My siblings were my responsibility. I was the one who cooked our meals, packed our lunch boxes, did my homework, and checked theirs. I made sure everyone bathed each night so jumping into our school clothes the next morning was easy. I didn't want to risk waking Daddy or Rachel.

"Walter was in first grade, and Clara and I no longer left him unprotected at home. He was so happy to leave each morning with us after we ate breakfast—a cold biscuit and jam. We rarely fought like other children. I guess our home life was so unsettling we knew we had to band together.

"Since Daddy and Rachel were usually asleep when we left for school, we could begin our day pleasantly. But in the evenings, Daddy seemed to be coughing a great deal, which brought back memories of my mother's illness and her persistent cough. After each coughing seizure, I pressed him to see a doctor, but he always said he felt okay and that I shouldn't worry. Then one day, I heard him coughing in the barn, and it seemed to be strangling him. It brought phlegm to his mouth. He pulled out his handkerchief to spit it out and, even though he quickly stuffed it back into his dungaree pocket, I saw blood on it. Still he kept telling me not to worry, that it was just a bad cold and he'd be fine in a day or two.

"But it didn't get better, and he continued to cough deeply and often. When I helped with the laundry, I saw more and more bloodstains on his handkerchiefs. He was spending more and more time in bed, and Rachel had stopped arguing with him.

"She was nicer to him, making potato soup, his favorite, and taking it to him if he said he didn't want to get up. If Walter got too loud, she'd scream at him to be quiet and quit running through the house. Just to be mean, she'd add, 'Do you want to kill your daddy with all that noise?'

"That always upset Walter, and he'd come crying to me, sobbing uncontrollably and saying Daddy was dying and it was his fault. I'd comfort him and tell him Rachel was just being mean as usual. In just a few weeks, Daddy died in bed. Rachel found him and ran from their bedroom raving like a crazy woman. We were terrified and huddled together in a corner of the living room. She composed herself enough to demand that I go to a neighbor's house for help. 'Tell them your daddy just died and we need the funeral director to come at once,' she wailed.

"It was late summer and very warm, but my insides turned to ice when Rachel announced his death. My teeth were chattering by the time I got the neighbor's house. All I could think of was getting back home. I'd left Clara in charge of Walter, and they were cowering in our bedroom, weeping softly in fear and confusion, when I left.

"The next few days were a blur. Daddy was laid out at home, just like Mama. Rachel keened and carried on until people coming for the wake could not stay in the room with her. The funeral was at the Baptist Church, and Daddy was buried next to Mama.

"Again, Clara, Walter, and I were not allowed to attend the funeral, but we heard people talking about how Rachel threw her body across the casket and tried to keep them from lowering it into the grave. Even as a child, I recognized Rachel's hypocrisy. I was mystified at how Rachel could have been so mean to Daddy when he was alive and act so distraught at his death.

"Instinctively, we three children knew Rachel would not want to continue to be our stepmother. I was ten, Clara was eight, and Walter had just turned six, and we had no idea what was next in our life. We just wondered what would become of us."

Although Mama never shed a tear as she recounted her childhood, Beth and I were teary-eyed. Mama appeared stoic, as if she was detached from all the sadness. Then she suddenly exclaimed, "I'm very tired and think I'll go to bed."

I walked Beth to her car. Both of us were sobbing, and we hugged each other tightly for several moments, as if trying to draw strength from each other. I said, "Mama's childhood was horrible. No wonder she has kept her emotions under wraps—must be a survival technique."

Beth replied, "Mama was the oldest, and we've seen how she was affected. Lord knows the scars that Aunt Clara and Uncle Walter carry from this ordeal."

That was our last conversation about Mama's childhood during my visit—as if the curtain had come down on a second act in a theatrical drama. The next morning, it was clear Mama was finished recounting her girlhood struggles for now and wanted to move on to more pleasant things. I was glad to have this insight into her past, yet couldn't help feeling regret that my questioning had opened this "Pandora's Box," forcing Mama to confront these early memories. But at least now Beth and I understood why she had so carefully hidden her upbringing from her children.

CHAPTER 68

With my Rockport visit over and Chloe and Janice back in Milan after Fashion Week, Lindsey and I went into high gear to wrap up purchase orders and confirm deliveries for the C&J and Bourne Innocence spring/summer lines. Our fall/winter lines of both brands had continued to gain market share, and we'd been sending positive weekly reports to Milan.

"I'll never get used to working on the spring/summer lines in the fall and the fall/winter lines in the spring," Lindsey muttered. Every day, I was more impressed at her performance. She'd proved to be a quick sturdy and was efficiently running the day-to-day business operations of both brands, as well as quickly learning the fashion design lingo. Her organizational skills were always in overdrive, and that allowed me to concentrate on trying to jump-start the lagging watch business. I aggressively began calling on jewelry store owners to personally show them our watch product lines and answer any questions.

The watch plan I'd developed with Lindsey for Chloe and Janice—the one they had chosen not to review—was a helpful guide. I used it to set goals so I would know exactly what I needed to do to increase our watch sales by year's end. I chose to act as if I were totally in charge of the New York watch business.

Lindsey finally asked, "Why in the world are you breaking your neck on the watch line? Isn't Toni, 'The White Knight from Zürich,' supposed to ride into town to save the day here in New York?"

Her sarcasm jolted me back to reality. I had to admit I had an ulterior motive for working so feverishly on the watch business. Secretly, I wanted to show Toni we didn't need him to magically develop the New York market. I'd also procrastinated about telling Manny that Toni was coming to New York. I didn't want to spoil the idyllic period we were experiencing in our relationship. The mention of Toni's name always sent Manny into a jealous rage, which I understood perfectly. I just didn't want to deal with it right now.

Not only were things with Manny going well in New York, but he also began prodding me to plan a long weekend trip to Rockport to visit family and friends. He reminded me that when I had returned from there in September, I'd vowed to go back soon. "Let's shoot for early November, before the snow season," he said. I finally caved in and wrote Mama to tell her Manny and I would be coming on November first but wouldn't need a ride from Nashville. Manny would rent a car.

When I called Mama to confirm the specifics of our Rockport getaway, she warned me she wanted to hear how Manny and I were doing as a couple. "I promise Beth and I won't take notes on your romance, but we want details," she girlishly giggled. Then she turned serious. "And Marilyn, I hope you and Beth give me another session with just the two of you. I do want to share my childhood memories with you. I want you both to understand me."

After I hung up, my first thought was that I didn't need another depressing session with her. I was already deflated emotionally from my heavy workload. Then I chided myself. *How selfish! After all, I was the one who urged her to share her childhood with Beth and me.* I remembered how in the past, she'd always been so guarded, never giving us details about her early years. Now she apparently believed we had every right to know her as a person as well as our mother.

When Manny and I boarded the plane for Nashville, he was giddy with excitement about our Rockport adventure. I instinctively knew I had to dial down my work stress and concentrate on a fun time with Manny and my family. The next three days were theirs.

Manny dropped me off at Mama's house and came in to say hello before going to Joe's house. Mama hugged him as if he were her own son—or maybe a future son-in-law. Manny's face lit up like a Christmas tree as he hugged her back and kissed her cheek. This spontaneous embrace of my two favorite people touched me profoundly.

"Manny, stay for dinner with us," Mama insisted. "You need to put a little weight on those bones," she chided as she pinched his cheek. Manny laughed and patted his stomach, assuring her that not eating enough was not one of his problems.

"Joe and Grace have dinner planned for me, so I'd better be shoving off before they wonder what happened to me," he said, giving Mama a farewell peck on the cheek. As he started out the door, he turned and winked at me. Typical Manny!

Mama had planned the weekend, and before dinner, she spelled out her itinerary for my visit. "Tonight, Marilyn, I want to hear all about your life and career in New York. And you'd better not leave out the details of your love life," she teased. "Tomorrow, Beth is coming to dinner, and we'll have another one of our family chats."

After we finished the dinner, I launched into an account of my life in New York—starting with work and ending with the limited time I shared with Manny. By 10:00, I was uncontrollably yawning. "It doesn't take long for me to relax when I'm home," I said. "Please excuse me, but I'm going to head on up to bed to get needed sleep. I'll see you in the morning."

I fell asleep that night at Mama's totally relaxed. As I dozed off, my last thought was that just being at home was so therapeutic.

CHAPTER 69

The next night, Mama put Maria to bed while Beth and I cleaned up the dinner dishes. We then settled into our regular seating pattern in the living room and waited for Mama to continue her story. She began after her father's funeral.

"Within a week of Daddy's death, Rachel told Clara, Walter, and me that she would not be able to take care of us. She said Daddy's last will and testament left the house and farmland to her, but we couldn't stay there, and someone was coming in the morning to take us to a better place.

"Walter started to cry, and I ran to comfort him. I kept saying everything would be okay—that we'd stick together, just like always. Clara jumped up and got right in Rachel's face. She screamed that our daddy would not want us to leave our home, and if anyone should leave, it was Rachel.

"Rachel drew back her hand and slapped Clara hard across her face, sending my sister reeling across the floor. As Clara put her hand to her stinging cheek, Rachel laughed, an evil, evil laugh and said daddy had never given a flip about who would take care of us if anything happened to him.

"I pulled Clara and Walter away from her wrath and cruelty,

and we scurried upstairs to my bedroom, our only safe haven from Rachel's meanness. We sat on the bed holding each other and weeping in fright. We were so confused and fearful and had no idea what would happen to us. As the oldest, I tried to comfort my sister and brother, telling them that it would be okay. I kept saying, 'This is good news. At least we won't have to live with that lazy devil-woman, Rachel.'

"Rachel followed us to our bedroom, pounding on the door and screeching that we should stop that wailing and do something useful, like pulling together all our personal belongings to take to our new home. She said the people to take us away would come early in the morning, and we would be attending a different school.

"Her words were chilling to me because I knew it was unlikely anyone would take in three children. I tried to keep my face as expressionless as I could. I didn't want Clara and Walter to see my apprehension and fear. I told them we needed to get busy so we'd be ready in the morning. It didn't take long to assemble the things we held dear to us.

"Our meager piles consisted of a few clothes, one pair of shoes each, and a special toy. Clara clutched her doll, and Walter held his red truck. I packed my small book collection, a gift from the librarian when they were discarded to make room for new books at the public library."

When she spoke of packing to leave, Mama began to cry. I squeezed Beth's hand for support. "Mama, you don't have to go on," I pleaded.

But she just shook her head. "No, you need to know. I need to tell you.

"I want you girls to know everything about my early childhood. You'll see from my story why Daddy and I worked so hard to give you girls the loving, safe, and happy childhood every child deserves."

Beth took the quilt we were sharing and wrapped it around Mama's shoulders like a shawl. Mama was rocking back and forth, trying to soothe herself. Again, I pleaded with her not to continue her story. We hated to see her so upset as she remembered her troubled past.

Finally, she collected herself, gained her composure, and continued speaking very softly. "Clara, Walter, and I awoke early that next morning, but we were afraid to go down to the kitchen to get something to eat. We just put our personal belongings on the bed and waited for them to be packed in suitcases. Then we sat in a circle in the middle of the bedroom awaiting our fate, like convicted criminals going to the gallows.

"Hearing the sound of tires on the gravel road in front of our farmhouse, we ran to the window. A black car had pulled into our dirt driveway, and a man and woman got out and walked toward the door. He had on a black overcoat, and his hat was pulled down over his eyes. The woman was so obese that her dark brown coat didn't button across her stomach. I'd never seen either of them before.

"Rachel let them in, and they began talking. We strained to hear what they were saying, but their words were muffled. Then they started up the stairs. Our hearts were pounding, and we cowered in the corner. Rachel opened the door, and the man and woman stood behind her. She introduced them as Mr. Olan Jordan and Mrs. Eula McAteer, adding that these were the nice people who would take us to a better place to live.

"In a sweet, sugary voice—one we'd never heard her use before—she told the man and woman how much she wanted to keep us precious children, but she didn't have enough income to provide for us. Then she took a handkerchief from her apron pocket and covered her face, feigning sobbing.

"We were amazed and horrified at her act. Clara and I looked at one another in total disbelief. Then, to my surprise, Clara jumped up, ran to Rachel, and kicked her in the shin, screaming, 'Liar, liar. You hate us.'

"Rachel dropped the handkerchief, exposing her dry-eyed face, now contorted in pain. We drew back, wondering what fury she'd unleash, but she kept up her deceptive act of a grieving stepmother for the visitors. She just brushed her eyes with the back of her hand and struck a sorrowful pose before she began putting our belongings into some brown sacks and boxes that were outside the door. I noticed she was careful to keep each pile separate. Then we all went downstairs to get in the big car. The man opened the trunk and put our belongings into it. As we drove away, I knew we were seeing our farm for the last time—and I hoped it would be the last time we ever saw Rachel."

Beth and I were both in tears, but Mama remained in total control of her emotions. "Please Mama," I begged, "you don't need to go on."

She responded quickly—and firmly. "Yes, I do need to go on. I need to get this sadness out of my mind and heart." Beth and I were silent. This was a Mama we had never seen.

"Listen to me, girls. The next time you think some petty, little problems in life are too much to handle, just think of what my siblings and I faced at this juncture in our young lives. Because of all I had to endure growing up, your Daddy and I did everything in our power to protect you girls from hardships in your growing-up years. You always knew you were loved."

The mask that Mama had always worn to hide her feelings was gone, and she soldiered on, continuing her heartbreaking tale. "The three of us sat as close as we could in the back seat of the big, black car. We didn't know these people and had no idea where they were taking us. But I didn't believe it was to a better place. I was sure we would be split up and that this car ride would be the last time we would be together as children.

"After what seemed like a long drive, the car stopped in front of a large, old, stone building. Over the front door, carved in the moss-covered stone, were the words 'Thompson Orphanage.' I couldn't believe this was happening. Clara screamed to the man and woman in the front seat that she was not going to an orphanage. Walter looked at me and asked, 'What's an orphanage?' Before I could answer, the back doors of the car opened on each side. The man helped Walter out of the car; the fat lady carried the sobbing Clara and, in a threatening tone, told me to stay in the car.

"I can still see Clara kicking and screaming as the fat lady dragged her into the building. Walter had begun to cry, too, and he kept turning around waiting for me to join them as the man pulled him into the building. In a few minutes, the man came back to the car for Walter's box and bags and then returned for Clara's belongings.

"That was my last remembrance of my little sister and brother. I wouldn't unite with them until years later, when they were released from the orphanage to live on their own. Clara was eighteen, and Walter was sixteen.

"As you know, I was sent to live with Aunt Myrtle. She volunteered to raise me, but didn't have the ability or stamina to take in Clara and Walter. And I've always had pangs of guilt that Aunt Myrtle could take me in, but not my sister and brother."

Mama's face softened as she continued her story. "I guess you can understand why your Aunt Clara is so feisty. I know she must have given them a fit in that orphanage. At least, I hope she did.

"Your Uncle Walter was such a sweet-natured and gentle little boy. But he changed. I guess what he endured in that orphanage at such a tender and impressionable age soured him for life. When he became a teenager, he turned to alcohol, like our father. It must have been his way to self-medicate the internal pain. And like our daddy, he never could shake his alcoholic habit. It was the only thing that let him escape from his sadness, if only temporarily. I know you girls are aware that sweet Uncle Walter died from his alcohol addiction—his coping mechanism—with cirrhosis of the liver."

Abruptly, Mama stood up, stretched her arms, and then took her straight-backed chair to the corner. Beth and I were relieved. We knew that act meant she was finished with her story for the night. She folded the quilt, making sure the edges and corners were perfect, and placed it exactly as she wanted it on the back of the sofa.

Mama was a perfectionist. Beth and I had often joked about it. Now I realized it was her coping mechanism. Her way to be in control of herself. Uncle Walter had had his alcohol. Aunt Clara had her scrappy personality. Mama had her spring-cleaning. How many times had Beth and I wondered why neither of us had inherited "Mama's spring-cleaning gene"?

Her cleaning ritual began by taking down all the curtains and window treatments, cleaning the windows, and painting the woodwork before putting everything back. She scrubbed the hardwood floors and then waxed them to a high polish. She emptied all the cabinets and washed all the items before replacing them. Each year, she added something to the spring-cleaning tradition.

After Beth went home, Mama read the Bible aloud to me, and I joined her for her nightly prayers. When we went to our bedrooms, I strongly suspected that she, like me, would have a difficult time falling asleep after our emotional roller coaster ride.

I lay in bed for a long time, reflecting on my growing-up years and trying to recall some of the traits and behaviors I had always found strange in Mama. Were her excessive cleanliness and insistence on order a psychological ramification of having to control her life to insure her survival? Was it a way to deal with a frightening and chaotic childhood?

I feel asleep thinking about the things in my life I could control and those things that were controlling me. *I know I have the courage to take risks and step out of my comfort zone. Yet, I resisted committing to a permanent relationship. I guess we all have our own hang-ups and personal obstacles. The trick is learning how to overcome them to gain maturity and make progress.*

CHAPTER 70

Manny arrived at Mama's early Monday to give us more than enough time to get the car back to the rental counter and catch our flight to New York. Typical Manny—he hugged and kissed Maria and Mama and then scarfed up a biscuit with honey before steering me out the door. I kissed Mama goodbye and said, "I'll be back home for Thanksgiving, my next big break from work. It's only a few weeks away."

Manny chattered all the way to the airport about his great weekend with Joe and his family, including his babysitting gig on Saturday. "She's adorable," he said. "I'm glad Joe and Grace got a chance to go to dinner and a movie, but mostly I'm glad for the time alone with my niece.

"I'm really envious of the life Joe's created for himself. Watching my little brother and Grace this weekend made me wonder why I wanted to open a music store in crazy New York. I grew up in New York and couldn't wait to get away, so why am I thinking of settling down there? Joe actually got the wheels spinning in my mind when he said he was surprised I hadn't considered relocating to Nashville—a musical mecca—even over New York City."

I was shocked and stunned at this declaration, but since we

were approaching the airport entrance in Nashville, I couldn't say anything. After we returned the car, checked in, and found the departure gate, we still had almost thirty minutes before boarding. Once we were seated, I questioned him about our conversation. "Manny, did I hear you correctly? Are you having second thoughts about opening your music business in the Village?"

He laughed the deep-throated laugh I'd come to associate with something unpleasant and almost crushed me in one of his signature bear hugs. "Wow, I did get your attention, didn't I?" Then he leaned back in his seat, locked his hands behind his head, and casually said, "What do you think, Marilyn? Could you adjust to living in Nashville after Milan and New York?"

What gall! I struggled to control my wrath before I answered him. "Have you ever considered how hard I've worked to establish myself in the fashion industry? You've always lived by the seat of your pants without much direction and certainly no dogged perseverance. You flunked out of Columbia Law School and drifted aimlessly until your father shipped you off to your mother in Milan so she could try to help you grow up.

"Meanwhile, I finished college and worked five years in Europe for your mother and Janice to establish my professional credentials and earn the opportunity to open a New York office for C&J and Bourne Innocence. Believe me, my professional path with them has never been easy! And when you arrived in Milan, I did everything in my power to encourage you in your music, including urging you to enroll in the University of Milan and get your music degree. I even backed you in your musical gigs there. Sometimes I had to work until dawn to finish my work after one of your late-night sessions. And I was supportive when your father, as usual, offered to set you up in a music store because you had proved yourself worthy."

By the end of my diatribe, Manny had dropped his casual pose, and there was no longer a smile on his face. His response was simple and direct. "Marilyn, you and I are so different. You're driven to prove yourself to everyone, especially yourself. I'm not. You have a passion; so do I—but mine is different. Despite our differences, I still think we make a great team. And I can't imagine my world without you in it. I only picked New York because you were there. I didn't give it much thought. Help me work through this tug-of-war between New York and Nashville. I can go either way. I've considered Joe's arguments for Nashville, but I value your insight as much as my brother's, so please give me your opinion. And whatever I decide, I want us to be together."

I was so relieved when our flight was called before I could answer. After we found our seats and clipped our safety belts, I turned to him. "I had another emotional weekend with Mama. I just can't think about your future for the music store and my place in those plans. I'm too exhausted and emotionally drained from the weekend—and your news isn't helping me."

He looked hurt, but I didn't care. I put my head back on the seat rest and closed my eyes, although I didn't get any rest. Instead, I found myself envisioning life in Nashville, close to my family in Rockport. Would living there be less stressful? Beth's life certainly seemed stress-free. My perception of New York City was that it was a place in which you constantly had to make order out of chaos. But the challenge of the city always made me feel alive.

When we got to my apartment, I told Manny to pay the cab and come upstairs so we could talk. His response was predictable. "I'll be glad to come up, but I bet we'll do more than talk." He grinned at me and laughed, trying to defuse the tension from the airport. I envied his ability to make major issues and raw emotions seem less significant.

"You go unwind. I'll get Chinese takeout for lunch," he said. As soon as he left, I called Lindsey to let her know I'd be in the office early the next day. She gave me a complete update on future orders and, just as I was about to hang up, added, "By the way, Chloe called about an hour ago and said to tell you Toni will arrive in New York this week." I thanked her, but all I could think was, *Why now?* Just one more worry, but one that would probably quickly move to the top of the pile.

Manny came back while I was on the phone, juggling the Chinese food and some fresh-cut daisies, which he put in a pitcher of water on the table. He said they would brighten my apartment and my mood.

He was being his most thoughtful self, laying the table with two colorful placemats, arranging the chopsticks and containers, and pulling a chair out for me. He'd already put the teakettle on the stove and, when it began to whistle, made two cups of Jasmine tea. We agreed to postpone any serious discussions until after lunch.

As soon as we finished eating, I asked Manny to explain his rationale for wanting to move his business to Nashville and be closer to Joe. I thought some of his thinking was "pie in the sky," but I wasn't about to throw cold water on his plans and dampen his enthusiasm. As I listened to him, I mentally considered his options before saying supportively, "I'll be glad to help you develop a business plan for opening a music shop in downtown Nashville."

Manny beamed and leaned forward. I held up my hand and said, "Wait, there's more." I wanted him to realize it wasn't going to happen without a serious commitment from him. "Your first step is to inform your dad about the new location. Nothing will happen unless he agrees to the change. And you'll have to make sure you can get out of the preliminary negotiations on the Village lease space. Thank goodness, you're not too far into planning details on the space and haven't selected a contractor."

I did my best to impress him with the number of steps necessary to prepare a comprehensive business plan for setting up a new business in a new location. Selfishly, I hoped the time it would take in brainstorming and research for the project would give me a reprieve and keep me—and Manny—from making any rash decisions.

Manny seemed content with my timetable, and I hated to risk upsetting him, but I had to tell him that Toni was coming to New York. I dreaded revealing that I'd known about this for weeks but had just never found the right time to tell him. I thought it might be better to talk about it in a public place, so I said, "Let's go for a walk and let our fried rice and egg rolls settle."

Neither of us spoke for the first few minutes. I was rehearsing my speech mentally, and when I looked up, we were passing my favorite café. I said impulsively, "Let's get an icy-cold drink. I'm parched from all that Chinese food." We took a table next to a window, so we could watch the street traffic, and ordered our drinks.

When the waitress left our table, I began by explaining how slowly the watch line was developing in New York and how disappointed Chloe was with the numbers. I told him Chloe and Janice had dismissed my business plan for increasing the business when they were in New York. "They didn't even look at the plan. And then Chloe surprised me and professionally offended me by saying she was sending Toni to New York. I've been doing everything I could to increase sales, so Toni wouldn't come, but it's not been fast enough to satisfy Chloe."

Manny slammed his hands down on the small, round table so hard that he knocked over his fountain glass of Coke. As I tried to mop up the liquid with napkins, he stood up abruptly and shouted at me, "I knew one day that son of a bitch would come back into your life. To hell with the watch business! He probably told Chloe the business needed him in New York. I know he still cares about you."

He continued, "So you kept this news from me for weeks.

Well, you're not the only one with a secret about Toni. One of my close Milan buddies wrote to me a few weeks ago that he saw Toni on a ski trip in Switzerland. Toni told him you'd soon be moving back to Zürich to work beside him in the watch business. Marilyn, are you blind or just naïve? Toni's convinced Chloe that only he can analyze the watch business in New York, but that's just a ploy to give him the time he needs to pursue you. He's not interested in watches; he just wants to whisk you off your feet and take you back to Zürich."

I blinked as Manny continued. "Chloe controls you in every area of your life. Don't you see that? You give her your best efforts, and what does she do? She slaps you in the face and sends Toni to do your work. Marilyn, I want to marry you and have children with you. I want us to move to Nashville and be near our family and friends. I want to raise our children there. I want our lives to be as authentic as Joe and Grace's. I want the life your family has."

Then he was silent, looking as if for the first time at the waitress who was helping to clean up the spill. He grabbed a towel and wiped his seat before he plopped down in the chair, exhausted. We sat in silence as the waitress took the soaked towels away and brought Manny another Coke.

When she left, I spoke in a very quiet voice. "Manny, I love you with all my heart. But there's another powerful force pulling on my heartstrings—my ambition. It drives me physically and emotionally. Right now, this ambition is a stronger force than any relationship.

"I can't abandon my work here in New York and move to Nashville because that's where you want to be—or think you want to be. Of course I know Chloe manipulates me. That's why I find it so difficult to work for her, and yet, working for her is my opportunity for professional advancement. I need her. And as a businesswoman, I understand and accept her decision to send Toni to New York. The watch business is not performing well. Toni is the expert in this field. He'll make it work or he'll shut it down.

"And on a personal level, don't forget I rejected Toni's marriage proposal. I haven't rejected yours."

Manny stood up, took my arm, and said forcefully, "Let's go." It was a silent walk back to my apartment.

CHAPTER 71

Toni arrived Thursday afternoon. I declined his offer to meet at his hotel, suggesting we meet at our office to review the past year's watch sales. I planned to present some data on the watch business, catch an early dinner, and then go our separate ways—keeping everything focused on business. I refused to consider the possibility that I was a little skittish about this first meeting.

I spent Thursday morning analyzing the past year's watch orders in the New York market. I'd already compiled a matrix of upscale jewelry shops in metro New York, what brands they carried, and which appeared to be our greatest competition and our best chance to gain market share.

I had surveyed our two largest accounts earlier, and my findings were not encouraging. The buyers thought our watches were overpriced and the designs boring—too conservative for their customers.

To confirm these findings, I sent Lindsey to Canal Street with orders to purchase some knockoff watches. "Be sure to get higher-end watches so we can study the design," I said emphatically. Her shopping expedition confirmed the buyer's criticism. For ninety-five dollars, she bought almost thirty watches. They had "Made in Japan" labels, and I suspected most wouldn't run after a week, but I was interested in their eye appeal, not the quality of the timepiece. I borrowed a display trick from high-end jewelers, and Lindsey and I stretched out a long, black velvet cloth to display the watches. We lined them up and used a desk lamp as a spotlight to highlight each watch individually. I wanted Toni to see all the different designs on the faces, hands, and bands of the watches.

Lindsey was wearing one of her brow-raising high-fashion outfits today in honor of Toni's arrival. She'd complemented her outfit with knee boots and chunky jewelry. The pièce de résistance to her ensemble was a large, knockoff watch that covered her wrist. "I bought this with my own money," she quickly assured me. "I just had to have it."

I laughed as I imagined her debating about the purchase and then giving in. However, I told her, "I think that watch on your wrist will send the wrong message. We're trying to promote our watches, not the appeal of a knockoff. Please put the watch on display with the others for Toni's inspection. And reimburse yourself from petty cash." I knew that wouldn't wipe out petty cash. The watch probably cost less than three dollars.

She looked a little crestfallen, so I complimented her on her enthusiasm. "You bring such energy and creativity to the business, whether it's our clothing lines or the watches. And you've been my lifesaver so many times during the past year. I could never have done this alone." Then I thought how Manny lifted my spirits after work. I couldn't exist without both of them in my life.

We had just added Lindsey's watch to the display when the downstairs buzzer sounded. I lifted the wall phone and caught my breath when I heard *"Buon pomeriggio"* in Toni's soft Italian accent. I pressed the button to open the door and then stood at the top of the stairs, peering over the handrail in front of our office. I watched him gracefully ascend the steps. He looked up at me, waved, and gave me his signature smile.

At the top of the stairs, he took me in his arms and kissed each of my cheeks, lingering much too long. I pulled away, somewhat shy with impressionable Lindsey looking on, and said, "Toni, I want you to meet Lindsey. She's been my amazing assistant this past year. Not only is she beautiful, but she's also smart, and her very high energy level keeps me motivated."

Toni extended his hand and pulled her close enough to kiss her on both cheeks. Lindsey, never at a loss for words, was suddenly speechless, and I smiled as her eyes flew wide open in this handsome man's embrace.

I directed Toni to the only comfortable chair in the office. "Please sit here. We call it the chair of honor because it's actually comfortable to sit in. Lindsey decorated the office on a pauper's budget," I said as Lindsey and I took the two desk chairs opposite him.

"She has a superb eye for color and design," he responded. Lindsey blushed. She couldn't take her eyes off Toni. And I remembered, a little too late, that I'd neglected to tell her how suave and charming Toni could be.

When Toni spotted the watch display, he asked, "Why do you have all these watches?"

I explained that Lindsey and I had tried to think of ways to illustrate how we'd worked with the watch line here in the city and also give him some idea of the problems we'd faced. "We have a full presentation for you, including this display, but perhaps we should just have a drink and an early dinner and tackle the presentation tomorrow morning, when you've recovered from jet lag," I said, keeping my tone as courteous—and impersonal—as possible.

"Wonderful idea. Nothing would please me more than to escort two beautiful women to dinner," he said, nodding to Lindsey and me and flashing that winsome smile. I looked over at Lindsey and could tell she was totally captivated—completely under Toni's very potent spell.

We walked to a small, quiet restaurant close to the office that was known for its exquisite seafood dishes and fresh vegetables. "You'll notice, Toni, I'm not steering you to one of our American-Italian restaurants to show you how we attempt your cuisine in this country," I said, laughing and touching his arm.

With Lindsey present as my shield, I felt I could relax. And after the three of us each downed two very dry martinis, we all relaxed. There was no sign of tension between Toni and me.

However, when I asked Toni about his mother, Zara, a shadow crept across his face. "Thank you, Marilyn, for inquiring about her. Sadly, she's not doing well. She requires twenty-four-hour care after suffering two more small strokes. She can't speak or use her hands. I shudder each time I think of her in that prison. She has no quality of life—just existence.

"She still lives with her sister, who often reads to her, and that seems to bring her peace. I've hired round-the-clock nurses for her. Even without speech, Mother can be demanding at times, so I'm very grateful my aunt is willing to share her residence with her under these depressing circumstances. I know it's a comfort for Mother to be with her sister."

Then, almost wistfully, Toni added, "She loved you and was so hopeful we would marry and live in the Zürich house that Father had designed and raise our family there. She loved that house so."

I felt Lindsey's leg press against mine under the table, sending a "girl code" to me. Leaning close to me, Toni said softly, "I wanted the same thing, you know."

Thank goodness, the mood was interrupted by the waiter with our dinners.

After dinner, Toni excused himself. "I'm exhausted. It was a long flight, and the best thing for me is to go back to the hotel and collapse," he said before flagging down a taxi. "I'll see you two tomorrow morning when I'm more rested," he promised.

Since it was still early, Lindsey and I decided to walk to our apartments. As soon as Toni's taxi was out of sight, Lindsey pounced. "You are crazy, really crazy, Marilyn White. You let that man get away?"

Lindsey spun around on the sidewalk, shaking her head from side to side and holding her hands up to the heavens as if in total disbelief, I laughed at my romantic protégée.

"Marilyn, he is the most handsome man I've ever seen. I could hardly take my eyes off him at dinner. If I were in your shoes right now, I'd marry him in a red-hot minute and live happily ever after just looking at him.

"Now I want all the details. What happened in Milan? Why didn't you accept his marriage proposal? Don't hold back now."

I began cautiously, "There were many reasons. Toni is connected to the hip with Chloe and Janice in many business dealings. His loyalty toward them goes way back. Those two women threw us together in a close working relationship, with Toni acting as my mentor. Like you, I was swept off my feet emotionally, and it was difficult to retain my professional balance because this close working relationship connected us personally and then romantically. I knew he had special feelings for me when he took me to Zürich to meet Zara, his mother. She was very dynamic, and I was just as fascinated with her as I was with Toni.

"Toni made himself vulnerable to me by sharing his sordid and sad past with me, especially his time as a university student and how he became alienated from his father when he dropped out of school. His drinking caused him to hit rock bottom, and he wound up as a janitor, sweeping floors in a fashion house.

"But he was smart, and after he finished sweeping, he studied the designs and learned to distinguish the characteristics of fabric. He really learned the fashion business from the ground floor up, and eventually, with help from a mentor who recognized his talent, he became a very savvy, sought-after fashion consultant with his own prominent firm in Milan."

I was about to continue when I realized I might be revealing too much about Toni. When we got to my apartment stoop, I ended the evening by saying, "You know, Lindsey, when a man shows weakness to a woman intentionally, it's a sign of trust and intimacy. I loved Toni but wasn't in love with him, and the more we saw one another, the more evident that became. Our relationship is complicated—and private. I'll see you tomorrow morning at the office."

Lindsey waved her hand goodbye and said, "I can't wait,"—almost as if she anticipated another installment in my story.

CHAPTER 72

I got to the office at sunrise the next morning. I wanted to flesh out our presentation before Toni and Lindsey arrived and derailed my train of thought.

Lindsey bounced in about fifteen minutes before Toni's scheduled arrival. She'd obviously dressed for Toni. Her outfit was strictly for the runway. "I'll have to sit most of the day. These three-inch heels look great, but they are definitely not made for walking. I keep wobbling," she explained. Looking at those red heels, I could only laugh and shake my head. I hoped Toni wouldn't ask her to bring him a watch.

"I set my alarm an hour early to get my outfit and makeup perfect for our presentation. What an Italian hunk! I just want him to know he's dealing with two contemporary fashion plates, not some novices." She giggled.

"You know, Lindsey, Toni is here to evaluate watches," I reminded her. Then I compared her outlandish outfit to my conservative sheath dress and thought we made a good team, representing fashion trends across the spectrum—just as we needed to do in the watch line if we wanted New York customers.

Toni arrived promptly at 9:00, looking as if he'd just stepped off the cover of *Esquire* magazine. Lindsey sat at her desk trying to catch my eye and, using another "girl code" by fanning her face with her hands, showing me her total approval of this soft-spoken, movie-star-looking man seated in our comfortable chair.

Toni looked at Lindsey and then me before he spoke. "Ladies, I know you've gone to a great deal of trouble to prepare this update on the watch market here in New York. I look forward to hearing your presentation."

I handed him a notebook chock-full of details, including information about the shops stocking our watch line, input from the shop owners on what they liked and did not like about our watches, and a rundown on our most serious competition. By the time we covered all that information, it was lunchtime. The three of us walked to a nearby deli for lunch, which I chose as much for the food as for Lindsey's footwear. I sat across from Toni in the booth, and Lindsey slid in next to him. Whenever she spoke to him, she unconsciously leaned toward him. I wondered if I had reacted the same way to his charms when I first met him.

When we returned to the office, I asked Lindsey to walk Toni through the knockoff watches she'd collected from Canal Street, explaining that this would allow him to see the latest designs in fashionable watches selling in the city. We worked as a team. As Lindsey described each watch, I spotlighted it with the desk lamp. When she lingered on the watch she had purchased for herself, I was careful to show no emotion, but I secretly laughed to myself. Lindsey really was a loveable "piece of work," and I was lucky to have her working beside me.

"Excellent presentation," Toni said, speaking directly to Lindsey. "I now have a real feel for the watch designs that are selling in New York. It was very clever of you to set this demonstration up for me."

Then he addressed me. "I need to get out on the street myself and visit some jewelry stores. Would you be my guide, Marilyn? You did such an exceptional job pulling all the data together in the notebook that I'm sure I'll be able to gain invaluable information through your contacts."

Lindsey looked crushed that she was not included in this field trip. I tried to soften her disappointment by suggesting, "Lindsey, how about meeting Toni and me for dinner at Michie's Bistro at eight tonight?"

Her face brightened, and she nodded in agreement, calling after us, "Have a terrific tour. I'll be here all afternoon holding down the fort."

As Toni and I walked toward Fifth Avenue and the three stores I wanted him to visit, he hooked his arm through mine in a most familiar way. Our conversation as we strolled along ranged from Chloe and Janice to his life in Zürich and my distress over his mother's condition. Four hours later, we had managed to interview three high-end jewelry store managers or shop owners.

"Marilyn, let's have a cocktail before we meet Lindsey for dinner."

There was a tiny moment of uncertainly before I heartily agreed with him. "I know just the place," I said.

I steered him to a small, quiet bar located within walking distance of the restaurant I'd chosen for dinner. After the bartender took our order, Toni reached across the small table and captured both my hands. "So much for business; now it's time for us to relax and enjoy one another," he said, oozing charm.

"You have no idea how much I have missed you since you left Milan," he began. "I could hardly believe what I heard when Chloe and Janice announced you would be going to New York. All I could think of was that we would no longer have wonderful chats and romantic times together in Milan or Zürich."

This was a perfect opening for me to finally question Toni

about something that had bothered me for some time. "Do you remember Chloe and Janice asking me if I would be interested in moving to Zürich to run their watch line there?" He bowed his head slightly and nodded sheepishly.

"Why in the world did you accept their offer and take the position yourself, knowing that I had been approached first? I would have moved to Zürich and been there when you set up your consulting business in your parents' home. That's what you planned to do after your mother suffered a stroke and moved to her sister's home—or at least, that's what I thought you planned to do. It would have been a perfect opportunity for you and me to be together and see how our relationship might have developed."

Before answering me, Toni took a long sip of his drink and leaned back in his chair. "Marilyn, when Chloe and Janice asked me to take over their watch business in Zürich, I knew they had asked you first, and I told them I wouldn't take the job away from you. But they told me that plans had changed and you would be moving to New York. You were no longer being considered for the Zürich position. That's why I accepted."

A rush of anger surged through me. Manny's warning about his mother flashed in my mind, and I realized how ruthlessly controlling and domineering she could be. And I knew she was dominating my life and would continue to do so as long as I allowed her to rule me.

I couldn't subdue the accusatory tone in my voice as I sat across from Toni. All I could think about was the many times I had wanted to call him and ask him the question I had just now asked him directly. But I had always stopped myself, rationalizing that Toni was not worth the cost of an international call.

"Did it ever occur to you that I would think your decision to take the position was a statement to me that the watch business was more important than our relationship? Why didn't you talk to me before you accepted their offer? At least then I would have known I meant something to you," I continued to rant. Toni remained silent during my tirade, looking down into his drink.

Then he lifted his head and looked into my eyes as he reached for my hands again. I pulled my hands from his as if I'd been scalded. I drew myself up, and with as much dignity as I could muster, I said emphatically, "Toni, we can be business colleagues, but I never want to rebuild a personal relationship with you. You hurt me irrevocably. I never believed the saying that 'Time heals all wounds,' but since moving to New York, I've learned it's true. I am very happy here with my work and my friends. I encourage you to move on with your personal life in Zürich."

A sense of release and relief washed over me. I had waited so long to say this to Toni, and now it was over. But my elation was short-lived as I succumbed to guilt, remembering how Toni had confided in me about his first love who had died, along with his unborn child, from an illegal abortion. That had triggered his withdrawal from the university and his alienation from his father. It had taken him years of destructive behavior to get over her death and the loss of their baby. I wasn't even sure if he was completely over all the emotional baggage that went with that chain of events.

My tone turned conciliatory. "I'm sorry I was so abrupt, but this has been bothering me since I left Milan. I'm glad you finally know how angry I was toward you and how hurt I was."

"I never meant to hurt you. Let me try to fix things between us," he begged. I heard the sincerity in his voice, but I couldn't respond. Instead, I looked at my watch and said, "Good grief, it's time to meet Lindsey. Toni, I think we should put this part of our lives behind us. Let's move on and build a supportive business relationship."

After Toni paid the bill, he turned to me and sadly said, "I'll try."

I was grateful that Lindsey was joining us for dinner because the mood lightened when she walked in. We brainstormed through dinner about ways to improve our watch sales. We also briefed Lindsey on the findings from our afternoon visits. By the time we finished dinner, I realized how physically and emotionally exhausted I was from our business visits and my conversation with Toni. Leaving Toni and Lindsey to enjoy a cup of coffee, I excused myself and headed to my flat.

I was just in time to answer my phone. It was Manny calling for reassurance. He badgered me for details and made snide remarks about my spending so much time with Toni. "I thought the watch business was his responsibility. Why does he need your help?"

At that point, my patience was as depleted as my energy. "Manny, I didn't know we had a contract that obligates me to report all my moves to you at the end of each day." The phone clicked as Manny hung up on me.

Waiting for a short time, I called Manny back to apologize for my rudeness and said, "Manny, this has been a rough working day, and my nerves are really frayed, but I shouldn't have taken it out on you. I left Toni and Lindsey at the restaurant because I was so exhausted. Lindsey is infatuated with him."

His response was simple and endearing. "Thanks for calling back, Marilyn. We'll talk tomorrow. I love you."

The next morning, Lindsey came into the office with a dreamy smile plastered on her face. "Toni is such a gentleman. We talked about the watch business, and I was so impressed at his knowledge. And you know what, Marilyn? I think I impressed him, too. He invited me to Zürich to study the watch business and learn about watch design and sales."

Remembering Chloe's cautioning me about "romantic Italian men" when I first met Toni, I felt I should repeat Chloe's warning to Lindsey, who paid no attention to me. Instead, she asked, "Do you think it would be possible for me to go to Zürich?"

I brought her back to reality by reminding her that Toni was in New York to evaluate the watch business. His findings would determine whether Chloe and Janice even continued with the line of watches in the States.

"Here's a file we need to study. It will help us deal with today's business; we'll talk about Zürich later," I said. I knew Lindsey's dream of going to Zürich would never materialize. Chloe was too shrewd a businesswoman to fly Lindsey to Zürich to study watches with Toni.

Toni came by the office about ten, and we made plans for the next week. He said he would be visiting friends in upstate New York for the weekend, which meant I could relax and recover over my weekend.

We met at the office on Monday morning, and Toni and I started our round of meetings. We'd scheduled many appointments with jewelry store owners and department store jewelry buyers every day. Toni, Lindsey, and I met for dinner each night and reviewed our day's progress. I excused myself as soon as we finished eating, leaving Lindsey and Toni to linger over coffee and liqueur. Neither seemed to mind.

When Toni returned to Europe, Lindsey was heartbroken. "He never said anything more about my coming to Zürich to visit him after that first night. I'll never see him again," she confided to me tearfully.

I didn't tell her I was relieved by his departure from both a work and personal standpoint. I'd neglected our clothing lines to devote time to the watch business, and that was risky. Fashion is a cutthroat business.

As the weeks passed, Lindsey continued to have a difficult time focusing on the day-to-day operations. She kept talking about Toni and how much she wanted to go to Zürich and spend time with him—and it was affecting her work and, in turn, mine. I needed her to focus. I was so aggravated at Toni. He had been disruptive during his time in New York, monopolizing our time and forcing us to concentrate on the watch business. Now he was gone, but the aftermath of his visit lingered.

I tried to corral Lindsey and get her focus back on her work responsibilities. Although both the C&J and Bourne Innocence lines had been selling steadily, we couldn't let our guard down. A competitive brand could replace us in a heartbeat, and I couldn't seem to impress that reality on Lindsey while she pined for Toni. And Chloe and Janice expected those relentless weekly reports to show a climb in sales each time. My days continued to be physically and mentally exhausting.

CHAPTER 73

After a particularly grueling day at work, the only thing I wanted to do was kick off my shoes, take a long, hot bath, and fall into bed. But as I opened my door, I heard soft guitar music and smelled the aroma of Italian food. Apparently, Manny had decided to use his key and make himself at home.

When I walked in, he stopped playing and smiled broadly. When I moved toward a chair, he patted the sofa and poured two glasses from the uncorked bottle of Chianti on the coffee table. As I sat down beside him, he raised his glass to salute me.

Nice gesture, but all I could think was, *Well, so much for my plans.* That relaxed evening alone had been trumped by Manny's plans for wine, music, and dinner. I also had a nagging question racing through my mind: *What's his real motive?*

"Tonight, I'm going to totally pamper you," he said. "Lean back, sip your wine, and let me remove your shoes, peel off those stockings, and give you a proper foot massage before dinner."

Lovely plan, but I was still suspicious and kept wondering, *When will the other shoe drop*? Of course, his offer was too enticing to refuse, so I scooted to the end of the sofa and put my feet in his lap. After the foot rub, we sat together, chatted about our day, and sipped our wine. "Don't move a muscle," he commanded. "It's time to sample my savory tomato and pasta concoction," he said over his shoulder as he went to the kitchen, returning quickly with two plates. Dinner was delicious, and I was beginning to feel guilty for my suspicions about his motives. Why couldn't I just believe he simply wanted to cook dinner and spend the evening with me?

I was feeling so comfortable as we cleaned up the kitchen dishes together that I almost confessed my suspicions. And that's when Manny said he wanted to discuss something serious, which involved me. I turned to face him, nodding my head in resignation, and said, "I should have known this wasn't a simple dinner—that there had to be another reason for this special evening."

He tried to mask the hurt from my comments and took a deep breath before continuing. "Marilyn, you know I've been toying with the idea of opening a music shop in Nashville instead of New York." Suddenly, the foot-dragging and finding fault with every location all made sense. He just didn't want to launch a New York shop.

"Dad's in total agreement, and he'll finance my operation there. He even thinks Nashville would be a perfect retirement spot when he decides to give up his practice. Plus, we'd be closer to Joe's family. Joe's really excited about the move and has already started looking for a good location for my shop."

Then he dropped to his knee, clasped my hands tightly, looked earnestly into my eyes and said, "Of course, you must come with me and be a part of my life there as my wife."

A marriage proposal! I must move to Nashville! What was he thinking? I jumped to my feet and began pacing, venting my anger. "Manny, did you even for one moment consider my feelings, what I would want to do, or where I would want to settle? You know how important my career is to me—and that means living in New York, not Nashville."

He sat quietly until, completely spent, I collapsed next to him on the sofa. He folded me in his arms and said softly, "Marilyn, what do you really want? Do you want my mother to rule your life and dictate what you must do?"

Before I could respond, he continued, "I thought I was more important to you than your work. All I wanted to do tonight was convince you that Nashville could be a wonderful beginning for our life together. And with our family members so close—it would be idyllic."

I was stunned. *Although he's never thought it important to discuss this plan with me, he had confided in his father and brother. Surely, he knew how important my career is to me? How could he have thought I'd just walk away from my life—a very together life in New York—to blindly follow him to Nashville?*

I slipped out of his embrace and walked to the door. "Manny, please leave." My request must have stunned him because he got to his feet quickly and walked through the door before turning and saying, "Marilyn, think about my proposal and then think about my mother's control over you. Ask yourself how much you actually do control your career." I slammed the door and collapsed on the sofa, sobbing uncontrollably.

I was emotionally exhausted from our evening and from the realization that our relationship might be over. I'd always expected to be with Manny eventually. Now I wasn't so sure. We were worlds apart in our thinking. I thought, *He should move to Nashville—or wherever he wants to go.* And I kept repeating to myself, *You're better off with him out of your life!*

When I finally finished my warm bath and fell into bed, I was completely exhausted. But sleep eluded me. Manny's proposal kept looping around my brain. There was little sleep for me.

CHAPTER 74

After Manny's infamous proposal, I filled my hours with work, work, and more work. Keeping busy, I thought, might give me time to make some rational decisions about my feelings for Manny. I also used work as an excuse to avoid seeing Manny. I was too busy to take his calls. Secretly, I hoped it would be easier to accept his absence if I distanced myself from him before he moved to Nashville. When we did see each other, Nashville was never mentioned, and our conversations were stilted and cautious.

Since I assumed Joseph would know about the rift between Manny and me, I was surprised when he called and invited me to dinner at his apartment. I expected Manny to be there and was a little apprehensive, but when I arrived, the table was set for two. The staff had prepared dinner but was gone by the time I arrived. I was uncomfortable but began to relax as we made small talk over dinner.

Then over coffee and dessert, Joseph said, "I'm sure you're wondering why Manny is not with us tonight." I nodded affirmatively. "I wanted to talk to you alone because I want to hear what you think of Manny's plans to move to Nashville. He told me you wouldn't be moving with him because your career is here in New York. Selfishly, I hope you'll reconsider.

"You've been such a positive influence on my son, and I'm grateful for that. I also know he's deeply in love with you. So, Marilyn, I have an offer I'd like you to consider." I squirmed in my chair as he continued.

"You know I've loaned money to Joe to buy your parents' farm and that I'm doing the same for Manny to purchase the Nashville music store. Since I look on you as the daughter I never had, I'd like to loan you the money to set up your own dress shop in Nashville."

Where did that come from? I needed a few minutes to process his offer and draft an answer that wouldn't seem rude or ungrateful. I was touched by his fondness toward me and had to acknowledge it was a generous offer.

He waited patiently while I took several deep breaths and then said, "Joseph, over the years, I've witnessed the close and endearing relationship you've developed with Joe and Manny. I respect you and appreciate your generous offer. However, I can't accept your loan. I'm happy with my career here in New York. One day, when I feel professionally ready to open my own business, I expect to arrange my own financing for it—wherever that may be."

Joseph looked down, studying his hands for a few seconds. I saw the hurt in his eyes as he apologized profusely. "I hope I didn't overstep my bounds in making my offer. It's just that Manny's happiness is paramount to me, and I know you care for him."

I smiled and reassured him that I was not offended. Then I got up and muttered something about the late hour and an early, busy day at the office tomorrow. At the door, I turned and said, "Thank you for dinner and your Nashville business offer, but I hope you understand why I can't accept your loan."

I raced home and my anger, this time directed toward Joseph, mounted with each step. His offer was a bribe. He had tried to buy me to keep his son happy in Nashville. I was already obligated to Manny's mother, Chloe; I didn't need to be indebted to Joseph too. What made the Bateson family think they could manipulate me with their wealth?

A note from Manny, slipped under my apartment door, sent me into another tirade. He wanted me to phone him when I got back from his father's dinner. I'd be damned if I'd call him tonight, or any other night, for that matter!

The next day at the office, Lindsey sensed my frustration but had no idea about the cause. "Good grief, Marilyn, you're racing through those orders and reports as if there was no tomorrow. What gives?"

"There are lots of things to get organized here," I snapped. "Chloe called before you came into the office. She and Janice are flying here at the end of this week after their business trip to Chicago," I peevishly complained. Secretly I thought, *Just what I need right now—another Bateson yanking me around.*

She didn't buy it and asked, "What's really the matter, Marilyn? You never get this upset over work." I didn't want to discuss the turmoil in my personal and professional life with the Batesons, so I apologized to her, pointing out how much we had to accomplish before Chloe and Janice descended on us.

I told her I was determined to be prepared for Chloe and Janice's arrival. I hinted that it was a matter of pride and then quickly said, "I need you to focus on these items because I have to focus on the watch business." Lindsey nodded and said she'd work as many hours as necessary. "You're the best—no wonder our customers love dealing with you," I said. She grinned and then dived into her assignments.

Lindsey was very good with people; she was just so likeable. However, she was weak in financial planning—really her only shortcoming—and that was my area of expertise. We were a good team. For the next several days, we both came early and stayed late. When Chloe and Janice arrived, we were ready. We had a complete review of our business activities and were sure we could answer any questions they raised.

Chloe and Janice breezed into our office, still glowing. They couldn't stop talking about their successful Chicago trip. They'd met with specialty shop owners and buyers for large department stores. Everyone had been impressed at the two fashion lines. We got a brief outline, and then Chloe said, "We can discuss this trip in detail over dinner. Meet us at the Rainbow Room at eight." As usual, Lindsey's level of excitement over the dinner invitation was much higher than mine. I suspected there was an underlying reason for dinner at a premier New York restaurant.

Chloe and Janice were very gracious throughout dinner. They talked about the business in Europe and New York, as well as the possibility of expanding into Chicago in the near future and Los Angeles a little later. Lindsey was genuinely engaged in their conversation. Her admiration for them came through, and you could see she was enthusiastic about their plans. How I wished I could share in her excitement. But I wanted to have more responsibility in my career. I didn't want to just follow their lead. I realized I was tired of being controlled by Chloe and Janice's business whims. Manny's assessment of my relationship with Chloe and Janice was too close to reality. That was why I had reacted so vehemently when he had pointed it out the other night.

We lingered after dinner for drinks, and that was when Chloe lowered her voice slightly to a more confidential level and said, "You two have proven to be highly effective in our New York enterprise. You both deserve and will receive a hefty financial bonus for your efforts."

Then she turned to Lindsey and said, "Janice and I are so impressed at your ability to make and keep strong customer relationships. Marilyn has been a wonderful mentor to you, helping you learn the fashion business. We think it's time you take on more responsibility here in New York—actually run the New York operations. We can hire someone to handle the financial side of the business."

Before Lindsey could recover from her surprise, Chloe turned to me. I braced for her announcement. Using the same persuasive voice, she continued, "Marilyn, there is no way Janice and I can thank you for your total commitment to us. Your business acumen has taken us to a totally different sphere. Because of your success here and your expertise, we want you to head the Chicago office and develop that market the same way you've done in New York."

Now I was surprised. Chloe continued, "We've discussed Toni's role here in the States and have concluded that this isn't the right market for a watch line. We're going to pull out of the watch business here."

I smiled but made no comment. Toni and I would not be dealing with one another, and Manny would be delighted with that development. Then I chided myself for even thinking of Manny. Chloe and Janice interpreted my smile as approval for the Chicago promotion.

Concealing my true emotions, I told Chloe and Janice I was grateful to them for their confidence in me and for all they had done to advance my career. "I'd be honored to be part of your business endeavors as we expand in the States." Chloe came around and hugged me. Janice said she was excited about our future together in the business world.

After we left the restaurant, I flagged a taxi instead of taking the subway home. Once in the cab, I dropped my charade and broke into such uncontrollable sobs that the driver had to ask me to repeat my address.

At home, I crawled into bed and pulled up the covers. I was

exhausted but couldn't sleep. I watched my clock tick off one hour after another. I kept going over my recent interactions with Manny and Joseph and now Chloe. I felt unsettled and confused. I had ventured well beyond my childhood fences, only to be corralled by other controlling forces.

The next day Chloe, Janice, Lindsey, and I made plans and set a timeline for transitioning the New York operations. Lindsey already had someone in mind to interview for the financial side of the business. The Chicago venture was an immediate launch. We'd open as soon as I could get there and find office space and an apartment. Chloe said there were orders in Chicago for the C&J fall line that would debut in the stores in the spring. Several department stores were interested in the fall Bourne Innocence line. Lack of sleep and the staggering number of things to do for the move to Chicago overwhelmed me—yet I knew how to react with an agreeable, robot smile. I made sure Chloe and Janice knew I was confident in my ability to tackle this new challenge.

After our planning session, Chloe invited me to dinner with her, Manny, and Janice. I wondered if she knew Manny and I had quarreled about his plans to move to Nashville. She probably didn't know Joseph had tried to woo me with a business loan to join Manny in Nashville. Since I didn't plan to enlighten her, I just nodded and said I'd be delighted to meet them for dinner.

I arrived at the restaurant early so I could try to settle my nerves before the others got there. My glass of wine arrived just as Chloe and Janice, impeccably dressed as always, were shown to the table.

After a short time, Chloe began tapping her fingers on the table, finally saying, "Where in the world is Manny? What am I thinking? He's always late." As if on cue, Manny charged into the restaurant and ignored the maître d' as he looked for our table. He was dressed like a bum—soiled blue jeans, a faded plaid shirt, and no jacket or tie. I knew he was making a statement to get under his mother's skin.

She fell for it. "You look like a homeless person from the Bowery," she observed. "I'm surprised the maître d' let you into the dining room looking that shabby." Manny just grinned at her criticism and said, "Mother, you have always been too wrapped up in outward appearances and too insensitive to people's inward feelings."

Their sparring lasted for a few uncomfortable minutes, although I couldn't help being secretly amused. I patted the seat next to me in the booth, and he sat down. He gave me a kiss on the cheek and said sarcastically and loud enough for Chloe and Janice to hear, "It sure has been a long time since I've seen or even talked to you, Marilyn. Is my mother keeping you *that* busy these days?" Then he lapsed into silence for the rest of the meal.

After the entrée had been served, Chloe unveiled the plans for the New York and Chicago businesses and the personnel changes in both locations. Manny looked stunned but recovered quickly, saying loudly, "The best news is that Toni—that conniving bastard—is no longer in the picture to pursue Marilyn." He threw down his napkin and said, "Good night, ladies. I'm finished here."

The topic of Nashville was never broached. Chloe apologized for Manny's rudeness. I waited a few minutes before thanking them again for dinner and the Chicago assignment. I told them I planned to go to Chicago in a few days to look for office space and an apartment. They were flying back to Milan the next day, so both gave me a goodbye hug.

"We look forward to hearing your plans for Chicago and have complete confidence in your ability to launch a successful business for us there," Chloe said with a reassuring smile.

When I got to the office the next day, Lindsey was already busily working at her desk. She looked up as I entered and grinned happily. “I hope you’re not upset that I’m taking over the New York operation from you,” she said.

“Of course not. You earned this position and the money that comes with it,” I said, placing my hand on her shoulder. “And I’m going to have a new challenge myself setting up a business in Chicago. The change will energize me. And the best part is that we’ll still remain in close professional contact.”

CHAPTER 75

Manny called the next day to check on me. "Marilyn, you looked so beaten up last night at dinner. Mother will do that to almost anyone! I just wanted to make sure you were okay. On another subject, would you be interested in a little getaway to Rockport this weekend before you fly to Chicago?"

The spontaneity of his offer seemed just like what the doctor ordered, and I agreed wholeheartedly.

Manny made all our arrangements, and Joe picked us up at the Nashville airport to drive us to Rockport. Our plan was that I would surprise Mama for a visit and Manny would stay with Joe and Grace.

I rapped on the kitchen door, watching Mama preparing dinner. Before turning to open the door, she wiped her hands on her apron. When she saw me standing there with my suitcase, she squealed with delight and rushed to give me a big hug. "What a wonderful surprise, Marilyn. I can't wait to hear all about your job and how you and Manny are getting along. How long can you stay?"

"Just until Monday. Where's Maria?"

"She's in front of the television—her favorite perch," Mama

replied. When I walked into the living room, Maria was sitting in front of the screen, intent on watching the movement of the pictures that entertained her for hours. She grinned broadly when I caught her eye, and I ran to her to give her a hug.

When I returned to the kitchen to help Mama prepare dinner, she updated me on her teaching, church activities, and what Beth and her family were doing. She stopped abruptly and asked with concern in her voice, "Marilyn, you look so tired. Have you lost weight? Is your work getting to you?"

It was my turn to catch her up on my life. In this safe environment, I told her about my new Chicago job promotion. I even confided that Manny and I had hit an impasse in our relationship, since he planned to move to Nashville to open a music shop there and not remain in New York. "Mama, keep this under your hat. Manny proposed marriage and asked me to join him in Nashville. His dad even offered to finance my opening a dress shop there. I have emphatically turned down both offers for many reasons. Then I received the Chicago challenge from Chloe and Janice. I came home to sort out these many options."

"Grace and I have so much fun gossiping about how great it would be if the two of you ended up marrying the Bateson brothers, but I had no idea that living in Nashville was also on the table," Mama admitted. "Maria and I would be over the moon if you came back to live in this area."

Like Manny, Mama didn't grasp how important my work was to my identity. "Mama, I love my job in the fashion industry. I have sacrificed so much to get where I am today. And as I've explained over and over, the real action for this industry is in major metropolitan areas in Europe and the States." I could feel myself getting worked up and decided to change the subject back to Rockport.

The next day, I visited Grace to see her and my little namesake godchild, Marilyn. Grace had a special glow about her. I listened patiently as Grace babbled on about Joe, Joseph, and Manny's plans for Nashville.

"Manny and Joe took off early this morning to visit Nashville for possibilities to set up a music shop," she said. "Now tell me all about your work in New York," she added with a smile. As she put her daughter down for her nap, I filled her in on my promotion to open the Chicago office. And I was grateful she did not ask me about my relationship with Manny.

My next stop was to see Beth. After I went through the same career litany and asked about her family, Beth said, "Mama telephoned me this morning and invited me to dinner tonight. It's just the three of us, since she wants to continue to tell us about her childhood—or, as she calls it, the next chapter in her memoirs."

Although I was not enthusiastic about this prospect, I didn't let on to either Mama or Beth. After dinner, Mama rushed through washing the dishes to proceed with her story. "You two don't know how cathartic it is for me to tell you the details of my background that I've guarded secretly all these years," she confessed. "What a brilliant idea of yours, Marilyn, so you two could learn my history firsthand."

After Maria was put to bed, the three of us took our usual places in the living room, waiting for Mama to begin.

"Now let me see, where was I? Oh yes, I was taken into my Aunt Myrtle's home, but Clara and Walter went to the orphanage. I felt guilty for being the lucky one to land in a relative's home. But my real distress came when I was forbidden by Auntie—as she wished to be called—to visit my sister and brother in the orphanage. Her reasoning was that it would depress me to see their living conditions. Little did I know that I would be learning from her what depression was.

"As time went on, Auntie's home became a psychological hell for me. She demonstrated the most bizarre and frightening ranges of behavior. Her dark moods sent her to bed for days and disabled her more than her manic states. Today, they would have diagnosed these symptoms as manic-depressive.

"My role was to be her personal servant in charge of the house cleaning, meal preparation, and helping her to bathe herself. She often would berate and scream at me incessantly to leave her alone. She continually reminded me how lucky I was to be in her home. And when she got used to my living with her, she would smack me and torment me in her mental states of mania or rage.

"I tried to attend school, acting as if nothing was wrong with Auntie and rarely sharing anything about myself or my siblings living in an orphanage. I could not connect to the other children in my class because I never wanted them to know about the abuse or guilt I lived with every day. Loneliness was my constant companion. My reliable friends were books, and I escaped from my daily drudgery by reading.

"One day, when I came home from school, I found the doors locked at Auntie's. This was odd because we never locked doors back then. I ran from the front door to the back, frantically knocking and screaming, 'Auntie, let me in. Are you okay?' There was no response. I tried to tap on windows, even tossing pebbles at her bedroom window.

"My terror grew as it became dark and very cold. I huddled in the doorway, trying to figure out what I should do next. Suddenly, the door flew open, and there was Auntie. She looked like a witch, with her hair wildly tangled and an angry look on her face. She grabbed me by the collar of my coat and shook me violently, screaming, "See what it's like if you have no shelter or food? Your laziness and ungratefulness are why I could not take your brother and sister into my home. I would have had three of you brats, bleeding me dry. Get in here now and get your chores done. And let this be a lesson to you, Missy."

Beth and I looked shocked. We both had known Auntie; she had visited our home when we were youngsters, but I had had no idea how cruel she had been to Mama. My only recollection of her was that I didn't like to be around her. She always had a stern look and paid no attention to me during her visits.

Mama continued. "Auntie was a big part of my childhood and teen years until I graduated from high school. I had been her caretaker, and sometimes she was contrite for her behavior with me. When I married your father, I was young, but I saw it as an opportunity to get away from her house and the sadness that lived there between us. Auntie disapproved of my marrying so young; I was only seventeen. She also disliked that my new husband had been given a small farm as a wedding gift from his father and I was now a common farmer's wife. It's the same farmhouse where Joe and Grace are raising their family.

"My upbringing by Auntie is painful to recall, but once I left her, I realized I loved her in a strange way—it was a misspent love built on pity. Life with my husband and then you girls showed me true love and fulfillment. As my circumstances changed, I spent hours in prayer to forgive Auntie. The older I got, the more I understood her mental illness could not be helped. Auntie taught me a valuable lesson as her constant caretaker. The lesson prepared me for our dear Maria—to be both patient and kind to those who are more vulnerable than us.

"There are many stories I could tell you girls about your Aunt Myrtle, but it's getting late, and Beth needs to head down the road to her family. We'll continue at another time."

When Beth left, Mama and I had a glass of milk and a slice of her sinful homemade chocolate cake. We talked for an hour or more before going to bed. She wanted to know all about my life in New York and how I felt about relocating to Chicago.

The timing seemed right to tell her how unsettled I felt in my career and my indebtedness to Chloe and Janice for everything that they had afforded me.

"Mama, I feel as if I'm at a crossroads in my life, and I'm unsure of what direction I should be going. Chloe and Janice have been terrific; they've given me a stellar career path. Their New York operation was an incredible proving ground for me. I even trained my protégée to take it over for me so I could graduate to a new challenge—like setting up their new business in Chicago. And now with this promotion, I feel guilty for thinking about what my professional ambition has cost me personally. Anyone my age in the fashion industry would be lucky to have Chloe and Janice as mentors and financial supporters. However, I have worked under pressure and stress for such a long time that I question my ambition and why I'm driven so hard to exceed. Could I be missing out on a personal life because of my job?"

Mama listened intently and then chose her words carefully. "Marilyn, as you mature, you will find that at different junctures of your life, you are forced to evaluate your choices. It can be a painful process. Obviously, you are at one of those junctures. Just know I am so proud of you and your achievements. You will make the right decision when the timing is right," she encouragingly remarked. "You'll see."

The next day, I went back to Grace and Joe's house. I wanted to spend time with their little Marilyn. I watched how Grace doted on Marilyn and how she basked in her role as a wife and mother. A smattering of envy washed over me in watching her interactions with her child and the way she lovingly described her life with Joe. She knew what she wanted, and she knew she had it.

Since Manny and Joe spent most of the day cutting trees and splitting logs for firewood, Grace and I had lots of one-on-one girl time to share in conversation. As Grace prepared dinner, I played with little Marilyn. Since cooking was not one of my skills, I confided in Grace I could not cook if my life depended on it.

"I'm definitely a takeout food aficionado, or Manny cooks for me. Do you have any simple recipes that I could attempt? What fun it would be for me to surprise Manny with a home-cooked meal," I said with a laugh.

With the mention of Manny, Grace jumped on the chance to ask me how things were going between the two of us. As she began to copy recipes for me, she listened to my explanation. To prove she was paying attention, she would interject questions.

"Grace, our relationship is very complicated. With my new job in Chicago and Manny intent on moving to Nashville, we are worlds apart. Manny is very skeptical of my working with his mother. He doesn't seem to understand that I'm ambitious and committed to my job. Manny is lackadaisical when it comes to work, and I'm a work fanatic. It causes quite a rift between the two of us. Now with us being in separate cities, I'm not sure if our relationship will last."

"Do you love Manny?" she asked simply.

"Well, Grace, that's what's really complicated. Manny brings both the best and worst out in me. What I value most about our relationship is that Manny accepts me being me," I said.

Grace smiled and said, "It sure sounds like true love to me."

Then I confessed to her Manny's reaction at the restaurant when Chloe had told him she was relocating me to Chicago to open a new office there. Grace jumped up from her kitchen table and cried out, "Don't do it! Don't go to Chicago! Don't let Chloe and Janice control your life and push you around!"

I began to cry as I shared with Grace all the pressure and sense of responsibility I felt toward my mentors and my work. She listened, hugged me, and reminded me that they would only take advantage of me as long as I allowed them to do it.

When Joe and Manny came in for an early evening dinner, Grace was putting little Marilyn to bed and I was setting the table. Manny put his arms around me, asking me how I would like to marry a lumberjack. It was typical of Manny to embarrass me in front of his brother. I squirmed out of his grasp, telling him to go wash up for dinner.

Like a little boy, he showed me his hands and with an impish grin said, "Look at these blistered hands, and all you want to do is reject me after a hard day's work with my Paul Bunyan axe." He went out of the kitchen to dutifully wash his hands, and I turned away from Joe so he would not catch the smile on my face.

Our dinner was perfect. We four laughed together and enjoyed one another's conversation. As Grace and I were doing the dishes and the fellows were relaxing in the living room, I told her I could not remember having a more fun and relaxed evening. Grace smiled, saying that she hoped the four of us could share many more evenings in Rockport like this one.

The next day at the airport, Manny and I chatted before our planes took off. Manny was going back to New York, and I was flying to Chicago to scout out that city.

"Manny, thank you so much for getting me home to Rockport to clear out the cobwebs from my head," I said before we hugged goodbye.

"By the way, Marilyn, I didn't tell you last night at dinner the good news. Joe and I have found two locations for my music shop in Nashville. I'll be returning in a few weeks with Joseph to show him these two sites and get his input."

As he departed for his gate, I sadly realized that Nashville was becoming his reality and Chicago mine. I felt alone as he turned and gave me a final wave goodbye.

CHAPTER 76

I rested my forehead on the plane's window, looking at the clouds and remembering that first plane trip to New York City when I was in college. Now plane rides were routine, but each, including this one, was still filled with excitement and anticipation. I knew thoughts of Manny and our future together—if there was one—would fade when we landed, replaced by my all-consuming professional life.

My first three days in the Windy City were spent apartment hunting with a real estate agent. I finally found a perfect one-bedroom flat on Michigan Avenue with a great view of that bustling thoroughfare. Although the rent was only a little cheaper than my New York apartment, I'd save on transportation costs. I could walk to most of my clients, and Chicago was a much closer plane ride to Mama and Maria. I signed the lease with a flourish—confident that my decision about Chicago was the right one.

Before I flew back to New York, I spent several days visiting shops and department stores, introducing myself to the contacts Chloe and Janice had made and checking out the merchandise they carried. I was delighted with the enthusiasm for the C&J upscale line and the more moderately priced Bourne Innocence. I began to relax and even wrote Chloe to update her on my progress and thank her for the inroads she and Janice had made in Chicago.

However, I was concerned about questions from the New York office. Even steep long-distance rates hadn't stopped Lindsey from calling my hotel with questions I thought she should be able to answer herself. I grew weary just thinking about trying to help New York while I was setting up the Chicago office.

Manny also called to see how I was faring, but I cut the conversation short by promising we'd catch up when I got back to New York. I needed to focus on the Chicago business, not my relationship with Manny. Once I got back to New York, Manny and I spent several evenings together talking about our future. But we didn't solve anything before he left for Nashville.

The days slipped into weeks. Manny was traveling between Nashville and New York, but I was busy trying to wrap up everything in New York and move to Chicago permanently. That translated into not having much time together. We planned a final weekend in Rockport before my apartment was ready.

Mama was still at school when I arrived and I took advantage of the sunny afternoon to stroll through my hometown. I stopped at the drugstore for a cherry Coke and a bag of chips—recreating my high school time there with Grace.

When I got home, Mama stopped her dinner preparations to give me a welcoming hug. "I think you could use a glass of sweet tea and a homemade biscuit," she said with a laugh. "The pot roast needs a little more time, so sit down, pretend you're enjoying high tea in London, and tell me how long you'll be here."

"I'm flying out on Monday. That's when my apartment becomes available," I said.

"Good, I'll continue my story on Sunday after dinner," she said. "Frank can feed the kids and put them to bed, since it's a school night."

On Saturday, I met Grace at our old haunt—Perry's Drugstore—for a Coke and a catch-up session. No chips this time. I was waiting in our favorite booth when she rushed in, beaming. "I'm so glad you're here. I'm pregnant, and I wanted you to be the first person outside the family to know," she blurted out before sitting down. "Little Marilyn is as thrilled as Joe and I. She can't wait to have a little brother or sister to boss around."

I leaned across the booth to hug her—then burst into tears. Grace looked startled. "Oh, Marilyn, what's wrong? I didn't mean to upset you."

"It's not you," I sobbed, blowing my nose and wiping my eyes. "It's me. I'm so happy for you. But your life seems to be predictably perfect for our age and mine is so unsettled. I'm just floundering."

For the next two hours, I confessed everything, starting with my love life with Manny. "You know, Grace, we've always had a complicated relationship, and now we're dealing with a long-distance romance. My new job is so stressful and challenging. I never thought I'd admit this, but I'm beginning to question my relationship with Chloe and Janice just when I should be relying on them more. And Joseph insulted me by offering to loan me money to open a dress shop in Nashville so I could be with Manny. You know how hard I've worked to get to where I am today. Does it make sense to begin questioning my career choices now?"

Grace just listened—once again my trusted confidante who let me babble on, pouring out all my fears and anger in Perry's back booth—before she said quietly, "Did you ever think the reason you're so angry with Manny is because you love him?" When I started to cry again, she took my hand and continued, "Could you be letting Manny go in a different direction because you're afraid of commitment?" I thought about this for several minutes before I nodded in agreement.

As we left the drugstore, Grace hugged me. "The only thing I want for you, Marilyn, is that you're happy within yourself. Don't give up on Manny. Come to dinner tonight. I promise—no serious discussions—just four friends enjoying one another's company."

Manny and Joe were feeding the livestock when I arrived. Little Marilyn ran to me with her arms wide open, expecting me to pick her up and twirl her around the kitchen. She smelled like Ivory soap and baby powder, and I had a twinge of longing for a baby of my own.

"My mommy's going to have a baby," she said solemnly.

I whispered in her ear, "If your mommy has a baby as perfect as you are, there will be two angels living in this house."

She whispered back to me, "Mommy's an angel, too." I nodded my head in total agreement.

Just then, the back door flew open, and Joe and Manny entered, both laughing and wearing "Farmer in the Dell" straw hats. Manny tipped his hat at me with a wink. "How are you, my little lady? Welcome to the farm of reproduction." We all laughed.

Manny kissed me on the forehead as if everything was fine between us. I envied him. How could he shake off unresolved issues so easily? I certainly couldn't.

After dinner, we played a game of cutthroat Monopoly and laughed at each other's financial luck or lack thereof. We also kept score about time in jail. Grace had delivered on her promise. It was an evening of sheer enjoyment—no worries or responsibilities intruded. The highlight of the evening for me was putting Marilyn to bed. When she kissed me goodnight after I had read her a story, my heart melted.

And then it was time to go. "It's getting late, and I'd better skedaddle before Mama wonders what's happened to me." Manny walked me to the car, but instead of opening the door, he put his arms around me and held me close, speaking softly in my ear. "Marilyn, you can't continue to let others control your life and make decisions for you. You are a strong, beautiful woman, and I love you. I want you to be happy. Of course, I want you to be with me in Nashville. My life would be complete if you moved there and we could begin to raise a family like Joe and Grace. But the decision is yours. I'm only asking one thing—please don't let your loyalty to my mother's business get in the way of us."

I knew—at that very moment—that I loved him. I began to cry. He put his hand under my chin and turned my face up to kiss away my tears. "Don't throw away our relationship. Take your time to decide and do what's right for you. I know Nashville is right for me, and I hope at some time it will be right for you. We would have an amazing life together."

I climbed into the car before answering, and then I only said we'd stay in close contact. As I drove away, I could hardly see the road for the tears in my eyes. That certainly wasn't the answer he was looking for. And, to be truthful, it wasn't the answer I wanted to give him. Why was I so conflicted about my relationship with Manny? Was I just stubbornly pursuing a childhood dream—one I'd already accomplished?

Mama was in bed when I got home, but the nightlights that had burned during my high school and college years were still burning brightly. I tiptoed through the house and quietly closed my bedroom door, relieved that I didn't have to talk to her in my weepy mood.

The wonderful aroma of brewing coffee woke me, and I joined Mama and Maria in the kitchen. I poured my coffee, and Mama fixed a biscuit with honey while she gave me the morning schedule. "Marilyn, I have to be at church early to help with the altar flowers. Do you mind walking to church after Mrs. Thompson comes to take care of Maria? I'll meet you in our regular pew for the 11:00 service."

There was a cool breeze as I walked to church, but the sun felt warm on my face. The Sunday morning silence of my small hometown was perfect for sweeping the cobwebs from the night before out of my head. I remembered, as a child, sitting high in the big oak tree on our farm's property and dreaming of the world "beyond the fences." I'd found that world, and now my life was ruled by the energy and speed of the big city's hustle and bustle—and my overzealous ambition to work. But today, I definitely felt the pull of the simple life here in my hometown.

When I joined Mama at church, I had a sense of calm and assurance. I knew I had to continue on my career path in Chicago. One day, I might settle down, get married, and have children like Joe and Grace—but not now.

CHAPTER 77

It was almost an after-dinner ritual. Beth and I took our places on the sofa opposite Mama in her straight-backed chair, waiting to hear the next installment of her life.

"Remember, I told you Auntie didn't want me to marry your father. In some ways, that decision could have seemed like a quiet rebellion against her wishes, but that wasn't true. I married Clark for all the right reasons—I loved him deeply and unconditionally. He was one of the brightest, most logical people I have ever known. As we grew together in our marriage, he also became one of the wisest—even without a formal college education.

"You girls have inherited his common-sense approach to life. I'm sure this is a gift that will guide you as you make future choices for yourselves and your families." I was sure Mama directed this statement to me. And so did Beth. She had a faint grin on her face when I sneaked a peek at her.

"Of course, Clark and I had no money, but we used the land from your granddaddy to secure a bank loan, and from that day on, we were never completely out of debt. Your daddy, always looking for ways to expand the farm business, called borrowing for positive improvements 'good' debt. I'd never lived on a farm and didn't know much about crops and livestock, but I trusted him. He grew up on a farm and was sure we'd have a secure life. In one area, though, I trusted my judgment over your father's. Clark only saw the best in people. I'd learned the hard way that not everyone in our lives was as honest, kind, and trustworthy as he believed."

That statement triggered a memory about our neighbor, Samuel Allison. I remembered the look of fear when I told Mama I'd talked to him about helping Joe with the farming after Daddy's heart attack. It seemed strange that she asked if I was ever alone with him and looked so concerned when I told her we rode horses to the river to check the water level and when we got back he promised to help Joe and Daddy. I never told her he said, "Your mama won't like this idea much."

Now I interrupted Mama to ask, "Are you talking about Samuel Allison?"

She bolted upright. "Why would you bring up his name, Marilyn? Did he ever bother you?"

"Of course not, Mama, but I felt uncomfortable when I visited his farm after Daddy's heart attack. Although he agreed to help, he warned me you would probably object to his interfering. That's all."

Mama hesitated a moment; then she continued, "I've never told anyone this. It's not something you'd want to share.

"Remember how each year at planting time, the farmers would come together and help each other? I was a young bride trying very hard to do all the right things. Every day, I prepared a big lunch, and afterward, when the sun was hottest, the men would find a shady spot under the trees in the backyard, away from the house, and stretch out to rest or nap.

"One summer day, there were four or five of them resting, and I was alone in the kitchen washing the lunch dishes. I had my back to the door but didn't turn around when I heard the screen door open and quietly close. I assumed it was Clark. Then I felt arms reach around me and hands move to my breasts, and I turned to kiss your father. Instead, I saw Samuel's face.

"Looking back, I should have screamed, but fear, shock and shyness stopped me. With all the force I could muster, I pushed on his chest, but he didn't budge. Instead, he leaned into my body and anchored himself firmly against me by putting each of his hands on the counter. He held me in place next to his erection and began rubbing up and down against me whispering, 'Be quiet and you won't get hurt.'

"I felt his hot breath next to my ear as he whispered, 'My wife Myrtle and I haven't had sex in years. But I get a lot of pleasure thinking about you and me coupling as I masturbate.'

"With that, he freed his left hand from the counter to expose his penis. He forced me to touch it and to do other distasteful things," she said, closing her eyes and shuddering as she recalled this shattering episode.

"Samuel finally released me, but as he slipped out the back door, he turned to warn me, 'If you breathe one word of this to anyone, you'll be sorry. I'll deny it and say you flirted with me and concocted this story when I rejected you. I will destroy you in this community—that you can count on.'

"I was afraid of him and ashamed of myself. I knew I could never tell Clark because he had such a quick temper. I didn't know what he would have done to Samuel or what he would have thought of me for not yelling. So I kept quiet and just stayed away from Samuel Allison. He was as evil as a poisonous snake."

Beth and I were shocked. We'd known Samuel until he died an old man. No wonder Mama had wanted to move away from the farm. Daddy always avoided the subject, but I'm sure he wondered why.

"Now you understand, Marilyn, why I was so alarmed when I

learned you had gone to his farm alone and his wife had sent you to the barn to see him. I always worried about you girls being alone with Samuel. Your daddy never understood why I hated to have Samuel around any of us, and I could never tell him."

When she finished, Mama stood up, and we knew this session was over. "I'm exhausted and really need to go to bed." She hugged Beth and me. "I love you girls so much. I've always wanted to protect you from any harm," she said. Then she added, "I'm telling you about my past so you'll understand me, but please know I never allowed this dark and sordid episode—or any of the bad times in my life—to totally define me or control my future. My life became bright when I married your daddy, and my three wonderful daughters added to that brightness."

Suddenly, my future decisions seemed so simple when measured against what Mama had endured and overcome. I also recognized how self-centered I'd been on so many different levels of my life.

As I walked Beth to her car, we talked about how privileged we felt that Mama was confiding in us. "We're getting to know her as a person, not just as our mother," Beth said.

I added, "Now we can understand why she was so often guarded with us—and so overly protective. It puts so many things in a different light."

CHAPTER 78

Before I settled permanently in Chicago, I flew back to New York to finish some business. At the office, Lindsey introduced me to Sloane, her new hire to handle the finances.

They couldn't wait to tell me their plans to expand the New York business together. They oozed enthusiasm when they told me Chloe had already met Sloane by phone and was looking forward to a face-to-face meeting soon. Sloane gushed about the conversation, obviously impressed at her new boss. Lindsey had reinforced this assessment by telling Sloane, "Just wait until you meet her in person."

I admitted to a tinge of jealousy as my two replacements boasted about their team approach to moving the needle in sales for the two fashion lines in New York.

They had quickly negated my role as the chief financial architect of the New York success. It seemed as if they had dismissed my role in developing a line of credit with the Bank of Milan and working countless hours to build the fashion lines into a thriving business abroad and in New York for Chloe and Janice.

I knew I was being foolish and shouldn't resent their enthusiasm, but I did. I collected my personal belongings quickly before they could see how hurt I was that they had shut me out and injured my professional feelings. I didn't want to appear petty, but I did think they could at least acknowledge me as one of the brains behind the operation—and the reason they could talk about moving the brands to a new level of penetration in the market.

As soon as I finished cleaning out my desk, I said, "The movers will be sending my stuff to Chicago in a few days. As soon as the office phone is installed next week, you can call me at this number." Then I picked up my briefcase, now stuffed with office incidentals, and walked out of the little office space I had found and worked in for so many months. I realized I'd been replaced, and it was quite an unsettling feeling—a real blow to my ego.

The movers came the next day and packed the few pieces of furniture and kitchen items I'd acquired. I would meet the moving van at my Chicago flat in five days. The following day, I flew to Chicago. The plane hit the runway at Midway Airport with a jolt, and I looked out the window with some anxiety, thinking, *Welcome to your new home—I sure hope you'll like it here.*

As soon as I was settled in my apartment and new office space, I began calling on buyers and taking orders at an amazing pace. The orders were coming in faster than I ever expected, and I frankly couldn't handle them. Obviously, I needed to hire an assistant—maybe two.

My daily phone calls and wires to Chloe about the success as well as the needs elated her, but she also had concerns. She was very worried about the ability of our Italian production houses to fill the volume of orders from Chicago and New York.

They had already expanded the production operation to accommodate the New York volume, and now Chicago's order flow was overwhelming them. She was afraid the shipments would be delayed and the American buyers would be unhappy. I tried to soothe Chloe by reminding her that this was really a good problem. "After all, if you didn't have such fabulous fashion designs in our two lines, we wouldn't be in this production snafu. It may not seem so easy right now, but we'll solve it."

Part of that solution surfaced quickly. They hired someone with experience in moderately priced lines to help with the Bourne Innocence line, admitting they did not understand this line, which was rapidly becoming our best seller. I tried not to show my exasperation with her amazement at the line's success. I was much more comfortable wearing Bourne Innocence instead of the high-end C&J clothes. Obviously, so were our customers.

During one of my phone conversations with Chloe, she asked how I felt about pulling the watch business from the States. "Toni was so disappointed in this decision. He says he misses traveling to New York and connecting with you there," she said, pausing and waiting for my reply.

"I think it was a wise business decision. The watch sales were too meager in the New York market to justify keeping it open.

"I think Toni still talks with Lindsey, although I can't say that positively," I said, hoping that would end the conversation.

I suspected her real reason for asking me about my opinion on pulling the watch lines here in the States was to bait me into my telling her how Manny and I were faring in our long-distance relationship and had nothing to do with watch decisions. After all, she was the master of manipulation.

Chloe finally authorized me to hire someone to help with the detail work so I could continue to be the point person with clients. I didn't waste any time in beginning to interview applicants and quickly offered the assistant's job to a woman named Jalee.

I appreciated her candidness during the interview. She made it clear that her husband and baby boy would come first—always over late office hours. "I'll have to leave at five every evening and will be unavailable to represent the company at social functions," she explained.

Her credentials, as well as her honesty and family focus, convinced me she would be perfect. When she asked if I had family in Chicago, I told her about my family in Rockport, which I described as a small town in Kentucky. "I'm close to my mother and sisters and try to visit when I can get away from work. But sometimes, it's hard to break away," I confessed.

When she replied, her voice was matter-of-fact, not judgmental. She was just very direct. "Then your family must not be as important as your job." I smiled at her and chalked this up as my first lesson in midwestern directness.

Her words lingered long after she left the office. I had put my personal life on hold to concentrate on my career goals. Not many of my girlfriends from high school or college shared my ambition and drive. Most of them had graduated and then married. They valued the title *Mrs.* more than any professional achievement.

The phone rang, bringing my attention back into the office setting. The caller was a client who wanted to increase his order. I swung into my professional mode, demonstrating how I prioritized career over family.

CHAPTER 79

Manny and I worked out our long-distance phone routine once we were both settled. Each Sunday, when prices were lowest, we took turns calling each other, so I was surprised when he called the office. "I'll be quick," he said. "I know you're busy. I'd like to come to Chicago next weekend if I can find someone to mind the store on Saturday."

My first, fleeting thought was, *With all the work I have to do, you want to come for a whole weekend?* Then I said, "Manny, that would be great. Get a flight for next weekend. I'd love to show off Chicago."

Manny arrived mid-afternoon on Friday and took a cab from Midway, knowing he'd arrive at my office at just about my quitting time. As usual, he burst into the office, startling Jalee and confusing her even more when he picked me up and swung me around the office. After he put me down, he stuck out his hand and said, "I'm Manny—better known as Marilyn's Prince Charming. Can't you tell?"

Typical Manny—but with a difference. Instead of ragged jeans and a T-shirt, he looked quite presentable in Western attire, authentic right down to his cowboy boots. Very much a successful music storeowner. It took a few minutes for Jalee to remember I'd mentioned my steady boyfriend was Chloe's son.

"I think the weekend has just begun," I said, turning off the office lights. Jalee immediately cleared her desk, and we headed out together. "See you Monday," I said.

Jalee responded, "You two have a terrific weekend."

The weekend was more than terrific—it was perfect. Even the weather cooperated. We had lovely warm days to walk around Chicago. I even showed him my newly discovered landmarks around the Chicago Loop before our Sunday afternoon ended with a lazy picnic lunch on the shore of Lake Michigan.

As I spread out my family's patchwork quilt for our picnic, Manny admired its unique design. "Tell me about this quilt," he said.

"This quilt is very special to me. Mama made it from pieces of dresses that Beth, Maria, and I wore as children. We each have one," I said.

After lunch, Manny rested his head in my lap, and I studied the different pieces of the quilt carefully as I stroked his hair. "This quilt is a picture of my childhood. Its color, texture and form are a remaking of my history," I said. "If you look carefully, you can see and feel that all the pieces woven into the quilt are not smooth. There are rough patches scattered throughout the design. I think Mama did that on purpose. The quilt—just like life—has smooth and rough patches."

"This quilt is also symbolic of your close-knit family," Manny said emphatically. "Hell, my family never stayed together long enough to have our patches sewn together. If the Batesons did have a family quilt—which we don't—our colors would be as vivid as colors in a kaleidoscope—but like a kaleidoscope, our connection would never stay constant enough to last as a piece of family art," he mused. I blinked. Rarely was Manny so introspective.

He rolled over on his stomach and looked into my eyes. "What do you see in your future?"

I robotically replied, "I don't have time now to think about the future."

"Well, if you could look into a crystal ball, would I be in it with you?" he asked, childlike, as he wove a cloverleaf ring. When he finished, he said, "Give me your left hand, please. I want to place this engagement ring on your ring finger to make my proposal official. But first, let me make this a formal proposal by getting on one knee."

I laughed when he ceremoniously knelt and placed the garland on my ring finger. "It's beautiful," I gasped facetiously. "I'll wear it forever."

Manny laughed too, but added, "Or at least until the damn thing falls apart."

As we packed up the picnic basket and shook out the quilt, Manny's tone turned more serious. "I have an idea I want to share with you, but I'll wait until we have a glass of wine together at your place."

Although I was eager to hear Manny's plan, I was also secretly dreading it. I hoped it would not involve a change in my career. Once back at the apartment, Manny opened a bottle of wine, and as we sipped it, he began to talk.

"You know more than anything I want us to be together. Good grief, I proposed unofficially in another city, and now this afternoon I've made it official with the ring. By the way, how's the ring holding up?" he asked as he glanced at my finger.

Then his tone became more serious. "I know you're loyal to my mother and her company. I'm also aware of how hard you've worked to succeed in a highly competitive field. I can't deny that you've been brilliant at it."

He began to pace before he continued, "I have great difficulty respecting my mother and everything she stands for—particularly the way she manipulates your life. She controls your future because she knows how ambitious you are.

"Earlier today, when I told you how jazzed I am about the Nashville music store—even naming it M&M for Manny and Marilyn—you listened intently and seemed genuinely happy for me. My mother has not called once to find out about my move to Nashville or how the opening was going.

"All my formative years, I acted out to get her attention—my parents never understood why I was so rebellious. As an adult, I've finally realized this behavior doesn't cut it. I'm so fortunate that my dad and I have made our separate peace. I enjoy having him in my life and value his parental support and friendship. And I realize he's been a victim too.

"Mother separated herself from all three of us. She chose Janice and career over family. And for years, we downplayed her lesbian relationship, even as it tore us more apart. But you know all that."

He knelt before me, taking my hands in his and saying earnestly, "I want M&M to have a family together. I know I'll have to learn to be a good parent, but I'm working on that. You'll be a terrific mother. You've had such good parental role models in your life. I really believe we would be awesome together with children."

I listened carefully as he continued. "I know you worked with Toni and watchmakers in Switzerland to develop the watch business. It was Chloe and Janice's design, but you were the one who got it to market. You told me the upscale watches didn't sell in New York because there was too much competition in the high-end market, so Mother shut down the operation. Now here comes the kicker—would you be interested in starting your own moderately priced watch business in the US with fun, playful, and colorful designs?

"Please be open to my idea," he said as I started to speak. "Why not start your own watch business in the States with affordable designs that are utilitarian enough for men and still playful and colorful enough for women and children? You could establish this business anywhere, but selfishly, I'm recommending you begin in Nashville."

I dropped his hands, and he joined me on the sofa. I chose my words carefully because I didn't want to dash his idea entirely. "Manny, I can't afford to leave Chicago and start over in Nashville—especially launching a new business. Chloe has paid me well, but I have limited savings. And my family doesn't have that kind of money. I couldn't ask for their help."

He'd obviously rehearsed his response because he interrupted me before I could list any other impediments. "I knew money would be the big issue. And I knew you refused financial support from my dad, but I have a totally different plan.

"I have a new friend. He's a regular at the store because he collects guitars. It's his hobby; his real work is as an investor for start-up businesses in Nashville. He's quite prominent and very successful. Now, don't get mad at me for telling him about my watch idea and about you and your career background. He likes the sound of it and wants to talk to you about a business loan when you come to visit me in Nashville."

My first reaction, as he suspected, was to get angry. He was his mother's son when it came to manipulation. But instead of tossing that at him, I closed my eyes and counted to ten before replying. "You know you've caught me off guard with this proposal. I'll need time to process your idea. It could be something I'd want to do in my future. I really will think about it."

I didn't want to squash his idea. I also was impressed at his display of maturity in working out the details. He was certainly single-minded in his quest to get me to Nashville. He truly believed we should be together permanently. And he certainly had confidence in my ability.

However, I was more honest with myself. I knew I hadn't achieved my professional success at this early stage on my own. Chloe and Janice had financed—and mentored—me at every step.

"Manny, I promise to carefully consider your idea. But I need to be realistic, too. I've made a commitment to establish the C&J and Bourne Innocence lines in Chicago. Your mother and Janice have made a sizable investment in me. I couldn't just walk away. But once I've accomplished my goals, I'll be in a better position to strike out on my own—maybe in Nashville." I smiled and, to stress the Nashville part, gave him a kiss.

Typical Manny, he abandoned our serious conversation, picking me up and heading toward the bedroom. "Okay, lady, but you'll have to seal that promise with more than a kiss."

After a glass of Chianti and pizza, Manny surprised me by pulling out a series of sketches from his suitcase. He had numerous designs to illustrate the unusual masculine utilitarian watch collection he proposed, as well as more fanciful and colorful designs for women and teens. The watch face designs had different band widths, and the colors were incredible. "Manny, you must have inherited your design sense from your mother!"

"Yes, she always admired my creative wardrobe," Manny replied, smiling impishly. We both burst out laughing.

As Manny packed to leave the next day, I confessed, "You're not even gone, and I already miss you." His response was a lingering goodbye kiss. At the door, he turned back to smile and wave. I stood alone in my apartment door for several minutes after he got in the cab.

It was a gloomy Monday morning, and my mental state matched the weather. Both Manny and I had to face the week's work in front of us—in very different places.

CHAPTER 80

The phone was ringing when I got to the office, and all thoughts of Manny scattered when I heard Chloe's voice. "I've confirmed our itinerary. Janice and I will be in New York next week. The following week, we'll fly to Chicago to meet Jalee. Arrange accommodations at the Ritz-Carlton and schedule appointments with your clients," she ordered. "We'll fly back to Milan from Chicago at the end of that week."

That surprised me, and I said, "Oh, I thought you might plan to see Joe and Manny after you finished your business here. It's such a short flight from Chicago to Nashville."

She quickly responded, "I'd really love to see the boys and Joe's family in Rockport if our time weren't so limited. There's just way too much to do. But I did send Manny a nice check for his new business. I hope it's going well. Joe sends me pictures of his little girl, Marilyn, and I understand they are expecting another baby soon, so I sent him a check, too. What I do for one, I always do for the other."

My blood pressure skyrocketed. How cold and calculating! How could a mother think sending a check could replace her presence and love? But all I said was, "I'll set up a full schedule of appointments for you and Janice. And I'll reserve the suite at the Ritz. Please let me know if there's anything else we need to do before you arrive."

I tried, but couldn't disguise my feelings, and Chloe was no fool. She sensed my aloof tone, but didn't acknowledge the reason. Instead, she said, "Marilyn, I know you and Jalee have been extremely busy. I want you to know how much we appreciate what you've done for our business. Janice and I are looking forward to spending time with you both in Chicago." That ended the conversation.

When Jalee arrived, I went over Chloe's agenda, and we put together a plan of action to ensure that we'd be ready for their arrival. Our next two weeks would be filled with work. By the end of the second week, we were ready for their visit.

With all the preparation, I hadn't thought about Chloe's cavalier attitude about seeing her sons. But suddenly, I was looking at her from another angle—mine. If Chloe had so little loyalty to her sons—her own flesh and blood—how much did she have for me? Probably none. She'd just assume, as she had with Joe and Manny, that a check would solve everything. For the first time, I thought I should be rethinking my commitment to her. Did the company deserve my unquestioned loyalty? I was still considering that at the office the next day while I waited for their arrival.

Chloe and Janice checked in at the Ritz, and when they arrived at the office, they looked, as usual, fashionably stylish. The minute I saw them, I panicked. I'd neglected to tell Jalee to wear her best professional outfit. They breezed into the office and then stopped short, looking at Jalee, before turning to me with a questioning look. As I made the introductions, I knew I'd have to do something about Jalee's wardrobe, but first I had to pacify Chloe and Janice, who continued to stare at Jalee.

"Jalee keeps the home fires burning here with her nose to the proverbial grindstone," I said quickly. "She's terrific with the financials and reports. I never worry about administrative details. I can call on buyers and storeowners every day because I know she's supporting all the important back shop tasks for all of us." I could see my explanations weren't working, so I moved on to their schedule.

The five-day visit passed quickly. Every morning, at a light breakfast at the Ritz, I went over the day's agenda, preparing them with dossiers on each client on their schedule. The three of us met for dinner each day to review and evaluate the day's performance.

Jalee was never included. I contrasted Chloe's behavior toward Jalee with how she had treated Lindsey at that first meeting in New York. And I was not surprised when on the last day at lunch, she said, "We need to talk about Jalee. She doesn't represent our clothing lines."

"What would you have me do about Jalee's appearance? Jalee is professionally very solid in the financial arena and has the maturity to handle any detail inside the office. I have great confidence in her skill level—more than I ever did when I hired Lindsey."

"That may be true, but the next time we come back to town, I want to see Jalee professionally dressed to meet anyone who comes to the office. If she doesn't measure up to our standards, I'll expect you to find someone else for her position. I'm sure there are any number of people with the skill level and the right appearance to represent our brands."

I flushed in anger but took a deep breath before responding. "Don't worry. I'll take care of it."

Chloe smiled but added a pointed barb. "I know you will. I don't think it's too much to ask that my Chicago staff appear as fashionably put-together as my New York girls."

I greeted Chloe and Janice's departure with profound relief. I was still smarting from Chloe's callous comments about Jalee—and her reference to New York. And now I had to confront Jalee about her wardrobe. The task was even more daunting because I knew Jalee's husband's hours had been cut recently and she was paying a larger share of her son's quite expensive nursery school. Her finances were very tight.

No way was I going to tell her that her job hinged on getting a new wardrobe. And I was livid at Chloe for questioning my ability to hire the right person—someone with extraordinary skills for the job. What was so important about looking stylish in the back office?

That night, I stewed about how to handle the situation. But when I pushed my clothes aside to hang up my sweater, I had an epiphany. I looked at my overstuffed closet and immediately started pulling out outfits that would look stylish with black shoes. I put together enough outfits to give Jalee several weeks of mix-and-match choices. We were almost the same size, but I'd pay for any needed alterations. Our shoe size was different, so I decided to buy her a pair of basic black leather pumps as a reward for all her hard work.

I smuggled the outfits into the office. I didn't want any questions from Jalee because I was still mulling over how to diplomatically address the issue without hurting or insulting her. By noon, I'd decided the sooner I dealt with Jalee and her office attire, the better for my sanity, and I asked her to join me for lunch. I'd practiced my speech; I just needed the right time to deliver it.

We settled on the deli near the office. While we were waiting for our sandwiches, I casually asked her, "So what did you think of Chloe and Janice?"

Her response surprised me. "I've been wondering how to tell you this. I found both those women to be condescending and snobbish. I told my husband last night that after being with them for a week, I planned to resign as soon as they left the country.

"They made it perfectly clear at our first meeting that I didn't fit their fashion mold. And after our introduction, neither woman acknowledged my presence—I was invisible to them. I'm not blind. I could see they didn't approve of me. I enjoy working for you, Marilyn, so I'll stay until you can hire my replacement."

I did not know how to respond. Obviously, this was not the time to tell her I had a new wardrobe for her back at the office. *Damn that Chloe for putting me in this position. Jalee's too good an employee to lose over something as trivial as her clothes, which are perfectly suited for her.*

"Jalee, you're an important person to this office. I respect your work ethic and financial knowledge. Please don't hastily quit. I promise I'll handle any issue that comes up between you and Chloe."

"You know, Marilyn, you're way too kind to be working for someone as insensitive as Chloe and her sidekick. But I'll stay as long as you shield me from any contact with Chloe going forward."

"You don't know how relieved I am to hear you say that, Jalee. Now let's forget Chloe and Janice and their offensive behavior and enjoy our sandwiches." I stayed past five and took the clothes back to my apartment.

It took a few days, but I finally came up with a way to handle the wardrobe issue. I invited Jalee to my apartment for lunch. I told her I had some personal things to share with her and thought not being in the office setting would be more relaxing for us.

Over the years, I'd discarded many things from my life in Rockport. But I'd kept one piece of the Samsonite luggage Mama and Daddy had given me when I graduated from high school. It was the resting place for the wool plaid skirt Mama had made for me in my freshman year at Wesley. I pulled out the luggage from the back of the closet and put it on the living room coffee table.

When Jalee arrived, we sat on the sofa like two friends, not employer and employee, to eat our chicken salad sandwiches and drink iced tea. Jalee confided that she was having difficulty meeting her family's bills. "It breaks my heart to see how my dear husband berates himself for not being a good provider. Nothing could be further from the truth, but he worries so much."

Talking about financial difficulties seemed an appropriate opening for me to tell her a little about my background—which certainly included financial difficulties. "Jalee, you must be wondering about the red Samsonite luggage on the coffee table. I placed it there to show you what's inside it. Its contents symbolize my modest upbringing."

I opened the suitcase and took out the homemade wool skirt. "I grew up on a farm, and money was always scarce, so Mama made our clothes. Although our home was filled with love, I always dreamed of a bigger and better life away from the farm.

"In my freshman year in college, my friend Joe Bateson invited me to his family's New York City apartment and their country home for Thanksgiving. I was wearing this homemade wool skirt when I first met his mother, Chloe, and her partner, Janice. Even the clothes I'd borrowed, which seemed so chic at Wesley, didn't cut it in New York. I was uncomfortable for the entire weekend. I felt out of place in the company of these people and their lifestyle. Yet I secretly coveted their lifestyle.

"I went back to Wesley dreaming about that weekend. Then I had an opportunity to study in Milan, and Chloe invited me to stay with them. My European experience was right out of *My Fair Lady*. These very prominent fashion designers became Professor Higgins to my Eliza Doolittle. They supplied my clothes and introduced me to the fashion world; I offered them my business and marketing acumen and helped grow their business.

"Of course, since then, Chloe has been able to control me for her benefit. She still does, and our successful collaboration shows in the company's soaring profits.

"But our business relationship began in Milan, when I modeled their fashionable clothing design lines for young, stylish women. I surveyed the reaction of students and young faculty and staff at the University of Milan, and did the same thing when I returned to Wesley for my senior year. I gave them constant feedback on how their clothing lines fared in Milan and in Kentucky small towns. In return, they picked my brains on business and marketing. However, their demands on me have moved far beyond—and become a lot more stressful than—our original relationship, which I'd have to describe as symbiotic. I wanted to get out of my small-town environment and go to the big city, and they needed a model with a business and sales marketing brain.

"Looking back, I realize Chloe and Janice were embarrassed by the way I dressed in the company of their sophisticated friends that Thanksgiving weekend. But I also realize they saw potential in me. That weekend changed my life in so many ways—and not just professionally. It was also the first time I met Joe's older brother Manny.

"From my first days in Milan, Chloe and Janice have provided me with the clothes I wear to represent their business. But I never want to forget my modest background, so I've kept this piece of luggage and my 'infamous' homemade wool skirt. In Milan, they replaced my luggage with an expensive leather suitcase, but they can never replace the values I learned from my Kentucky upbringing. Now I have something to show you in my bedroom."

Jalee had listened intently to my story about Chloe and Janice but was a little startled when she saw the pile of clothes on my bed. "These were given to me to represent the company, but I've continued to receive clothes, and my closets are bulging. I want you to have them now. You can represent the company by wearing them to work to reinforce our fashion brand. It's a marketing strategy, and I'll be glad to pay for any alterations. Think of them as your work uniform," I said, not without some irony.

"I don't know what to say," Jalee said as she held up the different outfits and looked in the mirror. "I've never had anything this beautiful to wear." To reinforce my need to pass the clothes along, I opened my closet door to show her how many of the clothes I'd been given for work were still hanging there, organized by season, fabric, and color, but unworn.

"Think of these clothes like I do—as perks of our employment with Chloe and Janice."

Jalee put the clothes down and hugged me, crying softly. "I've never had anyone be so kind or generous to me," she said. "We sure have pretty snazzy uniforms for work." She laughed as she brushed the tears from her eyes.

I carefully folded the outfits and packed them in another large suitcase, telling her she could return it at work the next day. "I can't wait to show my husband these clothes. His eyes will pop out of his head."

I didn't think either of us would accomplish much at work, so I added another perk—the afternoon off to compensate for our stressful week with our Milan visitors. In retrospect, I realized Chloe's ultimatum had ended well, but it still seemed petty and mean. The next day, Jalee appeared in one of the outfits. She looked smashing.

"My husband was upset when I showed him the clothes. He thought it was charity until I explained it was business. I was representing the company by showing off our fashion brands, and these outfits were a perk for working for these lines. I also told him about the wool skirt and red suitcase and how Chloe and Janice had taken you under their wing and benefitted from your clothes modeling. When I left home this morning, he whistled and said I looked like a fashion plate. He even offered to buy me another pair of leather pumps to go with the shoes you gave me."

Jalee did look like she had stepped out of *Glamour* magazine, and she seemed more confident. Maybe clothes did make the person. I applauded myself for pulling off this almost-catastrophe with such finesse. I had saved a valuable employee and also soothed Jalee's ruffled feathers from her first encounter with Chloe.

CHAPTER 81

Once I had solved the wardrobe problem and was sure of Jalee's loyalty to me and the company, I could concentrate on business. Or so I thought. But just as soon as Chloe got to Milan, she called in a state of panic. There was a problem with the quality of a shipment to one of the specialty shops carrying the C&J line on Michigan Avenue.

I made immediate arrangements to meet with the shop owner. He was furious and said the quality of the items he had received recently was unacceptable. I assured him the company would take care of the issue and it would never happen again. He continued in an enraged manner, saying there had been more than one quality issue with some of the shipments, and he had heard from other shop owners who had had similar problems.

When I returned to the office, I called Chloe to report my findings. Our clients were correct. The quality was terrible. There were dye streaks, as well as other imperfections.

I expected Chloe to be upset, but much to my surprise, she was furious. "That son of a bitch Toni did this on purpose. He's been sourcing our designs for your territory to the Philippines. He was angry with you when he returned from New York and warned me there would be consequences if things did not change."

My jaw dropped as Chloe continued her rant. "This is your fault, Marilyn. Would it have been so difficult for you to have an exclusive relationship with Toni? He certainly has more to offer you than my son, Manny."

I listened, dumbfounded. Blinded by my anger at how Chloe had belittled her own son and bullied me in my career, I erupted in a tirade I would later regret.

"Chloe, thank you for all you've done for me in the past, but I'm finished! You can tell Toni to go to hell. I will not allow you or anyone else to speak to me as you've just done. You've destroyed your relationship with your sons, and now you've done the same with me. What kind of cruel person are you? You insist on controlling everyone around you for your own benefit. You will no longer control me. I will have my personal items out of the office within twenty-four hours."

She screamed. "You can't walk out on me. You are nothing but a small-town hayseed. Believe me, I will see that you never have another job in the fashion industry."

As soon as I hung up with Chloe, I called Manny. When he answered the phone, I couldn't control my sobbing, and he asked in a panicked voice what was wrong. "Have you been in an accident? Are you okay? Please, Marilyn, calm down. Take a deep breath and tell me what's happened."

I finally gained control and told him, almost verbatim, about my screaming match with Chloe. I could tell by his tone of voice he was smiling. "Hang on. I'm taking the next flight to Chicago to help you plan your Chicago exit and future."

I responded, "That would be great. Let me know when you get in tomorrow."

The next call I needed to make was to Oakes Boden, the

attorney I had met with several weeks ago about the future possibility of starting my line of watches. He assured me there would be nothing Chloe could do legally to stop me, since she had pulled her watch lines out of the States. He encouraged me to be discreet should I decide to go in that direction.

Waking the next morning, I made a list of mandatory phone calls and a well-defined to-do list. Lindsey and Jalee were at the top of the list to be notified about my abrupt departure. After things settled a little, I'd phone my family and friends.

I'd certainly created a bittersweet predicament for myself—uncertainty coupled with unbridled excitement.

Manny arrived the next day. He swept into my apartment with his well-worn backpack over his right shoulder and his arms cradling a bottle of champagne. He bowed triumphantly and handed me a bouquet of fresh flowers.

He put down the champagne and his bag before picking me up and whirling me around the apartment. We landed breathless on the sofa, and he covered me with kisses. Laughing hysterically, we fell to the floor and hugged each other.

Manny insisted on hearing every little detail of what prompted my telling his mother to go to hell. I relayed the conversation but deleted his mother's vicious comparison of Toni and Manny. Although that comment had triggered my rage, I never wanted Manny to know his mother's cruel feelings about him.

As soon as I'd finished, Manny wanted to know when I'd be moving to Nashville. "Not so fast. Here's my to-do list. I won't be moving until I've accomplished all this. And I'd better get started now," I said, looking up the landlord's phone number to give him a month's vacancy notice.

Jalee was then briefed on the fateful conversation. She was supportive and didn't seem concerned about her job security. She simply applauded my bravery and said she was excited for my future. I had a hunch she'd probably leave the company soon. The demands of the job would never mesh with her family-first priority. Lindsey in New York was shocked and more concerned about what I planned to do next.

Once I had wrapped up loose ends in Chicago and Manny had helped me pack up the apartment, I decided to return to Nashville with him. It was time I had a change of scene, and I would be close enough to visit Rockport family and friends. Also, Manny was exuberant about showing me how his business had taken off. In addition, he hinted that he had a Nashville connection for me to get started on a new career path.

CHAPTER 82

Just as Manny had implied, M&M Music looked successful, thanks to Dr. Bateson's investment in the company. Since his opening, Manny had made headway in the recording studios' community and was working with several popular country singers to make custom-designed guitars and other special instruments for them.

The instruments and sound systems available at M&M were impressive, much larger than I'd imagined. Manny was knowledgeable about the instruments, especially guitars, and the sound systems he carried. "I visited every recording studio after I opened to introduce myself and tell them about the sound systems I carry. I'm using my music contacts in New York to bring cutting-edge sound technology to Nashville.

"My business really took off once the recording studios saw my stock," he continued. "I'm sure I can sustain my business as long as I continually educate myself about the music scene by going to musicians to find out what they want from their instruments. I'm always going to stock the best sound systems. They need the best so they can listen to their recordings and get an authentic sound."

As we were leaving the store, he lowered his voice and shyly said, "Now, don't laugh, but I'm getting ready to cut a record with a song I've written. It's all arranged."

I was thrilled for him. "Oh, that's fantastic. Can I hear it now?" I asked.

He took the chair from behind his desk and picked up a guitar. "Please be seated," he said. "I'm going to perform without the acoustical quality that I'll have in the recording studio, so cut me some slack."

He began with a musical introduction. The lyrics were about unrequited love, and his voice was beautiful—melodic and pure. His face was transformed as he sang. Clearly, Manny had found his calling—music.

As I watched him, I couldn't keep from thinking about the irony of life. The Columbia dropout law student, a rebellious nonconformist who took years to find his life's goal, had happily landed on his feet. What a contrast to my journey. The people pleaser, a conformist who made good grades in school, knew what she wanted to do, strived for it with focus and determination, and achieved her dreams of success in the sophisticated world of fashion at an early age, was regrettably now floundering.

When Manny finished his song, I applauded and kissed him. "I think you have a hit on your hands! I'm so proud of you and everything you've accomplished here in such a short time."

He said, "I feel good about things here, too. I know this is redundant, and I don't want to annoy you, but I've got to tell you one more time. My life here would be perfect if you were by my side as my wife."

"Oh, Manny. Our timing is so off in our career paths. Perhaps one day, but I simply can't marry you now without a job."

Manny smiled. "I told you I wanted you to meet my special friend Sean. Perhaps he might help change your mind about moving to Nashville with me."

After a full day walking through Nashville and driving in the country, we joined Sean Samuelson, Manny's friend, at a small bar near M&M Music.

Sean looked to be in his mid-forties. "What do you think of your man getting ready to record a single?" he asked me. "When he auditioned for me in the store, I immediately saw he was talented and agreed to front the cost of his recording with a written agreement to get a percentage of the sales when it takes off."

I was suddenly back in my business mode. "What happens if his single doesn't make more than the cash outlay you fronted?" I asked. "And have the two of you signed a contractual agreement specifying the percentage for residuals if it does become a hit?"

He turned to Manny and said, "You've got a real businesswoman here."

I responded quickly. "I'm sorry for interfering in your negotiations, but I know how easy it is to become committed to and confined by someone who's invested in your career."

Manny looked at me and smiled. "Could you be referring to a situation that I'm very familiar with?"

I nudged him and said, "This is not the place to discuss that situation."

It was easy to like Sean. He and Manny had obviously developed a comfortable friendship—they laughed easily with one another. Like Manny, Sean had come from an affluent family. An inheritance from his grandparents allowed him to move to Nashville and finance business ventures in the music field.

"I love everything about the music scene, and I've made a nice living helping young start-up performers. Manny has a rare talent—something that will resonate here in Nashville," Sean confided.

Sean and Manny explained the logistics of recording his single and marketing it to the radio stations. Sean had given Manny a marketing plan, and he emphasized the importance of following this tried-and-true course. I thought his recommendations were on target.

"How do you know so much about the music business?" I asked. "Is your background in music? Or did you learn the business through osmosis by living in Nashville?"

Sean laughed and said, "My music degree is from the College of Hard Knocks—strictly trial and error. My MBA was imposed by my successful businessman father. He was my mentor. When I struck out on my own, I worked for many different businesses and learned a variety of business practices. Eventually, I realized that I have a knack for reviewing business plans on products or services and determining their viability. Now I use my common sense and extensive business background to finance people and businesses I believe in. If I see a well-developed business plan and I believe the product or service will fly in the marketplace, I'll invest in it. It's that simple. By the way, Manny tells me you're the business brains of a company specializing in fashion."

"Manny is exaggerating about brains, but my background is in the fashion industry. Initially, my responsibilities were to develop business plans for the expansion of two women's clothing lines focused on sales and marketing, promoting the lines to buyers and storeowners. I started in Milan out of college, and the owners had me expand their business in New York and Chicago. I recently left this firm to explore new career opportunities."

Sean asked pointed questions about the fashion business. Because he seemed genuinely interested, I talked freely about what I'd learned from the beginning of my career in Milan to New York and Chicago, including differences between European and American consumers. Although he questioned me about all facets of the business, he was particularly interested in price points.

He said, "Your success in the women's apparel industry is quite impressive for your age." Then he added, "I hope that didn't sound condescending; I meant it as a compliment. Now tell me, have you ever met your Waterloo in the fashion arena?"

I smiled and said, "That's easy. Our high-end watch line launch in New York never made it off the ground. The competition was too ingrained in that marketplace. There were few buyers in the city at the price points we needed—and almost all of them stayed loyal to the old brands. We test marketed the line for two years and then abandoned it."

I wasn't ready to admit complete defeat, so I added, "However, this classic watch line does quite well in Europe. It's a different market, and there's not as much competition."

As we talked about the watch line, I remembered Manny saying he had a friend who might be interested in investing in a watch business and had even shown me some sketches of watches.

Manny had remained quiet as Sean and I discussed the fashion industry and my career. When we finished talking about watches, Manny admitted, "Sean is the person I thought might invest in your developing a line of fashion watches at a price point people could afford."

"It's an intriguing idea," I told Sean.

Sean smiled and said, "How about your putting together a prospectus for a start-up watch business based on the manufacturing location and price points? I'd like to see some designs and a detailed marketing plan. If your plan makes sense, I might be interested in financing it."

Sean looked at his watch—commenting that he could use a more fashionable one—and excused himself. "It's getting late, and I have to make a recording session for one of my artists, a new, young female talent. I believe she'll make it big in country music. By the way, she'd be a perfect person to promote the watch line if it becomes a go," he said, winking at me.

"You are one persuasive person." I smiled. He gave me a goodbye hug.

As he walked to the door, he turned and said, "My intuition is very good when it comes to spotting people who can be successful. I like investing in their dreams, and even more, I enjoy building our friendships as we fulfill those dreams. I'm looking forward to our developing friendship—and helping you realize your dreams."

Manny listened quietly, but he didn't offer any advice. Instead, he said, "Let's go back to the apartment. I'll fix coffee, and then I've got something to show you." After he poured the coffee, he started toward the bedroom, saying, "I'll be right back."

I could hear him rummaging around in the closet, and then he came back with a portfolio under his arm and sat down beside me. "I showed you a few sketches before, but this is the complete portfolio. Please look it over."

When he opened the portfolio, I realized it was full of color drawings of watches with square, round, and other geometric-shaped faces. There were different band widths and band colors, including some watches with interchangeable bands. Faces were a riot of colors, including copper, bronze, and black—dictated by the end purchaser—male or female. His earlier sketches had impressed me; now I was overwhelmed by the creativity in the designs and the professional renderings.

As I flipped through all the pages, I kept repeating, "Unbelievable. I had no idea you had such an artistic design talent."

"I guess I did inherit my mother's design gene. When I was a child, I drew all the time, just for fun. When Chloe realized I had talent, she kept pushing me to excel in school art projects. When I knew this was something she wanted me to do, I stopped doing it. I hadn't drawn for years, but then I started thinking about what fun it could be to design the watches. Could you put together a business plan to go along with my designs?"

With all this new input, the wheels were spinning in my head for my new career path, remembering the advice of the Chicago lawyer Oakes Boden to be discreet in my planning for a watch line.

CHAPTER 83

Manny drove me to Mama's house. I planned in detail how I would tell my family and friends of my decision to start my own company.

At Mama's house, Manny jumped out to help me with my suitcase. "I'll come in to say hi to your mother and sister before heading to Joe and Grace's place," Manny said.

He gave Mama a big hug before heading to the living room, but stopped at the door. Maria wasn't in her usual place in front of the television. Mama had followed him and said, "Oh, Maria's been under the weather for a few weeks. She's resting upstairs."

Manny nodded and said, "I'll check in with you later, Marilyn. You two have a great visit, and I hope Maria feels better."

When he left, I asked Mama, "What's wrong with Maria?

Wringing her hands, Mama said in a frightened tone, "She's had a fever for almost two weeks. The medicine Dr. Woods prescribed makes her very groggy. I'm so worried. She sleeps all day and night and has no appetite. This bug has gone on way too long. She's scheduled to go to the hospital tomorrow. Dr. Woods wants to run a battery of tests to find out what's wrong with her."

I vividly remembered the high fever that had severely disabled

Maria when she was two. The doctors had told Mama and Daddy she probably wouldn't live past six and recommended putting her in a children's institutional nursing home to get the special care she needed. My parents had said no and brought her home.

Maria was now thirty—beating all odds. And Mama was convinced she'd lived this long because of the loving care she'd received from her, Daddy, and the rest of the family. I agreed wholeheartedly. I was so glad I'd come home this weekend and could be close to Mama. She was obviously distraught over Maria's condition.

On Monday morning, Mama's panicky voice woke me. She was begging Dr. Woods to send an ambulance. I jumped out of bed, threw on a robe, and rushed to Maria's room. She was lying in bed listlessly. "The ambulance is on the way. Get dressed. I need your help," Mama yelled up the steps.

Mama had been up all night with Maria, trying to bring her fever down and stop the seizures that accompanied it. She'd applied cold compresses, and when Maria stabilized, she'd stayed awake for the rest of the night watching her. At sunrise, she called Dr. Woods.

"Why didn't you call me, Mama?" I asked helplessly as the sound of the ambulance's siren came up our drive. She simply said, "You have so much going on in your life that I thought you needed your rest."

I blushed, wishing I had never discussed my frustrations with her, realizing now that I had unknowingly, but still selfishly, contributed to Mama's worries. And I had let her down in this crisis.

The siren brought back memories of Daddy's death to us, but we quickly put them aside to deal with the current crisis. Mama had wrapped Maria in the quilt from the sofa and tucked her favorite doll next to her. As soon as the medics put Maria on the stretcher, Mama grabbed her pocketbook and coat and climbed into the ambulance.

"I'll call Beth and meet you at the hospital," I yelled after them.

I threw on some clothes and ran out the door. Beth was standing on her porch when I pulled up. Frank had already taken the kids to school.

We didn't talk on the way to the hospital. We were both wondering what Mama would do without Maria. Few people could understand Mama's unwavering love and commitment to Maria for all these years. But Beth and I knew Maria was Mama's lifelong purpose and loving priority.

The Rockport Hospital was an L-shaped, one-level brick building. We parked near the emergency entrance and rushed in. Maria was behind one of the white curtains waiting for Dr. Woods. Mama was filling out the admission papers, but as soon as she saw us, she stopped and said, "One of you girls finish this. I don't want to leave Maria alone one more second."

After Beth took the forms Mama moved, ghostlike, toward the curtain that shielded Maria. She appeared distant, almost removed from the urgency of the emergency room.

"I think Mama's in shock," Beth said. Once she completed the forms, a hospital staff member directed us to a family waiting room away from the emergency room.

Finally, Dr. Woods came out. "Maria is a very sick girl. Her organs have begun to shut down," he said sadly.

Beth and I clutched each other; we knew this was a fatal diagnosis. "We're doing everything we can, but it doesn't look good. Your mother needs your support. She's been through hell these past two weeks, and last night confirmed her worst fears."

Dr. Woods took us to Maria's private room. Mama was beside the bed. The overhead lighting cast a ghoulish, green light, and there were strange sounds coming from the large machine that was helping Maria breathe.

The hospital sheets were pulled up to Maria's chin, and her pallid face blended into the whiteness of the sheets. Mama looked so small, sitting in the straight-backed chair next to her dying daughter's head. She seemed to be counting each strained and intermittent breath from Maria.

Beth and I embraced her. I offered to get her something to eat or drink, and she turned her head toward me, but said nothing. Then she looked back at Maria, gently touching her forehead.

The nurse who came into the room to take Maria's vital signs told Mama she was going to call Dr. Woods to come back immediately.

In a muffled voice, Mama said, "Oh, that won't be necessary. Maria is going to be okay." She was in complete denial about Maria's condition.

Maria stopped breathing before Dr. Woods came back—not even the noisy ventilator could put air in her lungs and let it out. Maria's life had ended.

Beth and I watched as Mama stroked Maria's hair and said, "My beautiful Maria. You were always to be with me. Your daddy and I knew your sisters would go out into the world to make their way, but you would stay with us at home. Please, please don't leave me now."

Tears streamed down our faces. Each of us was alone in our sorrow.

Then I felt like an intruder who was invading Mama's private time with Maria, so I took Beth's hand and led her into the hall.

CHAPTER 84

When the Rockport community heard about Maria's death, they gathered around our family, as they had when Daddy died.

I was comforted by Manny. He stayed in Rockport to help Mama and me after the funeral. He was so dear, always trying to help without getting in the way. He even made me laugh with his observations about the tons of food and all the flowers our neighbors brought.

I spent ten days in Rockport before I finally admitted I had to confess to those close to me about my career change. I talked to Beth and Grace about my anxieties at leaving Mama to close up the apartment and office in Chicago and move to Nashville to perhaps start my new company. They both promised to keep in touch with Mama every day and reminded me her church circle would also be supporting her.

Chicago was cold, rainy, and dreary, mirroring my empty feelings. I missed my family, and I longed for Manny's comforting reassurance that my grief would pass.

Visiting the office for the last time, I realized my decision to hire Jalee had been a stroke of genius. All the orders were organized and ready to send to our manufacturing operations. The office was in good shape to turn over to Chloe and Janice's new manager.

On my last night in Chicago, Jalee had a personal dinner for me in her home with her husband and child. She presented me with a beautiful vase as a "going-away gift." Her career plans had changed, too, as she had accepted another job closer to her child-care with more realistic work hours. We both had tears in our eyes when I left this special evening.

Moving to Nashville was now a reality. A prospectus and watch design had been presented to Sean, who wanted to meet with me once I was settled in Nashville. Sean had reviewed my watch documentation and wanted to move ahead on my start-up watch business as soon as we worked out the details of his financing.

A meeting in Sean's office set up the initial draw and line of credit to begin. My head reeled. Moments of excitement were followed by total panic. This process was a lot easier when Chloe and Janice took the financial risks for my ideas. They always seemed so calm in their business dealings, and I wondered if they ever had the same anxieties I was now experiencing.

CHAPTER 85

After my finalization of business financing, I was eager to visit Rockport for a few days and spend time with Mama. When I called Beth to ask her how Mama was handling her grief, I was surprised at her assessment. "Mama is mentally distant. Her mind wanders when she talks to me, and I've caught her coming out of Maria's room with the saddest expression on her face. She's often inconsolable, saying over and over, 'Maria was such a sweet child and depended on me for everything. I miss her every minute of every day.' Mama questions her relevance now."

I went home the next day. Mama asked Beth and me to dinner. She said she wanted to talk about her struggle to deal with Maria's death.

Once again, Mama sat in her straight-backed chair. "Your daddy and I faced many challenges in our marriage. After Maria was born, Clark and I knew we couldn't afford any more children. However, there were few resources available to prevent pregnancy then, and I became pregnant when Maria was twenty months old.

"We worried about the financial burden, and two months later, I had a miscarriage. You girls were at school when it happened, and we decided not to tell you.

"I blamed myself for the miscarriage. I felt so guilty because the doctor had warned me about lifting heavy objects and said I should rest. I didn't follow his advice. Even after my doctor warned me about physical labor, I continued to work in the garden, often lifting and hauling plants and soil and pushing myself to total exhaustion.

"Then, on a hot, humid day, I was lifting a very heavy pot and began to cramp. By the time I got to the house, I'd begun to lose the fetus. Clark heard my screams from the garden and ran to help me. I was hysterical and kept blaming myself for the miscarriage.

"Clark always said that was foolish talk, but even to this day, I wonder if I subconsciously sabotaged my pregnancy because of the financial burden. This was before we knew the special needs our Maria would place on our family.

"For days, I cried about losing the baby. I even tried to bargain with God, promising if He gave us another child I'd do everything in my power to protect it. I guess God knew what He was doing by not blessing us with another child.

"Because of the rare virus that had attacked her brain and caused a high, prolonged fever, Maria was not walking or talking at two. Clark and I knew something was wrong, but we both were in denial about her condition. Even Dr. Johnson told us to give Maria time to develop.

"We finally had to admit something was wrong and took her to a specialist at Vanderbilt Hospital in Nashville. You may remember that Mrs. Thompson came to stay with you. The doctors at Vanderbilt performed a series of tests and finally came to us with the most heartbreaking news any parent could hear. They said our baby had brain damage that couldn't be corrected, and she would never have a normal life.

"I had had a very difficult labor with Maria. She was turned wrong in the birth canal, and the umbilical cord must have been around her neck, cutting off oxygen to her brain. I've always wondered if that also contributed to the debilitating damage that would later occur from the brain virus and the high fever.

"When Dr. Johnson used forceps to deliver her, she had already turned blue. She didn't cry at birth for what appeared to be minutes but was probably only seconds. The birth was so difficult that I thought she might have health problems, but I refused to accept that reality."

Mama could not go on. She was sobbing so hard and her body was shaking so uncontrollably that her chair moved. Beth and I jumped up to comfort her, putting our arms around her, but we didn't speak. The tears running down my cheeks dropped on Mama's head. We finally composed ourselves, but Beth was so visibly upset she could only murmur "Good night" as she left.

Mama started for her bedroom; then she turned and said, "I'm so pleased you decided to take control of your own life and no longer permit others to make your decisions. That's what your daddy and I did with Maria. The doctors said we should put her in an institution where she could get proper care. We talked it over and prayed a lot.

"Clark and I made the decision to keep Maria at home and give her our love and care. If we had allowed other people to make the decision for us, we would have missed out on the loving experience of having Maria in our life. Life is filled with one difficult decision after another—challenges that ultimately shape our lives. Don't let anyone make a decision for you, unless it's a decision you reach together with someone you deeply love and trust."

As I lay awake that night, I thought of the many difficult decisions my parents had made in their lives. As I drifted off to sleep, I concluded this was part of being an adult and learning to face challenges of different proportions along the way.

The next morning, while having coffee, Mama insisted I move in with her. I felt a sense of responsibility to be there for her but also knew this was not my home now.

CHAPTER 86

Although I was staying with Manny on a temporary basis, I declined at his invitation to move in with him permanently. It took me two days to find a fully furnished, one-bedroom garage apartment in a pleasant neighborhood within walking distance of Manny's place. I took this find as a sign of validation for my decision to move to Nashville. My landlady was a friendly, elderly woman who gave me a sweetheart deal on rent and let me use her telephone till I could get mine installed.

While unpacking my personal belongings, I realized how little I had acquired over the years. My wardrobe was the most expensive thing I owned—and the most extensive. I wasn't sure this wardrobe would work in my new city, but for now, it was my only option. I had limited funds and loads of other things to worry about.

Interrupting settling into my new place, my landlady said Manny had called to say Sean wanted to see us this afternoon and to come to his music store.

When I got to his shop, Manny's single was playing in the background, and I realized I'd never asked him how his recording was doing. "Manny, I'm sorry for being so self-centered. The recording sounds wonderful. How's it doing?"

He smiled and planted a kiss on my cheek before he said, "First we have to get to that meeting with Sean to talk about your business venture. After we get that settled, I'll tell you how it made number one on the local charts in Nashville."

I threw my arms around him and then released him. "Are you kidding? Your record is number one? That's wonderful. You're sure?"

Manny said, "Don't take my word for it. Just ask Jack here, my number one helper in the shop."

I looked at Jack for confirmation, and he nodded affirmatively and beamed. "It's been on the top ten list for the past two weeks in 'new country sounds' and just hit number one vocal this week."

"That's fantastic! Oh my God, I've picked up your mother's insensitive behavior by not asking you sooner," I moaned, hitting my forehead with my hand in self-punishment.

Manny laughed and said, "Don't be embarrassed. You have two good excuses, Marilyn. First, it's hard to get Chloe out of your life—although you're making great strides. And then there's that little thing about a new business venture. I'm going to cut you some slack on this one."

A few customers came into the store, and Manny moved toward them. I sat on an old rattan woven chair with camouflage cushions. Manny looked so in control of this environment. He moved around the store with such confidence, pointing out the differences in the guitars to these musicians. He knew his stuff.

I marveled at how Manny had made such a complete transformation since I met him more than a decade ago in Long Island. But so had I. Thinking back to our first encounter, I blushed at how Manny seduced me.

Manny finished with the customers and told Jack we wouldn't be back after we met Sean. Jack smiled. "I've got you covered, boss. See you tomorrow."

I liked the congenial and cooperative working relationship between Manny and Jack. Both had a kicked-back attitude, but they were completely professional when dealing with customers. They knew the instruments and music they sold, and it was obvious their customers trusted them. What a difference from the aggressive and competitive fashion world I came from.

As we walked to Sean's office, I gushed over Manny's accomplishments. "I'm so proud of what you've done. Your store's only been open for a short time, and it's doing great. And now you have a number one single!"

"I think I'm the luckiest guy in the world. I have you by my side, my dad and brother in my corner, and an exciting musical career ahead. Thank God, I'm not the attorney my parents wanted me to be." He pulled me close as we walked arm in arm.

CHAPTER 87

Sean's office was modest. When we arrived, he was with a client, and the receptionist was on the phone. We sat in two well-worn upholstered chairs in the corner. Water circles on the brown veneer table between the chairs were partly covered by the latest Nashville music magazines.

The cover of one magazine had the picture of an attractive young woman with long, silky blonde hair. She had a guitar in her hands and was sitting on a stool as if she were performing. Manny picked up the magazine and pointed to the cover. "Do you know who this lady is?"

I told him "I've no idea—not a clue."

He said, "She's the latest celeb in country music."

I punched him in the ribs and retorted, "I thought you were."

He laughed and explained that one single recording did not a celeb make. "She's got numerous recordings, and her upcoming national tour to promote her and her music is already sold out."

As he was talking, Sean's door opened, and the girl on the cover walked out. Manny stood, smiled broadly, and extended his hand, "Hello, Brittany. I want you to meet my friend, Marilyn White."

Brittany clasped his hand and then nodded at me. She was

prettier in person, and I was so proud when she congratulated Manny on his record reaching number one on the local charts. Then, to my surprise, she put her arm around his waist, guiding him toward the door. She was talking in a low voice, obviously meant for his ears alone, but I heard her invitation. "When can we get together again? It was such fun the last time we jammed together."

Had I heard correctly? My blood boiled. I was jealous. *How dare he spend time with another woman, especially one as talented and beautiful as Brittany? What did he mean by introducing me to Brittany as "my friend" Marilyn? How impersonal was that?*

Brittany dropped her arm from Manny's waist and kissed him lightly on the cheek. Manny gave her a friendly squeeze and said, "We'll talk later."

Manny turned toward me with a "shit-eatin' grin" across his face. I was fuming. My teeth were clenched so tightly my jaws were locked shut. All I wanted was to slap that smug smile off his face, but just then Sean walked out, grabbed both our hands, and, as he guided us toward his office, asked if we'd like coffee or water.

The only thing I wanted was to stomp out of the office and forget about the watch business, Nashville, and Manny. However, I'd learned my lesson on impulsive behavior, and instead of saying or doing anything rash, I began taking deep breaths. My logical side triumphed, and I adjusted my attitude to concentrate on Sean's business proposal. I'd deal with Manny later.

As Sean laid out the papers, I looked around his office. It was much like his reception area. There was an old brown leather couch with cushions indented by many previous clients. Sean and I sat on the couch, and Manny pulled up a wooden side chair from the very messy desk.

My gut reaction was negative, and I began to have serious reservations about Sean's acumen. His office certainly didn't look like the office of a highly successful businessman. M&M Music was more impressive—and cleaner. I wondered what Chloe and Janice would think if they saw this setup.

Sean spoke to Manny first. "Now that your first recording has traction, when do you think you'll be ready to put together an album?"

I relaxed a little as they talked about this production opportunity. And as they talked, I chided myself for judging Sean and his office on appearance. He obviously knew business financing. After a few minutes with Manny, Sean turned to me and said, "Sorry. We're not here to talk about Manny's music career, but you have to move fast to take advantage of success. I wanted him to be thinking about that album. Now to our real business—helping you set up a successful watch company."

I opened the portfolio to show Manny's comprehensive watch designs, since he had only seen one design with the prospectus. Sure of the visual impact, I spread out the extensive business plan I'd developed to accompany the designs. I'd outlined the start-up cost of production, marketing, and advertising and provided detailed budgets, expansion plans, and projections for the first, third, and fifth years.

Sean glanced at the plans and portfolio designs. "Very impressive, Marilyn. I wish everyone who came to me had such a well-developed concept and business plan. However, I have a confession—I loan money to people I believe in. Plans are nice; relationships and faith in the person are better."

Manny laughed and said, "Do you think I had a business plan when Sean loaned me money to take a shot at recording? You know me better than that."

I was uncomfortable with Sean's loose approach to financial lending. Relationships and gut reaction didn't seem like a sound investment philosophy. Plus, my business education and experience in the fashion industry had proved that analytical planning was a tried-and-true road map to successful growth in business. Perhaps Sean's route was not right for me—the high analyst.

I briefly thought about going the traditional route of seeking a bank loan. Bankers understood the importance of a well-prepared prospectus. It was only a brief thought because I immediately realized I had no assets and, therefore, no collateral for a loan.

I sat quietly stewing in my own juices while Sean and Manny discussed Brittany's recordings and upcoming tour. Since I had nothing to add to their conversation, I was mentally calculating a strategy to bring the discussion back to my business venture when Sean stood up, signaling the end of our meeting.

He shook Manny's hand and then mine, saying, "Marilyn, your loan papers will be ready for your signature tomorrow. If you need more money than you projected for your start-up, let me know."

I was totally surprised and blurted out, "Do you want me to leave my business plan with you?"

He shook his head. "No. All I need is your signature. I've seen enough."

When we left Sean's office, my head was spinning. I had mixed feelings. I'd expected Sean to study my plan in depth and then give me feedback. Instead, he had displayed total confidence in me, simply based on his initial exposure to my idea and a quick review of the plan. He'd only scanned the plan and sketches, but then I remembered he'd asked me several pointed questions. Maybe he had paid more attention than I thought.

Then it hit me. I'd never flown solo in business. I'd always had support and advice. But this business was mine—nobody else wasinvolved—I'd sink or swim on my own. I felt insecure, amazed, frightened and—best of all—incredibly eager to begin.

When we got out to the street, Manny looked at me and asked, "Marilyn, what's wrong? You look worried when you should feel liberated and happy. You're getting the loan. You're ready to start your own business—that's heady stuff."

I didn't know how to describe my feelings, so I confronted him about that cozy scene with Brittany. "What's with you and Brittany getting together? I heard her in Sean's office trying to make a date with you—and not a first one, either."

Manny laughed heartily before he asked, "Are you jealous of Brittany and me?" He sounded so pleased with himself.

"I just didn't realize there was another woman in your life," I said and turned on my heel, walking away from him.

He grabbed my arm and turned me to face him. "If you must know, Brittany and I are working on a record together. The meeting she mentioned will be in a recording studio. We need to collaborate on the recording before she leaves on tour, and we don't have much time."

Then he put his hands on my face and said, "I love you so much. I would never do anything to jeopardize our relationship."

I just broke down and tried to explain how inadequate I felt. "I'm so afraid I'll fail. Everything will depend on me—and my actions."

Manny held me close and said "Marilyn, as an entrepreneur, you'll always be afraid. Fear is your motivation. But the panic you feel now will leave once you're up and running and those first orders start coming in. That's what I've learned since I opened M&M. Trust me. Now, let's go get you some comfortable clothes." As we walked up the street, I wondered how Manny had gained so much wisdom since opening M&M.

Then I processed his last sentence and bristled. "What's wrong with my clothes?"

"For one thing, you look uptight and snobby for Nashville. People here are more relaxed and easygoing, and their clothes reflect that attitude. Your sophisticated outfits don't fit in. If you keep wearing those conceited-looking threads, people will think you don't want to fit in. We've got to get you some jeans and cowboy boots—pronto."

I told him I wasn't sure I would ever fit into his world, but he just laughed. "Wait till I get you into a wool plaid skirt, a cotton blouse, knee socks, and penny loafers. You'll be perfect."

I blushed, remembering my outfit for that New York weekend so long ago. I couldn't be angry with him. I slapped his chest and said, "Okay, but only because you've cleaned up your appearance. You always wore jeans and flannel shirts, but at least now they don't have big holes in them."

He started to dance on the sidewalk, mimicking Gene Kelly by spinning around a lamppost. I pulled off my high heels and ran ahead of him barefoot. It felt so good to be footloose and fancy-free. Manny yelled encouragement: "That's my girl!"

When I changed clothes for our shopping trip, I selected my most casual outfit—linen slacks, a silk shirt, and black flats. Manny was dressed in his usual jeans, crisp shirt, and cowboy boots. I smiled as I dressed because I wondered if Manny realized he was his mother's son—grooming me for his way of life as Chloe had groomed me for hers.

As we walked toward the shopping center, I said, "Sean really surprised me. It's hard for me to comprehend that someone who doesn't know me would invest in me so readily."

Manny said, "Stop imitating Chloe. That's what she'd think. You're going to have to learn to trust people and not be so suspicious. Tell me, how did your dad borrow money for the farm?"

I replied, "Daddy went to the bank, told them how much he needed, and agreed to pay it back with interest as soon as the crops were harvested. He and the banker shook hands and signed the papers. He never failed to pay back his loan in full.

"I get it. Sean's that banker, and he trusts people. And I'm my daddy's daughter. I'll pay Sean back in full if it's the last thing I do in my own business."

CHAPTER 88

Getting my watch business up and running was far more complicated than I'd anticipated. I was quickly bogged down in an avalanche of details and realized I needed expert help. Actually. I needed a Johann Zuddick, the Swiss watchmaker, but I couldn't call him because he dealt with Toni exclusively.

Then I remembered Dubie Frech, another talented Zürich watchmaker. He'd helped Toni and me with the internal movement specifications for Chloe's watch design, but it wasn't a continuing relationship. I rummaged through my New York files, found his business card and called him in Switzerland.

I was cautious in briefing Dubie about my new business venture, and I didn't elaborate on my relationship with Toni or Chloe, simply saying I was no longer affiliated with them. I did, however, say I'd expect complete confidentiality for anything we discussed going forward.

"I'm calling because I need your expertise. I'd like you to advise me about resources I should be considering in the manufacturing process."

We talked briefly and then agreed I should come to Zürich for at least a week to fully explore my options. Before I hung up,

I reminded him that Toni, Chloe, and Janice didn't need to know about my plans to open a watch business in the States. "Please don't let anyone know I'll be meeting with you," I said.

Once Dubie and I settled on a date, I flew to Switzerland and booked a room in a small, out-of-the-way hotel. Upon arrival at the hotel, I dropped off my bags before going to Dubie's office. We greeted each other with the customary kiss on each cheek, and since it had been some time since we'd seen each other, we took a few minutes to catch up. He said he'd missed seeing me in Zürich and was delighted I'd sought his help in my new business.

Before we addressed my business venture, we talked briefly about Toni and Chloe. Dubie knew Chloe's watches were selling in Europe and wanted to hear my take on why the designs had failed in New York.

"Dubie, Toni was in charge of the watch line operation in New York—not me. I was assigned to market the product in the States beginning with New York, our test market. However, we faced stiff competition from many other high-end lines with brand recognition, and most retail outlets were uncertain about adding another unknown, expensive line to their offerings. The few retailers who placed orders didn't reorder. Our watch line had a poor sales performance, and Chloe decided to pull the plug. Toni and Chloe might have another explanation for its failure," I added, choosing my words carefully.

Dubie nodded and then asked, "How are things with you and Toni?"

Again, I was circumspect. "I hope Toni and I will always be on friendly terms, but since we live and work on separate continents, we don't have much reason for communication."

Dubie obviously picked up on my reluctance to elaborate and changed the subject. However, the conversation still centered on Toni when he pointedly asked, "The last time I saw Toni, he told me about some quality problems in a shipment of the C&J line to Chicago—do you know anything about it?"

"I was responsible for the Chicago shops that carried the C&J brand. When Chloe called about the quality problems, I immediately used all efforts for damage control. That quality issue was probably the main reason I decided to resign, although I'd been considering leaving the company and starting my watch business for some time."

Dubie lowered his voice as if telling a secret. "When Toni advised Chloe to have this expensive clothing line manufactured in the Philippines to save money, I warned him there could be problems because the workmanship would not meet the standards expected in fine clothing. However, Toni simply said, 'The silver-tongued "Great Marilyn" will be capable of damage control if something goes wrong with any shipments.' There was such undeniable sarcasm in his voice when he mentioned your name that I suspected you were no longer on the best of terms."

I flushed in anger but quickly recovered and smiled. I didn't want Dubie to know he had disclosed information I shouldn't have. He continued, "I found out about the clothing line because Toni was also outsourcing some of Chloe's watch business. He thought he could save money by moving it from Switzerland. Toni is an arrogant man who thinks he has all the answers," Dubie confided.

It didn't take much prodding to keep Dubie expanding on Toni's lack of business scruples and integrity in his dealings with Chloe and Janice's company. "The watches you were putting in the New York stores were of inferior quality—not the same Swiss-made quality watches we sell here in Europe," he added. "The only thing that was the same was the high price tag."

Apparently, Toni had sabotaged the watch design in the States and now intended to sabotage the high-end clothing line. No one had complained about the watch quality, but I had wondered why we never got repeat orders or why so many retailers refused to even consider stocking our brand. If the first stores that carried the watches had found the quality unacceptable, they would have talked with other retailers. That would explain a lot of the problems I had in marketing the line.

I was shocked and asked Dubie if Chloe was aware of Toni's activities in the States. "Of course," he replied. "She's greedy and backed him in his plan to make more profit in the States by supplying inferior quality merchandise. Chloe said Americans wouldn't know the difference and would pay a higher price for lower quality because of her established brand name."

"Well, I guess you know why I've left Chloe's company and am venturing out on my own," I replied. I was now confident Dubie would keep my business a secret. Based on our exchanges, I knew I could rely on his support. I was so glad I'd come to Zürich and talked with Dubie in person. We would never have reached this level of trust so quickly through phone calls.

Now it was time to talk about my business. We quickly moved to the drafting table, and I spread out the drawings. Dubie responded enthusiastically and with complete approval for the unique colors, shapes, and sizes. I was thrilled with his few suggestions and relieved when he approved my proposal.

Then he began to educate me about the internal mechanics of timepieces, explaining that the movement, whether for an expensive Swiss watch or a less expensive version, was made up of many moving parts. The movement could be designed to fit into different watch case sizes. Cost differences came from the materials used for the watch cases, faces, and bands.

"Precision Designs is a reputable watch manufacturer located in the Blue Ridge Mountains of North Carolina, in the village of Charter, outside Asheville. They specialize in cases, faces, and bands," Dubie said. "I've used their watch products when the movement was specified in size here in Switzerland to fit a case, face, and band manufactured in the States. I'll be glad to call and introduce you to them."

Dubie and I agreed on the number of internal working movements he could provide for my initial order if we standardized the case size and worked with Precision Design.

He smiled broadly and moved toward a small refrigerator in the corner. "Let's celebrate our new business collaboration and our bright future with a glass of champagne. We will do well together."

I held my glass flute as he poured the sparkling liquid. My heart was racing with excitement as we lifted our glasses. My new business venture was now a reality.

After we toasted, Dubie turned serious. "Marilyn, you should have solid legal counseling in case Chloe and Toni try to interfere or stop your new watch venture. You know I was involved in their start-up watch design business and still work with them. It's just a feeling, but I keep seeing caution flags that they might try to sabotage your business endeavor."

"I had those same flags, Dubie. Even before I got my financial backing, I had legal counsel from a corporate law firm in Chicago. I was worried that Chloe might become vindictive and sue me for conflict of interest. My attorney advised me that there was no precedent for a conflict of interest lawsuit, since my watches would be different in both design and price point, plus sold in a non-competitive market on a different continent. Basically, she can't thwart free enterprise.

"And now that I know the full story, I don't see how they could even think of doing anything to hurt my fledgling business after they knowingly sabotaged the quality of watches they sent to New York!" I said. This time, I didn't try to hide my anger.

Dubie smiled and patted me on the shoulder. "Marilyn, you are no longer Chloe's protégée. Now you know how she and Toni operate in business. Personally, I believe you are smart to be out of their clutches. They used you to gain a foothold in the States. But I warn you—when your business becomes successful, as I'm sure it will, those two wolves in sheep's clothing will try to interfere with your operation."

Dubie's comments proved to me that he didn't approve of how Chloe and Toni operated. I also believed Dubie was in my corner, pulling for my success.

I met with Dubie several more times to discuss my business launch, and I got the customary kiss and a big hug before I left Zürich. On the plane back to the States, I knew I'd made the right decision to go to Zürich for help—even if it had cost me a pretty penny. But now at least it was *my* penny!

CHAPTER 89

Manny met me at the airport and eagerly questioned me about my meetings with Dubie and what I had learned in Zürich.

"I want all the details," he said. "Tell me exactly what happened and where you go from here."

I briefed him on the agreement and the next steps but said nothing about how his mother and Toni's greed had undermined the American market with inferior quality products. It would only increase his disdain for them.

Once I'd answered his questions, I had a question of my own. "How did the album release go?"

He grinned almost sheepishly and said, "An overnight success. I really don't deserve all this musical recognition—at least, not this quickly."

I kissed him on the cheek and teased him, "I think you're talented enough to sing me to sleep tonight."

He laughed and said, "Singing will not be on my mind when we tumble into bed."

Back at Manny's apartment, I said, "Right now, I just want to take a hot shower to get rid of my travel dust. It's also the best way to recover from jet lag and will give you time to finish dinner."

"Perfect," he said. "My terrycloth bathrobe is on the back of the door. Use it when you finish. It will speed up my seducing you later," he said, twirling an imaginary mustache and laughing.

While I showered, Manny added the final touches to a very romantic dinner. By the time I stepped into the living room, wrapped in his robe and feeling like a new person, he'd created the perfect setting for our romantic reunion. The room was bathed in candlelight, soft music was playing, a glass of wine was waiting for me on the coffee table, and the aroma of the food was so inviting we sat down immediately.

After a delicious dinner, Manny pulled out his sketchbook to show me some additional watch designs. I was deeply touched that he was taking such an active interest in my new business, especially since his own career was taking off. His new designs were more playful, with each face having a unique personality. And, much to my delight, he'd given many of these new creations whimsical names: Critical Time, Playtime, Two-Time, Watch Out, and Watch This. I laughed and added my own timepiece-themed tag lines to several watches.

Manny just smiled as he picked up the sketchbook again. "Don't waste all that enthusiasm. Keep some for my final design, which, in keeping with the watch taglines, is called Time 4 Love." He flipped to the last page and, instead of a watch, revealed an engagement ring design. I was stunned—and speechless—as Manny forged on. "Marilyn White, I have loved you for years and plan to love you for all my years to come. Will you marry me?"

This was so right. With tears of happiness rolling down my cheeks, I flung my arms around his neck and said, "Yes, Manny Bateson, I want nothing more than to spend the rest of my life with you."

He picked me up and carried me to the bedroom, and as he placed me on the bed, he reached into the nightstand drawer for a small velveteen box. It held a stunning diamond engagement ring—a duplicate of the sketch he'd just shown me.

"My father's friend in New York's Diamond District used my sketch to design this ring especially for you. Like you, it's one of a kind and has a special brilliance." As he slipped the ring on my finger, I pulled him close to seal our promise in a lovemaking session of pure unbridled joy and intimacy. The evening marked a definite change in our relationship. There was no second guessing, only a deep sense of optimism about our future together. We both knew we'd finally arrived at a level of maturity to know our own hearts and minds.

I woke jubilant the next morning. Over coffee, we discussed the family dynamics of a traditional wedding in either Rockport or Nashville.

Manny speculated on how our wedding would play out. "If you think Joe and Grace's wedding was a circus, I guarantee if Chloe and Janice show up, ours will be ten times more of a Barnum and Bailey show. I'd love to be the proverbial fly on the wall when Chloe receives a wedding invitation from the son she scorns and his ungrateful fiancée who resigned from her company." Although we laughed about it, there was an element of sadness as we recognized the truth of his words.

But Chloe and Janice were not a priority. Number one on our to-do list was a trip to Rockport to tell my family and Joe and Grace before calling Manny's father in New York City.

We left right after breakfast, and our first stop was Mama's white bungalow. As we pulled into the driveway, I was struck by the appearance of her yard. It was neglected. The flowers were wilted, the grass was overgrown, and the shrubbery needed trimming. "I wonder what's going on," I said to Manny. "Mama always kept her place neat as a pin inside and out."

I'd been so totally absorbed in launching my business that I hadn't been home for quite some time, but I recalled a phone conversation with Beth. Now I tried to reconstruct it verbatim for Manny.

"Beth said she was worried about Mama, who has appeared lost since Maria's death. She's forgetful and depressed. She's not keeping up with her teaching responsibilities, either. She uses poor health as an excuse to request a substitute teacher. Beth wanted me to know so I wouldn't be shocked when I came home."

I'd glossed over Beth's remarks at the time, thinking it was normal grief that would eventually subside. I had also thought Beth might be making a mountain out of a molehill. She could be overly dramatic at times.

As we walked to the house, I kept thinking I'd made a mistake—a serious one—when I ignored Beth's warning.

"I'm almost afraid to walk through the back door," I confessed. "I'm not even sure if we should tell Mama our news. I don't know how she'll react."

"We'll play it by ear," Manny said.

The kitchen was in total disarray. There were dishes in the sink, opened containers on the drain board, and clutter on every surface. When I called out, there was no response. When Mama finally came out, she seemed dazed, rubbing her eyes as if she'd been asleep. She was still in her flannel nightgown with pink plastic bubble rollers in her hair, and she apologized, "Oh, Marilyn, did you tell me you were coming this morning? I'm so sorry. I guess I just plain forgot. Let me fix you two something to eat."

Now I was alarmed. She didn't look like Mama, and she looked unsure about fixing breakfast. I thought she needed some time to collect her thoughts, so I said, "Manny, why don't you and Mama go in the living room for a visit while I tidy up the kitchen and brew a pot of coffee?" Manny took Mama's arm and gently led her into the living room.

I lunged for the kitchen phone to call Beth, and as soon as she answered, I unfairly accused her of neglecting Mama. "Beth, why haven't you taken better care of Mama? I've never seen her like this. She's a wreck, and so is her house."

Beth responded with her own accusation about my neglectful absence. After a few tense moments, we calmed down, and Beth gave me an update.

"Marilyn, I tried to warn you. Things have continued to decline since Maria's death, especially Mama's mental state. I was planning to call you because the principal of Mama's school called me last week and said he thought it would be best if Mama retired or took a leave of absence.

"Since then, I've talked to Mama about retiring, explaining how it would help if the school system could replace her instead of trying to find substitutes for her absences. I didn't say anything about her mental confusion in the classroom, but that's certainly a factor. I haven't had much luck. Now that you're here, we should talk to her and make some decisions about her future."

I agreed. "I'll call you, Beth, after I've had a chance to assess the situation."

After I fixed coffee, Manny drank a cup in record time and left to check in with Joe and Grace and let them know he'd be spending the night with them. I walked him to the door, and he whispered that he didn't think it was the right time to announce our engagement. I wholeheartedly agreed.

I tried to talk with Mama during the day, but she barely responded. She just sat and stared blankly out the window. I fixed a light supper and then helped her to bed early. I gave the house a superficial cleaning, since I didn't want to disturb her sleep by running the vacuum cleaner. When I took the last load of laundry out of the dryer, I collapsed on the sofa. This was not the joyous homecoming I'd imagined.

Instead of joy, there was sadness. I shut my eyes and lay on the couch, wondering how we would ever bring Mama back from the abyss she seemed to be in. Mama was slipping away, and I didn't see any hope. I felt incredibly sad—and not just for Mama. How could I deal with the loss of my mother? I'd finally admitted I'd not recovered from the loss of Daddy and Maria. I vowed I would fight for Mama.

I sat up, picked up a magazine on the coffee table, and began to mindlessly leaf through it when an article caught my attention. It described how aging could weaken brain functionality and cause cognitive decline, severely diminishing a person's quality of life. The article said the disease, called dementia, was marked by a loss of mental skills and memory as it progressed. I read the entire article before calling Beth to read parts of it to her.

"I think we should find out more about this and have Mama's cognitive ability tested. Let's call Dr. Johnson tomorrow and ask him what we should do. I'd like to have some plan before Manny and I go back to Nashville. And Beth, we're in this together."

I woke the next morning to the familiar smell of coffee wafting up to my second- floor bedroom. Had I overreacted to Mama last night? I dressed quickly and rushed downstairs. Mama was dressed, her hair was combed, and she was sitting at the table having coffee and toast. She smiled as I walked toward the coffee maker and said, as she always did, "Did you sleep well, Marilyn?"

We talked about the mundane things happening in Rockport for a few minutes before I asked her directly how she was feeling.

"Are you all right, Mama? I was so surprised yesterday to find the house and yard in such disarray. Have you been ill?"

"Not really, but I'm getting so forgetful that I sometimes

frighten myself. I'm so tired, too. I can hardly get out of bed some mornings, and I have to call the school and tell them I just can't come in."

"Mama, Beth and I want to tell Dr. Johnson what's happening. This is so unlike you. We can ask him to recommend someone who specializes in memory loss. We need to make sure you'll be safe living here independently." Mama nodded her head in agreement.

There would be no engagement announcement until we could figure out how to help Mama. My beautiful ring stayed in its box in my suitcase during my Rockport visit.

Beth and I eventually had Mama tested by a neurologist at Vanderbilt Medical Center in Nashville. Dr. Johnson said she was among the best in the country, and we accepted her findings after her assessment, which confirmed our fears.

The neurologist explained that Mama had progressive memory loss and said that we should have someone with her if she stayed in her house. She also said we should locate a facility that could care for her as the disease progressed.

"Your mother will have good days when she's lucid and bad days when she'll be totally confused. Even if she stays at home with help, that will only be a temporary solution. Fortunately, there's a relatively new facility, the Baptist Home for Seniors, just outside Rockport. I recommend the three of you visit it as soon as you can and find out if your mother would like to live there."

When Beth and I asked Mama about visiting the facility, she agreed at once. She said, "I just know that things are not right with my memory and I need help. I'm so grateful you girls are here."

We visited the Baptist Home as soon as we got back to Rockport. Mama saw several people she knew there, and we put her name on a waiting list. We hoped she'd be living there within the year.

When we got back to Mama's house after our tour, I called Manny to meet us at Mama's. I was sure this was the right time to give my family some happy news after our struggles and worries about Mama over the past two months.

Manny and I asked Beth and Frank, Joe and Grace, and all their children to join us at Mama's house for a family meeting, without disclosing the subject. Once we were assembled in the living room, I slipped the engagement ring on my finger and slowly moved my hand around the circle. I was so proud of my beautiful ring and the commitment it symbolized.

Everyone squealed with delight. Mama's face lit up, and her smile swept across her face. It was a perfect dose of medicine for her and our families. Mama said she expected to help with all the wedding preparations. I assured her I'd be depending on her for advice and much-needed help. "You'll be front and center, Mama. Don't you worry."

Of course, the first questions all involved our timetable for the ceremony, and I had to admit it would be a lengthy engagement. "I've got a business to launch, and Manny's got to continue to grow his business—and build his music career. Give us some time. Now I'm just happy to know that Manny and I will be together for the rest of our lives."

CHAPTER 90

Manny insisted I talk with his landlord about a small, empty space next to his store. He thought it would be a perfect office. I knew I couldn't conduct business from my one-bedroom garage apartment, but I worried about the cost of an office. When I talked with Sean, he agreed with Manny. "Marilyn, you included rental in your budget, so why are you worried?"

Reluctantly, I called Manny's landlord and was surprised when he eagerly agreed to lease the space for a hundred dollars a month plus utilities. As soon as I signed the lease, I measured the office and decided it was large enough for a desk, two chairs, and a filing cabinet. Best of all, I had a mailing address, not a post office box; my company appeared stable. I combed through the yellow pages and found a nearby consignment store. As I rummaged through the offerings, I kept thinking that this was how Lindsey and I had started out in New York. Once I'd selected the furniture, I borrowed the Jeep and enlisted Manny and Jack to move the furniture and set up the office.

To get my marketing communications program initiated for my company, I met with a small advertising firm in Nashville. We discussed the company name; I wanted a unique name that was personal and made me smile. I came up with "Jalee Watches, Inc." as the brand name, which would be shortened to "Jalee" with a tag line of "The Just-In-Time Company."

Although I had to control the bursts of apprehension when I thought about what I'd gotten myself into, I woke every day eager to get to my office and continue putting together the pieces of the business puzzle from my plan. I knew it was a good plan, but sometimes I needed reassurance. That's when I leaned on my two strong support systems—Manny and Sean.

Just as everything seemed to be falling into place, the unexpected happened. One afternoon, I was out of my office storing things in Manny's basement storage unit. When I stopped by his store to return his keys, he met me at the door.

"Thank God, you're back," he said. "Beth called me when you didn't answer your office phone. Your mother is in the hospital. There was an accident in her kitchen. Beth wants us to drive to Rockport immediately. I'll fill you in on the details once we get on the road."

I locked my office door, and Manny called Jack to cover for him in the store. When I got in the Jeep, Manny said, "I'll drive you to your apartment so you can pack a bag. I'm not sure how long you'll need to stay in Rockport."

Although Nashville was only an hour from Rockport, it was the longest hour I could remember, and I was grateful that Manny was driving me there, especially after he told me the rest of Beth's conversation.

"Marilyn, your mother was cooking something and set herself on fire at the stove. Beth had no idea how bad the burns were when we talked. She just wanted you to come quickly and asked me to tell you how serious this could be."

We arrived at the Rockport Hospital in record time, and I rushed through the front doors while Manny parked the car. A kind lady at the reception desk directed me to Mama's room. Beth was sitting at Mama's bedside, and she signaled me to join her in the corridor, since Mama was sleeping.

"All we know is that Mama should be okay with rest, but she was badly shaken up from the incident. Apparently, she was cooking soup and reached across the stove to the back burner. Her sleeve got too close to the gas flame and burst into flame. She ran to the sink and turned on the water to put out the fire, but when she reached for the phone to call for help, she slipped and fell. Thank goodness she did reach me. I was there in a few minutes. She was lying on the kitchen floor shaking, and I called an ambulance.

I grabbed Beth's arm and said, "Beth, thank goodness you were home!"

Beth took a deep breath and continued, "The attending emergency doctor examined Mama and said they would keep her overnight for observation, but she should be well enough to go home tomorrow. He expects her to be fine but did say she needs to be watched carefully for several days to make sure the arm doesn't become infected and that there are no other injuries, such as a concussion from the fall."

Beth comforted me when I began to cry. "Marilyn, we can't ignore this. We don't have a choice. We must get Mama into a safe place."

"You're right. I think we should go to the Baptist Home to see if Mama can be moved up on the admission list."

We called from the hospital and set up an appointment for the next day after we took Mama home. We also called Mrs. Thompson. She had always helped with Maria, and she agreed to stay with Mama when she got home from the hospital.

With Mrs. Thompson's help, this allowed us to keep our appointment at the Baptist Home. Once we told the administrator about the accident, she said she'd move Mama to the top of the list. "Her safety is now a critical factor," she said, before adding, "I know that sometimes older people are apprehensive about moving, so why don't you bring her for lunch soon? She can get to know the facility and meet our residents before she comes to live with us permanently."

When we told Mama about our visit to the Baptist Home, she looked relieved that she'd be in a place with people around her day and night. And she readily agreed to visit for lunch and another tour once she recuperated.

Beth and I knew she would have the primary role in getting Mama settled in the Baptist Home, breaking down her house, and selling the furnishings. But I wanted her to know she wouldn't be alone.

CHAPTER 91

Setting up my business was complicated. Lots of letters, wires, and even a few expensive international phone calls to Dubie helped me navigate the maze of designers, manufacturers, and distribution points that overlapped. Getting Jalee Watches produced and finally marketed was challenging—but also very exciting.

I spent my days following up with Dubie's resources in the States while he worked his magic in Switzerland. At last, he wired that he was sending five prototypes for approval before manufacturing the inner workings for shipment. I panicked. Now it was up to me to figure out how to get the product to market quickly and begin to recoup the large outlay of money I'd made so far.

I'd already set up my campaign strategy: a small, targeted print advertising program in Nashville; follow-up visits to shops and boutiques in the region once I had the product in hand; and a grassroots personal endorsement from Brittany, now a friend of mine.

Brittany was a celebrated rising star in the country music scene in Nashville, and her music had taken off nationally. I couldn't believe how lucky I was when she offered to let me capitalize on her fame: she would wear Jalee Watches on her upcoming world tour and plug them to her fans. I knew how important her support would be.

Manny and I would sit for hours and brainstorm about other ways to market the watches. I was working solo to launch my business, but I wasn't isolated. Manny was right next door to my office. I could pop into the music store and talk to Manny or Jack. They were both so supportive. I'd also been in the habit of calling Mama from the office every morning—although sometimes the calls were disturbing. That was one reason I'd call Beth most nights after she put the children to bed, to get her take on Mama's condition.

Beth's observations confirmed what my phone calls were revealing. Mama's loss of memory was escalating much faster for her age than either of us had anticipated. Mama had no concept of time or place. She no longer recognized the faces or recalled the names of longtime friends in Rockport. Her ability to work with numbers was gone, and Beth was now paying her bills and handling other financial matters. The day Mama didn't recognize Beth's children when she took them to visit their grandmother was traumatic. Beth described the scene as devastating to her and her children.

For me, the saddest thing about my many weekends home was that Mama no longer read. Beth said she couldn't comprehend the words on the page. Mama had become Maria. Her only pastime now was staring at the television—just like Maria. When I visited, our conversations were often simply repeating the same topics over and over. She couldn't even remember that Manny and I planned to get married.

Mama had always been a voracious reader and book collector. She had instilled the love of reading in Beth and me when we were growing up. When Mama moved from the farm to the in-town bungalow, we had hired a carpenter to build bookcases in the living room to house her collection, which she always called her greatest treasure. Now they were untouched.

Just as we were about out of options for Mama's care, we finally got some encouraging news. Beth called to tell me Mama would finally be moving into the Baptist Home. "The administrator called a few hours ago and said a room was now available. They're painting it, and Mama can move in at the end of the week. But listen to this: when I told Mama the news this afternoon, she was so befuddled she thought I was moving her to her Baptist Church." Beth and I both laughed, but it was a laugh tinged with sadness, picturing Mama unpacking her belongings in the sanctuary and watching her select a pew for her bed.

"Beth," I said, moving into my organizational mode, "I'll be in Rockport by mid-morning Friday to help you move Mama and get her settled. We'll have to make sure we get all her personal belongings."

I continued, "I'll stay at Mama's house over this weekend and sort through her other things, so we can decide jointly what to keep and what to give away. You've had most of the burden caring for Mama, and I'm so grateful for all you've done. But at least I can be there for you with this. I'm ready to pick up the slack."

Beth had already made some decisions about this move and responded quickly, "Let's put the house up for sale as soon as we clear out the furnishings. I've studied Mama's bedroom and plan to create an identical setting in the Baptist Home. Her nightstand will be in the same place, with her Bible on it, and she'll be sleeping on her same linens. I've painted an old bookcase from the children's room, so we can move some of her favorite books and knickknacks to remind her of home."

I agreed with Beth. "You're so right. If we can create a familiar space for Mama, it will make the transition easier. Hopefully, she'll soon adjust to her new surroundings."

After getting Mama set up in her new location, Beth and I both wept silent tears on our drive home. The enormity of what we had just done was overwhelming. We knew we had placed Mama in a safe environment where she would be surrounded by people who would care for her and alleviate her loneliness. But we also knew her old way of life—the one she had dearly treasured—had slipped away much too rapidly for her chronological age. Mama was experiencing a form of a living death, but she could not totally comprehend her condition. However, her family and friends fully understood it but could only look on helplessly.

When Beth dropped me off at Mama's house, I opened the back door and looked at the familiar kitchen, now so forlorn and silent without Mama's presence. I forced myself to make a sandwich and drink a glass of milk before going to bed. I hoped I'd get a good night's sleep, so I'd be ready to tackle my first dismantling chores before heading back to Nashville.

As I was drinking my morning coffee, Mama's dear neighbor and friend, Mildred Robinson, tapped on the kitchen door. "I saw you and Beth moving things out of your mother's house the past two days, but I didn't want to bother you. Did you get her settled in the Baptist Home?" I nodded and asked her in for coffee.

As Mrs. Robinson settled at the kitchen table, I realized I was glad to have company before I started my chores. "Your mother and I go back a long way in this community," she said as she brought her coffee cup to her lips. "We met here as brides. But that wasn't what kept us together. That glue was our love of reading. She was the most intellectual friend I had, and I'm sure going to miss her. We never tired of dropping in on one another to share books and talk about them—alone or with the Rockport Literary Club's members.

"We noticed how your mother was failing mentally for quite some time. When we learned she would be moving to the Baptist Home, we were relieved. All the members will miss her, but me especially. I always loved her book recommendations and the way she made the discussions at the club so interesting. Now, don't you worry, we'll drop in to see your mother. She was one of our most popular members."

Mrs. Robinson finished her coffee and checked her watch. "I've got to get myself ready for church. Anything I can do to help, you and Beth just let me know. I'm right across the street."

Before heading back to Nashville, I called Beth to give her a progress report and share my plans for the following weekend. Then I told her about Mrs. Robinson's comforting visit. "She talked about Mama's leadership in the literary club and said they would all be visiting Mama at the Baptist Home."

CHAPTER 92

It's not easy to dispose of a lifetime of furnishings and treasures. But sometimes sifting through a household can be rewarding. Beth and I called the work "Mama's household project," and it did two things: brought us closer together as sisters and ensured that Mama's house would sell as soon as we put it on the market.

We kept Mama's library for last. The shelves in her living room were filled with books, and we just had to look at the photos and letters stuck between the pages. We laughed at the childhood photos in the family albums—and wondered how we could have ever worn those clothes. The cookbooks were fun, especially the handwritten recipes filed in the proper places. Beth took most of those books, vowing to try to make Mama's favorite dinner the next time I came to Rockport.

I got a ladder to reach the higher shelves, and I'd just about finished bringing down these top-tiered books when I found an odd-looking nine-by-twelve-inch slipcase. I was curious, so I jumped down and opened it. Inside was a handwritten manuscript, and I recognized Mama's neat handwriting.

"Beth, look at this," I squealed. Her title page simply read, *"The*

Patchwork Living Quilt: A Memoir of a Kentucky Woman by Mary Beth White." Here was Mama's life story unfolding for us again, but in far more detail than her oral recitation. The original manuscript was well written, but her hand edits in the margins showed that she'd reviewed it many times. "I wonder when she wrote this manuscript," I said. "Before or after our evening sessions?

"Do you mind if I take this back to Nashville to read this week?" I asked. "I'll get it back to you next weekend."

"Be my guest," Beth said.

Back in Nashville, I told Manny about our surprising find, and he asked to read it with me. We met after work and took turns reading it page by page.

"Marilyn, your mother is a gifted writer. I love her colorful descriptions of the farm and the small town of Rockport. Because she writes with such great restraint about her personal life, it adds strength to her amazing story of survival."

Manny was right. Mama was a gifted writer, but Beth and I had her true back story. Many of the things she had shared with us were in the book, but without the intimate and emotional details from our family sessions. The pain and suffering were there, but—as she had done in our sessions—balanced with the good. Yes, her life story was in these pages, but it was a softer version of the rough times and perhaps a little more focus on the loving times. Still, she had so aptly likened her life to a quilt composed of both rough and smooth colorful materials.

Since the book ended with Mama's dive into depression after Maria's death, I made a mental note that Beth and I should write an epilogue to the memoir about the challenge of dementia that placed her in the Baptist Home.

Manny suggested that we find someone to type the manuscript professionally and try to find a publisher. He thought we should pitch the memoir to Mama's alma mater, the University Press of Wesley.

I couldn't wait to tell Beth about our ideas, and she added her own idea on how to proceed. "Once it's typed professionally, why don't we ask Mrs. Robinson to have Rockport's literary club critique it?"

For the present, the "Mama project" would have to eclipse promoting my own watch business and deciding when Manny and I should marry. Of course, I couldn't completely ignore my business; it was just a lower priority. And I still thought about my future with Manny.

I knew that in time, my business and marriage would become a reality—just not right now.

CHAPTER 93

Two months after Beth and I finished downsizing Mama's house, it sold. We celebrated the successful closing—and a few days later celebrated the first shipment of watches from Dubie. I needed to begin marketing my product; it was now a reality, a big reality. I found myself climbing over boxes in my small office. I just had no place to store the watch inventory.

Once more, Manny came to my rescue. He offered to store the watches in the storage unit assigned to M&M Music. My office was too small to rate additional storage.

However, once I contacted the Nashville area stores and boutiques that I'd visited with the prototypes, storage was much less of a problem. We sold the entire initial shipment of five different watch designs within two weeks. I called Dubie immediately to send another shipment. It looked as if storage would not be an issue.

My watch line rocketed to success—thanks in part to Brittany's tour and popularity. She wore a different watch for each of her performances. When she signed autographs after her concerts, her young fans wanted a watch just like Brittany's, and she'd give them my business card to order directly from Jalee Watches. Orders from her fans were coming in faster than I could handle, and the stores in Nashville wanted more watches. They couldn't keep them in stock.

Now I could relate to Manny's feelings about his first song's success. My watch line was an overnight success, and I was feeling overwhelmed—of course, in a good way. But it was evident that I needed a larger space to showcase the watches and handle distribution and shipping. However, I didn't want to feel too confident, so each time I mailed a watch, I included a customer survey postcard and asked the buyers to return them with their comments. Their feedback helped me select new designs and concentrate on bestsellers when I ordered cases, faces, and bands from my American suppliers to send for the final assembly.

In just three months, Jalee Watches had reached the sales projection for its first year in business. Sean was proud of me and extremely pleased with his business investment.

The grassroots promotion of Jalee Watches really paid off. Not only were gift shops and jewelry stores placing repeat orders, but department stores also now wanted to carry the line. I needed more office and shop space and more help. I hired a business major from Vanderbilt as a part-time employee to help me call on established customers and potential ones.

One night, at a quiet dinner with Manny in our favorite little Chinese restaurant, I confessed I was overwhelmed by all the demands on my business. "I know it's a good problem to have," I said, "but keeping all the balls in the air without dropping one is exhausting."

Manny laughed and offered a solution. "Why not call Toni and ask for help? You know how reliable he is at juggling." He grimaced as I kicked his leg.

Then the pain left his face, and he fiddled with the fortune cookies. When he looked up to reach for the check, his facial expression was serious. "Marilyn, have you given any thought about when and where we should get married?"

"I think about it all the time. And I think we should make our wedding date very soon, before Mama's condition gets worse." Manny whipped out his calendar, and we set the date for a Saturday three months away.

"Ordinarily, the bride is married in her hometown, but because of Mama's dementia, I'd be more comfortable having a small destination wedding in New York City with just your family. We could have a private ceremony for Mama at the Baptist Home with her minister officiating and Beth and Frank, Joe and Grace, and their kids attending after we return from New York. What do you think?"

Manny smiled and kissed my hand. "I think that sounds like a very reasonable plan. Let's make it happen. Now, let me show you your fortune," he said, passing me the paper. His fortune read, "Future happiness is in front of you."

Just as we planned that night, in three months, Manny, Joe, Grace, and I flew to New York City, and with Joseph, Chloe, and Janice present, we were married in a small side chapel of St. Peter's Cathedral. Joseph hosted a reception for us at his apartment.

Chloe and Janice flew in from Milan, but only for the wedding day. They were reserved with Manny and me, and neither my business nor Manny's success in the music world came up. But they were more animated with Joe and Grace, who acted as our buffer in this small wedding party. They left the reception early to fly to Los Angeles to check on their accounts. Before they left, they gave Manny and me a wedding present check—and then another to Joe and Grace. Chloe always said she never did for one without the other.

Once they left, Joseph rose to toast "The two most favorite women in my life—Grace and Marilyn. I'm proud to have you as my daughters." His toast was more authentic than the checks bestowed on us by Chloe. We spent our brief honeymoon at the country house on Long Island, returning to Nashville midweek. On Saturday, we had the small wedding party at the Baptist Home for Mama's blessing.

Following our two wedding ceremonies, Manny and I returned to Nashville as Mr. and Mrs. Bateson—exhausted but blissfully happy.

CHAPTER 94

Manny and I had a double reason to celebrate our first wedding anniversary. First and foremost, we were happy in an extended "honeymoon glow," and when Beth called to congratulate us, she added to our happiness with some exciting news about Mama's memoir. Mrs. Robinson had taken copies of the typed manuscript to the Rockport Literary Club and asked the members to review it and give us feedback.

After reading Mama's memoir, they were so impressed at her manuscript that they voted to create a scholarship in her name at Wesley University. They also submitted the memoir to the University Press of Wesley, which now planned to publish it as a book on the region by a Wesley graduate.

The University Press staff also arranged to honor Mama at a special, invitation-only event at the Rockport Library to present Mama with the first copy to give to the library's collection.

When that Sunday afternoon arrived, Beth and I picked up Mama at the Baptist Home for the event. She looked radiant wearing her light pink dress Beth and I had bought her for my wedding and the pearl earrings and necklace Daddy had given her the Christmas before his death. She—or someone at the home—had applied makeup, and her hair had been shampooed and curled into a soft style that framed her face. Best of all, though, she was lucid and excited. I asked Beth if Mama's medication had been changed for her to be so alert; she shook her head negatively.

The library parking lot was filled, and cars were parked all along the street. When we walked in, Mama seemed to revert to the person she had been before her memory loss. It was as if this familiar place, where she'd spent so many hours in the past, triggered good long-term memories and pulled her from her current dim reality into the present. She looked completely at home surrounded by the books she'd revered all her life and smiled happily at the people who were there to celebrate with her.

The Rockport Literary Club had contacted the local newspaper and radio station, as well as a television station in Nashville whose general manager was one of Mama's former high school students. All planned to interview her.

Mama stepped to the podium and spoke into the microphone softly, glancing around the audience of her many friends, neighbors, and Rockport students. They had turned out to honor her literary accomplishment but also to acknowledge her contribution to educating the children of Rockport and to purchase her book.

Her words of appreciation were profound and, like her book, well crafted. "Thank you all for coming out today to acknowledge me and my book. For many years, I escaped from my own life to live in the world of books and the lives of others. Today, I give you my life in the pages of *The Patchwork Living Quilt: A Memoir of a Kentucky Woman*. By writing about my life, I am now free to live as I have never lived before as one of you."

After her interviews, Mama signed books for everyone who purchased one—almost the entire audience. Proceeds were to go to the Wesley University scholarship in her name, which pleased her greatly. But perhaps she got the most pleasure from her former students who told her how much she had influenced their lives by instilling in them a love of reading.

I will always remember Mama as she was that day—gentle and humble. She was truly as beautiful as a carefully stitched Kentucky patchwork quilt crafted from fabrics that are rough and smooth with unforgettable colors and shapes.

I reached for Manny's hand and squeezed it. I wanted him to know we were both a part of her patchwork quilt—literally and figuratively—stitched together for life in its grand design.

ACKNOWLEDGMENTS

Although this story and its characters are my invention, it is loosely inspired by the experiences of my rural life growing up in Kentucky and then graduating to the world-at-large. As I look back on the disciplined hours when I sat down to write about the characters and plot, I remembered how I would hear Ernest Hemingway's encouraging quote resounding in my novice writer's ear, "We are all apprentices in a craft where no one ever becomes a master."

To that end, I am indebted to my two editors, Fran Mathay and Rosalie Spaniel. They did magic to my initial manuscript that went beyond anything I had ever imagined as I embarked upon writing my first novel. Together we journeyed through many drafts where red ink often masked the black. My appreciation to Fran who spearheaded the editing process and to Rosalie who continually polished the manuscript after Fran's input. Admittedly, our collective and harmonious process made me a better writer.

Also, many thanks to the book club, "The Readers@The Lake" who willingly read and critiqued Part I giving me valuable feedback and encouragement to continue writing the second part of the book. Annie Pott helped with reading a later version of the manuscript with fresh eyes and provided valuable input and corrections. Also, I am grateful for the input Irene Burnett gave after diligent reading of the manuscript and Vickie Crafton who gave me advice on publishing.

Thank you to Lindsey Lindquist the illustrator of the book cover. The little girl on the cover is Sloane the daughter of Lindsey and Bill Lindquist.

Finally, for the past five years I worked on the manuscript, I had the loving support of my husband Rich who always gave me his attention and counsel when I said, "Listen to this part and tell me your reaction to it."

CPSIA information can be obtained
at www.ICGtesting.com
Printed in the USA
LVHW111320100719
623675LV00001B/84/P